DATE DUE

THE BOY,
THE DEVIL
AND DIVORCE

The Boy, the Devil and Divorce

Richard Frede

POCKET BOOKS

New York   London   Toronto   Sydney   Tokyo   Singapore

POCKET BOOKS, a division of Simon & Schuster Inc.
1230 Avenue of the Americas, New York, NY 10020

Frede, Richard.
    The boy, the devil and divorce / Richard Frede.
      p. cm.
    ISBN 0-671-77658-4
    I. Title.
  PS3556.R37B68 1993
  813'.54—dc20   92-25326
                                            CIP

First Pocket Books hardcover printing May 1993

10 9 8 7 6 5 4 3 2 1

POCKET and colophon are registered trademarks
of Simon & Schuster Inc.

Printed in the U.S.A.

To my sons,
Ari and Dov,
with love

*The heart has its reasons which reason
knows nothing of.*

—Pascal

THE BOY,
THE DEVIL
AND DIVORCE

1

THE DEVIL

WHAT JUSTIN WHITNEY, AGED TEN AND A HALF, WOULD most remember later was something he hardly noticed at the time.

Gamble, his mother, called home about six to say she was stuck with a client who had showed up late and there was a frozen chicken pie in the fridge for Justin to put in the oven for himself and he should have some sliced tomatoes with it and don't forget to have a glass of milk.

Skip, his father, had helped out at soccer practice after school and had already told Justin he was going back to his office and would be working into the evening.

It was nearly seven, nearly time for "Dr. Who," and Justin had brought his dinner into the TV room on a tray and turned on the set. The channel that came on was the one his parents had last been watching and there was a picture of one of the meanest-looking men Justin had ever seen. It was a news program, and the segment was something about a lawyer from Boston who had just won a giant divorce case involving children and money in San Francisco and his client, a woman, was kissing him and hugging him and the lawyer was trying to push her away.

The lawyer had a name that Justin might have remembered later anyway just because it was so funny. Weld Pennyworth.

All of a sudden the lawyer was standing there alone on the screen—a very close shot of him—and he was looking directly at Justin with angry eyes behind black-rimmed spectacles, and he said, "That's right, I'm through with this. I'd rather clean toilets. Divorce, domestic law, is the pits, and I'm through with it."

Justin turned to "Dr. Who."

That night, coincidentally, there were no sounds of anger from downstairs or from his parents' bedroom. Nor were there any sounds of anger during the nights that followed. Justin began to sleep well again.

2

HELL

A FINE FALL DAY, A BRILLIANT DAY, A DAY IN WHICH THE scent of brightly colored leaves hung in air that was warm and golden with sunlight.

Late in the morning, a backhoe at work on road repairs near the elementary school had dislodged and broken a water main. There was no water for the school. The school buses were called to an early dismissal of the children at noon.

There was a mood of rowdy celebration on Justin Whitney's bus. Justin sat with his best friend, Ryan MacKenzie. They were discussing the business project they had to do for Mr. Dunphy, their fifth-grade teacher. They were to decide upon a business and write a report about what the product or service would be and how they would fund it, promote it, and get it to the public.

Justin and Ryan had overcapitalized their business, the MacKenzie and Whitney Worm Company, with hilarity, and they were presently suffering physical discomfort from this overcapitalization, their bodies twisting in agonies of self-induced laughter.

"There are worms in your future!" Justin cried. "Our product cannot fail, Mr. Dunphy, there are worms in *everybody's* future!"

"Our products will worm their way into your heart!" Ryan said.

When Justin got his breath, he said, "A worm can be your friend when there is no one else to turn to! *Turn to,* get it? Get it?"

"I got it, but I don't want it," Ryan managed before he was again overcome with laughter.

"Worms get along great with your pets!"

"Worms can help you with your homework!"

"Worms will help clean your room!"

" 'Worms and You,' " Ryan said. "That's the name of our report."

"Presented by the MacKenzie and Whitney Train-a-Worm Company."

"Train a worm?"

"Trust me. I know about these things," said the president of the company. Justin was president because both of his parents were in business, whereas Ryan's father was a doctor and his mother didn't work at all.

The bus had stopped at the blacktop driveway to Justin's house, but the two boys were so submerged in laughter that the driver and other passengers had to yell at Justin to get off the bus.

"See you at soccer practice!" Ryan called after him.

"Hang loose!" Justin called back, bouncing down the two steps of the bus. He circled in front, stopped, peered both ways down the back road off of which he lived, and then ran across to his driveway, a raid on one of the Chex boxes in the kitchen occurring to him even though he had eaten his lunch just an hour before. Or maybe some Ben and Jerry's or Steve's, what his parents called designer ice creams. Strikers need all the energy they can get, as long as they don't get fat getting it.

The woods between the town road and the house were largely pine and the air was so warm that it had drawn resin and the smell of pine was everywhere. Even in the shadow of the pines, Justin could feel the heat of the sun on his bare arms and through his jersey.

He was accustomed to coming home to an empty house, but usually he was only home for an hour or so before someone picked him up for soccer or baseball or something like that. Now he'd have almost four hours alone.

Well, he could work on the business report. Or his reading. Maybe even straighten his room, the way he'd promised. He considered computer games, TV games, and the train table in the basement. Or see what his parents had rented for the VCR. That sounded best. Watch a movie.

The pine forest broke and there was open land, a meadow, hardwood beyond near the lake, maple, oak, cherry, and birch, the leaves gay as butterflies in the sunlight. And his house all golden and aglow in the light with the blue of the lake behind it.

The house, however, was odd today. There were cars in front of it. That shouldn't be, not at noon on a weekday.

It was a house that was unique in the area, a house that startled people even when they were familiar with it. Two floors of glass and bronze-colored wood that had been sealed but not stained, and not a single simple plane to any side, as if the rooms within the house were boxes that had been stacked so that some were recessed and some jutted out from among the others. And then, atop it all, the slanting solar panels gazing up at the sky.

His parents had designed all of that themselves, expanding and modifying it year after year as their financial fortunes improved and allowed, until now it stood there done.

The house sat on twenty of its own acres and many of the acres fronted on the lake.

Real estate taxes were paid to Town of Carlton, New Hampshire. The town had never been larger than the population of 3800 to which it had now grown. It had grown to that number because it had become a bedroom community for affluent professionals. The land to one side of the Whitneys was owned by a lawyer who practiced in Manchester, ten miles away, and who kept horses and rode in international competitions. The land to the other side was owned by an investment banker who drove daily fifty miles to Boston for his work; beyond him was another Boston commuter, a radio talk-show host who was heard all over New England and beyond. There was the chief pilot of an airline and across from him a retired general who had been famous in World War II. On the same road there was also a publisher, an architect, two more lawyers, and a surgeon.

"Mainstream professionals," Skip Whitney would say. And then he would proudly say, "I'm in an *oddball* profession. I counsel lists. It's a service for people who want to sell something to other people through mail-order marketing. I don't actually sell the lists. I advise. It's not dissimilar to what a stockbroker does. I advise people what lists to buy. I match the profile of a list with the profile of the buyer the seller wants to reach. I'm sort of the broker for the list. Also, I manage some lists." No one ever understood what his father did.

Everyone always understood what Gamble Whitney did. She was a realtor who, in Carlton and adjoining communities, had managed to continue to do very well even in a terrible market. She specialized in luxury properties and affluent clientele. She had been bragging about it recently, something Justin found unlike her. "There's a lot of money to be made in these hills of New Hampshire," she told visitors from out of state. "In fact, there's gold in these here hills." Gamble was from Boston, but Skip would say of her, admiringly, "She has the instincts of a swamp Yankee."

Today they should both have been at work or at the things they did at lunchtime—aerobics, squash—but it looked as if they were home. There was his father's black Mercedes and his mother's eight-seat, paneled Chrysler station wagon that she hauled potential buyers and their families around in. And a third car.

Gamble and Skip Whitney had been married for twelve years. Justin was their only child. Gamble was thirty-four years old, Skip, thirty-eight. It was hard for Justin to imagine them in their offices— he rarely went there. Mostly he saw them playing sports. During the summer and early fall they played tennis outdoors on their own court or on the courts of neighbors, and they sailed on the lake. In the winter they played tennis at an indoor court that they and some of their neighbors had constructed and they skied from a condominium they owned up north.

"A golden couple," Justin had more than once heard them referred to as. "A golden couple with a golden boy. For some people life comes down beautifully."

The third car was a little red Subaru station wagon and so that meant that his parents' real good friend Nelle Vance, who was a lawyer and wasn't married and who his father had said to his mother probably didn't get laid enough, was there. Justin knew what getting laid was—or thought he knew—but he didn't know what not getting enough was or why it should concern anyone.

Getting laid sounded sort of gross to Justin sometimes. Other times it didn't. There was a girl in his class named Amanda he could imagine doing it with. Sometimes he daydreamed that he had scored the winning goal in soccer and Amanda would get him to her house all alone and kiss him.

Anyway, his mom and dad and Nelle were all home and he hoped there was nothing wrong. Maybe they'd gotten the new sailboat his mom and dad had talked about and they were showing it to Nelle.

Justin dropped his backpack by the front door where he wasn't supposed to leave it, passed the sun-filled living room area on the right and the cantilevered stairs on the left, entered the cool, dark hallway between the TV room and the office on one side and the formal dining room on the other, and sailed on down the hall toward the blaze of light at the other end where the hall joined the kitchen and dining area at the back of the house, a sliding glass door and screened-in feeding facility his parents had redesigned, expanded, and added on when Justin had just been old enough to notice and be able to remember it later. He had been in day care then. His parents had paid the highest rates because they made so much money. They even *gave* money to the day-care center.

And then he hadn't been too much older than that when they had built a deck onto the kitchen. People sat out there and had drinks and his father had a propane gas grill out there and cooked steaks and things like that, even in winter.

Justin liked the house very much.

The sliding glass doors to the deck were open. The sliding screen doors—rectangles of faint gray between the kitchen and the brilliance outside—were closed.

Justin saw his father and mother and Nelle seated at a table on the deck. The odd thing was, there was no food or drink on the table. Justin was going to keep sailing right out the hall, through the kitchen, and onto the deck.

It was his father's voice that stopped him. *"No, I will not leave this house."* Justin did not enter the sunny kitchen. He remained in the shadows of the hallway.

"Look," Nelle said, "I'm here as your friend. And I'm here as an attorney. Please remember I don't represent either of you. I'm here to try to mediate—"

"That's your idea, Nelle, not mine, not Gamble's."

"Still, it's a good idea," his mother said.

"Work out something now so that you don't hurt Justin any more than you have to. Also if you can come to some mutual agreements now, it will save you both a lot of grief later. And a lot of expense."

"All right," his father said. "Mediate."

"That's what I've been trying to do, Skip. But neither of you have given me a whole lot to work with." Justin saw that Nelle had a long yellow pad in front of her and a pen in her hand. "The immediate issue is the question of who is going to reside in this house until the court makes a permanent disposition."

"But you want to make a disposition now," his father said. "You want me out of the house *right* now."

"Skip, let me explain again. I know it sounds hard to you, I know it sounds harsh—"

"I'll burn it down, I'll burn the house down before I'll just hand it over to her like that."

"You're not handing it over, Skip. Undoubtedly Ted Bagley has filed a libel of divorce that asks the Court to order you off the premises."

"He has," his mother said.

"On what grounds?"

"Physical endangerment to myself—"

"I've never touched you in my life! Not to hurt you—"

"There's the possibility. Under all this stress. *And* to mitigate an emotional atmosphere that is detrimental to Justin's health."

"My God!"

"Well, don't you agree, Skip, the way we treat each other, the way we speak to each other, all the arguing, isn't that detrimental to Justin's health?"

His father was silent.

Nelle said, "The court will undoubtedly accede to Gamble's request. That's just the way of things, Skip. The mother remains in the home with the child. For now, anyway. Unless you and Stu Bredwell allege and prove some serious misconduct on Gamble's part that affects Justin. Or that Justin would be in jeopardy if left in his mother's care."

"God, this is a nightmare."

"From which I am attempting to extricate you both to the extent that I am able. Some of the nightmare needn't continue."

"My thinking exactly," his mother said. "Marriage is a recurrent bad dream. I'm tired of it."

"Well," his father said, "I'm goddamn tired of *you*."

"If you were honest, Skip, you'd say the same thing I did. You're just as tired of marriage as I am."

"I'm goddamn tired of *our* marriage. The way it is."

"What way is that?" Nelle said.

"Neither of us is ever here for the other," his mother said. "Physically *or* emotionally."

"That's the god's honest truth."

"What about for Justin?" Nelle said.

His father said, "We each make our own time for Justin."

"We each give him a lot of time," his mother said. "Separately."

"Good time. Good for each of us. Justin and me, Justin and Gamble. I don't fault Gamble on being a mother."

"Nor I Skip. Skip is a fine father."

Justin didn't quite believe what he saw happen then. He didn't quite believe anything he was seeing or hearing, but he saw his mother reach out and place her hand on his father's hand. Then his mother and father looked at each other. Justin almost cried out then: *Don't move! Stay that way! I'm here!*

But then his mother removed her hand. "I think, between the two of us, the time we each spend with Justin, I think Justin may not even be aware of the strain between Skip and me."

"He'd have to be deaf sometimes," his father said.

Nelle said, "Have you considered staying together for Justin?"

"What do you think kept us together this long. Isn't that right, Skip? We never discussed it, but isn't that right?"

"That's right. *Oh,* that's so right."

"What is it you two have against each other?"

"Personality differences," his mother said. "Skip wants to be the dominant male. He wants everything done his way. He's got to be in charge. Even when we play tennis—he can't relax, he's got to be in charge. I'm so very tired of all that."

His father said to Nelle, "She's got to be so goddamn independent. I don't know why she ever got married."

"I failed to understand the institution. Or you."

"C'mon, Gamble. We did pretty well at first. Together."

"Then I got pregnant," his mother said to Nelle.

His father said, "You didn't *get* pregnant. You said you wanted to have a child."

"I did. I didn't. I did say I wanted to have a child. I didn't say I wanted to have a child *right then*. You insisted."

Justin already *knew* it was his fault, it *must* be something *he* had done—

"We have a wonderful child," his father said.

"Yes, we do. We have one of the most wonderful children in the world."

"We both have to take care of him."

"Yes," his mother said. "I've thought about this a lot. I went to some lectures on divorce and children—"

"You never said—"

"Of course not. I wasn't certain then. What I learned, Skip, whatever *our* arguments are, *our* conflicts, we have to exclude Justin from them."

"I totally agree."

"Okay, Skip, we can get on with this. God, we haven't talked this well in months, maybe years."

"Years. Can I ask you something?"

"You can ask."

"Are you sleeping with someone else?"

"I think we ought to just exclude that from our conversation. I'm not going to hold *your* personal life up in court and I hope you're not—"

"What personal life? What *personal life of mine?*"

"Folks," Nelle said, "you're not giving this your best effort." Justin saw her turn to his father. "Skip, the reality is that the court is going to order you out of here. At least till the temporary hearing. It's far better for everyone, especially Justin, if—" Nelle stopped. "I swore to myself I wouldn't interject myself personally in this . . . this, this *dispute* of yours. But I do want to say one thing. If I had a son like Justin, I would *fight* like hell to keep my marriage *together*."

"But you're not married," said his mother.

"And you don't have a son like Justin," said his father.

"The mediator acknowledges both assertions and resumes her role."

"Yeah, and if I move out, the court's going to see that as some sort of acknowledgment on my part. That the house goes to Gamble."

"No. That's why I propose this temporary stipulation." Nelle picked up the yellow pad and read from it. " 'Both parties acknowledge that the interests of their minor child Justin are best served if he is not daily exposed to the disharmony that exists between the two parties. Therefore, pending future orders from the court, Mr. Whitney voluntarily agrees to withdraw from the homestead property and take up interim residence elsewhere and that he does so without prejudice to his claims upon the homestead property. Both parties agree that Mr. Whitney retains the right to raise the issue later without prejudice and Mrs. Whitney gives assurance that she will not pursue an argument based upon such prejudice."

"Homestead property?" his mother said.

"That's the legal phrase."

"Why don't you just say *home?*"

"I'll just say *home.*" Nelle put the pad down. "Skip, you're simply telling the court you're removing yourself from this house for Justin's benefit. Until the court makes a disposition."

"That makes him look awfully good," his mother said.

"Would you prefer to exchange places with him, Gamble?"

"No."

Now his father stood up and looked down at his mother and the intensity in his father's voice frightened Justin. "If you think I'm going to let you live here with another man, you're crazy."

"Skip, I'll live with whomever I want *wherever* I want. But not till this thing is over. And as far as that goes, if you think another *woman* is going to live in this house after all the work and money I've put into it—"

"Please, folks," Nelle said gently. "Let's get back to the constructive side. You know you're going to have to do that sometime. You're going to have to manage some sort of mutual accommodation for Justin's sake. The court will order it and you'll have to abide by it. Can you both sign this? You're agreeing to this draft. I'll have it typed and you'll sign it again when we have the final copy. You'll have a chance to review it once more at that time."

"All right," his father said.

"All right," his mother said.

"I feel uneasy," his father said. "Like I'm signing the house away."

"I know it's difficult for you, Skip," his mother said.

"I know you're screwing around," his father said.

"You know no such thing."

"Please, folks—"

"I know that's why you want the divorce."

His mother said, "I wouldn't be the first in this marriage, would I?"

"I told you," his father said, "that never happened."

"You told me that on several occasions."

"And I never lied. It didn't happen."

"Your flirtations, they happened often enough to hurt, even if it didn't happen."

"I can say the same about you."

"And have."

Justin hadn't heard their voices like this in weeks. He had thought all that was over. The house had been quiet at night for weeks.

"Look, Skip, I just want out. Forget about all the rest."

"Then let's come to some reasonable solution about the house."

"The reasonable solution is, I get it. Or half of it. That's the law in this state. Half and half. The court will decide which half each of us gets. The half that gets lived in or the half that gets bought out."

"Folks, we're going in circles."

Nelle stood up, and Justin felt a sudden terror. Nelle was his only hope and she was leaving.

"I came here with the object of helping to mediate. For Justin's sake. But you two won't have it. You're more interested in accusations and allegations about *each other*. I'm not here to be an audience to that. And, frankly, I'm tired of listening to it."

"Nelle, sit down," his mother said. "I guess both Skip and I could be a bit more mature. You're right. You could help us. For Justin's sake. Skip?"

"Yeah. Let's see what we can do. For Justin."

Nelle sat down, and Justin felt that his heart could beat again.

He looked at the three of them out there, held them motionless, as if they were in a photograph, his mother with her long blond hair and slim features, his father also slim and blond, but sort of a rugged look to him where his mother was sort of glamorous, both of them athletic looking and tan from summer sports. His father was a little taller than most men and his mother a little taller than most women. They sat opposite each other, and Nelle, between them, looked as if she still had some more growing to do. She had very dark hair tied up in a bun. That's the way she always was, except when she came to a party or sports. Then her hair was down. What Justin liked especially about the way she looked, though, was her funny smile. It seemed to go up on one side and down on the other, and whenever she smiled at Justin, it seemed to him that she had wonderful secrets she was saving to tell just him. But she had her lawyer-look on now, no smile at all.

Nelle said, "Now, if we could come to some agreement about visitation. That would be a wonderful accomplishment."

"I don't see that as a problem," his mother said. "We'll handle it the way we always have."

"What's that?"

"I take Justin when I can and Skip takes him when he can. It depends on our business commitments."

"And if neither of you can?"

"A sitter."

"But you're going to have two separate domiciles now. It won't be a matter of who can get home and who can't."

"Well," his father said, "we'll work out a schedule."

"I'd like to get it written down," Nelle said.

"That's not possible," his mother said. "Our schedules are erratic."

"It's best that Justin knows what to expect and where he's going to be. If you can't construct a visitation schedule because of your other commitments, let me suggest that you make out a visitation schedule week by week. I'll meet with you on Fridays. For half an hour, say. You look at your schedules for the next week and we'll work out Justin's schedule. And his care."

"For the time being," his mother said, "it's best that Justin stay here, where all his surroundings are familiar and reassuring. Skip doesn't even have a place yet."

His father said, "I think you're using Justin as a cat's-paw to get this house now."

"Look, Skip, in all probability I'll be getting Justin. I think your own lawyer will tell you that. In this state the award always goes to the mother. Unless she's a drug-addicted, alcoholic whore—and even then she's got to do it in front of the children. That's what Ted Bagley told me. But I'll give you as much time with Justin as you want. I really mean that. We'll share our time with him the same as we always have. As soon as you get settled, you can have him over there a lot. I promise you. That won't be a problem for us. Justin will not be a problem for us."

"Gamble, I'm not going to let you use Justin to get this house."

Justin found that he was backing away from the grown-ups, backing away from their voices.

When he got to the front door, he let himself out very quietly.

The sunshine was warm on his bare arms, but he had never felt so cold in his life. Whatever he looked at blurred. He wiped his eyes and wiped his face. He found that his legs and arms were quivering.

A few minutes later Nelle came out on the porch and saw Justin —so small, as if his body had contracted within itself—so small and huddled in racking grief against the side of the house.

Oh, God! Nelle said, not knowing if she said it out loud or only inside herself.

3

JUSTIN IS ADVISED BY OTHER TORMENTED SOULS

THE FEELING OF COLD WOULD NOT GO AWAY. BLANKETS did not help. They made his body hot. The cold was inside him. But in the darkness, as soon as he shoved the blankets off, his skin got cold too.

His father was gone. The house was silent. Justin wouldn't have believed even that morning that he would ever wish to hear his parents arguing late at night again, but now he did.

His father had talked to him. "Your mom and I aren't getting along. It's better that we don't live together. We both love you." His father had told him things were going to work out okay and had hugged him. And Justin had said, "I love you. Don't you love me enough to stay together?"

At bedtime his mother had talked to him in almost the same words and had told him everything was going to work out okay and had hugged him. And Justin had said, "I love you. Don't you love me enough to stay together?" His mother had said, "Justin, it doesn't work that way."

Justin heard these words in the darkness. But if they both loved him, why weren't they going to stay together? And why were they going to send him back and forth between them? Didn't they *want* him? *What had he done that they weren't going to be married anymore?*

In the darkness he closed his eyes, and when he opened them he thought maybe everything would be over, he'd just wake up from a bad dream, a very, very scary bad dream.

But that did not happen. Whenever he opened his eyes, he knew he had not slept, had not dreamed. Still he could not get rid of a feeling of disbelief.

He felt tears on his cheeks, dampness on his pillow. They shouldn't be *doing* this to him. It wasn't right! He was their son and they should be taking care of him. That's what parents *have* to do for their kids—unless they're *rotten* parents—take care of their kids, not *hurt* them and mess them up.

He was so *angry* at his mother and father. And when he felt that anger flood through him, Justin hid down underneath the blankets where no one could see him.

The next day, at first recess, Justin asked his classmate Amanda to sit down alone with him and talk.

"What about?" Amanda said. She wanted to go off with her friends.

"Divorce. My parents are getting divorced." Justin tried to say it straight out and cold, but he felt tears coming to his eyes and he turned his head.

"Well, sure, Justin. That's sad. I remember." Amanda was divorced. "This just happen?"

"Yeah."

"See it coming?"

"No."

"Sad."

They sat down on a bank above the school's playground and playing field.

"I bet half the kids in this school are divorced. Did you know that?"

"No. I just thought, you know, you and Derek and Heather and . . . I didn't know that many."

"Yeah. See, kids ask me like you are. About divorce. It's a wicked bad time. I know. But, like, you want me to listen to you about it? Or you want me to tell you about it?"

"You tell me."

"Okay, Justin. I've been divorced three years now. Since second grade. I got a lot of good ideas about it. From experience. I'm really gonna tell you if you want to hear."

"I want to."

"Okay. This is going to sound wicked bad. But here goes. The kid has got to start out right away and make divorce work for *her*. Or him. But you've got to get on it right now, while they're separated. They separated?"

"Yes."

"*Right now,* Justin. You've got to get on it right now. Before it's too late. Right now you've got the chance. They feel guilty, real guilty, what they're doing to you."

"Really?"

"Trust me. You can get them to give in on certain things."

"Like getting back together?"

"No, stupid. On things you want. I don't mean Disneyland or things like that, either, but you can go after that, too. I mean, the things you figure are going to be *important*."

"Like what?"

"I don't know. Who you're going to live with. How much time you're going to spend with your mom and how much with your dad. Where they're going to be. How they're going to guarantee your happiness and take care of you and make up for this rotten thing they're doing to you. See, you've got to get things going your way now. Before the lawyers and the judge do their thing. You've got to be hard-hearted, Justin. You've got to be real mean."

And Justin saw Amanda begin to cry and she didn't hide it. Justin felt a new worry—that someone would look over and think he was making Amanda cry.

"Get your stuff started now," Amanda said. "Sure, they fight over custody of you. But the trial's about the parents. They don't look to see what's best for the kid. It's just what's best for the grown-ups." Amanda looked straight at Justin and said, "It's fucking ageist is what it is," and she stopped crying as soon as she'd said the swear and just that she had said it almost blew Justin away.

At lunchtime Amanda invited Justin to sit at her table. She had her friend Heather there and Adam and Derek, and a few other divorced kids from their own class.

"You'll get used to it," Derek said between bites of a peanut butter sandwich. "I got used to it."

"Yeah," Heather said, pausing in her attack on an apple, "you sorta get used to it."

"It's a lot of work being a kid," Derek said, mixing up his yogurt. "It really is. Parents don't realize that."

"They forget," Adam said.

"They forget everything," Heather said.

For a moment Justin thought maybe he was taking divorce too seriously. All the other divorced kids were talking about divorce and eating lunch and he was *hungry* but he couldn't eat. Food made him feel sick in his stomach. Well, there was one kid, Chick, who wasn't talking. He just sat there with his head down, picking at his lunch.

"Just don't expect much from your parents," Derek said. "That's my philosophy."

"Pay attention," Kira said. "Listen to what they say. Like, what they say to you. And, like, what they say when they don't know you can hear them. Sometimes you can use it on them."

"For what?" Justin said.

"To get your way. Like, what do you want?"

"I don't want them to get a divorce."

"Lotsaluck."

"Justin, you've got to start planning your life now," Amanda said. "You've got to start planning ahead. You can't feel sorry for your parents."

"The child should get the choice of who they live with. Not all these judges or courts," Adam said.

"The kid should have the biggest say," Heather said. "Not all these people talking. They don't know what the child knows. All these lawyers are saying they do, and they don't know."

Chick, the boy who had been silent, quietly said, "Sometimes the kid doesn't even know what's going on."

"Yeah, I know," Heather said. "My father had this lady friend. She acted so sweet and good around me. She was just wicked phony."

"What did she do?"

"She took my father away from my mother, and that's why they got a divorce."

"There's this guy?" Adam said. "The one my mother's with now? He's always trying to act like he's my father, all buddy-buddy. My *father* doesn't act that way. This guy's always bringing me presents. Presents make me sick."

"How long have you been divorced?" Amanda said.

"Two years," Adam said. "It was just when school was starting they got their divorce."

"What I hate is, you're home alone a lot," Derek said.

"I'm used to that," Justin said.

"You can come over to my house anytime," Derek said.

"Thanks, Derek."

"Divorced kids shouldn't have to be home alone so much, that's the way I feel," Kira said.

"I don't expect much from my parents," Derek said again. "That's what you learn."

"But, see, my parents are *great*," Justin said. "I mean, they've always been great to me."

"That'll probably change," Amanda said. "They get interested in other things."

Justin sat very still. He could feel the cold creeping up around him again. "But I love my mom and dad."

"That doesn't mean a thing," Amanda said. "Not in divorce."

"Which one do you want to live with?" Kira said.

"I want to live with both of them."

"Yeah, but which one do you want to have custody?" Heather said. "That's the person you mainly live with. The other person gets visitation."

"They toss you back and forth like a football," Adam said. "That's what visitation is."

"Lots of times they fight over whose turn it is to get the football," Derek said. "Even after the divorce, they keep fighting over the same things."

"You can't do anything about it," Kira said. "It's the pits. You just feel awful, awful, awful."

Amanda turned to Justin. "You better figure out who you want to live with mostly."

"Don't bother," Adam said. "Everyone else will decide it, not the kid. How can someone decide what's better for the kid than the kid?"

"See," said Derek, "it's all the parents and the lawyers and the judge. There's no one there for the kid."

"Sometimes there is," Kira said. "Like I had a guardian for a while. He's called a guardian ad litem. He's sort of a lawyer for the child. He's *supposed* to be, anyway. He's supposed to find out what's going on with the parents, you know, the things that have to do with the child, like how they each take care of the child and what the child thinks of them and like that. And he's supposed to listen to what the child says and what the child wants and he's supposed to take that to the judge. You know, be the lawyer there for what the child wants."

"That sounds good," Justin said.

"Yeah, just hope you don't get the loser I got. No matter what I said to him, he turned it around. If I said I wanted to be with my father mostly, he'd say, 'Do you realize that means taking time away from your mother?' I mean, I just told him what I wanted, why did he have to say that to me?" And Kira began to cry.

"That's okay," Adam said. "That's okay," the other kids said to Kira.

"I think my mother was screwing the guardian, that's what I think," Kira said. The divorced kids began to laugh. Kira looked at them in bewilderment and then with anger. And then she laughed loudest of all.

"The thing is," Amanda said, "get some control while you can." The bell to return to the classroom sounded.

Chick, his head still down, said, "Sometimes the kid doesn't even know what's going on. Don't get down on yourself. Don't blame yourself. It's not your fault. Sometimes the kid even wets his bed.

But that's okay, it's not the kid's fault." He got up and pushed his uneaten lunch into the paper bag and crushed it together and walked away.

When Justin got back to Mr. Dunphy's room, Ryan came over to him. "How come you had lunch with *those* kids?"

"I just felt like it."

"And you spent the whole recess with *Amanda.*"

"I just felt like it."

"You know, you're acting wicked weird today, Justin."

On the bus Ryan didn't sit with Justin, but then he did a strange thing. He started to get off the bus with Justin.

"Just a minute, Ryan," Mrs. Collingsworth, the bus driver, said. "Where's your note?"

"Oh," Ryan said. *"Drat!"* He struck his forehead with his open hand. "It was in my lunch bag and I threw my lunch bag out."

"Well, I can't let—"

"I forgot, I'm sorry. See, there's no one home at my house and I'm supposed to have dinner with Justin and—isn't that right, Justin?"

Justin was standing down on the road. There were two cars behind the school bus and one of them honked.

"Yeah," Justin said. "I guess."

"Well, I don't know, I'm not supposed—" There was more honking and in her rearview mirror Mrs. Collingsworth saw a second school bus pull up and stop behind the two waiting cars. She was used to Ryan getting off with Justin or Justin getting off with Ryan at Ryan's house. And there was the traffic she was holding up. "All right," she said to the boys, *"scat, scat,"* and Ryan bounded down the stairs and he and Justin raced across the road.

"Why did you do that?" Justin asked.

Ryan didn't say anything for a few seconds. "When are we going to work on our worm project?"

Justin was walking along, studying the blacktop of the driveway. "I don't know, Ryan."

"Why not?"

"I just don't feel like it."

"It's not what you *feel* like, Justin, it's what Mr. Dunphy *expects.* We told him we'd do it. I'm in this too, Justin."

"Not right now, *okay, Ryan?"*

"No. Not okay."

They came out of the woods into the meadow. Justin looked up. The house did not look the same. It wasn't his house anymore. It wasn't anybody's.

And at the same time, he felt a terrible loss, as if the house were his pet and it had died. Or as if the house were telling him to go away. Or as if there were no safe place in the whole world for him anymore.

"Why are you just standing there?" Ryan said to Justin.

"Why'd you get off the bus?"

Ryan looked at the house. "Is there anyone inside?"

"I don't know. How should I know?" Justin didn't like his own tone of voice and he said, "I guess not. There aren't any cars. Why?"

"I just want to tell you something. I don't want anyone else to hear it."

"So tell me here."

"I don't know."

"Jeezum, Ryan. What's the big mystery?"

"I never told anyone this."

"Okay, so don't tell *me*." Justin started to walk away.

"Hey, hold it," Ryan said, not moving. Justin walked back to him. Ryan looked at the pine forest where it ran down to the lake off to the side. "See, the thing is, Marcia isn't my mother."

"I always wondered why you call her Marcia. Instead of Mom."

"See, my mother didn't even come home from the hospital with me. She just wrote my dad a note and got dressed and left the hospital."

"What did the note say?"

"I don't know."

"Where is she?"

"I don't know."

"Doesn't your dad know?"

"He says he doesn't."

The two boys both studied the blacktop.

"So you see," Ryan said, "you're not the only one."

"That's sad," Justin said. "That's pitiful."

"It's not so bad. I mean, Marcia's wonderful. She could be my real mom. But it's just sort of odd when your own mom doesn't want you."

4

THE *YAR* AND PLANS
FOR SATURDAY

THE TELEPHONE WAS RINGING WHEN THE BOYS ENTERED the house, but it stopped before Justin could get to it. They set their backpacks on the floor of the kitchen. Usually they would have started to get food out. But Ryan climbed up on a stool and Justin just sat at the kitchen table.

"Do the other kids know about me?" Justin said.

"Everybody does now, I guess."

"It feels strange being divorced."

"You're not divorced yet, Justin."

"Yeah."

"Your guys, they want you though, don't they?"

"Yeah."

"Then things aren't so bad, Justin."

"I guess not. They just feel bad. . . . In a way, I'd rather be like you."

"No, you wouldn't."

"Okay. I guess not."

The telephone rang. Justin got it. "Justin," his father said.

"Hi, Dad."

"I was worried. You should have been home—"

"I was just a few minutes late—"

"I know. I just got concerned because of everything and—"

"Ryan's here."

"That's good. I'm glad you've got company. Listen, Justin, I was going to be there to pick you up for soccer, but—"

"You're not? You're not going to?"

"I don't think I should, Justin. Let me explain. Mom served papers on me this morning. Right here in my office."

"What's that? Papers."

"That's when one person is suing the other person for divorce. The sheriff delivers a notice about the divorce. Anyway, Mom asked for temporary sole custody of you and the court said okay."

"Does that mean I don't get to see you?"

"No, no. I just want to explain why I won't be there to take you to soccer. I don't know what the rules are. And Mom's out of her office, so I can't ask her. I don't want the court to get angry at me. I don't want to do something wrong right at the beginning."

"What if *I* ask you to take me to soccer? I mean, that's what you'd be doing anyway. If we were still together."

"I don't know, Justin. I have to be careful. I asked Stu Bredwell —you know, my lawyer—and he said check with Mom, and he said no matter what, don't do anything involving you that might upset Mom."

Justin didn't say anything. He looked at the base of the phone as if evil spirits were inside it.

"Justin, are you there?"

"Yes."

"I have something else I want to tell you. I got a place to live. Temporarily. While I look for something else. The Graysons' summer place. It'll be fine. As long as the weather holds. As long as we don't need anything more than the fireplace for heat. We can sail from their dock and—"

"Are you gonna have the *Yar?*"

"Well, it's mine."

"I thought it was yours and Mom's."

"Well, she's never been into sailing the way I am. I'm sure she'll let me have it."

"What if she won't?"

"Why, Justin?"

"I'm just interested. I want to know."

"I don't know. Just one more thing for the lawyers."

"We could use the Graysons' boat."

"It's drydocked for the winter."

"Please take me to soccer, Dad."

"Didn't Mom say anything to you about it? That she was going to take you to soccer? Or someone else was?"

"No."

His father was silent. Then his father said, *"All right,"* in a way that sounded *mean* to Justin, but Justin didn't think it was meant to be mean for him. It was just so intense. "All right. I'll be goddamned if I'm not going to take my son to soccer practice. Listen, Justin, you write your mother a note. Explain to her I'm going to pick you up. Explain to her I'm going to bring you home."

"Okay. That's great, Dad. And Dad?"

"Yes?"

"Get here early, hunh? Cause of Ryan? We'll have to stop by his house so he can get into his soccer stuff."

Justin hung up. "Oh, boy," Ryan said. "I better call home right away. Marcia'll have the police out when I don't get off the bus."

"I almost called the police," Gamble said to Skip.

There were so many partitions and openings in the house, so many levels and balconies, you could be almost anywhere and see and hear whatever was happening somewhere else if you wanted to. Justin hadn't quite made it to his room when he heard his parents at the front door and could just glimpse them if he stopped where he was around a corner.

"I almost called the police. I get home and there's no Justin and—"

"He was supposed to leave you a note."

"There was no note. I left the office early just so I could take him to soccer and—"

"I tried to get you about it. But you were out."

"I won't put up with this sort of thing, Skip. The first thing that crossed my mind was that you'd kidnapped him."

"Kidnapped him? Where would I take him?"

"How should I know? I have sole custody—"

"Temporary sole custody—"

"—and I won't put up with aggravation and worry where Justin is concerned."

"I had no such intention, Gamble. I was just trying to take care of Justin."

"Just trying to seduce him."

"*What?*"

"I know the games that start now. I've read all about them."

"What games? I'm not doing anything differently than I ever have."

"I think you had better start doing things differently, Skip. This is a different sort of situation. An entirely different sort of situation."

"God, don't I know it."

Justin heard his mother's voice change. "I'm sorry. Do you know that? Can you believe that? I'm truly sorry."

"I am, too."

"We both worked so hard at it. I *know* we *both* worked so hard at it."

"I'll agree with you about that. And it got to be too much work."

"Much too much work," his mother said. "We both deserve a good rest."

"Yes."

"I just wish . . . you know, *Justin*."

"I know. Let's not fight over him, Gamble. Okay? Let's make it as easy on him as we can."

Justin saw his mother place her hand on his father's once again. "Okay."

"I'd like to have him this weekend," his father said.

"Okay, that's fine. I've got to work Saturday. I'm planning something special. Some people are interested in buying property on the lake to convert to a year-round house and I've got just the thing. But they're looking all over the state. I want to impress them with this area."

"I'm sure you'll do it."

"You've got a place to stay already?"

"Yes. That's the other thing. I'd like to use the station wagon tomorrow and take some things over—"

"Okay. Or do you want to take it now?"

"That would be fine. Thank you."

"No problem."

"Now, if we could just work out everything else as easily."

"We can try," his mother said.

"All right. Also, I'm going to take the *Yar* for the weekend."

"No, Skip, I am."

"It belongs to me, Gamble."

"It *belongs* to both of us. And I have plans for it already."

"I'll simply take it."

"I don't know how, Skip. The sails are all neatly stowed in that great neat box you built in the basement and you are specifically *ordered* by the court not to remove anything from this house except personal property."

"I note that the same applies to you."

"Yes. But I have, in effect, temporary sole custody of the house. And I am not going to approve of you taking the *Yar* or the sails on Friday or Saturday. Maybe on Sunday. I'll think about it."

"You *bitch*."

"I wondered when that sort of thing was going to start."

"You *started* it."

"Skip, why don't you just *take* the station wagon and come back tomorrow when Justin and I aren't here. I'll trust you to take just your personal possessions. Not the sails, not the boat."

"*God.*"

"Skip, we were going to work on this, remember? To make it easier on Justin."

"*God*, Gamble—"

"Look, you can pick Justin up after school anytime on Friday."

"He has a game Friday afternoon."

"Good. Take him to it. I'll have his things ready. Have fun. You can take the *Yar* on Sunday. Okay? Isn't that fair?"

His father was silent.

"Skip, where's your place? I want to know where Justin will be. And the telephone number. Have you got a telephone?"

"It's being reconnected. I've got the Graysons' place till I find—"

"That's *delightful*. How do you propose to get the key?"

"I have it. Jean told me where to find it under the deck."

"Ah." His mother's voice had a strangeness to it, a sort of weariness.

"Now what, Gamble?"

"We should have an interesting Saturday. Are you planning on being around on Saturday? Maybe you could take Justin somewhere. Around lunchtime, early afternoon?"

"No, we were going to go sailing."

"Well, you see, the Graysons' house is on the market—"

"So Jean told me."

"I'm representing it."

"She didn't mention that. She just said she'd be in touch with the realtors."

"Well, now I know why she left a message to call her . . . And so, Skip, it will be a bit difficult on Saturday if you stay around."

"Why?"

"Because I'm showing the house on Saturday. It's perfect for my prospects. I'm going to pack the picnic hamper, sail them over so they can see how beautiful the lake is, how undeveloped. Then we'll have some drinks on the deck—"

"If it's a nice day—"

"There's a fine forecast. And then I'll show them the house and we'll have lunch on the deck."

"With a bottle of wine, no doubt."

"With two, if they want."

"What are you serving?"

"Bread, cheese, paté, some salad—"

"I meant the wine."

"A Pouilly-Fuissé."

"What year?"

"Eighty-six."

"One of *our* Eighty-sixes?"

"Why yes."

"That's not personal property, goddamn it, Gamble. That's joint property."

"There's not time for me to go to Boston and find something as good as we already have. It's in the line of business. Don't worry, Skip, I'll replace it."

"Goddamn it, Gamble, I selected that wine, I arranged for—"

"I'll replace it, Skip."

"You may not be able to get a Chateau Fuissé, it's—"

"Well, I'll get something comparable."

"That's not the point. It's joint property, you're removing something you probably won't be able to replace, a Chateau Fui—"

"Oh, Skip, don't be so rigid."

"Then go to the liquor store and get—"

"I won't be able to get anything comparable here, Skip, you know that. And these people are from New York."

"You really do piss me off, Gamble."

"Yes, I know. You've made me fully aware of that. Do you know why the Graysons are selling?"

"No, we didn't discuss it, Jean said she didn't want to."

"They're getting a divorce."

"I thought they had such a good marriage."

"That's what people thought about us. A golden couple."

"What about their kids?"

"That's why they waited till now. Till the twins were in college. Sam says they planned it better than they knew. Selling the house will put the twins through college."

Justin thought, if only his parents would wait until *he* was in college.

"How long had they been planning this?"

"Two or three years."

"I don't see how they could wait that long. Once they'd decided on it."

"Nor do I." There was a silence and then his mother said, "Skip, things will be very uncomfortable if you remain in the house while I'm showing it."

"Christ, Gamble, you force me out of *this* house, and as soon as I find a place of my own, you want to shove me out of there, too."

"Oh, Skip, you are truly *unbearable*. I'm just asking you to facilitate a business situation I—"

"Justin and I will be there, unless you want to let me have the *Yar*—"

"Absolutely not! I have made these plans very carefully—"

"Then perhaps you'd like to bring along enough lunch for Justin and me—"

"Skip, you may not have yet appreciated that I haven't asked for any money from you, no alimony, no child support—"

"Also, bring along another bottle of our joint property."

"You can take a bottle right now and fuck off! But be out of that house when I show it or—"

"*Or?*"

"I will go after every cent you have."

"You won't get it."

"I'll make a dent in it."

"See you Saturday, love. Mind you bring enough for all of us." Justin heard his father call up to him, *"Justin? I'm going. I love you. Pick you up here after school on Friday."*

"The Grayson house better be neat when I get there," his mother said.

"That will depend entirely upon how I feel about you Saturday morning."

"Neat, clean, and straight. Or I'll have you out of there so fast you'll think you were never there. One call to the Graysons that you screwed up a strong prospect. I might do that anyway. If the house is neat or not. It depends on how I feel about you Saturday afternoon."

5

SPACEY

"YOU KNOW YOU'RE GOING TO BE WITH YOUR FATHER THIS weekend."

"I know."

His mother was sitting by Justin's bed. Every night, before he went to sleep, his father or his mother read to him. Justin wished his mother would get on with it, but she hadn't even opened the book in her lap.

"I know this is a very difficult time for you, Justin."

Justin didn't say anything. He concentrated on a spot where the wall met the ceiling.

"I wish it wasn't. I mean, I wish it didn't have to be."

Justin kept looking at the line between the ceiling and the wall. "If you wish it didn't have to be, why are you doing it? You don't *have* to do it."

"It's not just me, Justin. It's your dad, too. I swore I wouldn't say anything bad about him, but you have to realize he contributed *mightily* to this situation. I'm just actualizing it. I mean, the divorce. Your dad made it happen as much as if he'd gone out and gotten the divorce himself."

Justin was silent.

"Either one of us could have gone out and started the divorce."

"But you were the one. You could stop it."

"No, Justin. It would be bad for you. When children's parents are fighting all the time, it's bad for them. It's better that their parents don't live together. That means getting a divorce. Do you realize that fifty percent of the marriages in this country end in divorce now? Do you know that means that fifty percent of the kids in this country have divorced parents?"

"I don't want to be divorced."

"You're not the one who's getting divorced."

"Yes I am!"

"Well, I'm sorry to disagree. I understand what you're saying, but you're not using the word properly. *You* are not getting divorced. Dad and I are. We're *both* still there for *you*."

Justin thought for a few seconds. "When you made me, you and Dad?"

"Yes?"

"Didn't you have like an agreement? I mean, in your minds, that you'd stay together and take care of me?"

"Well, I guess every parent *intends* that . . . I was so worried about you, when I was carrying you. That I might do something wrong and you wouldn't come out right."

"I think you're doing something wrong now. Something wrong to me."

"Justin, don't try to lay a guilt trip on me. This is hard enough."

"What about me?"

"How so?"

"You pretend like I'm not getting divorced, but it's *my* family that's getting messed up. And you're doing it!"

"I told you, Justin, cut that out. I'll discuss it with you reasonably, but—"

"I'm getting split up!"

"I know, I know, Justin—" She tried to put her arms around him, but he rolled away.

"I don't even know where I'm going to live."

"Well, of course I'm asking for you."

"Asking?"

"Well, mothers usually get the children. You don't have to worry about that, I'm not. It's the other things. Oh, you know, who gets what, like the house, that sort of thing . . . Ready for me to read?"

"I don't care."

His mother read to him for longer than usual. Then she put a guitar tape in the box by his bed. Justin always went to sleep listening to guitar music. He had been playing the guitar since first grade. Tonight it was Julian Bream. He rotated Bream with Segovia and Montoya. But as he lay there and tried to listen in the darkness, he thought the music belonged to some other child. Some other child who was far away somewhere and couldn't hear it. He, Justin, was a fake Justin. What was happening wouldn't happen to the real Justin.

When it was time for first recess the next day, Mr. Dunphy asked Justin to stay in the classroom. He came over and sat down on a child's chair next to Justin's desk. Mr. Dunphy had been a semipro basketball player and he looked silly in the little chair with his knees coming up to his chest. Like a great big child. Justin felt sorry for him.

"I know what's going on at home, Justin. I'm sorry about that. It's a rough time, isn't it?"

"Yeah."

"Not much anyone can do, I guess. But you let me know if I can, all right?"

"Sure."

"Past couple of days, you've been spaced out, you know that, Justin?"

Justin knew he felt far away a lot of times. No, like the classroom was far away. He was sitting there, but everything around him was a long ways away.

"That's okay. That's to be expected. But I'm not going to go along with it after this weekend. I'm gonna be on your case, Justin."

Justin looked at Mr. Dunphy and Mr. Dunphy saw the anger.

"Thing is, Justin, a kid's parents get divorced, the kid goes down the tube for a while. How far and how long—the way I see it, a lot of that's my responsibility. Here in the classroom. A student can just slip and keep slipping. A kid's got so much on his mind, right?

Unfortunately, most kids let their brains slip backward—with all the pressure and all, you understand? And most grown-ups just stand around and say, 'Isn't that too bad, such a bright young kid, and look what's happening to him, but who can blame him, his folks getting a divorce and all.' So the kid just goes down the tube. You understand what I'm saying at all?"

"I guess."

"Okay. But that's not the way it happens in my classroom. I have standards here for everyone—and that includes divorced kids and kids who are getting a divorce, and kids with families that bum them out, and kids with regular families. In this classroom, Justin, the commandment is, Thou shalt not regress intellectually. That means—"

"I know what it means."

"Okay. You have a good weekend. If you can. Have a good game this afternoon. Win it, we're in first place, did you know that?"

"Ryan said."

"Tie it, we're tied for first place."

"Ryan says they're the best in our league."

"I think we're the best in the league. Anyway, have a good week-end." Mr. Dunphy stood. "Rest up. Give your head a rest if you can. But get your homework done. Because come Monday, things are back to normal here. As far as what I expect of you."

Justin looked up at Mr. Dunphy.

"Justin, what I'm telling you, I didn't learn this from a book, I didn't learn it in an education class in college. I learned it in my classroom when *I* was in fifth grade and *my* parents got a divorce. Truth is, I had to *repeat* fifth grade, so it made a lasting impression on me. I thought I'd never want to see a fifth-grade class again."

"That's funny."

"You're right. See what can happen to you if you're not careful? You can end up in fifth grade the rest of your life . . . I don't think you want to do that. In any event, I'm not going to let you."

"What if I wanted to be a fifth-grade teacher?"

"Teacher, that's different. Not student. Come Monday, Justin. You're smart, Justin, you've never had to work too hard. You're still smart, but now you're going to have to work."

"It isn't fair."

"My words exactly. How's the business project going?"

"With Ryan? The worms?"

"Yes."

"He wanted to work on it, but I didn't."

"It's a team project, Justin. Don't make Ryan suffer because of the way you feel. His mark depends on your work, you know, just the way you depend on his work." Mr. Dunphy listened to the sounds of two classes coming down the hall. "Recess over so soon? It isn't fair."

Justin wanted to run and kick. *He wanted to kick ass.* The sound of the words in his mind made him feel better. Even Mr. Dunphy had made him feel better, sort of. But the feeling didn't last very long and then the classroom was far away again.

6
THE SEX GODDESS AND THE EARTH MOTHER

AT THIRTY-ONE, AND A MEMBER OF THE FIRM FOR ONLY three years, Nelle Vance already generated a cash flow at Colby, Whitcomb, Beebe & Bean that all but assured her of a partnership in the near future. She had as clients both personal injury victims *and* insurance companies. She was a respected—and expensive— mediator in labor–management disputes. Her present caseload involved big pieces of change for the firm, except for the usual pieces of divorce work that befell every lawyer in the state who didn't have the extraordinary energy necessary to avoid them. Nelle did not quite understand—or approve of—domestic law hotshots like Weld Pennyworth, the Boston Devil, who extracted fortunes from each piece of domestic litigation in which they involved themselves.

The two men were looking her over as a possible bedmate, Nelle realized, as she sat down. It was something that men did out of a misguided sense of sexual superiority. No matter how successful she was as an attorney, most of her male colleagues comparison-shopped her physical assets before getting down to whatever issue was at hand. It was a form of condescension, Nelle thought.

Herein, well and good. The gentlemen's condescension would serve her purposes.

"Sorry I'm late," Nelle said. "The judge wanted to see us in chambers."

"Carnegie Trucking?" Ted Bagley, appearing for Gamble Whitney, said.

"Yes."

"How's it going?" Stu Bredwell for Skip Whitney.

"I'm confident." She placed a yogurt, an apple, and a mug of coffee on the conference table.

"Opening statement was impressive, I hear," Ted Bagley said.

"There's coffee anytime you want," Nelle said, tapping the phone by her seat. She sat at the head of the table. Little lady or not, they were on her turf.

The three of them were less distinguished by their apparel than by what they had brought to eat. Bagley wore a dark blue blazer and a rep tie. Bredwell wore a medium gray suit and a paisley tie. Nelle wore a dark gray suit and a white blouse tied at the neck. Bagley had brought a grinder and soda, Bredwell a croissant sandwich and tea.

And here I am, Nelle thought, the granola lady.

"We are here, brothers, on the matter of Whitney v. Whitney."

"Don't brother me, Nelle," Bagley said. "I don't like entertaining ideas of incest."

"Your wife might be equally uncomfortable about it."

"Nelle, why don't you just be a woman?"

Why don't you just be a man? Nelle thought, and then realized that was exactly what he *was* being. "Can we cut out the sexual games, Ted? I'm sure they'd be *lots* of fun—if I were the least bit attracted to you."

"Nelle," Bagley said, "most of law is a bore. Most of life is a bore. I can't flirt with my brothers, it wouldn't be seemly. You cheer up the day for me, that's all. I'm expressing my admiration."

In spite of herself, Nelle felt complimented. "That was pleasantly said." She saw herself as she had been when she was a little girl, all dressed up the way her mother wanted her to be, hoping for her parents' approval. She immediately became annoyed again at Bagley.

Bredwell put his croissant down and wiped his fingers. "Precisely what are we here for, Nelle?"

"You boys are representing the Whitneys. Nobody's representing Justin. I want to represent Justin."

"Justin's not getting the divorce," Bagley said, "Gamble is."

"You've been meddling in this already," Bredwell said.

"Trying to mediate. On behalf of Justin's well-being."

"I don't like that. You have no position in this action," Bredwell said.

"But I want one. I want to be appointed guardian ad litem. I want you two to agree to it and I want your clients to stipulate it."

"Look, Nelle," Bagley said, "I've got no objection that I can think of, not right now, but aren't you too close to these people? Where's your objectivity?"

"That's just it. I'm close to all three of them. I know the situation. I don't have to spend hours and days investigating it properly."

"I don't know how my client will react," Bredwell said. "I can't speak for him. What does young Justin say?"

"I haven't spoken to him about it."

"Oughtn't you?"

"To my knowledge the court does not have the minor child interview potential guardians before appointing one. I want you to agree to me and move it to the court."

"If Gamble goes along with it, I have no objection. Stu?"

"It bothers me."

"Why?" Nelle said.

"You're not dispassionate enough. You know these people too well."

"Does that disqualify you two from representing them?" Nelle said.

"We're hired guns," Bagley said. "You know that. Our social relations with the clients don't make any difference."

"You'll plea passionately on behalf of your clients."

"Of course," Bagley said. "Uh-oh."

"Exactly. Justin ought not to be deprived of passionate pleading on his behalf. Or deprived of someone who knows the family as well as you two do."

"I'm not comfortable with it," Bredwell said. "I can't recommend it to my client."

"There's this to consider, Stu. If I'm not there as guardian ad litem, I will ask the court to hear me as amicus curiae." She let him consider that. "In that role, if the court is so disposed, I can advise the court. Since I will have no prior official standing with your clients or Justin, you will not have the benefit of any input as to what I might say. I may say anything I want."

"Jesus, Nelle," Bagley said.

"What do you perceive to be your role as guardian?" Bredwell said.

"To represent Justin's best interests as I see them."

"Does that mean whether or not Justin sees his best interests in the same way you do?" Bagley said.

"A child in this situation cannot be asked or be expected to perceive or understand his own best interests. That is what the guardian ad litem is for. To take the weight off the child. I want to do that for Justin. You know as well as I do how the child is placed in the middle, dragged this way by one parent, the opposite way by the other parent. I want to help Justin escape that. I want him to know he doesn't have to decide. I'll represent his best interests."

"What if he *wants* to decide?"

"What child wants to be placed in that position?"

Bredwell had finished his croissant. "Neat move, counselor. Amicus curiae. Amicus curiae indeed." He stood up. "You come in a neat package, Nelle, but you carry a big, mean stick. I perceive that you won't hesitate to use it."

"Not where Justin is concerned."

Bredwell looked at Bagley. "God help our clients." He looked at Nelle. "All right, I'll recommend your appointment to Skip."

"I thank you. Ted?"

"Likewise. I don't see any problem there. The contest's going to be over the house."

"That's an irreconcilable difference," Nelle said. "Why don't you suggest to the court that it be sold and the proceeds divided equally?"

"It's an emotional issue," Bredwell said. "And as we speak of it, my dear amicus, you probably did a good job of mediation getting that agreement drawn up between Skip and Gamble. I'm sure it was good for Justin and I'm positive it was good for Gamble. Probably not so good for my client."

"It says that Gamble agrees the issue may be raised without prejudice—"

"Yes, yes, but you see, dear, my client is already *out* of the house now. As you know, it's so much easier for the court to leave things as they are rather than move Skip back in. In the future, I would appreciate consultation when you feel an attack of mediation coming on. The facts of the matter are that you have moved my client out of his house, you have undermined his position vis-à-vis his express desire to remain in the house with his son or to return there. In short, Nelle, consciously or unconsciously, you have conspired with Gamble and her interests against my client and his interests."

"Absolutely not. All of this was done in Justin's best interests."

"You've chosen one parent over the other. That's why Skip is out and Gamble is in."

"No, Stu, Gamble is in the house and Skip is out of the house because Gamble had already filed the divorce libel and asked for temporary custody and received temporary custody. Was I to suggest that she and Justin move out and Skip stay there?"

"I take your point, Nelle."

So much for the sex goddess and the earth mother, Nelle thought after Bagley and Bredwell had gone. She knew the truth well enough, but every so often, when the boys were playing boys-and-girls games, she forgot it: that once you got down in the trenches, it was mind against mind.

7

IN A HOUSE THAT IS NOT HIS HOME

"BUT I DON'T WANT NELLE TO BE MY GUARDIAN," JUSTIN said.

His father was driving him to the soccer game. Justin's weekend possessions were in the trunk—the clothes his mother had packed for him, his sleeping bag, a big box of Legos he hadn't played with in a long time but insisted on bringing along now, a bunch of comics, his collection of sports cards, his guitar, his boom box and guitar tapes. "You don't need so much stuff," his mother had said. "It's just like staying overnight with Ryan." "No it isn't. Ryan's not my dad. Why can't Dad stay here?" "Then where would I go?" his mother had said.

"I don't want Nelle to be my guardian. I don't want a *guardian*. I want you and Mom."

"I understand, Justin. But Mom doesn't want it that way."

"She says you don't either. I *know* you don't, so don't blame it on Mom."

"My God, Justin."

"My God, what?"

"You've grown up about twenty years the past few days, and I don't like it."

Justin thought that was funny. His father thought he was getting to be about thirty and Mr. Dunphy was afraid he was going to *regress* to kindergarten or something.

"Anyway," his father said, "it's not like Mom and I aren't your parents anymore. Guardian, in this case, is just a legal term."

"I know what *guardian* is."

"You do?"

"Yes."

"How do you know that?"

"The kids in school. We had a meeting." Justin recognized that he had said something that threatened his father in some way. "They explained what a guardian is. I don't want one."

"It's for you, Justin. I'm afraid the court's going to insist on one sooner or later. That's the way things are done."

Whatever happened in his life now, Justin realized, it had nothing to do with him. The court made all the decisions. Even his parents couldn't make the decisions.

Justin sat on the bench and tied his cleats on the way the English pros had taught him during the summer when they'd had soccer camp in town. His hands did the job, but they were separate from him. He tried to get closer to them, but they functioned independently. They did what the English pros had taught them, not what Justin was telling them, though it was the same thing. Everything was inside out, upside down.

The air was cool and the afternoon was as bright as an apple. Across the field the Manchester Cosmos, in their maroon jerseys, were listening to their coach.

On the Carlton side of the field Mr. Dunphy had stood back, and now there was a circle of players, boys and girls, on either side of Ryan, who was captain, center, and one of the best players in the league.

"We can beat these suckers," Ryan said. "I know people say they're the best and all that, but Justin and me saw 'em play Hollis, and we can beat 'em, can't we, Justin?"

Ryan banged Justin's back. Justin played right inside, and he and Ryan, passing to each other, setting each other up, made most of the goals on the team. "I guess," Justin said.

"We got to *want* it," Ryan said. That's not enough, Justin thought. He'd never thought that way before. "If we don't beat ourselves, they won't beat us." Bullcocky, Justin thought. "Okay," Ryan said, "let's *do* it!"

The players placed their hands on top of Mr. Dunphy's and counted out, "One! Two! Three! Break!" and took their positions.

Ryan stopped by Justin. "You okay, Justin?"

"I'm fine, okay?"

Manchester scored almost immediately. Thirty seconds, no more. Justin saw it happening. They passed around him, went down the middle of the field, passed out to a wing who had gotten in close, and scored. Justin knew it was his fault.

"Okay," Ryan said, "let's get it back."

But at the quarter they hadn't. "We've got to *want* to win, you guys," Ryan said to everyone, but looking at Justin.

Justin's hands had felt strange. Now his body felt strange. Nothing belonged to him anymore, including his body. Even his mind wasn't his anymore. It kept thinking about things he didn't want it to think about. And as to his heart, it was filled with the foreign matter of sadness and fear.

At the half they were still behind by the one goal. *"Great* defense," Mr. Dunphy said. "Get some offense going and you can win this game." He talked to individual players about what they were doing or not doing, Justin no more than anyone else. "Justin, you tired? You want to rest?"

"No."

"Because you look half awake out there."

Justin just nodded. He was almost as good as Ryan. Everyone got to play at least a half, but people like Ryan and Justin and Amanda got to play the whole game if they wanted to. Justin felt like asking to be taken out. But he couldn't get himself to do it. He couldn't get himself to do anything. Just like in class.

Suddenly he saw the ball. Ryan had made a *beautiful* pass to him, led him just right, Ryan had tricked their goalie over to one side, Justin had almost an open goal in front of him and he—he kicked it wide of the entire goal. Ryan walked away, shaking his head. "Jeezum. Wake up, Justin."

Then there was a player down and a time-out with two minutes to go, still 1–0. *"C'mon, everyone, you've got to want it,"* Ryan said fiercely. Time-in.

Justin was seeing everything clearly now. But it was in a sort of slow motion and as if from a great distance. He was hot. He felt things were going to explode. But he sort of didn't care either way. Ryan was on a breakaway. Justin used that great long-distance-seeing to pace himself down the field with Ryan, keeping himself wide but close enough and open for a pass. They got to the penalty box and Justin knew the game-ending whistle was about to blow and there was no one between Ryan and himself and the goal except the goalie and Ryan kicked a perfect goal that was still rising as it shot beneath the crossbar and then the official was in front of them blowing his whistle and waving his arms, but he was waving his arms to make X's, *no goal.*

"Offsides!" the official called out and pointed at Justin. Then he raised his arms outward. "Game."

* * *

Justin had been to the Graysons' house many times, but he had rarely entered it through the front door. Usually he'd come over in the *Yar* with his parents and then he'd come into the house through the lakeside deck door.

But now his father parked on the dirt driveway that led past the front door. There was no light in the house and very little light left in the sky. The air was cold. His father unlocked the door and turned on a light, and then Justin started carrying in his own things while his father brought in bags of groceries.

When Justin had finished, his father was putting things away in the fridge. The kitchen, dining area, and living room were all one big room. Justin had spent a lot of time there for as long as he could remember. But the house was strange to him now that he was going to live in it sometimes, now that it was going to be "his" house sometimes, now that it was going to be a home of his sometimes. And this home wasn't to last either. It was just till his father found another place.

"You remember the twins' room?"

"Yes," Justin said. He had slept there a few times.

"That'll be your room. I've got the big bedroom down the hall."

"Okay."

"Why don't you take your stuff up there now?"

Justin felt very sad again, putting his good things in this room that didn't belong to him. When he went back down he carried the box of Legos with him. His father had made a fire. Justin could smell it and hear it.

His father had a bottle of beer in one hand. "Justin, c'mon over here, my boy." His father was in the living room area. On the floor there were several packages, two of them big ones, some of them gift wrapped. "Start with the smallest."

Justin opened it. It was a toothbrush and toothpaste. "Us bachelors have got to start setting up our own digs. Till we get back to our own place."

There was a book that looked like a grown-up book—*Favorite Folktales from Around the World*. "That's what I'll read you at bedtime," his father said. "One each night."

There was a new rugby shirt, a sweater, a dress-up shirt, and three pairs of pants. "You'll have clothes here," his father said. "I'll have to get the pants shortened." There were socks and handkerchiefs and underwear. They were all for him, but they belonged to some boy he didn't know. The more boxes Justin opened, the more rotten he felt about the new boy who was getting outfitted.

There was a new sleeping bag and then there were still two packages to go. "Open the big one," his father said. He handed Justin his Swiss Army knife to cut through the tape around the cardboard box. Inside there was another box. *Super Nintendo.*

"I've heard of this. The graphics are awesome!"

"I saw a demonstration at the store. Awesome. Much better than the one at home."

Justin was glad he'd have the company of Nintendo in the new place, but the second set just made the split feel more hopeless.

"Open the last package."

There were all the new cartridges Justin had heard about. "Wow! Some of these aren't even out yet, Dad."

"They'd just got a shipment in. I got one of everything."

"Thanks!"

"C'mon, let's set this sucker up."

Justin remembered his birthday when he'd gotten the first Nintendo. His father must have been thinking about the same thing because he said, "Remember in *Duck Hunt* how Mom kept missing and the dog kept coming up to the screen and laughing at her?"

Dad, Justin wanted to say, please don't talk about Mom. Just don't.

His father made a salad and did frozen french fries in the oven and then grilled a steak. His father always thought that grilling a steak made everything all right. They had designer ice cream for dessert.

The new Super Nintendo really was awesome, but Justin didn't have the energy to play it after dinner and couldn't figure out why. All of a sudden there were so many things he couldn't figure out about himself.

When Justin went to brush his teeth, there were towels from home in the bathroom. The same look, the same feel, the same smell. He held a towel to his face and breathed deeply. For a few seconds he felt safe and secure, and then he felt absolutely desolate. He had to stay in the bathroom for a few minutes before going to bed just so he could stop crying.

His father was sitting beside the bed, the folktale book on his lap, when Justin came into the twins' room.

"I thought you'd fallen in," his father said. "I was going to come in and flush a rope down the toilet and see if I could pull you out."

Justin smiled a little. He settled into the new sleeping bag on top of the bed and zipped it up.

"Pretty good dinner, great new game," his father said. "See, us guys can make out okay on our own."

"Dad?"

"Yeah?"

"How come you bought me that big new game? I mean, it's not Christmas or my birthday or anything."

"So we can have something to do together. All the stuff we usually play is back at the house."

"Oh."

"That was a funny question."

"I was just wondering."

"I've got to get a bike rack or something. I want you to have your bike with you when you're with me. So we can go riding together."

"Dad?"

"Yes?"

"What did you mean before when you said till we get back to our own place?"

"Wouldn't it be nice if we were back there together?"

"Us and Mom?"

"You and me."

"Are you going to get the house?"

"I don't know. The court decides that."

"What about Mom? If you get the house."

"She'll have to find a place of her own. Like she's making me do now."

"I don't care if I live there," Justin's ears heard Justin saying.

"Don't you like the house? Your room? The things we have there, the—"

"I don't know."

"That shocks and surprises me, Justin."

"You and Mom, you're just fighting over the house."

"That's true. We can't agree about it."

"But what about me? *Who am I going to be with?*"

"Mom and I'll work that out. The same as if we were married."

"I thought the judge decides, the lawyers decide."

"It's up to the judge, that's right. But Mom and I have something to say about that. We're not fighting over you."

Why not? Justin wanted to know.

"You ready for me to read?"

"Yes."

When his father kissed him good night and turned on the Segovia that Justin had already loaded, his father said, "Big day tomorrow. Your mother's coming to call."

"Oh, yeah," Justin said.

Alone again in the dark, the very familiar going-to-sleep music seemed to be coming from his room at home at the other end of the lake. Maybe another Justin was going to sleep there, someone who had taken his place. Maybe the other Justin was the real Justin. Justin cried quietly. He cried for the Justin who had been displaced, the Justin who lay in this new sleeping bag with its brand-new smell.

8

A BIG DAY LAKESIDE
WITH MOM AND DAD

JUSTIN GOT UP EARLY AND PLAYED NINTENDO. THEN HE put it away. He didn't want his mother to know about it. He did not understand why he felt that way.

"A *perfect* day to be out on the water," his father said. It was a little after nine and his father was standing on the deck looking out at the lake, a mug of coffee in his hand. "Sunny. Breezy. A *perfect* day for sailing."

Justin did not like the sound of his father's voice. There was something strange in the way his father had said it.

"Where are you going, Justin?"

"Inside."

"What are you going to do?"

"Watch cartoons."

"Not on a day like this."

"That's what I'd do at home. On a Saturday morning. When there isn't soccer. What's different about here?"

"Everything," his father said quietly. "Go ahead."

"Unless there's something you want me to do?"

"Watch cartoons. Scramble your brains."

But the trouble was, the cartoons wouldn't scramble his brains. And his father was acting really weird, which further distracted Justin from the cartoons. First his father swept the downstairs. Then the deck. Then the upstairs. Then he was moving things around. Justin asked again if he could help, but his father just said no.

Justin got up and turned off the TV and went out on the deck. At home he could have been fooling with things. Or he would have biked over to Ryan's. But this was his dad's time now, not his own. Time got divided between Mom and Dad, Amanda had said, and the person who got the most time with you was the person who let you have the most time on your own.

Bart Murganwheeler was in his late forties, Sue Murganwheeler just about forty, Gamble guessed. The Murganwheelers stood in the two-story foyer of the Whitney house where on a day such as this sunlight exploded everywhere without dazzling. Gamble saw that they were impressed and that was half her intent in making a voyage from the house to the Grayson house rather than just driving over.

"What a marvelous house!" Sue Murganwheeler said.

"Driving up, well, it *is* astounding. For this part of the country. I've seen some places like it in California."

"It *is* nice," Gamble said.

"Sue would buy it."

"It's not for sale."

"Good. It's not quite my style. I like something a little bit more traditional."

"You'll feel more comfortable in the Grayson house."

"But this house is fascinating," Bart said.

"Could we see it?" Sue said. "Or would that be an imposition? Or an intrusion?"

"Come along," Gamble said. "Would you like some coffee first? Tea?"

The Murganwheelers followed Gamble through the house with gratifying expressions of wonder and appreciation. The master bedroom, however, was still more than they were prepared for. Twenty feet wide, it jutted out above the lake with an expanse of windows and sliding glass panels. The lake and the autumn foliage seemed to fill the room. And then Gamble had them step out onto the bedroom's narrow balcony above the lake.

"How did a house like this ever come to be?" Sue said.

"It grew with the marriage," Gamble said.

"Some marriage," Bart said.

"Yes. Skip and I were just married. We were living in Manchester and looking for what folks in New Hampshire call 'a camp.' That can be anything from a lean-to to an entire estate—just so long as it's on a lake or off in the woods and you use it for recreation instead of your primary residence. Well, we found this place. It was just a kitchen and a bedroom and bath then. No heat. But it was so gloriously situated and it had all this lovely land. That was twelve years ago, just before land started to be at a premium here. Even so, the price was dear for a couple starting off. But Skip and I fell in love with it—the lake, the view, the forest. Well, we couldn't afford a place in Manchester *and* a camp at that price, even if it was only a shack then, so we came out here and roughed it year-round. We put in propane heat and started *doing* things—taking out a wall here, laying a new floor there. Skip did very well very quickly in his business and I saw the opportunities in local real estate immediately. The house grew right along with our careers. It wasn't long after we started adding on and building upward from the additions that we realized it made the best sense to simply raze the original place rather than trying to preserve it. And so we did and built over it. And here we are."

They all had a good look at the lake—as if they had not noticed it before.

The *Yar* slipped through the water eagerly before a following breeze, the hull making a satisfying hiss and gurgle.

The house had done its work on the Murganwheelers, Gamble knew. She was no longer cast in the role of the real estate agent dependent on her betters' pleasure for a sale and commission. She had demonstrated, through the house, that she herself was landed and affluent, that she was, at the very least, the Murganwheelers' equal. And all that was as it had to be because she was asking a steep price for the Grayson house, though not an inappropriate one.

Gamble looked to the far end of the lake, where the Graysons' house would appear, with all the nervousness of a first-voyage seaman on watch and warned of mountainous seas ahead.

His father had come out on the deck and stood still, an instant of dead calm, a pause in all the to-ing and fro-ing that had been going on.

Justin looked out on the water where his father was looking. There was a sail in the distance. There were other sails, but Justin knew this sail was his, although he would not have been able to say what distinguished it from the other sails. A sail against the blue of the water, the red and orange and yellow of the leaves along the shore.

When it was nearer, Justin saw three figures in the sailboat. One, he saw, was his mother, though, like the sail, there was no definition that accounted for his knowing that it was his mother. And when it got nearer and he saw that it definitely was the *Yar* and his mother, Justin had a sudden fear. His mother was coming here deliberately to his father's house. There would be a big fight in front of the other people. For an instant he hated his mother. Then he hated his father, too.

The *Yar* made good speed toward the Graysons' dock, too much speed, Justin thought; his mother was going to slam in and his father was going to be furious.

But his mother dropped sail just at the right instant and the *Yar* slipped in slowly to the dock. At the bow his father kept the boat from bumping, stepped down onto it, and threw Justin a line to be secured on a dock post. Then his father hopped up on the dock and went to the stern. His mother threw her line to his father and he pulled the stern in and secured it. Then his mother got up and his father gave her a hand up onto the dock. Justin watched with fascination as if what he was watching were taking place in slow motion.

His father said to his mother, "Hello, dear."

"Why, hello to you, *dear*," his mother said with surprise and warmth and a smile.

Justin couldn't believe it. He felt the way he had when he had hoped he would wake from the bad dream. He knew now that that wouldn't happen. *But* . . . But maybe all the bad stuff was a game his parents had been playing and they were calling the game off now.

His mother said to the two other people, "This is Skip. And this is our son Justin. They're baching it this weekend, camping out. Sue and Bart Murganwheeler. Skip, would you help me with the hamper? *And* the wine?"

"I'll get the hamper. You get the wine."

On the deck, Sue said, "It *is* a lovely house. Just as you said."

"I'll show you through it in a few minutes."

"It's *so* attractive from the lake."

"It's equally attractive inside. And it's been *impeccably* cared for and maintained." His mother shot a look at his father.

"It has," his father said.

"Before I show you around, why don't we have a drink first? Sit down and enjoy the dock and the view? I've brought some Bloody Marys."

"Just the thing," Bart Murganwheeler said.

"Just the thing," his father said.

"I hope so," his mother said. She turned to Justin. "Sweetie, I've brought you your favorite root beer."

Justin studied the grown-ups. The Murganwheelers were older than his parents. Mr. Murganwheeler wore plaid pants and a jersey with a logo on it. Mrs. Murganwheeler wore a khaki skirt and a pink button-down shirt with the sleeves rolled up.

His mother was wearing white canvas Bermudas, white sneakers, and a short-sleeved blue-checked shirt. There was a blue bandana holding her blond hair back. His father had on white canvas slacks, a blue-checked short-sleeved shirt, and espadrilles. He had a blue bandana tied casually around his neck beneath the collar of the shirt.

Justin sipped his root beer and stared at the matching images, mother and father, husband and wife. His father had his hip cocked against the deck railing. His mother sat against the railing.

It was just like always, except they were in a different house.

His mother put her empty glass down on the picnic table. "I've brought some awfully nice wine. I mean, Skip and I think it is—I hope you will. So let me show you the house and then we'll have some lunch."

"Splendid," Bart said. "What a pleasure to have a realtor treat you as a friend rather than a mark, eh, Sue?"

"Absolutely."

His father said, "Shall I unpack the hamper, dear?"

"Thank you, Skip, would you do that while I show Sue and Bart the house?"

"Happy to."

"Thank you."

"No problem."

Justin could not understand them. They were getting on so well. He felt an emotion he could not identify at first. Then he recognized it. It was rage. He wanted to scream at his parents—because they were being so good together and he was not part of it.

Justin watched his father pour from the third bottle of wine. There had been espresso and tiny cakes for dessert, but the wine kept going.

"Awfully decent wine," his father said, for about the fifth time.

"Extremely," Sue said.

"My wife's choice," his father said. "Impeccable taste."

"In men as well as wine," Sue said.

"Thank you, thank you," his father said.

"I'm the one to say thank you," his mother said.

Bart had been lying back on a lounger, but now he stood up and said to his wife, "My God, these people are *incredible*. With this house and neighbors like these, I'm ready to settle in right now."

"Bart," his wife said.

"Nothing like it in New York. Isn't this the best place we've seen? Aren't these the nicest people we've met?"

"Bart, be cautious. Remember, we have to be in a bargaining position." She laughed. "He didn't build a business doing business this way."

"Sold it," Bart said. "Built it from nothing to—well, a lot of money. Now don't hold me up on this house because I said that."

"Oh, no," his mother said.

"He's got an idea for a new business," Sue said. "He wants to set it up in Manchester. He thinks he can do it there."

"I do, and my business comes from all over the country," his father said.

"We better bargain about this place, Sue. Don't you agree?"

"Well, yes, but maybe this good wine—we ought to think about it."

His father poured the last of the wine into Bart's glass and, when Sue shook her head, into his own. "Yes, you ought to think about it. Needs a lot of work. Winterizing."

"Skip, I've told them about that."

"Probably cost you as much again as the house."

"Oh, Skip, don't be ridiculous. The property value alone—"

"You like to fish, Bart?"

"He *adores* it," Sue said.

"Skip and I have caught landlocked salmon here," his mother added quickly.

"Because, if you like to fish," his father said, "I'll tell you something about this lake. In all honesty. The goddamn acid rain is killing off everything worth catching."

"Really?"

"Really. Honest to God."

"Skip," his mother said with the approximation of a smile, "you paint such a bleak picture. I'm sure—"

"Property values on this lake are just way overinflated. Take our house, dear."

"What?"

"Isn't that your intention? I couldn't afford that house if I had to buy it."

Justin found that he had gotten so small no one could see him. The Murganwheelers were still smiling but they looked at each other as if for guidance.

"The wine and the sun," his mother said. "We're not making any sense."

"But I can recommend the leaves," his father said. "The leaves in the fall are splendid. And they're free."

"I think Sue and Bart and I will be heading back now, Skip."

"Bon voyage!" His father shook hands with Bart and kissed Sue with his arms around her. He said to Gamble, "Our new friends are just delicious." His father turned to Bart. "Another thing about the leaves, some people say the acid rain's been improving them."

The Murganwheelers went down to the dock. His mother held back, stopped, and spoke to his father at the foot of the steps to the deck.

"If I lose this sale—"

"I can lose you that sale anytime I want."

"If you do—"

"I'll be over for the *sail*boat tomorrow morning. Early."

"The sails may not be available."

"If they're not, I guarantee you, you'll lose this sale."

"You've gone a long way on that already, Skip."

"I can undo it with a telephone call. Bart and I are buddies, didn't you see?"

"I saw the way you hit on Sue. Bart saw it, too. Don't count on his being your buddy."

"Well, *you* better. If you want this sale."

"Make that call."

"Give me the number. I'll find a phone booth."

It had gotten dark outside. His father was cooking dinner. "Anything good on TV? Look in *TV Guide.* I wish they had a VCR here, I'd have gotten us some movies. I'll have to get one of the VCRs from home. Justin? Are you listening to me? Why are you stalking around? Why aren't you playing Nintendo or your guitar or something?"

"Dad? How come you did that to Mom?"

His father put down a wooden spoon. "Oh, boy. Are you taking sides?"

"I just want to know. Why?"

"Because of what she did to me. What she's *doing.* Sometimes you have to stand up for yourself."

9

A STRANGE CAR

THE NEXT DAY THERE WAS A COLD, CONTINUOUS RAIN, AND Justin was glad that it was so. They wouldn't go over to the house for the *Yar.* There wouldn't be a fight over the sailboat.

Instead he and his father ran. When they came back in, they tried to make the house warm by building a fire in the fireplace. "Useless," his father said. "A fireplace sucks all the warm air out of the rest of the house. It'll be freezing here tonight. I have to buy some wood, there's almost nothing left. I may take you back early."

Justin shrugged. He had no idea what time he was supposed to be home.

Justin and his father played some Nintendo games. Then they played chess. Then they had lunch. Then they played checkers. His father put on the Patriots game and they watched that. The Patriots lost. The house was cold. His father was fidgety. "It's early, but I better take you ho—, I better take you back to your mother."

It wasn't four o'clock yet.

Justin went up to the twins' room and got his stuff together.

There was a car Justin didn't recognize parked outside the house.

Inside there was light upstairs coming from the doorway to his parents' bedroom, but the rest of the house was dark with the grayness that creeps in when there's dank weather outside.

His father switched on the hanging light inside the entrance. "*Hello?*" his father called, "*Hello?*"

They were standing at the foot of the open-step stairway, the blond flight rising up to the garrison balcony, the open library, and the bedrooms beyond the balcony.

There was no sound from upstairs. No sound from anywhere in the house.

"*Hello?*" his father called again. "*Hello?* You up there, Gamble?"

Justin heard a door close upstairs. He thought he heard his mother's voice.

"What?" his father said.

"Just a minute," Justin thought he heard. His mother's voice, from wherever it was coming, was faint.

"What?"

"Just a minute!" His mother appeared on the balcony tying a robe closed around her. She came down the stairs. She was barefoot. "I didn't expect you till five." She looked kind of wet, the way she did when she came in from running with his father.

"The house got too cold," his father said.

His mother came all the way down the stairs and bent and kissed Justin. "Hello, sweetie." She rubbed his hair. "Did you have a good time?"

"Sure."

She stood up. "I tried to call you. I wanted to tell you you could have Justin late or even overnight if you wanted."

"Is that so? The telephone isn't—"

"I know. I found that out. You can still take him back, if you want."

"I explained. The house is cold. And I'm running out of wood."

His mother had hugged her arms around herself as if *she* were cold. "You could have called from a pay phone or something. That would have been the responsible thing to do."

"I'm sorry you find it irresponsible that I bring Justin back a little early so he can be in a warm house. I'm sorry it seems to inconvenience you."

"I didn't say it was an inconvenience. Where are you going?"

His father had started up the stairs. "I want to get some of my stuff from the bedroom."

His mother went a stair higher than his father. "Tell me what you want and I'll get it for you."

His father stepped around his mother. "That's all right, I'll get it for myself."

His mother went up and stood directly in front of his father on the same step. "I said, I'll get it for you. Just tell me what you want."

"There are several things. I'll get them for myself. You couldn't find them."

His father started up the stairs. His mother went two steps above and faced him, looking down. It was like some sort of dance that Justin had never seen before. "It's my bedroom now, Skip, and I won't have you in it."

"It's still my house and *my* bedroom, even if I don't sleep in it and—"

"*Our* house, if you want to be legal about—"

"I'll go up there if I want to and remove whatever personal possessions of mine I want—"

"Stay out of my bedroom!" His mother was on the same step as his father and she had grabbed his wrists. "You just go *right back downstairs,* do you hear me, and I'll get—"

"I hear you—" His father was trying to remove his mother's hands from his wrists.

It had been a sort of no-touch dance and then the couple got together for the end. It was also scary because they were struggling up there.

"*Skip,* look at Justin."

He was staring up at his parents.

His father spoke to his mother in a very low, even voice. "Gamble, I'm going up to the bedroom if I have to drag you along with me."

His mother stayed on the stairs while his father went up. She began to cry. After a moment she came down the stairs. "Got a handkerchief?" she said to Justin. Justin gave her his handkerchief. She wiped her eyes. "Thanks."

Then they waited together and the house was utterly silent again.

After a while his father appeared on the balcony and came slowly and quietly down the stairs. He carried a wet suit, two business suits, and a jacket on hangers and he had some folded shirts in plastic bags under his arm and some ties slung over his arm.

"Find what you wanted?" Gamble said.

"More or less."

"Good. Now get out."

His father stood at the bottom of the steps, somewhat imprisoned by all the clothes he was transporting. "Hey, Justin, give me a hug." His father bent his knees. Justin hugged him. "I love you," his father said.

Justin gave him a very tight hug. "I love you, too."

"I guess you'll have to open the door for me."

Justin did so, but his father did not go out. His father said to his mother, "Whose car is that out there?"

Justin was very surprised because his mother began to laugh. "The wagon's in the shop, Skip. Because you messed it up by overloading it. That's a loaner."

His father nodded a little looking down at the floor and then went out.

His mother went to the door and there was silence for a few seconds and then Justin heard her call out to his father, *"My secret loaner, you bastard!"*

"I'm sorry, Justin. I'm sorry you have to be exposed to all that."

"Yeah."

"It's part of this. It's part of people breaking up. There's a lot of resentment and suspicion."

"Why can't you just be friends if you can't be anything else?"

"It doesn't work that way."

"How come you wanted me to stay with Dad? Don't you want me here?"

"Of course I do, honey." Gamble knelt down and hugged Justin. "I love you more than anything in the world, you know that."

"More than anything?"

"Yes. And your dad does, too. I want you to know that, no matter what goes on between him and me. I respect that part of him—"

"Then why—?"

"Shhh, Justin." His mother stood up again. "Of course I want you here. But something's come up." She touched her hair. "Damn, I wanted to wash my hair and—Oh, it's just too late now. Look, Bart and Sue Murganwheeler invited me to dinner at the inn. I think it means they want to make a deal on the Graysons' house—"

"Does that mean Dad has to move out?"

"No, no, sweetie. They've got to winterize it before they can move in. I hate to do this to you, but I need to get them while they're hot. This will put me over the two million mark for the second year in a row. You and I can use the money. We can keep this house then. You know I'm not asking your dad for any money."

Justin shrugged.

"What I did was, I drove into Manchester and got you fried rice and that Szechuan chicken you like—"

"With the peanuts?"

"Yes and—"

"Awesome!"

"So dinner won't be so bad even if you are alone. And I taped *Romancing the Stone* for you last night and—"

"Awesome!"

"I'll be back by nine. I'll be back in time to read to you. Now I've got to get ready. Everything's out, you just have to heat it up—"

"I know, gently."

"Yes. We're having an early dinner so I can get back here and be with you. But first, *ta-da!*, a surprise!"

"What?"

"Come into the TV room."

There was a gift-wrapped box. He opened it and found another set of the new Nintendo games. Justin stared at them and then he realized he wasn't displaying the enthusiasm, the excitement, his mother expected to see. He tried to. "Really, Mom, they're great." But he knew he wasn't bringing it off.

"What's wrong?"

"Nothing. They're really great."

"They told me you'd *love* these new games—"

"They're just great. Chinese food, new games, *Romancing the Stone,* I'll have a *great* evening."

10

THE DEVIL BECKONS

GAMBLE HAD WRITTEN DOWN THE NUMBER OF THE INN, kissed Justin, and gone out. She had been wearing perfume. The smell of it had transported Justin back to special evenings when his parents had been all dressed up and he had been little and there had been a babysitter and his parents were going off to do something special with other grown-ups that grown-ups did when they got all dressed up and had perfume on.

The house was quiet again. There was an emptiness to it as if it were uninhabited in spite of Justin's presence. It wasn't his home anymore. It was a battleground. And the battle was being fought *for* the battleground. Justin wished it was just his home again.

He didn't want to play Nintendo, he didn't want to eat dinner, he didn't want to watch *Romancing the Stone*. The best he could think of doing was to play with his Legos. And he wanted *company*.

He took his big box of Legos into the TV room and turned on the TV and sat down on the floor in front of it.

There was that angry-looking man he had seen on the news a little while back.

"The New England Show" . . . Tonight, the Boston Devil himself, Boston's superlawyer, Weld Pennyworth. His offices are in Boston, but he's known in courtrooms around the country, most recently in San Francisco where he represented Cornelia Canby in her divorce action against her husband Senator Gordon Canby, the recent heir to one of California's largest fortunes, involving a timber and mining empire, controlling interest in the film studio American International, and private ownership of Rienzi Brothers Vineyards. Also at issue was custody of the Canbys' two children, Melissa, aged eleven, and Warren, aged five . . .

It was just another one of those news specials to which Justin was exposed, rather passively, each day. Often he didn't hear them—they were just background noise—or he switched channels. But now that he knew what custody was and he had a little idea of what it must be for grown-ups to be battling over an empire, he was vaguely interested, although most of his concentration remained on his Legos.

This is Weld Pennyworth's private Lear Jet, which, incidentally, he pilots himself.

Pennyworth: If someone else flew it, I'd have to sit back there reading all the drivel I have to read anyway. It's a good way to make money, but it's not a fit occupation for a grown man. Divorce litigation means toiling in [bleep]. So I sit up front and leave the flying to myself. It's a marvelous way to get from place to place, flying is, and doing it yourself is more than half the fun, it's all the fun.

Voice-Over: One recent week, while arguing the Canby trial in San Francisco, Pennyworth also managed to consult in person with clients in Atlanta and Houston.

Pennyworth: You do it on weekends, when court isn't in session. It's a great advantage of not being married—your weekends are free. Of course, my clients seek to emulate my condition and are willing to pay great amounts of money to achieve that end. They are trying not to be married. And they want to exit that condition in the best possible circumstances. That means money, property, and children, usually in that order.

Voice-Over: But Mr. Pennyworth does not favor one sex over the other.

Pennyworth: I am gender-blind. If you need me, I will represent you.

Voice-Over: If you have the money. Or if you had the money. Even the money isn't enough now, as we shall see. We'll continue this "New England Profile" of Attorney Weld Pennyworth after this.

Justin hadn't watched too closely, but he had heard every word. Now he leaned back on his elbows and looked at the ads, not hearing a word that was said. Pennyworth knew all about this stuff.

Justin was thinking about that when the program resumed.

Voice-Over: Very little is known about Weld Pennyworth— and he will not talk about himself—prior to 1976 when he graduated from Harvard Law School and celebrated the occasion by flying a light plane upside down under the Mystic River

Bridge, a feat for which he had his pilot's license suspended. That was the abrupt beginning of his public history.

In 1978 he was a Boston city prosecutor. In 1979 he gravitated to juvenile court where he was a public defender for two years.

Pennyworth: The dregs of the profession. Divorce law is the pits, but juvenile law runs a close second.

Voice-Over: A stint of another two years in criminal law, representing clients as diverse as Carmine "Crazy-head" Rappoli, the reputed Mafia hit man; the Philadelphia Three, who allegedly blew up federal offices where draft registrations were kept; and American Standard Chemical, charged with criminally polluting seventy thousand acres of forest in northern Wisconsin, served as a bridge to—

Pennyworth: It was a natural transition from juvenile law to criminal law and from criminal law to divorce litigation.

Voice-Over: I get the impression that you regret it.

Pennyworth: I regret that I didn't charge more.

Voice-Over: Your fee in the Canby case is reputed to exceed one million dollars.

Pennyworth: I worked very hard on the Canby case.

Voice-Over: This is Weld Pennyworth's home, a townhouse with its own cobblestone courtyard off Joy Street. Not as famed a townhouse residence as Louisburg Square, but perhaps more exclusive.

Pennyworth: I can walk to and from my office. That sometimes is the only joy in my day.

Voice-Over: Up there on the thirty-third floor of One Beacon Street, on the riverside corner of the building, high above most other buildings in Boston, are Weld Pennyworth's offices. They are opulent offices, decorated by people who charge opulent prices for their services, but the furnishings have an unmistakable Pennyworth touch: a mixture of the antique and the contemporary, the plain and the ornate. The glass doorway reads, simply, Weld Pennyworth, Attorney.

Inside there is a staff of fourteen. Three attorneys who assist Mr. Pennyworth, seven assistants who assist the attorneys and run the office, and four people who assist Mr. Pennyworth.

Voice-Over, addressing Pennyworth: Your staff is very fond of you. They gave you a surprise party last year for your fortieth birthday.

Pennyworth: I believe that is so.

Voice-Over: There is a story that the party displeased you.

Pennyworth: It was thoughtful of them.

Justin was now studying Pennyworth carefully. The man was cold. He was thin. He had black hair carefully combed to one side. He had cold eyes behind black, wire-rimmed spectacles. He looked a little older than Justin's parents and ready to live forever on simple meanness. He interested Justin.

Voice-Over: Known for dramatic and aggressive tactics in the courtroom, Weld Pennyworth is, in person, polite and ultra-controlled. But, as *Time* magazine wrote of him after *Jonathan versus Jonathan*, where he won custody of three school-age children for the stepfather from the biological mother, "If Pennyworth is the adversary, you quickly realize that something out of your own worst nightmare is coming straight at you."

Time went on to conclude that "Daniel Webster himself might not have triumphed against *this* Devil-at-Law," and so it is that in the years since the Jonathan case, Pennyworth has been regularly referred to as the Boston Devil. He does nothing to discourage that characterization.

Indeed, in *Canby versus Canby*, when it was alleged that both litigants had been members of a satanic cult and had participated in its ceremonies, Pennyworth's opposing counsel suggested that Pennyworth himself was the supreme authority in the courtroom on Satanism and Pennyworth replied, mildly, that that was probably so.

Canby was certainly the sort of litigation one would have thought Pennyworth would revel in—it did appear, as the trial progressed through its seventeen days, that he *was* reveling in it: the young children, the vast fortune, the many residences around the world, and finally Senator Canby's own career and presidential prospects at stake. Mistresses, lovers, alleged homosexual liaisons by both parties, sadomasochism, Satanism—children, sex, money, property, political power. And here is what Pennyworth had to say after it was all over and he had won.

Pennyworth: I am exhausted.

Reporter: The devil exhausted?

Pennyworth (with considerable hostility): The devil never sleeps.

Looking at him, Justin could believe that Pennyworth never slept.

Reporter: Does it bother you that, almost as a side issue in this litigation, you've probably cost the senator the next election?

Pennyworth: I cost him no such thing. The senator cost himself the next election. The people of California will be well rid of him, and the people of the United States will be spared the obscenity of seeing him in the garb of a presidential aspirant. Neither the people of California nor the people of the United States deserve him.

Voice-Over: Senator Canby told a reporter at the trial that he imagines that you have a limited life expectancy. Does that concern you?

Pennyworth: No, it doesn't bother me at all that my life was threatened by Gordon Canby. I've been threatened as a prosecutor, I've been threatened by opposing counsel and by their clients, I've even been threatened by my own clients. I would not be practicing law if I were concerned about threats.

Voice-Over: These are the faces of some of the beautiful and celebrated women who have, for varying lengths of time, shared Weld Pennyworth's life with him. Each one of them complained bitterly about his disaffection when he broke off their relationship but, soon enough, each one became a steadfast friend. Never married, Pennyworth has some interesting views on marriage and himself.

Pennyworth: I consider marriage to be the root cause of divorce, domestic strife, domestic ill. I have avoided it carefully and successfully. I am much better at friendship than I am at a continuing relationship that requires my daily participation. Regrettably, I do not have the energy for both domestic law and domestic bliss.

Pennyworth looked entirely satisfied with himself, Justin saw.

Voice-Over: But now the devil may have found time for domestic bliss. Returning from San Francisco and the Canby trial, our own Mary Heath caught Weld Pennyworth moments after he'd stepped down from his Lear Jet.

Pennyworth: That's right, I'm through with this. I'd rather clean toilets. Divorce, domestic law, is the pits, and I'm through with it. I will stick to defending corporations, insurance companies, and such. Great impersonalities. No more domestic employment.

Heath: Not even for the rich and famous?

Pennyworth: For absolutely no one.

There was more sound, but Justin did not hear it. He was concentrated on the black hair combed straight across the head, the narrow face, and the eyes that were dark and swift and without compassion. He *was* the coldest man Justin had ever seen. Justin decided to go to the devil. He had no one else to go to.

He looked down and discovered he had made a house out of his Legos. A home. He hadn't even realized he was doing so.

11

THE DEVIL'S BIRTHDAY

PENNYWORTH WAS CELEBRATING HIS FORTY-FIRST BIRTHday, if *celebrate* were not too radical a word to apply to so solitary and unfestive an occasion.

He had spent the past few days, including the weekend, divesting himself and his office of all domestic litigation.

He was a little drunk on a silver pitcher of martinis, a life-giving force to which he rarely subscribed—apart from this one day of the year.

Something about birthdays, his own in particular, made him tremble. He trembled with both fear and rage, neither of which he acknowledged, just as he did not acknowledge their source. Instead, he called up the spirits from the silver pitcher to protect him, and that they did.

In summation on behalf of a client who went into a several-days' incapacitating seizure of fear and trembling each year around the time of a car crash in which the client had been a victim, Pennyworth had quoted his own expert psychiatric witness and said, "The anniversary of a trauma can re-create the trauma."

Pennyworth was alone for the evening and he found that situation entirely agreeable. The year before he had not been so fortunate. His birthday of the year before had been an even more than usually miserable time for him, made that way by his closest associates.

His office staff had given him a surprise party. They had hired a favorite restaurant and closed it to outsiders for the evening. They had hired a favorite pianist and a favorite jazz band. They had invited friends, acquaintances, and even those few clients whose company

Pennyworth held in esteem. The staff and guests had sung a thrilling "Happy Birthday to You" at dessert.

Pennyworth had passed the evening in smiles and champagne and friendly animation. Before he begged forgiveness to retire rather early in the evening, he had made a parting toast, a notable summation of gratitude to everyone on his staff not only for the party but also for the mainstay of their support in his professional life. Then he bade them a cheery good night, embraced a woman here, a woman there, shook hands all about, and went home to write a memo on his computer, which he immediately dispatched by modem to his office, priority notice, to be delivered to every member of the staff as the first piece of business the next morning, to wit:

> Thanks again to one and all for the thoughtfulness of the party and please be advised, collectively and individually, never, never again to intrude upon my birthday, not even to acknowledge it with a greeting.

Pennyworth felt especially fortunate that he did not have a wife to complicate his birthdays. A wife's company would be especially difficult to escape on a birthday. Deborah, the most recent to want to be his wife, was gone from his life—for the time being. (If she ran true to the form of the others, she would return after a while as something of a long-lost friend and be greeted and prized as such.) Sonja would probably spend the night with him tomorrow, unless she had given him a false signal, in which case she had wasted his time and wouldn't get another chance. Actually Pennyworth could have had her company this very evening—and probably very nearly any other company he might have desired—but tonight he desired only the company of the spirits from the silver pitcher.

Yes, his birthdays severely taxed Pennyworth's emotional stamina. That much he recognized. But it was not accumulating age—not the accumulation of years at all. What he perceived (or allowed himself to perceive) was a sadness and a foreboding for which he could find no explanation, not even the serial sense of his own mortality. He could not remember when this yearly sense of helplessness and hopelessness, of utter defeat, had begun.

That put Pennyworth in mind of life insurance and insurance companies in general, and with it came the first happy thought of the day: New England Mutual had insured a client corporation, National Logistics, against claims under default of contract, and the government of the United States, on behalf of the Department of Defense, was suing NL for one hundred million dollars for failure to procure, distribute, maintain, and replace certain materiel vital to national defense. Pennyworth loved the case. He didn't like any of the litigants. The litigation would ultimately be decided upon the basis of tactical error committed by one of the teams of attorneys involved. The case would take years to prepare and there would be many continuances. It was an intellectual challenge devoid of personal lives. Pennyworth just loved it.

12
SUMMONING THE DEVIL

JUSTIN'S FATHER CALLED ABOUT EIGHT O'CLOCK TO SEE IF Justin was all right and to apologize for the scene with his mother that afternoon. Justin felt uncomfortable when his father apologized to him. He didn't know how to accept it or what to say. "That's okay, Dad." He hoped that was the right sort of thing to say.

His mother called a few minutes later to say she had some exciting news. She'd closed the deal, she was just having a nightcap with the Murganwheelers, they said to say hello to him, what a wonderful boy he was, they hoped he'd visit them in the house when they were settled in next year. Did you have a bath? Well, take it now, I'll be home by nine, and, oh, did anyone call?

"Just Dad."

"What did he want?"

"Nothing."

"Okay. See you soon."

When Gamble got home, Justin was in his pajamas and already in bed trying to read the second volume of *The Chronicles of Prydain* and unable to settle into the fantasy, a state of mind he had not experienced before.

His mother was very excited. She hugged him and then brought the chair over to his bedside and took a book off the shelf and held it in her lap. She smelled a little of wine or something.

"This is just the most wonderful thing, Justin. They are so lovely. They have a lot of friends in New York who're interested in property up here, I mean *very* wealthy people. They had one of them with them at dinner tonight. A very famous doctor, a cardiologist—"

"What's that?"

"A heart surgeon."

"Oh."

"A very handsome man. And not married. He *liked* me. See, my life isn't over just because I'm getting a divorce—"

"But you're still married to Dad."

"I don't mean it *that* way, silly." She tousled Justin's hair.

"Quit it. I shampooed and combed it real careful."

"And it won't get messed up while you're asleep, silly?"

"Not like that."

"Anyway, I just meant that it's nice to know that twelve years of marriage haven't turned me into an old witch. But *listen, Justin,* this could be *so much money,* you wouldn't believe it. We could be so well off, you and I. We could have all kinds of things we wanted—"

"Like what? More Nintendo games?"

"Just like that. Regular trips to Europe and vacations in the Caribbean and skiing in Vale and Switzerland—"

"The skiing here is fine. Besides, I can't take the time off from school."

"Oh, yes, you could. You're smart enough. Traveling is educational. I could get you a tutor if you needed one."

"I don't want a tutor. I want things to be the same."

"They'll be *better,* Justin. Look at right now. Isn't it cozy here alone, just the two of us?"

Justin turned his head away. "I just wish you'd read."

Carlos Montoya had long since clicked off automatically at the end of the cassette. In the darkness Justin looked up with his eyes open and saw the cold, narrow face of Weld Pennyworth. *The lawyer he must get.*

But he had no money, and it wasn't like he was a prince or something, somebody famous like a child actor on TV. He had no connection with Pennyworth and no way of meeting him. And Pennyworth had said he was through with divorce, it was the pits.

Justin agreed with him about that. He got up and went to his desk and turned on the light. He wrote the letter three times before he got it the way he wanted. Then he had to decide whether to write it in cursive or block. His block was easier to read, but the cursive would look more grown-up, as if the writer of the letter knew what he was doing.

He took a piece of the lined paper from school that he did his homework on and wrote in cursive and in pencil so that he could erase his mistakes:

Dear Mr. Pennyworth,

I heard you say on TV tonight that you are fed up disgusted with divorce and custody. Me too.

I am 10½ years old and in fifth grade. My mom and dad are getting a divorce and fighting about the house and things. I am against it.

Please call me at this number which is my regular home: 603 597 9095. You can call collect. The best time to call is when I'm here alone. I get home from school at 2:30 and nobody's here and then I go to soccer practice unless it's raining. So any time in there would be good. Friday is a Teachers Workshop Day which is No School, so I will stay home all day.

Justin wrote Sincerely, and signed his name, then wrote:

PS. Please call.

He studied the letter for mistakes. Then he read it over several times. It felt good.

He had a rubber stamp for his name and address and he inked it and stamped the letter and the envelope. He remembered the address, it was simple: #1 Beacon Street, 33rd Floor, Boston, MA, and for the ZIP, which he didn't know, he used his grandmother's who lived in Boston, where they could probably figure out the ZIP for him.

He sealed the envelope and put a stamp on, turned out the light, and went to bed with his heart sending little thrills through his body that kept him awake the way it did on Christmas Eve and the night before his birthday.

13

CLYDE

BUT THE LETTER WOULDN'T GET THERE FOR *DAYS* MAYBE. That thought woke Justin a good hour before he had to get up at six-thirty for his seven-fifteen bus to school. He knew it was childish to want something *right away,* but he wanted the letter to get to Mr. Pennyworth *right away.*

At breakfast he rushed through the microwave pancakes and went back upstairs while his mother, in her robe, was still drowsily sipping at coffee and waiting to see him off. Justin made it seem like he was going back upstairs to go to the bathroom, but at the top of the stairs he tiptoed into his parents' bedroom and picked up the phone and hoped with the fear of a thief that his mother wouldn't hear him.

He dialed a number he was familiar with from having called it occasionally for rides to Boston to see his grandmother.

"Mr. Giambelli? This is your neighbor Justin."

"Hello there, Justin. Need a ride to Boston?"

"No, but I have something that does. Are you going to Boston today, Mr. Giambelli?"

"Unless my show's been canceled."

Mr. Giambelli had a radio talk show that aired from one to four every day. It was perfect for going in and coming back from Boston. "Are you leaving soon?"

"Right now."

"See, I've got this letter I've got to get to Boston right away. Would you take it in for me? I'll run right up to the mailbox and put it there for you. Okay? You can pick it up. Okay?"

"What's your rush, Justin?" his mother said, but he didn't explain, kissed her in passing, and tore up the driveway. "Did you pack your lunch?" she called after him.

"Yes!" he called back and ran so fast he could feel the cool air parting around his face.

He was about to put the letter in the mailbox when Mr. Giambelli drove up in his black Corvette. "Federal Express, Mr. Whitney. You have an overnight letter?"

"No, for today."

"Let's have it. I'll mail it from the studio. It's for Boston?"

"Yes."

"It'll get delivered tomorrow. God willing."

Justin handed it in through the open window.

Mr. Giambelli glanced at the address. He laughed. "Well, Justin, you getting divorced? I didn't even know you were married."

"My parents are getting divorced."

Mr. Giambelli's manner changed immediately. "I didn't know that. I'm sorry to hear that."

"That's okay."

Mr. Giambelli looked at the envelope again. "He's not doing divorce anymore, anyway. I was just making a joke. I'm sorry."

"That's okay."

"You know what? I've never been divorced. I'm one of the few people I know like that. Amazing."

"I guess."

"I'm sorry for you, Justin. It's a mean time. Anything Mrs. Giambelli or I can do for you, you let us know."

"Okay. Thanks."

Mr. Giambelli flipped the envelope a little. "Had Pennyworth on the show . . . *twice*. Once when I was starting out, and he was, too, and once a couple of years ago. He's a good interview. Everything goes *zing* when he's on."

"Are you a friend of his, Mr. Giambelli?"

"Justin, my lad, no one is a friend of Mr. Pennyworth's. I'm sorry to say, in fact, that I don't think Mr. Pennyworth is a friend of Mr. Pennyworth."

Justin thought that was odd and then decided it was impossible.

Mr. Giambelli said, "Your package will be delivered to the postal authorities before ten-thirty this morning. Thank you for calling Giambelli Express."

After school Justin went home with Ryan to Ryan's house to work on their worm project.

They paused in the enclosed breezeway to say hello to Blackie, their pet rabbit. At the school fair in the spring they had won enough prize tickets so that, pooled together, they could get the black rabbit. Originally, the rabbit was to spend one week at Ryan's house and the next at Justin's, and then back and forth. But Justin's parents, who had some extreme prejudice against having any pet in the house—a dog Justin had always wanted, or a cat, or even a gerbil or hamster—of course wouldn't have the rabbit, even though Justin had gotten it on his own and swore he'd take care of it entirely by himself and besides the rabbit would be at Ryan's half the time. But his parents were so extreme about it that they spent eighty dollars and bought a rabbit cage and other stuff and gave it to the MacKenzies just "as a house gift," Justin's mother said, "so Blackie can stay at the MacKenzies' forever."

"Can't he ever come here? Even if he stays outside?"

"His home is at the MacKenzies'. He'll feel safe there. If you bring him here, he might get scared. He might run away."

Bogus, Justin had thought.

Before they went to work on the worms, Justin sat on the floor with Blackie on his lap and stroked the smooth fur.

"Sometimes I think he purrs," Justin said.

"I think so, too."

They dug for worms in Ryan's mother's herb garden. "There's always a big motherload of worms here," Ryan said.

When they had gotten a can full, Ryan went into the house and came back with a salt shaker.

"What's that for?"

"Experiment. MacKenzie and Whitney Worm Company R and D." He removed a worm from the can and placed it on one of the bricks that made the border of the herb garden. "Observe. Someone told me, if you pour salt on a worm, it like boils."

Ryan picked up the salt shaker, and Justin screamed at him, *"Stop it! Don't!"*

"Hey, what is it?"

Justin had come over to Ryan and pushed him away. "You don't have to take a hyper!" Ryan said.

"Leave the worm alone. Don't do it. Don't do it to *any* worm. *Any*time. Even if I'm not here."

"Jeezum, Justin!"

"Just don't."

"You push me again, I'll clobber you, Justin."

"Maybe your mom has a glass jar or something."

"Huh?"

"A glass jar. Could you get me a glass jar, *please?*"

"Bonkers, Justin, bonkers. The divorce is making you crazy. You need a shrink."

"I need a glass jar."

Ryan went into the kitchen again and came back with a glass jar. He handed it to Justin.

"I need something to poke holes in the top."

"I think someone poked holes in your top." Ryan went away a third time and Justin filled the jar three-quarters of the way up with damp earth. "Here," Ryan said and handed Justin a hammer and a nail.

Justin put some holes in the metal top. Then he placed the worm that had been about to be the subject of the experiment into the jar, pulled some grass and put the grass on top, and screwed the top on.

"What are you going to do with that?"

"It's not *that*, it's Clyde."

"How come it's Clyde?"

"Because that's what I'm going to call it."

"What are you going to do with Clyde?"

"I'm going to take him home."

"What for?"

"To be my pet."

Ryan's mother drove the boys to soccer practice and Justin took Clyde along, but then hid him in his backpack. When his mother picked up the boys to take them home after practice, he didn't tell her about Clyde.

He put Clyde in his room under the bed and went back to the library to do his guitar practice. But first he used the phone up there.

"Who're you calling?" his mother said from downstairs.

"Dr. Blanchette."

"Dr. Blanchette?"

"For my worm project. Don't listen. It'll gross you out."

"You don't have to tell me twice."

"Mrs. Blanchette? Is Dr. Blanchette there? This is Justin Whitney." When the veterinarian got on, Justin said, "I've got this earthworm, and I know it sounds kinda stupid, but he's sort of a pet I want to raise and I want to know what I should do for him, you know, what to feed him, how to take care of him, what sort of home to make for him."

"You mean an earthworm from the grass?"

"From a garden."

"All right. What I'd do is get a shoebox and punch holes in the sides and top to let air in. Get dirt and grass clippings and put them in. Keep the soil moist, but don't overdo it."

"What should I feed it?"

"Justin, it's been a long time since I took care of an earthworm, but I'm pretty sure they eat cereals, grains—I don't mean cereals with sugar. And, oh, yes, they love eggshells and coffee grounds—"

"Really?"

"Really. Especially eggshells. You can give it table scraps—garbage."

"Is that all?"

"Keep it in a cool, dark place. That's the kind of environment they're used to."

"Could I build it a house? I mean, like with wood?"

"I don't see why not. Sure. A shoebox'll get damp and moldy. Just make sure you have the holes in it. You can use some holes in the bottom, too, for drainage."

"Thanks, Dr. Blanchette."

Justin went into his room and got the glass jar out, but he couldn't see Clyde anywhere inside. Clyde had gone to bed early, Justin decided. He went downstairs to get a pinch of cornflakes to put in

Clyde's jar so that when Clyde woke up he'd have a good breakfast. But before he got to the kitchen, he heard his mother on the phone. From her tone of voice he knew she must be talking to his father.

"Did you have a good swim?" his mother asked flatly. Then his mother's voice flattened even more. "I came into the kitchen to make dinner and I happened to glance out the window and there's the *Yar* without a mast— . . . I'm looking at it right now, Skip. There's the *Yar* and the mast is gone. What did you do, swim over in your wet suit and swim it back? Or did you have a motorbo— . . . You have no right to take *anything* from this house except personal— . . . I think the court order *means,* Skip, that you can't take anything that belongs to this house whether it's in the house or outsi— . . . If you carry on like this, things are going to be very difficult between you and me, I'm trying to do this as decently as I can but you— . . . That's right, I'm *in* the house and you're *out,* that's just the breaks of the game, buddy, but you damn well better play by the rules . . . The *court's* rules . . . So if *you* can't use the *Yar, I* can't use the *Yar.* How childish can you get, Skip? . . . Sick? You want to know what sick is? Stealing the mast, Skip. How phallic can you get? How *threatened?* Stealing a mast? . . . Well, you know where you can shove it, Skip."

When it was over, Justin went back upstairs and did his guitar practice. Then he came down and got the cereal for Clyde.

14

AWAITING THE DEVIL

ON TUESDAY JUSTIN RAN ALL THE WAY HOME FROM THE bus to be there for the call from Mr. Pennyworth, but the only call in all the waiting he did after that was from his father to say that he'd talked to his mother and that he'd be taking Justin to his soccer game and bringing him back.

"Am I going to be with you this weekend?"

"You'll be with Mom this weekend. It goes back and forth. For now. Why?"

"I want to build something with you. I drew up the plans. Do you think you could come over sometime? So we could use your tools?"

"What do you want to build?"

"Oh, just something. I'll explain in the car. A sort of box with holes in it. It's only about a foot long and maybe six inches wide and it doesn't have to be very tall. Maybe four inches. Would you ask Mom about it? About coming over to build it with me?"

"There's a better chance if you ask."

"Sure," his mom said when Justin asked her. "As long as I'm not here while he's here. And as long as he doesn't steal anything from the house."

Justin bowed his head.

On Wednesday, as soon as he got home from school, Justin cooked himself an egg so he could have the shell. The telephone did not ring at all, but his father came by early so they could make the wooden box at his father's workbench in the cellar before the soccer game.

"What's this for, Justin?"

"Oh, it's for my worm project."

Before they left for soccer, his father went into the kitchen and came back with a big wooden salad bowl, a yellow enamel Dutch oven, and two of the copper pots that hung over the butcher-block table in the kitchen.

Justin looked at the floor. "Mom said you aren't supposed to take anything."

"That's between Mom and me. The Graysons don't have much to cook with." His father was about to go out but stopped. "You see these pots? They're twelve hundred dollars for the whole set. They've just hung there since we got them. They've just been for show. Mom and I don't do twelve-hundred-dollar cooking. We hardly cook at all, you know that. But now I'm cooking, young man, and if Mom—"

"I don't want to hear about it."

As soon as he got back from soccer, Justin dug soft earth from the flower garden—making sure there were no worms in it—and put the earth and some grass clippings in the box he and his father had made, and he added broken pieces of eggshell and took the box up to his room and transferred Clyde to it. Then he sat on the floor and cradled the box in his arms, and gently rocked it back and forth and hummed some Segovia.

Afterward he put Clyde to bed under his own bed.

On Thursday Justin sat by the silent phone for as long as he could bear it and then he went to the room his parents used as an at-home office and got out the Boston telephone directory and looked up *Pennyworth* and there it was: Pennyworth, Weld, One Beacon Street . . . 555-3268.

Justin got it wrong the first time, forgetting to dial 1 and the area code. But then he *did* get it and a woman's voice said, "Weld Pennyworth's office . . . Hello?"

Justin hadn't figured out what to say, and further, he was struck dumb by being in contact with the great man's telephone.

"Hello?"

"Yeah," Justin said. "Hello. My name is Justin Whitney. I wrote Mr. Pennyworth a letter and I was wondering, did he get it?"

"Justin, did you say?"

"Yes, ma'am, Justin Whitney."

"Let me ask Mr. Pennyworth's secretary, Justin. Will you hold on? I'll have to put you on hold."

"Thanks." Justin looked at the stacks of business magazines his parents kept near the desk.

"Justin?"

"Yes."

"Yes, Mr. Pennyworth did receive your letter."

"Well, can I talk to him?"

"Mr. Pennyworth is in conference."

"Is he going to call me?"

"All I know is that he got your letter. Excuse me, I'm the receptionist here and there are some people waiting."

"Thanks," Justin said, bowing his head without realizing it.

He took Clyde for a walk. Ryan was wicked mad at him for not working on the worm business this afternoon, but Justin had told Ryan he had something so important to do it was even more important than getting the work done for Mr. Dunphy, and besides, it wasn't due till the end of next week. Ryan had threatened to dissolve their business partnership.

When he came back in, he called Pennyworth again. "Hello, this is Justin."

"Hello, Justin. Mr. Pennyworth's still in conference."

"Okay."

Justin called Amanda's mother, who was going to take him to soccer practice and bring him back home, and told her he felt a little sick to his stomach, he wasn't going to go.

"Did you tell your mother?"

"I'll be all right."

"Well, it's going around."

"I'm just going to rest."

"Okay. I hope you feel better."

Justin waited till five o'clock and then called Pennyworth again.

The woman who did the phone answering said, "I'm sorry, Justin, but Mr. Pennyworth is a very busy man. I don't think he's going to be able to return your call."

"Ever?"

"I'm sorry, Justin."

"Oh . . . I see . . . Well, thanks," and he hung up.

He sat there for a long time and he really did feel sick to his stomach.

15

BESEECHING THE DEVIL

DURING THE NIGHT JUSTIN DECIDED TO GO TO BOSTON. HE decided he would go to Pennyworth's office and try to see him in person.

He looked at his bedside clock. Ten minutes after eleven. His mother would still be up—watching the eleven o'clock news. She was a news junkie. Both his parents were. She said it had something to do with Watergate. For a long time Justin thought that had to do with her waters breaking when she had him.

She was sitting up in bed watching TV. "Justin, what's wrong?"

"Nothing."

She waved the remote control at the set and the set went *hss-blonk*.

"See," he said, "I was lying in bed and I was thinking—you know, tomorrow's Teachers Workshop, no school."

"I know. I told you I was sorry I can't be with you, but—"

"That's all right. So I was thinking, would it be all right if I got a ride in with Mr. Giambelli?"

"Go to Boston?"

"Yeah."

"See Granny?"

"Well, maybe. I mean, no."

"What then?"

"Remember you let me and Ryan go in to the Science Museum?"

"Ryan's going to go with you?"

"Well, no."

"What are you planning to do?"

"Just go to Boston."

"Justin, I'm not going to have you wandering around Boston alone. Not at ten years old—"

"Ten and a half."

"I know. I have every reason to remember. I don't think your father would approve, either."

"You guys let me go in with Ryan and you let me go in alone to see Granny—"

"Of course I'll let you go in if you're going to see Granny. At least I'll know where you are."

"Sure, I'll go see Granny."

"I'll call her now. She'll be delighted."

On the way in, there was usually very little talking with Mr. Giambelli. He was always listening to tapes of background material on people who were going to be his guests, or parts of their books or something. This morning it was about a bill that was going up before the Massachusetts legislature and Justin went to sleep. He needed the sleep. He had not been getting his usual good night's sleep and he had been awake most of last night planning his talk with Mr. Pennyworth and how he would convince Mr. Pennyworth to be his lawyer.

Granny was his mother's mother. She lived in an apartment on Commonwealth Avenue down near the Garden. His mother always gave him money to take a cab from the radio station to Granny's, but Justin found it was easier to walk than to get a cab to stop for him.

He got to his grandmother's at nine-thirty and she had some chocolate and fruit croissants for him. "Fresh baked," she said. "I went out and got them from the baker first thing."

"They're good."

"What do you think of what's going on, Justin?"

"I don't like it. I don't want it to happen."

"That's what I think. A pox on both their houses is what I think."

"What's a pox?"

"It's an expression. I thought I'd take you out for Chinese for lunch or we could—"

"Actually, Granny, I've got to go somewhere right now."

"Your mother didn't tell me anything about that."

"I didn't tell her anything about that." Justin had decided he'd

just walk out, run away from Granny's if he had to. But he wasn't
going to lie to her.

"I don't like that. Where is it you'd go?"

"I'd rather not say."

"Why not?"

"It's to stop the divorce."

"Well, I'm all for that, Justin. Do you think it's possible?"

"I've got an idea. It's okay, Granny. Really, I'll be fine."

"I'll take you, wherever it is. And I'll wait."

"That won't work out."

"Why not?"

"It just won't."

"Justin, I can't let you go alone, much less to some place you won't
even tell me about."

"I've got to go, Granny." Justin went over and kissed her. "I've
got to."

"Justin? Justin, you can't just leave . . . *Justin!*"

Justin stepped out of the elevator. A panoramic window gave him
a view of the Charles and the river basin. The water was as blue as
the cloudless sky above it. Here on the thirty-third floor Justin felt
as if he were in the sky.

He recognized the glass doors to Mr. Pennyworth's office from the
television program. He went in to a woman at the reception desk.
She had a fancy console beside the desk and she answered the phone
and said, "Weld Pennyworth's office," and then pushed a button.
"Yes, young man?"

"My name is Justin Whitney and I'd like to see Mr. Pennyworth,
please."

"Justin Whit—? *Oh*, Justin. We spoke on the phone yesterday."

"Yes, ma'am."

"I explained to you that Mr. Pennyworth is unavailable."

"I came all the way in from New Hampshire."

"Just a minute." She picked up her phone and pushed a button.
"Eleanor? Justin Whitney from New Hampshire is here to see Mr.
Pennyworth . . . Yes, I know he doesn't have an appointment . . ."
She listened and replaced the receiver. "Mr. Pennyworth is in con-
ference with clients all day today."

"I'll just wait," Justin said. "In case." He went over and sat on a
couch. He looked around and felt as if he were on a sort of spaceship
that was carrying antiques through the galaxy. There wasn't anything
good to read, but then he remembered there were cartoons in *The
New Yorker*. From time to time people went in to or came out from

offices beyond a large black door with a gold knob. Justin was starting on a third *New Yorker* when a woman's voice said to him, "You must be young Justin Whitney."

He looked up and then stood. "Yes, ma'am." The woman was all dressed up the way his mother got for business sometimes.

"I'm Mr. Pennyworth's secretary, Justin, and I'm sorry to have to tell you that he just won't be able to see you. It's going to be a waste of time for you to stay here."

"I don't have anything else to do. My ride back isn't till five."

"We'd prefer that you wait somewhere else."

"I don't have any other place to wait."

"All right. As long as you realize it's a waste of your time." She went back through the black door.

Justin went through *Boston Magazine* and dipped into *Time*s and *Newsweek*s.

A new woman came in and took the place of the woman at the desk. The woman who had been sitting at the desk came over and said, "Justin, it's one o'clock and I'm going to lunch. You must be hungry."

Justin shrugged.

"Would you like me to bring something back for you?"

"That's okay." He looked down at the magazine. "Thanks, though."

There wasn't *anything* to read or look at in *U.S. News & World Report*. Justin got up and looked around. He found some *Sports Illustrated*s on another table. Usually they would have excited him. But he was all magazined-out. He could hardly relate the pictures to anything he knew about.

"Here, Justin." The woman who had been at the desk had returned. She handed him a waxed paper bag. "Chicken salad sandwich, milk, cookies, and a nectarine." She spread out two paper napkins on the table in front of the couch.

"Gee, thanks." He reached into his pocket for money.

"My treat," the woman said. "You've got the stamina of a lawyer."

Justin did not know if that was good or bad.

Three o'clock and Justin was too bored to look at magazines. He just sat and looked up whenever the black door opened. He never saw Mr. Pennyworth. He would have to leave at four to be sure to be on time for Mr. Giambelli. The office was air-conditioned, but Justin felt hot and sweaty.

Three-thirty. Justin was having difficulty keeping himself awake. But the later it got, the more rapidly his heart beat. He couldn't remember what he was going to say to Mr. Pennyworth.

The black door opened and Mr. Pennyworth came out. He wore a charcoal suit, blue shirt, bright red tie, and shiny black shoes. He was taller than Justin had thought, but there were the cold eyes behind the black-rimmed glasses. His black hair was immaculately combed across his head. He wasn't as old-looking as he had been on TV. He seemed startled when he saw Justin.

Justin went over to him right away before he could go back through the black door.

"I'm Justin Whitney, Mr. Pennyworth, and I wrote you a letter and—"

"I know who you are. I read your letter. I left instructions that I have no interest in your case."

"I know you won't do divorce, but I want to sue my parents *not* to get a divorce."

"Don't be stupid, young man." Pennyworth's voice was so loud the receptionist looked over. The voice embarrassed and frightened Justin. "If your parents are getting a divorce, they have split up, and that's the reality. Your parents have a right to get a divorce. You have no right in that at all. What you're looking for isn't realistic." Justin felt near to crying. Why was he *so loud?* "The suit you contemplate has no basis. You can't make it into an issue. It isn't an issue. Never has been before and won't be now. There is nothing you can do."

"Has anyone ever tried it?"

"Not that I know. I repeat, there is nothing you can do."

Justin stood in front of Pennyworth so that Pennyworth couldn't get by him. It was like guarding a seventh- or eighth-grader in basketball, except that Pennyworth was bigger.

"The court makes the appropriate disposition of the child."

"I'm the child."

"That has not escaped me." Pennyworth peered at the blond-haired boy. He was briefly touched by a distant resemblance—other than for the color of the hair—to himself at that age. Except that, Pennyworth thought, at that age I would not have had the daring or the resolve to do what this boy is doing. Certainly I did not have the imagination. "It is not your stature that's at issue, it's your thinking. Your thinking is *dumb*. It's never-never land."

Justin wanted to cry out, *Please don't yell at me! Please!*

But Pennyworth went on in the loud, angry voice, not the cool voice of the man on TV. "All right, Justin. Let's see exactly how dumb, how *stupid*. Let us say the court, in an equally stupid frame of mind even for New Hampshire, let us say the court entertains your suit that your parents not get a divorce. Then what's to happen? You have two parents in the same household who do not want to be there—"

"They *both* want to be there! They're *fighting* over the house—"

"Two parents in the same household who do not want to be there together, who despise each other. What is the court to do about that? Who is going to supervise them?"

"I will."

"The idea is impertinent. Bear this in mind. The court acts to keep people from doing wrong. There is little the court can do to make people do things right."

"Who says?"

"You are being insolent, you are being snotty."

"If you'd just let me explain what I figured out—"

Pennyworth looked at his watch. "Young man, my fee is three hundred dollars an hour and expenses. We have been in consultation now for seven minutes. Thirty-five dollars. And that is just small talk."

"I couldn't—"

"I also require a retainer of ten thousand dollars."

"What's a retainer?"

"Some money in advance to keep me in your employ. Otherwise I go to work for someone else. Meanwhile, young man, as we stand here chitchatting, the meter is running. It is costing you five dollars a minute, for which I would certainly bill you, were I to take you on, and that I have no intention of doing. So, in this brief consultation, I have saved you a great deal of money. Now, I don't wish to be rude, but *get off*. The court will make whatever award of you it sees fit."

"Award? How can I be awarded? I'm not some stupid soccer trophy!"

Pennyworth went rapidly out of his reception room to the bank of elevators outside. He rang for an elevator and glanced back through the glass doors and saw the boy looking at him and coming toward him.

Pennyworth did not hesitate. In full, swift stride he rounded a corner, opened a door, and went down the fire stairs as quickly as he could.

"Your mother wants you to call her right away," Mr. Giambelli said when Justin got to his office. "She's worried. And upset."

Justin called her. She said, "Justin, are you all right?"

"Yes."

"All right." She hung up. That's all she had to say. Justin thought there would have been more.

He was still pretty much all right until he got into Mr. Giambelli's Corvette and they were driving and he realized that he was going home, or rather that he would never have a home to go to again, not *his* home, and that Mr. Pennyworth not only wouldn't help him, but *didn't like him,* and that was the way he, Justin, had thought the divorce had started anyway, because he had done something bad, *his parents didn't like him,* and that's why they were getting a divorce.

"Hey," Mr. Giambelli said, "it's okay to cry, Justin, but tell me what's hurting?"

"Nothing. *Everything.*"

Dumb, stupid. That's what Mr. Pennyworth had said. And Justin trusted Mr. Pennyworth entirely.

Pennyworth got home to his house off Joy Street at seven. All the curtains and all the drapes were drawn.

Pennyworth spent much of his life up in the air: in his office thirty-three stories above the ground, in his airplane miles above the ground. But at night he wanted to be closed in, the drapes and curtains drawn against the night, the house in which he slept firmly footed upon the earth and not so tall that it could not be protected by its neighbors in a storm.

He had run from the child, that much was plain.

He called Sonja and said he would not see her that evening. She was angry. It was Friday. He was to have taken her to dinner with friends, he had accepted the invitation. He asked her to call and make his apologies. He shut the phone off.

He did not drink and he did not eat.

He did not know what the problem was. He did not suspect that there was a problem. He was tired. That was all. He showered and brushed his teeth and was content to be in bed before nine.

He felt as he had as a boy when night itself was a curtain and he drew it up over himself and hid in it until it rewarded him with sleep.

But thoughts that were odd and alien intruded and interfered with Pennyworth's getting to sleep.

Why had he used such a loud voice with the boy? He had heard his own voice and it had frightened even himself for an instant.

Why had he *run* from the boy instead of merely dismissing him?

Because you panicked, the Voice said.

It was a voice Pennyworth had not heard in a long time, but it was not an unfamiliar voice. It was a voice that he had heard ever since he was a schoolboy, a voice that sometimes spoke as a friend, sometimes not; sometimes mocked, sometimes cajoled, sometimes warned or even provided a running commentary on Pennyworth's most inner life, a sort of single-voiced Greek chorus that Pennyworth had lugged around with himself all these years, a voice he was used to. It was very much like his own.

Happy birthday to you, the Voice sang, happy birthday to you, happy birthday, dear We-eld, happy birthday to you.

It was getting on to midnight. Pennyworth got up and went to his den and poured himself a very large cognac, a piece of business entirely uncustomary for him once he had retired. And when, ready to return to his bed once more, he heard, or thought he heard, the Voice beginning to hum the happy birthday tune in some dismal part of his mind, Pennyworth opted for the cognac once again and turned on the television with enough volume to white out any sounds going on in his mind. It was not until a little after two in the morning—with considerable assistance from the brandy bottle—that Pennyworth felt safe and secure that any and all voices in his mind had been stilled for the night.

16

THE MORNING AFTER
ON JOY STREET

PENNYWORTH SLEPT FITFULLY.

He awoke to the sound and smell of heat rising into his bedroom through the registers. It must have turned chilly during the night. Although it was still dark in the room, there was a line of gray light at one end of the drapes. He looked at his bedside clock. A few minutes after six.

He made a weary journey to the bathroom and then got under the covers again. He was *so* tired. But he discovered he had no intention of letting himself sleep. There were questions before the court, questions that Pennyworth was charged with both asking and answering, and charged to do so by Pennyworth himself.

He heard himself saying to the boy, You cannot sue your parents not to get a divorce. The suit you contemplate has no basis. There is nothing you can do.

Has anyone ever tried it? the boy had said.

No. I repeat, there is nothing you can do.

Sue parents not to get a divorce? Maybe a child ought to be able to do that. Alone, enjoying his own counsel, Pennyworth found it a legal and intellectual challenge. Maybe the child ought to be able to do that.

In *Surviving the Breakup,* Wallerstein and Kelly had reported following fifteen hundred family breakups in California and had come to a conclusion at odds with traditional wisdom. Tradition said that when parents were in abrasive disharmony with each other over a long and continuous period of time, divorce provided a corrective that benefited the child. Wallerstein and Kelly, however, found that though children perceived the unhappiness at home, it had a different impact on them than it did upon the warring spouses. There was a lingering injury from divorce more profound than any injury suffered when the parents remained together.

Pennyworth ticked off a note on the yellow legal notepad in his mind: spousal v. parental responsibilities (and rights).

Rights of the parents over the rights of the child—a nice legal conflict. *Tic.*

In a divorce, custody and visitation are the only child-directed issues. *Tic.* Might I introduce other issues on behalf of the child?

No, no, no: This is *craziness,* Pennyworth, the Voice said.

Make other things the base issue? What? Yes, there's a path to be explored: make something other than Custody and Visitation the base issues. But what?

Ah, getting intellectually interested, Pennyworth. A legal challenge to your mind, the Voice said. In law school, Pennyworth had found the Voice to be especially useful. By then it had matured and he had often disputed with it.

It's never happened, he had told the boy. Can you make it happen, Pennyworth? he asked himself.

Parents have a statutory right to divorce.

What rights does a child have in a divorce?

Pennyworth got up and brushed his teeth and paused to examine himself in the mirror for signs of irrationality. As ever, he found none.

When he arrived in the kitchen, wearing his silk foulard robe, the coffee—programmed by his housekeeper the day before—had already perked. He sat down with a cup at the kitchen table. He was mightily hungry from not having eaten the night before, but he did not want to interrupt his mind with food. His stomach would just have to wait its turn.

The Court will make its disposition of the child, after it has heard out the merits of the divorce disputes, according to what it has determined to be in the best interests of the minor child.

Tactic: Don't wait for the disposition; don't wait for the guardian ad litem; don't wait for psychiatric evaluation—Get in there before the parents get to court. Tell the Court that *the conflict itself is not in the best interests of the child.*

The Court will laugh you out of court, Pennyworth, the Voice said.

Don't be so sure. It depends how I frame it—and when I get it in.

Oh, are you going to do it then, Pennyworth?

It's interesting, it's interesting, Pennyworth thought.

Pennyworth searched his mind for precedents, the more remote the better.

Tinker v. Independent School System of Des Moines (1969), in which the Court found that a student has the same rights in school as out of school. Let's reverse that, Pennyworth said to the Voice. A student has the same rights out of school as in school. If a teacher abused or neglected young Justin Whitney in such a psychological manner, if *two* teachers did so . . .

The Voice said, Parents have superior rights to teachers.

Parents do not have the right to abuse. Parents do not have the right to neglect.

Pennyworth found that he was getting fidgety. He also found that he had drunk half the pot of coffee. What he had already drunk was continuing to perk in his veins and arteries. Nevertheless he poured another cup. He gave thought to homeowner's insurance.

If a child is injured in his parents' house, if the insurance settlement proves to be unsatisfactory, the child may sue the parent (even at the parent's behest) because the insurance is in the name of the parent. . . . *Tic.* Show that this child has been injured, but there is no insurance to cover his injury. The parents must be held accountable—it is a matter of personal injury.

If a child is injured in his parents' house . . . Certainly I was injured in my parents' house, Pennyworth thought. He had a fleeting recollection of his parents' divorce, a subject to which he devoted so little reflection that it almost might not have happened at all, at least not to Pennyworth, though perhaps to a distant relative he had once known, a boy who was unfortunate enough, or irresponsible enough, or unloved enough, to have lost his parents to new families and lost his home, his boyhood, to people he didn't even know. Pennyworth once again dismissed the boy.

Pennyworth poured the last cup of coffee. The kitchen was ablaze with light from outside. Pennyworth was ablaze with light from inside. Pennyworth envisioned something daring, something extravagant, and original. A two-pronged attack. *Two* courts. One court versus the other. Now *there* was an interesting idea.

The Voice said to him, Why isn't there punishment for the parents because of what has been done to the child?

Frivolous, Pennyworth responded, though he liked the idea.

Strategy: Get the parents to reconcile in some fashion.

But the concept of reconciliation, Pennyworth suddenly found, to his utter surprise, really *galled* him. For all these years, Pennyworth realized, he had thoroughly enjoyed seeing parents destroy each other. Odd that he had just realized that now.

Q: How to convince the judge there's a hope of reconciliation?

Alternative objective: Assert control of Justin's life by Justin.

Justin's objective: That his parents not get divorced.

Your Honor, Pennyworth said in his mind, we have three people here. The father/husband, the mother/wife, and the child. The child is the most vulnerable of them all. The child is the one most in need of the Court's protection. The child's emotional health and mental well-being are jeopardized by the parents' capriciousness.

Pennyworth found himself standing. As he did so, he thought of the reluctant gunfighter of his boyhood, Shane, strapping on his gun at the end of the movie.

"Your Honor," Pennyworth said aloud, "there is a presumption by society and by the court that a child's parents are the best persons to protect the child and promote his welfare.

"Your Honor, we will not dispute that. We will, in fact, stipulate that it is so."

Pennyworth found his hands at his waist, cinching the gunbelt, placing the prong through the hole and drawing the tongue through the buckle. He patted his hips where the guns would be.

"My client prays, *May it please the Court, I want to sue my parents not to get divorced,* signed Justin Whitney, age ten and a half. And that, Your Honor, is what I am here to do on his behalf."

Pennyworth patted the butts of the six-guns on his hips again. But he wasn't only a gunfighter, Pennyworth realized. He was—once more to his surprise—a little boy in league with another little boy, and oh what meanness they would conspire to do together.

17
ENCOUNTERS

THE MORNING WAS NOT VERY PLEASANT FOR JUSTIN AND the evening before had not been pleasant either.

When Justin had gotten home, his mother said, "You had me very worried."

"I'm sorry."

"Granny said you left early."

"Yes."

"Where did you go?"

"Out."

"What did you do?"

"Nothing." Justin found himself bitterly shocked that he had told a lie.

"I don't believe you, Justin."

"I just had to get out. I just had to be on my own."

His mother scared him by laughing. "We're all the same in this family," she said.

"I felt like everything was pushing in on me. Wherever I go, there's divorce."

"You scared Granny and you scared me. We had no idea where you were, what might have happened to you—"

"I'm sorry."

"I can't let you go to Boston again."

Justin thought of Mr. Pennyworth. "I don't care."

"I know this is a difficult time for you, Justin—"

"Don't keep saying that."

"But the rules would be the same if your father and I were together. He'd be just as upset as I am."

"All right! All right?"

"Don't talk to me that way."

"Well, you make me!" Justin ran to his room and slammed the door. He had never done that.

He dove onto his bed. He felt like crying and sleeping both. He cried a little, but he didn't sleep at all.

He got Clyde's home out and moved the eggshells and grass cuttings and other stuff on top around a little, but no Clyde. He hoped Clyde hadn't gotten out through one of the holes and run away.

He took a popsicle stick and gently parted the soil here and there until he got a partial glimpse of Clyde's brown and pink body. Then he tucked Clyde in again.

After a while his mother opened the door and said, "Come down to dinner."

But all she wanted to do was try to find out where he had been after he had left Granny's and Justin wouldn't tell her and neither of them ate much dinner. Both of them were sulking. Justin was disappointed that grown-ups could sulk, too.

When he got up in the morning, Justin was cautious. He couldn't tell *what* his mother was—cautious? sulky? sleepy?

"I want you to come with me," his mother said. "We're going shopping. I want you to help me pick what we'll have this weekend and some things for next week. Snacks after school, desserts, things I can get in that won't spoil."

"I'd rather go over to Ryan's." But Justin went along unenthusiastically.

"This is my weekend with you. I want you to spend it with me. I see you little enough during the week."

"I've got a game."

"I know that. It's not till ten-thirty. I'll get you there by then."

"I'm supposed to be there half an hour early."

"I know that. I have some experience as your mother." She tousled his hair. "The mother of a soccer player. I'll have you there for warm-up."

"Dad's coming to see the game. I just hope you don't have a fight in front of everybody."

"We don't have fights in front of everybody."

"Yeah, just at home."

"Yes, just at home."

"What about in front of . . . in front of those people last weekend?"

"That wasn't a fight. Don't be unfair, Justin. Your father did the whole thing. I was a victim, can't you see that?"

I'm the victim, Justin thought. *Can't you see that?*

Justin saw his father's car parked across the street from Al's Market. He didn't know if his mother saw it.

They went into the market and his mother bought two lobsters. "A terrible extravagance," she always said, but she smiled with complete pleasure as Al bagged the lobsters and handed them across the counter to her. His mother always thought everything would be okay if she cooked lobsters.

Justin drove the shopping cart as it accumulated both staples and an impressive array of foods his mother characterized as "treats" for him and "extravagances" for her. As they rounded the paper goods aisle and headed into fresh vegetables and frozen foods, Justin almost ran his cart into his father's.

"Hey there, my boy." His father gave him a one-armed hug so as not to embarrass him. "Big game. See you out there. Soon as I get my supplies. Hello, Gamble."

"Hello, Skip."

His parents looked at each other.

"Separate shopping," his father said.

"Yes, it's weird, isn't it?"

"Anything you want me to get for next weekend?" his father said to Justin.

Justin began to tense. That wasn't a neutral topic. "No, nothing. Anything, I guess."

"Well, I'll talk to you later in the week about it. Maybe you'll have some ideas then."

"Nice day, isn't it?" his mother said to his father.

The tension took a nicer hold on Justin.

His father looked to the front of the store and the windows. "Beautiful. Perfect fall day."

"Right," his mother said. "Nice breeze and just warm enough."

Now Justin thought his mother's voice could probably be heard in every aisle in the store. He remained absolutely still as if, if he didn't move, no one would know he was there.

"Perfect day for sailing," his mother said.

"I guess it is." His father seemed amused.

"I thought Justin and I would go sailing today—"

"I thought Justin and I would go sailing *last weekend*—"

"If you don't get that mast back today, Skip, you're not getting Justin next weekend."

"You signed a stipulation that—"

"*Screw* the stipulation," his mother said in a whispery, mean voice. "Justin and I go sailing in the *Yar* today or—"

Justin was withdrawing, as motionlessly as he could, until he rounded the last of the lettuce and headed by the cheese and past the cookies and cakes and through the checkout aisle and back to his mother's station wagon where he scrunched down so no one could see him.

*   *   *

"I'm sorry about that," his mother said after the groceries had been loaded in the wayback and she had settled into the driver's seat.

"No problem," Justin said.

After the first quarter, Mr. Dunphy took Justin out. "You're not paying attention out there, Justin."

Justin didn't reply.

"You're one of our best players. But you're just not helping. You're getting in the way."

Then I'll quit, Justin thought.

"You'll still get at least a half. Show me something in the third period and I'll keep you in the fourth."

I won't show you anything! Justin thought.

They lost the game, and after it was over his mother and father started to face off again.

His mother had that ice-cold sound in her voice. "You removed property from the house, Skip. There's a court order—"

"I did not remove property from the house."

"From the lake. The mast. Property that belongs in the house. I've told Ted Bagley to ask for a Contempt of Court—"

"I wish he'd do that. But I doubt he'd go after anything so trivial that way—"

"The mast?"

"You asked me how phallic can I get? I don't know, Gamble. It's a long time since you let me find out."

Justin saw that other parents and his teammates were glancing at his parents.

"You took the mast."

"I did not."

"It's missing."

"Missing doesn't mean it's taken."

"*God damn you,* Skip Whitney! Don't play games! Where is that mast?"

"You'd keep Justin from me because of a mast?"

"You're goddamn right. Because of the *Yar.* If you removed—"

"But I didn't," his father said. Justin couldn't understand why his father's voice was so pleasant. "I took care of it. I placed it in the cellar for safekeeping. Right down the bulkhead. You'd have found it if you'd just looked. All safe right *inside* the house."

*   *   *

"The sonofabitch!" his mother said as they drove home. "That bastard! Let me *tell* you about your father."

"I don't want to hear it." Justin could hardly hear his own voice.

"There are some things you need to know about your father for your own good."

"I don't want to hear it!"

Of course, the mast was no good inside the house without help to get it on the *Yar*. The problem was setting and raising it, his mother said. "It's as good as not having it at all. Don't you see what your father did? He *screwed* us. As far as sailing. Well, the mast just stays there. Locked up. *No one* sails."

His mother took him to Manchester and they went to Toys "Я" Us and they looked for games they could play together, but then she bought him Laser Tag, which she'd sworn she would never buy because it was like real killing, and she said *she* wouldn't play it with him, she couldn't bring herself to shoot him, but he and Ryan could play it during the week, and then she took him to a movie and then they went home and Gamble cooked the lobsters and frozen french fries and made a salad.

Sunday his mother was going to call a friend to help raise the mast, but the weather was cold and drizzly. The envelope of the house was warm with stored solar heat, but it *felt* cold nonetheless. "It must be the look of things outside," his mother said.

Justin went to sleep that night ready to sink into the blackness of the house and the blackness of the night forever.

18

A GATHERING OF EXPERTS

THE DIVORCED CHILDREN GATHERED AT LUNCH AGAIN. It was the third time and each time there were more of them. They occupied three tables. It was nothing planned. It just seemed that, after that first time when Amanda had gotten them together, it was a good thing to get together at lunch every few days and talk things over—hardships, parents, divorce, "and other grubby things like that," as Heather explained to a classmate who was not divorced.

Ryan told Justin that some of the other kids, who weren't divorced, considered that the divorced kids had formed a clique. Cliques were generally despised by anyone who wasn't in them. If you were a member of a clique it was sort of like being a traitor to the school. Justin told Ryan anyone could sit with the divorced kids. So Ryan joined the suspected clique.

In spite of the subject of their luncheon conversation, there was no self-pity. Defiance, anger, hurt, and even misery (depending upon what had gone on between the divorced parents most recently, and what the fallout had been upon the child), but no self-pity.

"I hope you're thinking about the decisions you're going to make," Amanda said.

"Like what?" Justin said.

"Who you're going to live with. Like that."

"The kid doesn't have any choice in that," Derek said.

"Sometimes she does," Amanda said.

"They ask you," Kira said, "but they don't pay any attention."

"They just pretend to listen to the kid," Derek said, "but they don't really."

Adam said, "It shouldn't be that way, but it's true. The kid can't do anything about it. The kid can't do anything about anything when it comes to divorce."

Amanda said, "Justin, listen. Don't let the judge or the lawyer or your parents do something you don't want them to do."

"Yeah," Heather said. "Scream out loud. Make them listen."

"Make *everyone* listen," Derek said.

"How?" Justin asked. He looked around the table for an answer, but everyone had their heads down, like the silent Chick, pretending to concentrate on lunch.

"You just have to do it," Derek said.

"If you want something done," Kira said. "Like I have to go back and forth on the bus to Boston to see my dad—"

"Going back and forth really sucks," Adam said.

"And then they tell you you can't take your things back and forth," Amanda said. "Like this thing belongs here and that thing stays there and it's things you've always had or they just gave you."

"They split up all your things," Heather said, "and they hate each other so much, they split you up, too."

"I'm not going to let that happen," Justin said.

"Yeah, sure," Derek said.

"When I grow up," Adam said, "one thing I'm not going to be, and that's a pilot or a traveling salesman or something. I'm going to stay in one place."

"Say you don't want to be put on the bus," Kira said to Justin. "You want someone to drive you. Say it. Throw a hyper."

"Or if you want to spend more time with one parent," Derek said.

"Or even if you want to spend no time at all with one parent," Adam said.

"Don't be afraid to say stuff," Amanda said. "Go right out and say it. No matter what."

"Things couldn't get worse," Heather said.

"Yes they could," Derek said. "They could get mad at you. If you need to talk, it's very important to talk to the right person."

"Who's that?" Justin asked.

"How should I know? What're you, dumb or something, Justin?"

Mr. Pennyworth had said he was. Mr. Pennyworth hadn't been the right person to talk to.

Amanda said, "If you need to ask questions, Justin, ask them. No matter who to."

"And don't hold back from knowing information," Adam said. "That's very important. If you're being held back from knowing information, you've got to do something. You should have the right to know everything that's happening."

"They'll try to trick you," Heather said.

"Or get real nice to you," Amanda said.

"Be sure about who you're talking to," Derek said.

"Listen, Justin," Amanda said, "don't let any of the divorce interfere with the good things in your life. Or school. Don't be afraid to talk about it. Or else you'll go into a depression."

"My mom and dad keep arguing. Even though they're crashed and split, they keep arguing. Anywhere at all. They yelled at each other in Al's Market and at the soccer game and back at the house—"

"If you don't want to hear about it," Adam said, "just cut off from the divorce—"

"Like when they talk to you at night when you're trying to go to sleep," Amanda said.

Adam went on. "Just cut off from the divorce. Go to someone else's house. See if you can take a vacation from your parents."

"Do exercise," the usually silent Chick said, not looking up.

Derek said, "See if you can get a psychologist who'll see what you really want."

"Yeah, but kids can really be manipulated," Adam said, "depending on their age. You got to be wicked careful."

"But if a kid doesn't want to see a psychologist, she shouldn't have to go," Heather said.

The silent boy spoke again. "Just give up and let them do to you whatever they want."

Kira said, "Someone should really scare the parents. Like if they love the child, and they don't stay married, something terrible would happen."

"Like what?" Justin said.

"You know," Kira said, "the child would die or get kidnapped or something."

19
THE DEVIL RESPONDS

JUSTIN WAS EATING A BOWL OF CEREAL AND LOOKING OUT at the lake and the mastless *Yar*. He did not expect the telephone to ring and when it did he thought it was probably his mother checking to see if he was home from school. He got up and answered the kitchen phone.

"Master Whitney?"

"Who? Mr. Whitney?"

"*Master* Whitney. Justin Whitney."

"That's me."

"I suspected as much. This is Mr. Pennyworth."

"Gee."

"A deft response. I'm calling to see if you remain interested in my services."

"*Me?*" Justin started to cry. It just burst out of him and there was nothing he could do. He couldn't even talk to Mr. Pennyworth and he was afraid Mr. Pennyworth would hang up and that made it even harder to stop crying.

"Justin, I will call back in five minutes." And Mr. Pennyworth hung up.

Justin made a bowl of his hands several times and filled them with cold water and pressed his face into it and then rubbed his face hard with paper towels. When he had finished, and the crying had gone away, he found that his arms were trembling—and his back and his legs, everything.

But the telephone *did* ring again.

"I should like to discuss this," Mr. Pennyworth said. "Is there any inconvenience? A parent about? A chum?"

"No one."

"Then let us explore this, Justin. I'd prefer consultation in my office, but since that is not opportune, we'll do the thing over the phone."

"Sure."

"Wipe your nose. I can hear it. No sniveling."

"I'm not."

"Let's start with your parents. Full names. Present addresses. Occupations." Pennyworth listened and grunted. "How does their work affect the time each spends with you?" Another grunt. "Who takes care of you?" Pennyworth did not say a word as Justin answered the questions and explained.

"Who filed for divorce?"

"My mom."

"Do you know the grounds?"

"Nothing. Some sort of differences."

"*Irreconcilable* differences."

"Yes."

"And that was when?"

"Two weeks ago about."

"Do you know if your dad filed for divorce, too?"

"He did. My mom was real mad. She said he had no right to file for divorce."

"Do you know the grounds?"

"Same thing. Those differences."

"Tell me about your parents. How you get along with each of them, what you like about each, what you don't like."

"Up until the divorce, I liked just about everything. Now they're . . . They say mean things to each other, they do mean things to each other—and they try to get me to take sides. I don't like that at all."

"Why not?"

"*I love them both.*"

"That puts you between a rock and a hard place, Justin. I want to know more about them. Them and you."

"Isn't this a real expensive call?"

"We will discuss money later. Do you wish to pursue this conversation or not?"

Justin told Pennyworth more than he realized he had known about his parents' relationship with him.

"They seem to be kind, loving parents," Pennyworth said coolly after listening for a long while. "They seem to care about you a good deal."

"Not right now they don't."

"Divorce tends to warp all the relationships it touches. Now, Justin, you have got this thoroughly absurd notion of suing your parents not to get divorced."

"Yes."

"It is senseless and grotesque. Preposterous. And the Court will see it that way."

"I thought you were going to help me."

"New Hampshire has a no-fault divorce law. That means that one person alone can get a divorce if she, or he, wants it. The impediment is whatever people fight over. Custody—"

"They're not fighting over custody."

"They're cooperating about that?"

"I guess."

"What are they fighting over?"

"The house. And who gets to use the sailboat. And some kitchen stuff."

"But not about you."

"No. That's why I want to sue them not to get divorced. They're my mom and dad. They always loved me. Till now. Till this and the stupid house. If I can get them together, they'll love me again."

"Divorce creates bitterness all around, Justin. In some cases it lasts many years. In some cases it lasts entire lifetimes. If you bring suit against your parents, that will at the very least cause friction between you and your parents. Or worse."

"I guess."

"You may be certain."

"Well, I have to do it anyhow."

"This is not a game, Justin. Do you understand that?"

"Yes."

"If you say you want to do it, I will expect you to stick with it. Otherwise I do not wish to participate."

"I'll stick with it, Mr. Pennyworth."

"You will make your parents' lives very difficult. That's not going to make them love you. Divorce is bitter. For everyone."

"I understand."

"You will have to be fearless. That is *the* word. *Fearless.*"

"I will."

"We are going to have to discuss compensation. My fee."

"I haven't got any money."

"We will discuss that. I will attempt to structure the fee accordingly. I'm not happy with this telephone conversation, Justin. It would be much better if we were to have our conversations in person."

"I'm not supposed to go to Boston. I could skip school, I guess."

"No. And as an adversary, I don't wish to come to your parents' house. You do, however, live in the same town as an acquaintance of mine."

"Who's that?"

"Jim Giambelli."

"Mr. Giambelli is the one who drives me into Boston."

"Does he know what's going on?"

"About the divorce. But I didn't say anything about you. He said, if I wanted anything, with the divorce stuff going on and all, just to ask him or Mrs. Giambelli."

"Good. He owes me a favor. For doing his show. I'll give him a call. We might meet at his house."

"You're going to be in New Hampshire?"

"If I'm going to represent you, I'm going to have to be in New Hampshire quite a bit, aren't I?"

"You'll do it?"

"I have a question. I require an honest answer. I will know if it is an honest answer or not."

Justin felt nervous. And he felt another presence in the room. He turned. There was Ryan. Time for soccer practice. Ryan's mother must be waiting outside and he didn't even have his soccer clothes on. He'd been on the phone with Mr. Pennyworth for over an hour.

"Why did you pick me, Justin?"

"I saw you on television."

"That is an insufficient answer."

"You said you were fed up with divorce."

"Still insufficient."

"Because you look mean."

After he had hung up, the Voice said, Why are you doing this, Pennyworth?

Pennyworth pressed his intercom. "Eleanor, get me Bryce Tuttle.

That's Morison, Abbot, Shire & Tuttle in Manchester, New Hampshire."

Up in Justin's room, as Justin got into his shorts and jersey and warm-ups, Ryan said, "That was real heavy stuff, huh?"

"You shouldn't have heard. You snuck in on me."

"Did not! I called from the front door about ten times."

"Okay, okay. You think you know what I was talking about?"

"Stuff to do with the divorce?"

"Yeah. Don't tell anyone."

"Of course not. Can I see Clyde?"

"He's under the bed."

"Dear Bryce."

"Dear Weld. Why do I find a chill wind in my office just because you've called?"

"Look to your conscience, Bryce."

"That's right. It makes cowards of us all, does it not?"

"Not that I've noticed. I am in need of the courtesy of your offices, Bryce."

"How so?"

"I wish to do some research in your library."

"But of course."

"And I want to shop for a judge while I'm there."

"We have some of those here. Not so exotic a selection as you have in Massachusetts."

"What you have will do."

"That's been our experience here."

"I require some information from the clerk of court."

"I will see what can be done."

"A copy of a divorce libel. Gamble G. Whitney v. Conrad J. Whitney. Notice was served about two weeks ago. Presumably there is a cross-libel. I would like a copy of that as well. If a hearing has been set, what is the date? Who is the judge? Have there been temporary orders? If so, a copy thereof."

"Weld, why is it that you always make me feel like a clerk?"

"Look to your conscience, Bryce. I am simply asking for the courtesy of your assistance. I would extend the same to you."

"No doubt. But this is intriguing, Weld. It would seem that you are not representing either of the Whitneys. Upon whose behalf might you be acting then?"

"A mystery client."

"Ah, one of those. When would you like to come by?"

"Nine tomorrow morning."

"It is reputed that the office is indeed open at that hour. I wouldn't know."

"Most appreciative of everything, Bryce."

After Pennyworth had hung up, the Voice said, This will change nothing.

20

THE DEVIL RETURNS TO DANIEL WEBSTER COUNTRY

THE OFFICES OF MORISON, ABBOT, SHIRE & TUTTLE, IN downtown Manchester, were two blocks away from the main street and four blocks away from Hillsborough County Superior Court where Whitney v. Whitney would be heard. And when it was heard, Pennyworth had decided, his client's voice, in the person of Weld Pennyworth, would be the loudest.

A number of attorneys' offices—Morison, Abbot's among them—occupied a line of red-brick Federal row houses with simple but elegant white-columned entry porches, buildings neatly plucked from the nineteenth century (when they had been the homes of mill overseers) and affectionately restored. There was an aspect to them, Pennyworth reflected, of courteous advocacy—no suggestion of housing incivility or any adversarial position that might tend to be antagonistic, belligerent, or combative. Very pleasant to look at and to work in, Pennyworth reflected—a reminder of those pleasant times when gentlemen practiced law in a gentlemanly fashion, times that probably had never existed and certainly did not exist now.

Pennyworth parked his black Porsche Targa in a space at the rear of the Morison, Abbot building reserved for members of the firm.

The carpeted reception area was set with hard black chairs bearing the crests of the law schools from which the partners and their associates had graduated. There was the homey smell of coffee, the soft sounds of easy-listening music, and, from somewhere, the harsh chainsaw sound of a computer printer already hard at work one minute after nine.

The receptionist got on her phone and in a moment a woman came out from the inner offices and said, "I'm Dena, Mr. Tuttle's secretary, Mr. Pennyworth. Mr. Tuttle sends his apologies. He won't be in till later, but here are the materials you requested." She handed him a large manila envelope. "The library is this way. I'm at extension 44. If there is anything you want—"

"Tea with milk and a little sugar," Pennyworth said. By the time she had brought it, Pennyworth was settled at the large conference table, all dark and shiny as if it were never used, his Mont Blanc pen already making black notations on the yellow legal pad he had set down between the volumes he had come to consult: *State of New Hampshire Revised Statutes Annotated* and Volume 3 of *New Hampshire Practice, Family Law,* by Hon. Charles G. Douglas, III, Associate Justice, Supreme Court of New Hampshire. "If my office calls," Pennyworth said to Dena, "I am unavailable."

When Bryce Tuttle came in later to welcome him, Pennyworth did not look up. He simply said, "Later," and continued to read and write.

He did not take lunch or even notice that he had not.

Butterick v. Butterick . . . Perreault v. Cook . . . He particularly liked *Butterick v. Butterick . . .*

Attorneys and secretaries consulted the library. Pennyworth's awareness of them was almost nonexistent. Pennyworth had discovered what any first-rate explorer or astronomer will discover: that what he already expects to be there is there.

Pennyworth had discovered RSA 169C, a celestial black hole in the domestic law of New Hampshire that, if properly exploited, might reasonably be expected to suck vast amounts of the Whitney v. Whitney divorce action into a time warp of indefinite duration, thus causing Whitney *parentae* frustration, desperation, and infinite exasperation, which made it, to Pennyworth's mind, all the sweeter.

Tactics, he had written: *embroil the parents—confuse, disorganize, and exhaust them.*

He picked up the library phone and punched in 44. "Dena, Pennyworth. Please provide me with several copies of the petition for 169C. I'm ready to see Bryce now if he is available."

Tuttle's office, all splendid with brass, teak, etchings, and other nautical memorabilia, had been fitted out like a naval museum right down to the captain's chairs that faced his desk.

"169C," Tuttle said. "Abuse or neglect. I grant you it's a novel approach, but I don't think our judges will go for it."

"I think they have no choice. They will have to give it consideration.

Proper consideration will require time and investigation, reasonable intrusion into the private lives of the parents, additional legal and professional expenses the Whitneys did not anticipate—all these extra inconveniences that people getting a divorce simply don't want to be bothered with."

Tuttle handed a sheaf of forms across the desk: The State of New Hampshire Petition for Abuse or Neglect.

"You are going to maintain," Tuttle said, with the politeness of someone addressing a deranged and possibly dangerous mind, "that your client will suffer serious neglect as a result of a divorce being granted to his parents."

"Serious emotional harm is already being done him. The problem, of course, is that you can't seek an injunction against divorce. And so I avoid that by placing my client under the gentle and protective umbrella of 169C."

"You are not dealing with an umbrella, Weld. All you have there is a statute and a theory."

"A viable theory. The petition meets the standards of the statute. The court will not be able to ignore the petition." Pennyworth smiled, a tender, gentle smile—and any smile at all from Pennyworth would have shocked Tuttle. With an even rarer display of affection, Pennyworth said, "I *love* this statute, 169C. I adore it. It's so very nonspecific."

"How do you propose to apply it? *No, wait.* The divorce will be heard in superior court."

"Yes, yes."

"You are quick to be irritable. I'm getting at something here I'm not sure you appreciate."

"What is it?"

"Your 169C is heard in juvenile court."

"I'm aware."

"Juvenile court is district court."

"District court with the doors closed for the protection of minors. Yes, I'm aware of the distinction."

"Are you proposing to pursue the Whitneys in *two* different courts?"

"Absolutely. Superior court *and* district court. I shall hound them into pliancy."

"What effect is that going to have on your client and his relationship with his parents?"

"Whatever effect it has, it is to his advantage. If they agree to our terms, so much the better—if they agree by taking better care of their child. If they contest with him at home and make him feel worse than he already does, they are only underlining our case of neglect. My client is in a no-lose situation."

"I wish I could be so cold-blooded."

"You haven't the necessary background."

"All right then, how *do* you propose to apply 169C?"

"Impartially—to both parents. Here we have a clear case of interference with a child's well-being."

"The parents' divorce."

"Exactly."

"You realize that if you win this case, it will have a chilling effect upon the whole structure of divorce. The court will not allow it. The court relies upon divorce for much of its employ."

"I appreciate your jocularity."

"It's a good deal more than jocularity."

"Let us look at 169C. The divorce provides clear interference with the minor child's well-being. No one can argue with that. The child may suffer serious emotional impairment. In granting a divorce, the court is party to both of these acts of neglect. In divorcing each other, the parents show clear neglect of the care necessary for the child's mental and emotional health."

"That's true for all children of divorce."

"Ah, but, to my knowledge, no other child has sought the shield of 169C, which explicitly provides for the protection of the child and the protection of the parent–child relationship. I already see and can foresee serious impairment of the child's emotional health. Does divorce not constitute conduct that is injurious to the child?"

"I don't think the intent of the statute encompasses divorce."

"But, brother Tuttle, the statute does not rule it out. The petition and pleadings meet the standards of the statute."

"So you say, so you said."

"The Court will have to overrule me on that."

"Then you are done."

"No, then I appeal. If judges in New Hampshire are like judges elsewhere, they do not like to be overturned."

"I'm not sure that some of our judges in New Hampshire *are* like judges elsewhere."

"I think your judge will want to let me slog it out in his court— let the process run."

"And then what?"

"Meanwhile I am putting Whitney and Whitney through the tortures of the damned in superior court. My client and I will grind them small with the law's delays. They will be happy to escape with whatever I allow them."

"That seems harsh, Weld. Very harsh. All they want is a divorce."

"It has been my personal experience that parents who divorce deserve everything they get. And everything they lose."

"You are downright gleeful, Weld."

"Oh, this is a special case. I have never had the opportunity before of clobbering *both* parents."

"This is an amazing conversation, Weld. The devil against divorce?"

"How could I be? For years I've thrived on it. No, I am not against divorce. It is a most useful institution. It keeps the incidence of homicide down. I have, though—I have discovered because of young Justin Whitney—a singular antipathy to parents who get divorced. Now, let's get on with it. Tell me about the district judge in this bosky hamlet of Carlton, New Hampshire."

"He's an old fart. Rutherford B. Stickney. Ford for short, which he is, very short in the management of his court. Cynical. Been sitting on that bench so long he's got calluses from it. Known to be abusive. Little patience. Roll 'em in, roll 'em out. You can expect early dismissal from him."

"When does he sit?"

"Mondays and Wednesdays. Though he has to appear for arraignments."

"Might he consider other business on an alternate day?"

"Such as a petition for neglect?"

"Precisely."

"I don't know. I could give him a call."

"I'd rather you don't. Tomorrow's Wednesday and he's liable to say bring it in tomorrow."

"What's wrong with that?"

"I want it done on Friday. I want my client safely out of both parents' houses when the order of notice is delivered by the police."

"I can understand that. I'll call him on Thursday. Doesn't mean he'll do it."

"Give it the try."

Tuttle sat back in his chair and clasped his hands across his belly. "Stickney will not allow his court to be used."

"Presumably his court will be as responsive to the statutes of the state of New Hampshire as any other."

"Stickney is a little crazy. A little arbitrary. Colleagues come back from his court with strange tales. Back-to-back decisions in virtually identical cases and each decision the opposite of the other. A kind description is that Stickney has turned *restless*. Well, I would say that he's more than a *little* restless. I listened to him at the last bar association convention. Had a drink with him. Maybe he was just drunk."

"Is he a drinker?"

"Heavens, no. Sober as a judge. And that's what makes his behavior on the bench so odd. Let me rephrase. I withdraw the word 'crazy.' There seems to be a new and strong tendency toward quirkiness. Yes, that's it—quirkiness. You don't know which way he's going to bounce."

Pennyworth looked at his watch. A few minutes before four. "If you'll forgive me, Bryce, I need to consult with my client. Before he goes to soccer practice."

Tuttle stood up. "I was just going to beg leave to go to the gents' anyway. Use my phone." But then he didn't leave. He fixed Pennyworth with close attention. "Weld, I want to say this again. I want to *emphasize* it. I am deeply concerned for the well-being of your client. I am concerned that you are surely going to exacerbate the natural emotional trauma of the divorce. You are having him *sue his parents*. How are they going to react to that, do you think?"

"They're going to be pissed off."

"Yes. And pissed off at whom?"

"Yours truly."

"Sorry. You're not available. You're in Boston. Young Justin is immediately at hand for being pissed off at."

"Then perhaps the parents will unite to deliver their beloved son from the clutches of the devil."

21

SHOPPING FOR A JUDGE

"JUSTIN, PENNYWORTH. WE HAVE MATTERS TO DISCUSS."

"*Sure.*"

"I require your assistance after school on Friday. With whom are you going to be this weekend?"

"I don't know. They haven't decided. I was supposed to be with my dad, but my mom says unless he puts the mast back up on the sailboat I can't go. But she's got to go out of town on Saturday and Dad won't put the mast back up."

"What do you want?"

"I want to go to my friend Ryan's. He invited me over for the weekend. We have a soccer game Saturday morning and then his folks want to take us to the circus in Boston."

"What do *your* folks say?"

"Fine with them. Except my dad wants to go along to the circus, but my mom says if he goes, I can't go."

"What did he say to that?"

"Shit."

"I beg your pardon?"

"He said *Shit*. About that."

"Ah."

"He said he doesn't want to miss seeing me, but if Mom keeps me from seeing him, that helps him, especially if she's not even with me but ships me off to someone else."

"How do you feel about that?"

"I'm just tired of it. I need a vacation from it. I just want them to get back together. But right now I'm glad to go to Ryan's."

"You make sure you do. Can you do that?"

"I think so."

"Now I want you to think carefully about what I'm about to ask you. Do you still wish to sue your parents?"

"Not to get divorced? *Sure!*"

"You won't be suing them not to get divorced. You can't do that. They have a legal right to get divorced. I told you that. You are going to sue them and say that by getting this divorce they are harmfully neglecting you."

"What will that do?"

"That will block the divorce for a while, if the judge will accept your suit. It will also give you some power in the divorce. Instead of two players in the game, there will be three. You will be the third."

"Will it keep them from getting a divorce?"

"Possibly, but probably not. It will give you a say in the divorce."

"But it's possible? It might keep them from getting the divorce?"

"I don't want to mislead you, Justin. It is only a possibility. I am seeking a different sort of outcome."

"Like what?"

"It shall unfold. Now, if you sue your parents, they're not going to like it very much. I imagine they'll be angry with you."

"They'll be ripshit."

"Exactly."

"It's what they deserve."

"My feelings exactly. You may call me in Boston before Friday if you change your mind. Now, what will you do on Friday? How would you get to Ryan's?"

"On the bus."

"There's a delicate situation here. I don't want to be perceived as kidnapping you."

"How can my lawyer kidnap me?"

"Lawyers have done worse by clients. Perhaps you could meet me at the entrance to your home. After school. Bring whatever you need for the weekend at Ryan's. I'll take you over after we've done our business."

"What business?"

"I want you to hand-deliver your petition to the judge."

"Let's go to superior court now," Pennyworth said to Tuttle. He flicked the libel and cross-libel for divorce in Whitney v. Whitney. "Irreconcilable differences have caused the irremediable breakdown of the marriage, wherefore Gamble G. Whitney prays that a divorce from the bonds of matrimony be decreed. Ahunh, ahunh, ahunh . . . To which Conrad J. Whitney answers in the same vein and prays the court one better than his wife—for an *absolute* divorce from the bonds of matrimony. Does that little flourish tell me something about Conrad J. Whitney or about his lawyer?"

"Stuart Bredwell would go one up on his own mother. All in the most precise language, of course."

"And his adversary?"

"Ted Bagley prefers to play the bumpkin. But that's all it is— playacting. The man has considerable intelligence."

"I will further acquaint myself with the gentlemen later." Pennyworth returned to the libels. "Ahunh, ahunh, ahunh . . . Usual allegations and disclaimers about who owns what and who should get what. Nothing exotic there. When's it scheduled and who's hearing it?"

"Two weeks. Jack St. Marie's the judge."

"What about him?"

"Nothing exotic there either. A good enough workhorse, not very interested in domestic litigation."

"I intend to raise Justin's stature to that of a full participant in his parents' divorce."

"I've never heard of that."

"Stay tuned. The Whitneys would be well advised to beware of forthcoming impediments to their divorce. They might find themselves in marriage counseling. They might find themselves in psychiatric evaluation. I have a number of other troubles in mind for them. The judge in superior court is the authorized representative of the boy."

"An interesting concept."

"It's not a concept, it's part of a statute. 167B."

"You're a quick study, Weld."

"The judge is the authorized representative of the boy. I hazard judges need reminding of that. I hazard they don't think of it very often. Not in that way. I hazard they don't think of it at all. I shall remind the judge. It should give him pause. It will please me to tinker with the timing and rhythm of this divorce. And the judge's concept of himself and his relationship to my client—he might be more willing to entertain and order other unlikely motions on behalf of my client. As my client's representative."

"Weld, the judge is not going to take kindly to this attempted exploitation."

"I will merely remind His Honor of a specific trust invested in him. Whitney and Whitney are litigants. But His Honor is the state-appointed representative of Justin Whitney. As such, certain discretions have been placed within his authority."

"To wit?"

"Never mind. I will bring them to His Honor's attention. But first, I will attack the grounds for divorce."

Tuttle laughed. "That certainly goes to the heart of it."

Pennyworth nodded in serious agreement. "Yes. In order for the court to grant the divorce, there has to be grounds for the divorce."

"Irreconcilable differences have always proved sufficient."

"Ah, but are the Whitneys' differences irreconcilable?"

"The Whitneys think so."

"It's more important that the Court think so. If there is some doubt in the Court's mind . . ."

"How do you expect to do that?"

"Simple. I'll convince the judge there's hope for reconciliation."

"I'm not hearing this. No. I'm not. And that's what the judge is going to say."

"And that is why I came all this way to shop for a judge. I need a judge who is imaginative and creative."

"I don't think you want Jack St. Marie then. No, Jack's not your man. He won't listen to the nuances. He'll give you a predictable decree. Children to the mother, reasonable visitation to the father, if you consider Saturday and Sunday twice a month reasonable, and two weeks in the summer—everything else split down the middle, with child support to the mother probably not quite adequate. Jack prefers criminal and corporate materials to play with. He loves in-surance fraud."

"Who else is there?"

"You might have a shot at four others. Sophocles Kazantscouras has been known to make decisions for either parent regardless of sex."

"I'm not looking for a decision for a parent, regardless of sex."

"Francis Feeney. He likes domestic cases. I'd say he probably has a one hundred percent record on the side of the female parent."

"Bryce, I don't believe you heard what I said about parental preference."

"Oh, yes, dear brother, I did. But I'm giving you the most pertinent information I can."

"Go on."

"Graham Houghton. Newly appointed."

"Background?"

"Real estate and tax law."

"None of them speak to me so far."

"That brings us inevitably and finally to Turner Haskins. Judge Haskins has demonstrated compassion in domestic cases, has a rep-utation for listening closely, caring, and knowing the law, here and out of state."

"That's my man."

"No."

"Why not?"

"Judge Haskins is of the female persuasion."

"What of it?"

"Your well-known male chauvinism—"

"It is *not* male chauvinism—"

"Your prejudice against women colleagues—"

"It is not a prejudice against women colleagues, it's a prejudice against incompetence."

"Your impatience, condescension, rudeness—"

"All of which I exhibit indiscriminately, regardless of sex—"

"But which is perceived as being *particularly* inappropriate when the object of your derision is a woman—"

"Are you telling me a colleague is looking for favorable treatment because of gender?"

"No. But you have a reputation, Weld. I can't see Turner Haskins being oblivious to that reputation. Or to the foundation for it."

"Is she a good judge? You said as much."

"Yes. But let me quote Mr. Pennyworth: 'Justice is blind, but she isn't deaf.' Turner Haskins will have heard all about you. You're an insult, Weld, to our brothers who are sisters."

"I believe I have been evenhanded in my treatment of colleagues."

"Ignorance is not an excuse."

"Is she imaginative?"

"Yes."

"Is she creative?"

"Yes."

"How do I get to her?"

"You mean how do you bypass Jack St. Marie?"

"Yes."

"The usual. Turner becomes available the middle of next month. Jack St. Marie starts hearing cases up north the end of next month."

"Very well. I'll file an appearance in superior court on behalf of Justin Whitney. I will move for a continuance of Whitney v. Whitney on the basis that I have to appear in federal district court in Boston that week. The following week I will be out of the country, and so I shall be—I owe myself a week's vacation somewhere. Will that be sufficient?"

"For the continuances?"

"Yes. So that I get Turner Haskins."

"I think we can arrange that."

"Goody, Bryce."

"Will you have enough time for the case here, Weld? With your other work and—?"

"I will have all the time in the world. I will divorce myself from everything else. I've owed it to myself for years."

Tuttle rose. "I assist you in this with considerable reservation."

"So you've stated."

"Because of your efforts, Justin Whitney is going to suffer needless distress."

"I will protect him from what I can. He is already suffering needlessly."

"You're going to increase his suffering, Weld."

"In the short run."

"And in the long run?"

"The long run is what this is all about."

"Weld, you're in over your head. You're in New Hampshire, man."

"I've been there before. And I've been here before."

22
SOMETHING TERRIBLE

PENNYWORTH DID NOT GO HOME THAT EVENING BUT WENT to his office.

On the way he taped instructions for his secretary: "Get me a living room/bedroom suite at the Center of New Hampshire in Manchester. Book it for the Monday of my return from vacation and for an indefinite period thereafter. Have a private telephone installed with two holds. There is a state-sponsored guardian ad litem course given once a year in New Hampshire. If it is available before the end of October, enroll me. If not, make arrangements for an equivalency. It is a one-day course."

He worked until midnight, at which time he was finally alone in the offices, and a deep foreboding swept through him—something that was not part of his maturity but something that he vaguely recalled from his childhood.

Pennyworth was occasionally subject to attacks of an emotional nature—foreboding, sadness—that seemed to leap out at him from the distant days of childhood and that he ascribed as properly belonging to the child he had once been. He admonished the child to keep these childish emotions where they properly belonged—back with the child. Grown-up Pennyworth had been at pains to teach young Pennyworth control and mastery of young Pennyworth's vagrant emotions. Usually that control worked splendidly.

But now that he was alone in his office, embarked upon the campaign on behalf of young Justin Whitney, and with no one there to answer to but himself, there was this damn foreboding—as if something very terrible might happen to young Justin—or to himself.

Something terrible was already happening, Pennyworth reminded himself, and that was why he was in the campaign. It seemed an insufficient reason. Something quite terrible was at stake—otherwise, why the foreboding?—and Pennyworth did not know what it was. Something quite terrible, something malevolent and threatening, had gotten alone with him in his office.

He glanced over—his glance was *pulled* over—to a shelf on which had accumulated certain trophies and relics of celebrated trials in which he had been victorious. What drew his attention did not actually belong there, but there was no place else for it. It was something that had been with him for a number of years: a paperweight of the sort that is a clear globe and contains a scene that may be animated by tipping the globe back and forth. This one contained a cozy little house with a few pine trees scattered about it. When the globe was agitated, a mock snowstorm swirled about, almost obscuring the house and trees until the motion slowed and the snow settled gently on the roof and tree limbs. There was a birthday party going on inside the cozy little house. Of that Pennyworth was certain. Fear and foreboding surged through him again.

Pennyworth put on his jacket and his overcoat, locked the office, went down in the elevator, and fled the building, only vaguely aware that he was running away once again and not at all questioning from what it was that he might be running.

In the safety of the dark and deserted street, he hit upon it. Low blood sugar. He had not eaten since breakfast and that had been only tea and toast. The sense of foreboding was simply his body warning him that the fuel supply was becoming critical.

He altered course and destination to The Last Hurrah, a nearby late-night bar and eatery. There he settled into a banquette, fended off acquaintances who asked him to join them, drank some wine, and ate some fish, and the foreboding that had been within him was dissolved as completely as if it had never been there.

So much for the ghosts, the emotional debris of childhood, Pennyworth thought. Now we get down to hard facts.

And it is true that he slept well that night, Tuesday night, and again well on Wednesday night. But on Thursday night, the night before the afternoon he was to meet Justin, he slept hardly at all and wrestled through the entire night with what devil? For surely it was no angel; and the only devil with whom he was personally acquainted was himself.

A splendid fall day, a brilliant day in which the colors of the leaves—the browns and reds and yellows—leapt out in the cool air beneath a clear blue sky. Pennyworth drove with the window beside him down. A leather envelope containing pertinent papers lay on the seat next to him. He wore prescription aviator sunglasses against the brilliance of the day, and he was dressed for country court—an old tweed jacket, a rep tie, button-down shirt, beige slacks, brown loafers—nothing that would appear to the court to be particularly tailored, monied, or clever. As the road signs indicated a growing proximity to Carlton, Pennyworth's heart increased its pace and resonance noticeably. Pennyworth was uneasy and he did not like that in himself. It was not his heart that was making him uneasy. Rather, his heart was providing the cadence of his uneasiness.

Pennyworth resolved that, at the first opportunity, he would dump Justin Whitney.

What? said the Voice, run again?

"Now we get down to hard facts," Pennyworth said to Justin. "Everything bad. Nothing good happens from here on in. If you hesitate, I'll walk out on you."

They were in the office that Jim Giambelli kept at home, Pennyworth seated behind the desk, the leather envelope in front of him, Justin in front of the desk in a hard chair that was much too big for him. Justin felt that now-familiar chill steal across his arms and shoulders and he felt his heart pick up the way it did when he heard his parents fighting.

"Do you know the word *adversary?*"

"It's someone on the other side," Justin said.

"Yes, an opponent. It also means enemy. You are going to become your parents' enemy."

"I just want to get them together."

"In the legal process, you are going to be their enemy. That is the way they are going to perceive you. Probably not all the time. But certainly *sometimes*. Are you strong enough for that?"

"Will it get them together?"

"That is part of my strategy. To see if they will join forces in their opposition to you."

"Can't I just *ask* them not to get a divorce?"

"Haven't you done that?"

Justin nodded.

"I don't want any hedging here, Justin. No holding back."

"No, sir. It's just that this is pretty scary."

"Indeed it is. And it will become more so. Here, read this." Pennyworth unzipped the leather envelope and took out a multipage form. The top page was the original and the other pages were duplicates. The word at the bottom of the original was COURT. It was a white page. The next page was pink: PARENT. An extra PARENT copy had been made. A yellow page: JUVENILE/ATTORNEY. An aqua page: PROBATION. Another aqua page: WELFARE. Justin saw that things that had to do with him had been typed into blanks.

THE STATE OF NEW HAMPSHIRE

PETITION FOR ABUSE OR NEGLECT

To the Justice of Said District Court: The undersigned represents that *Justin Whitney* of *49 Old Town Road, Carlton, N.H.*, being *ten* years of age, and whose date of birth is *January 21, 1981*, is ( ) abused (/) neglected in that *Gamble G. Whitney* of *49 Old Town Road, Carlton, N.H., and Conrad J. Whitney also of 49 Old Town Road, Carlton, N.H., but currently residing at 104 Lake Road, Carlton, N.H.*, did on *as set forth below* at *as set forth below* [ ] abuse [/] neglect said child, to wit:

And what Justin then read chilled him more than anything he had felt before.

"Where it says Petitioner, Justin, you will sign there. Before a notary public. You will see that it says, 'Subscribed and sworned to by the petitioner, before me,' and the Notary Public signs there."

"I have to *swear this* against my parents?"

"Only if you agree with it."

"I guess I agree with it."

"That's not good enough. There will be no guessing in this. You either agree with it or you don't."

"I agree with it." Justin stared at it. "It's just so strong."

"Does it represent your position or not? Does it represent the facts, or does it not?"

"Yes. Both ways."

"You will sign it only if you agree with it *and only if you wish to carry it forward*. Do you understand?"

"Yes."

"You can drop the whole thing now."

"Do you want me to?"

"I am the attorney, you are the client. I have advised you of the situation. The decision to carry forward or not is yours."

"I guess."

Pennyworth arose. "That is not good enough—"

Justin stood up sharply. "*Yes! yes! yes!* Do it! Carry it forward!"

Justin turned away, tears of rage forcing themselves from him, a rage he felt at Mr. Pennyworth for being against his parents and making *him* be against his parents. And rage against his parents for making *him* be their enemy.

* * *

In Mr. Pennyworth's car—which was just the sort of awesome set of wheels he would expect of the Devil—Justin said, "Why do I have to sign it? Why don't you sign it?"

"I like it better if you sign it."

"But you're the lawyer. You're the grown-up."

"Yes. But you're the minor child. There's an expressiveness in your signing it yourself."

"What's a minor child?"

"A child who has not yet achieved his majority. A child who has not yet reached the age of eighteen."

"Can a minor child sign something like that?"

"Good question. The judge is going to say the minor child can sign it all he wants and it has no significance, it doesn't amount to a hill of beans."

"Then why don't *you* sign it?"

"I like it better if you do. It's more poignant that way."

"What's poignant?"

"Something that wrenches the guts."

Downtown Carlton consisted of a cluster of shops and professional offices in white frame or red brick. The town hall was brick. The wood floors were brown with age and bright with varnish. Justin had always thought of it as a friendly place. He had been brought there on day-care trips and on school trips to learn about the history of the town and how it worked, and once to meet the chief of police, and another time to meet Judge Stickney and hear about what the court did. In the fall (and pretty soon again) there would be the town Halloween party with all the kids in costumes and cider and donuts upstairs in the town meeting room. A friendly, familiar place and now, on this mission, as frightening and foreign as any castle that housed warriors and serpents.

Mr. Pennyworth took him into the town clerk's office. "Why, hello there, Justin," the woman behind the counter said cheerfully.

"Hello, Mrs. Winter."

"Something wrong, Justin?"

"No, Mrs. Winter."

"You look like something scared the wits out of you."

"No, ma'am. I'm fine."

"Well then, what can I do for you today?"

"I understand you're a notary?" Mr. Pennyworth said.

"Indeed I am."

"This young gentleman would like you to witness his signature."

"Certainly." Pennyworth placed the petition on the counter. The town clerk looked at it. "Come around here, Justin. Come over to my desk. The counter's too high." When Justin was around the counter and safely within Mrs. Winter's protection, she said, "Now, Justin, who is this gentleman with you?"

"That's Mr. Pennyworth."

"Who might Mr. Pennyworth be?"

"He's a lawyer from Boston. He's my lawyer."

"Have you read this, Justin?"

"Yes, Mrs. Winter."

"And you want to sign it?"

"Yes, Mrs. Winter."

"Is anyone forcing you into this?"

"No."

She glanced at Pennyworth. "But this says *terrible* things about your mother and father, Justin."

"I know—"

"Madam," Pennyworth said, overriding Justin, "your obligation does not include an appraisal of the contents of the document. I believe you are charged with witnessing signatures."

"I won't witness this one. The child has been turned against his parents."

"I am unaware that there is a category of signature that you are restrained from witnessing."

"Well, no—"

"If there is, kindly enlighten me. Otherwise carry out your obligation or I will bring a complaint."

Mrs. Winter's voice became formal and cool as if, Justin thought, she didn't like him anymore. "Read this over, Justin."

"Okay . . . I did."

"Do you solemnly swear that what's in there is true?"

Justin heard the silence all around himself. "Yes."

"Sign it then."

Justin signed. Mrs. Winter applied her stamp and signed it herself.

"What is the fee?" Pennyworth said.

"None whatsoever," Mrs. Winter said and turned her back.

Pennyworth walked Justin across the street to a red-brick building; outside, the most prominent plaque read STICKNEY & GRAVES, AT-TORNEYS. They entered the building and then turned through a door that led to the offices. Secretaries were busy at typewriters. Pennyworth approached the reception desk. "Justin Whitney and counsel to see Judge Stickney."

"The judge isn't here."

"There was supposed to have been an appointment."

"I know, but the judge isn't here."

"When will he return?"

"I don't know. He's across the street at an arraignment."

"Ah."

Pennyworth took Justin back to the town hall. They went to the clerk of court's office. Justin stepped forward to the woman behind the desk and stood there for a moment, the petition down at his side, almost as if he wished to hide it.

The woman looked at him. "Is that something for me?"

"The judge," Justin said and handed her the petition.

The woman glanced at it, then settled real attention on it. She looked up beyond Justin. "You are Mr. Pennyworth?"

"Yes."

"Judge Stickney is in court. He's here now."

"That is my understanding."

"If you want to wait, I'll bring this to his attention."

"Thank you."

23

A NOVEL THEORY

THE JUDGE WAS A SCRAWNY MAN AND NOT VERY TALL. His robes seemed too big for him, but he stood straight in them—rigidly straight, Pennyworth noted. He emerged from his office and mounted to the bench and peered down first at Pennyworth and then at Justin and then at Pennyworth again, like a bird entertaining thoughts of attack.

"This is a curious document," the judge said. "The petition is brought by the minor child and is attested to by him. But there is a change of person here. The wording is in the third person. It lacks the innocent grammar of a child. It has something to it of the . . . ah . . . *sophistication* of the legal mind. I note that you have represented yourself to this Court as the minor child's attorney."

"I have, I am. The allegation was worded by me on behalf of my client, Your Honor."

"Your client."

"Yes. Justin Whitney. On his behalf I framed the allegation within the legal context."

"You have made an error, Mr. Pennyworth."

"I will gladly be instructed by the Court, Your Honor."

"I recognize that you are from Massachusetts." Stickney made it sound like a territory in orbit somewhere in the vicinity of Mars. "But here the minor child has no standing before the court and therefore cannot petition the court."

"Your Honor, I would not presume to correct the honorable Court in regard to the statutes of its own state, but if you will permit me to jog the Court's no doubt excellent memory?"

"Certainly, Mr. Pennyworth. No matter how familiar the Court may be with the pertinent statutes, I suspect that a more recent review has provided you with a perspective with which the Court is unfamiliar. I await with interest."

"The question is, Does the minor child have standing before the Court or does he not?"

"Well put. The answer is, He does not."

"Your Honor, RSA 169C reads that *any person* may bring a petition of abuse or neglect before the Court. *Any* person. Nothing in RSA 169C prohibits or is contrary to the minor child presenting the petition himself."

"Thank you, Mr. Pennyworth, for jogging the Court's memory. Do you intend to practice in this state for any length of time?"

"I intend to practice in this state and in this courtroom and in superior court—"

"Los supers? You will trot your act out before los supers?"

"I will ignore the Court's characterization of my professional comportment—"

"Please don't, Mr. Pennyworth."

"I intend to pursue the pleadings in this case here and in superior court, yes."

The judge directed his attention to Justin. "Justin Whitney?"

"Yes. I was here on a field trip and—"

"Yes. I fed you all a lot of balderdash about how the legal system works. I told you about how it's supposed to work. Now, if you keep on with this nonsense, you'll find out how it *actually* works."

"Yes, sir."

"Yes, *Your Honor*."

"Yes, *Your Honor*."

"That's lesson number one. Does this man Pennyworth represent you? Is he your lawyer? Would you describe him as such? Would you say, 'Mr. Pennyworth is my lawyer'?"

"Yes, Your Honor."

"Would you also say, 'I want Mr. Pennyworth to sue the dickens out of my parents because they're getting a divorce'?"

"Yes."

"Mr. Pennyworth, did you mesmerize this child? Did you seek him out?"

"He called me. He beseeched me, Your Honor. He hung out in my office like the albatross."

"Is that true, Justin?"

"I don't know about the albatross thing, but the rest is true."

"Justin, I'm going to read your allegation here. The charge you make against your parents. I want you to listen closely. Are you ready?"

"Yes, Your Honor."

"Hmmmm . . . 'Gamble G. Whitney and Conrad J. Whitney did neglect said child,' that's you, 'to wit,' which means, here's what you're saying about your parents: 'That said parents in the process of divorce proceedings before the Superior Court have created such circumstances that said child has been psychologically injured so that said child exhibits symptoms of emotional problems presently and which will continue to affect him throughout his life.' " Judge Stickney sat back. "Have you got that, Justin?"

"Yes, Your Honor."

"Explain it to me."

Justin looked at Pennyworth. Pennyworth showed him no response. Justin looked back to the judge. "It means that what they're doing is ruining my life. It's going to ruin it forever."

Stickney looked at Pennyworth. "An admirable précis."

"My client is determined."

"I will grant you this, Mr. Pennyworth. This is an interesting proposition. But Justin is well clothed, he appears to have been fed regularly—are they feeding you regularly, son?"

"Yes, Your Honor."

"They're not beating him. At least there's no allegation of such. Are your parents, either of them, beating you, Justin? Hitting you, mistreating you physically?"

"No, Your Honor."

"So you see, Mr. Pennyworth."

"Your Honor, the parents are putting the minor child through emotional turmoil that will fester in him the rest of his life. I pray this honorable Court to grant young Justin relief from that."

"I understand the boy is upset, Mr. Pennyworth. We cannot put aside the parents' right to a divorce, though."

"That is not what is being asked here, Your Honor. Juvenile court is being asked to respond to demonstrable neglect. Questions of divorce, as Your Honor fully comprehends, are not the province of juvenile court. Questions of divorce are the province of superior court, are they not?"

"Indeed, Mr. Pennyworth. They are the province of los supers."

"We pray the Court to look at the circumstances of the minor child. Your Honor, the parents are failing to provide the minor child with necessary emotional and mental care. These elements are necessary for the protection of the child. It is reasonable to posit, on the basis of clinical findings, that there will be substantial emotional damage to Justin Whitney. He is being beaten up emotionally, if not physically, and that requires a judicial response under 169C."

"Taking a neglect position. A novel theory, Mr. Pennyworth. I have a question, Mr. Pennyworth."

"I await, Your Honor."

"Why did you not sign this petition yourself, Mr. Pennyworth? As attorney for the minor child?"

"The minor child is the witness in this, Your Honor. I am his representative."

"You have no personal knowledge of this alleged neglect?"

"My knowledge is of what my client has informed me. I have questioned him closely. I have no reason to doubt it. Justin brings this petition on his own behalf. I assist him with it."

"Interesting. Quite interesting. And you are prepared to act on his behalf before los supers as well?"

"I am. I have filed an appearance."

"You don't trot, Mr. Pennyworth, you run." To Justin he said, "This will be presented to each of your parents by a member of the Police Department, Justin, unless you decide to withdraw your petition." Judge Stickney read to Justin, " 'Order of Notice of Hearing—The foregoing petition having been presented, it is ordered that a hearing be held at three o'clock P.M.,' Justin, 'one week hence,' here in this district court, 'and that Gamble G. Whitney and Conrad J. Whitney, the persons having custody of the child, are hereby summoned to appear with the child at the hearing.' It goes on to say, in a statement of rights, 'You are advised that the child will be represented by an attorney appointed by the Court.' "

"I'm glad you got to that, Your Honor."

"Yes. I see that you have prayed the Court that Weld Pennyworth, attorney, be appointed guardian ad litem."

"Under 169C a guardian ad litem is to be appointed immediately by the juvenile court judge. As you know, Your Honor, the appointment is automatic once the petition is filed."

"And there you are, Mr. Pennyworth."

"Here I am, Your Honor."

"You're already his attorney. What more do you want?"

"Exactly as I have requested. That I be appointed guardian ad litem."

"But you have already failed to make a thorough investigation of this matter, Mr. Pennyworth."

"I have not had the opportunity. That is why I wish to be appointed guardian ad litem. That I may do so."

"You wish to be both advocate and finder of facts for the child?"

"Those two roles are embodied in the office of guardian ad litem."

"You are bound and determined, are you not, Mr. Pennyworth?"

"In the instant case, I am most bound and determined, Your Honor."

"*In the instant case,*" the judge said, his voice leveling with sarcasm. "Very well, Mr. Pennyworth, I will consider it."

"I wish to begin the investigation immediately. Before the preliminary."

"Investigate then, Mr. Pennyworth, by all means investigate."

"If it please the Court, the task would be more readily accomplished if I had the authority of guardian ad litem."

"I must say, you are overwhelming me with interesting proposals, Mr. Pennyworth. A novelty in this court."

"Your Honor, it is all in the best interests of the minor child."

"So you say. Let us look to the future, Mr. Pennyworth. If I were to find for young Justin, what sort of disposition might I make? Los supers will make the final order relative to the divorce action. There is no disposition I might make that would affect the outcome there."

"I am sure a wise and appropriate disposition will disclose itself to this honorable Court in due course, Your Honor."

"With some assistance from the guardian ad litem, I gather."

"It is the function of the guardian ad litem to advise the honorable Court as to the best interests of the minor child."

"The Court is bewitched with the prospect of advice from learned counsel." Judge Stickney paused and looked out the windows of his courtroom.

He looked out and was silent for so long that it seemed to Justin that he and Mr. Pennyworth ought to leave, the judge was signaling them to leave. But Pennyworth remained where he was, his hands in the pockets of his jacket, and watched the judge steadily.

After a while the judge looked back at Pennyworth. "All right. The Court will appoint you guardian ad litem to Justin Whitney."

"Thank you, Your Honor."

"A word with you, Mr. Pennyworth. If you'll request your client to await you outside?" The judge handed the signed Notice of Hearing to the clerk of court. "Stella, type up the notice and get it to the chief."

"Yes, Judge. Justin, you can come with me."

When the two men were alone, Judge Stickney said, "You are fortunate that I am bored just now, Mr. Pennyworth."

"No, Judge, young Justin is fortunate in that."

24

PLACED ON NOTICE

PENNYWORTH JOINED JUSTIN IN THE CLERK OF COURT'S OF-fice. He stood by her desk, as if she worked for him, while she typed the Notices of Hearing.

"You'll be taking them to the chief now?"

"Yes."

"Very well, we'll accompany you."

They followed her downstairs to the town police station. There were some desks and a lot of informational posters and notices on the walls. A uniformed woman was at a telephone console.

"Chief in? I've got some paper for him and these folks want to see him."

The chief's office was a small room with a lot of athletic trophies on the shelves. The chief remained seated at his desk and read the paperwork. Justin knew the chief from a field trip, and even better from his being one of Justin's coaches in baseball. He was used to the chief smiling and kidding, but this time he looked at Justin without expression and he looked at Mr. Pennyworth with outright suspicion—as if Mr. Pennyworth were *a criminal.*

Pennyworth reached across the desk with his hand extended and held it out there in front of the chief. The chief looked at Justin again and then stood up. Pennyworth kept his hand extended. Outdone, the chief shook hands. Pennyworth explained his position as guardian.

"I know this feller," the chief said, finally smiling at Justin. "A real desperado. We've had to lock him up several times."

"Now he has a lawyer."

"I see."

Pennyworth nodded at the paperwork on the chief's desk. "When will delivery of notice take place?"

"This afternoon if they're at home."

"Maybe they won't be home till six or seven," Justin offered.

Pennyworth looked at Justin with interest.

"Late this afternoon or early evening," the chief said. "If we don't have something more important come up." He looked down at the notice and then back at Pennyworth. "In abuse or neglect, we try to deliver these things as soon as we get them."

"Good for you."

The chief walked them back into the other room. "Lorna, get hold of Morris and tell him to go by Judge Stickney's office and get filled in on this before the judge goes home." He placed the Notices of Hearing on her desk.

And as the notices dropped to the desk, a great weight seemed to drop from Justin's heart or, more exactly, from his stomach, which is where he had felt its presence most strongly.

He was going to do it. He was doing it already. With Mr. Pennyworth's help. He was going to *stop* the divorce.

He didn't feel afraid anymore about what his parents might think or how they might get at him (they were already getting at him) or guilty that he was doing something bad to them.

Justin was glad.

In his car, Mr. Pennyworth said, "I noted your participation and I am pleased with it."

"Yeah, but what gets me is, now I have to be out of my house, out of my bedroom."

"Yes. Till the shock is over."

"Yeah, but why does everyone have to leave their house? Why can't we all just live together? Even if they're divorced."

"Something of the sort has already occurred to me. Patience, Justin, patience. But for now I want you out of the way."

"They're sure not going to be thrilled with this, are they?"

"They are not going to be pleased. I forewarned you this would be a rough voyage if you embarked upon it."

"But not rougher than the one I was already on. That's what you said."

"Not rougher, but longer." Pennyworth looked off to fields and forest. "Where does Ryan live, Canada?"

"No. Old Common Road. It's new. It's up ahead. What are you doing to my mom and dad?"

"I'm making them examine themselves. That's *one* of the things I'm doing."

"Tell me something else."

"I'm going to make them sweat. I'm going to make them sweat very hard."

Justin nodded again. He was smiling to himself. "I was right. You're *wicked* mean. That's why I hired you."

"You did no such thing. You're not paying me a cent."

"I can afford a cent."

"I'll draw up a contract."

"Good. Turn here."

"It's going to cost you more than a one-cent retainer. It's going to cost you one-cent-on-the-dollar legal fees. You could end up owing me a thousand dollars."

Justin felt trapped. "Where will I get a thousand dollars?"

"Mow lawns, rake leaves, shovel snow, push drugs, whatever a child your age does to earn money these days. But not a cent from your parents. Not your allowance money, presents, and so forth."

"Yeah, well, I was going to talk to you about the allowance they give me—"

"Young man, I do not negotiate children's allowances."

"It was just an *idea*." Justin was silent for a moment. "I was okay till you said this thing about a thousand dollars."

"Nothing in life is free, Justin."

"Yeah, but where will I get a thousand dollars?"

"Oh, someday you will. You might even get a thousand dollars or more in *compensation* from your parents."

"You just said not a cent from my parents."

"And that's right. Not a cent of anything they give you of their own volition. But anything the Court may order them to give you, that's different. A penny on the dollar up to whatever my legal fees have grown to by then. And by the way, this ride is not free. It's part of my professional time."

"Jeezum, Mr. Pennyworth. Anyway, I'd rather earn the money myself."

"Go to it. I encourage you. Admirable, admirable. Admirable but impractical."

"That's Ryan's house there."

On the way back, attempting to follow Ryan's and Justin's instructions for the best way to get to the highway, Pennyworth became lost. Not just lost, but lost on a road that had no houses, one on which he was unable to retrace his route.

He found himself driving down old paths, remembered roads, from when he had been a little passenger. He placed his foot on the pedal and accelerated away from such thoughts, much as he did when he applied full thrust to the twin jets of his Lear and lifted himself away from all earthly cares, as if the speed of the car could deliver him from unwanted thoughts and the renewed cannonade of his heart. And he maintained the acceleration until he almost lost control of the car. When he had regained control and slowed, he found he was wet all over with his own sweat.

Gamble had just noticed the quiet of the house, the quiet of Justin's absence. It was a different kind of quiet from that of Skip's absence (for which she was grateful). Justin's absence, when she was home alone with it, left an absence within herself.

She had just noticed that quiet and absence when she became aware of some motion out across the meadow and then she saw the police cruiser emerge from the pines. *My God,* she thought with instant terror, *Justin!* Something had happened to Justin.

She was in the drive in front of the house when the young police officer got out of the cruiser. His facial expression and physical manner were such that Gamble felt relief. No one so unconcerned would be bringing bad news.

He was not an officer Gamble knew. And so terribly young. As fresh-faced as . . . almost as fresh-faced as Justin. But there was the silver glint of his badge and the black metal of his holstered gun.

"Mrs. Whitney? Gamble G. Whitney?"

"Yes?"

"I'm Officer Morris. David Morris. And I've been asked to deliver this to you." He handed her the notice.

"What is it?" Gamble said. She started to read it.

"I'm here to answer any questions, explain the situation—"

"What the hell *is* this?"

"Well, ma'am, you're being charged with neglect of your son Justin."

"*Neglect?*"

"Yes, ma'am. There are the details, that's the petition. And this is the judge's Order of Notice of Hearing. So you're to be in court on that date—"

"It says I'm being *summoned.*"

"Yes, ma'am. You're to appear in court as it says and bring the child with you."

"Who *says* I neglected Justin, who would dare say—? Oh. Oh. I understand. Skip. *Skip—*"

"If you mean Mr. Whitney, no, ma'am, he's charged, too."

"Who then?"

"Where it says Petitioner, the name is right there."

"But that says Justin Whitney!"

"Yes, ma'am. He's the petitioner."

"This is incredible. *He's my child.*"

"Yes, ma'am."

"Someone put him up to this. He wouldn't do it on his own. He wouldn't know about such things. Charging *his own mother* with *neglect?*"

"He was accompanied by an attorney. But anyway, Judge Stickney found probable cause. That means—"

"I *know* what it means."

"You may want a lawyer to represent your interests. At the hearing. If you need an attorney—"

"This is bullshit," Gamble said. "You know that."

"It's not for me to decide. The judge will."

"Bullshit," Gamble said quietly.

"Well, have a good evening, Mrs. Whitney."

When Gamble picked up the phone, she was trembling with anger. She tried to get Justin at the MacKenzies', but there was no answer. It was just as well. She would have *screamed* at him. She called Ted Bagley.

"Can he do this?" Gamble said.

"Justin? I guess so. There's a statute that covers it. Neglect. I'm not overly familiar with it. I don't run into it. Not usually. Not with my sort of clients."

"I'm your sort of clients," Gamble said. "Please remember that. Especially as my office provides you with so much real estate work."

"No offense intended, Gamble. Just take it easy."

"I asked you, *can he do it?*"

"I don't know. Usually an attorney or a witness or the Division of Child and Youth Services signs the petition."

"I told you. *Justin* signed the petition."

"And Ford Stickney signed the Order of Notice of Hearing. So I guess it's all right with the judge for Justin to bring the complaint."

"But you know that I would never neglect Justin. Even Skip wouldn't—"

"We'll just have to address the matter in court. I'm going to want to see you about this. And I want to study the petition. And Stu Bredwell better do the same with Skip. Then I think the four of us had better get together, as uncomfortable as that may be, and see if we can come to some sort of agreement on how to approach this. Unless you want to back Justin up on his complaint against Skip?"

Skip had just entered the chill and silent Grayson house, bleak with fading daylight, and bleak with the absence of Justin. God *damn* Gamble for not letting him have Justin when she wasn't going to have him herself, and damn her for not letting him go to the circus with Justin.

Well, he'd see Justin at his soccer game the next morning, and he'd have Justin with him next weekend, and by then he'd be in the furnished place he'd found.

Except for Justin's absence, Skip was beginning to enjoy the breakup of his marriage. His fantasies of other women—of playtime with them and even of a deeper relationship—need no longer be constrained, unacted upon, because of his marriage to Gamble. Stu Bredwell said a normal sex life would not have any adverse weight against him in court. Just so long as it didn't interfere with his relationship with Justin.

"What about the house?"

"How do you mean?" Stu asked.

"Will my sex life have any weight about who gets the house?"

"I imagine the award of the house is going to have a lot to do with whoever gets primary custody of Justin."

"I want that house, Stu."

"I know, Skip. But so does Gamble. You can't both have it."

Skip heard a car outside and realized that he hadn't yet turned on the lights. The house was almost completely dark, but there was flashing light from outside.

He opened the door. A young officer stood there, a cruiser behind him. *My God, Justin!* Skip thought and felt a rush of something painful through his body.

"Mr. Conrad J. Whitney?"

"Yes, yes! My God, what is it?"

"Just this, sir." He handed Skip the notice.

Skip reached inside and turned on the hall light and the outside light. He began to read the notice.

"My name is David Morris. I'll be glad to explain the situation and answer any questions—"

"*What the fuck is this?*"

"A complaint of neglect—"

"Oh, I get it. I get it. The underhanded bitch—"

"—brought by Justin Whitney, who is your son, I believe, sir."

"Justin?"

"Yes, sir. He's your son, isn't he?"

"He says I *neglect* him?"

"You and Mrs. Whitney. Because of the divorce you neglect him."

"I see him every chance I get. He'd be here now except that bitch his mother—"

"Please, sir, I'm not here to judge a domestic dispute. Just to deliver the notice and make sure you understand. You're summoned to court on the—"

"I see it, I see it. I can't believe this."

"Yes, sir. And if there are any questions, I'll try to answer them."

"I'd like to know what the fuck this really is."

"I'm afraid I can't answer that, sir."

"Do you know?"

"Just what it says, sir. But you may want to retain an attorney to represent you at the hearing. Perhaps he can find out for you what the f—, what this really is."

"Shit. That's what it really is. Shit."

"Yes, sir."

"Shit."

There was no answer at the MacKenzies'. A sitter answered at Stu Bredwell's. The Bredwells were out, they wouldn't be home till late.

"How late is late?" Skip said.

"They didn't say. Midnight? Do you want to leave a message?"

"I want to talk to Mr. Bredwell—"

"I have to go. One of the babies is crying."

"Didn't they leave a number? For an emergency?"

"Just for me. Not for clients."

Skip hung up. Goddamn attorneys. They had no right to have fun when a client was suffering.

25

A CONFERENCE OF ADVERSARIES

THERE WAS NO SOCCER ON SATURDAY MORNING. SOCCER was played in rain, snow, sleet, and subfreezing temperatures, but not when there was lightning about. On Saturday morning there were thunderstorms and lightning flashes.

The MacKenzies, with Ryan and Justin, took an early start to Boston for lunch at Quincy Market before the circus.

The Whitneys, Gamble G. and Conrad J., at the earnest summons of their attorneys, came together in Stuart Bredwell's conference room. Both lawyers had offices in the same professional building. Ted Bagley's conference room was being painted that day. However, it made little difference which legal turf they were on. The Whitneys were meeting in common cause, though they did not know it yet.

Seated at the conference table, Gamble said, "I don't understand why you insist on bringing Skip and me together."

"You face a common enemy," Bredwell said.

"Justin?" Skip asked.

"Weld Pennyworth," Bredwell said. "The Devil himself. We've conferred with Ford Stickney and you're dealing with Weld Pennyworth, not Justin, but Weld Pennyworth."

"I don't like that at all," Skip said.

"Nor I," Bredwell said.

"Ditto," Bagley said.

"Pardon me," Gamble said to Bredwell, "but I believe the way you phrased it was, *you* face a common enemy. What about you and Ted?"

"Well, of course, us too," Bagley said.

"Are you up to it?" Gamble asked Bagley.

"I'd like an answer to that as well," Skip said to Bredwell.

"Up to it?" Bredwell said. "Up to it? My dear Gamble. Skip, if you have any doubts, you may bring in outside counsel."

Bagley said to Gamble, "Ditto to you."

"But," Bredwell said, "I'm as good a trial lawyer as you'll find in this state. Together Ted and I know a good deal more about New

Hampshire law and practice than Pennyworth—or two Penny-worths."

"Not about neglect apparently," Gamble said to both lawyers.

"I've corrected my recent lack of knowledge," Bagley said to his client. "And Stu recognized where Pennyworth is coming from immediately."

"Yes," said Gamble. "From our own worst nightmares, if I recall the description."

"He does have that effect," Bredwell said. "But does he have the substance?"

"Well," Skip said, *"does* he?"

"169C is an interesting statute," Bredwell said. "It's open to in-dulgent interpretation. And visionary application."

Skip said, "So much for Pennyworth's lack of familiarity with New Hampshire law."

"He stepped right in, didn't he?" Bagley said.

Bredwell said, "There is no precedent *whatever* for this application. I shall point that out to Judge Stickney."

"What happens now?" Gamble asked.

"You've been ordered to a preliminary hearing," Bredwell said. "The Court will listen to you and to Pennyworth and Justin and then decide whether the evidence supports the petition or not."

"Stu and I will contend that the petition is unfounded. There's a little problem with that, though."

"Such as?" Skip said.

"Well, the evidence in these hearings under 169C, the evidence isn't bounded by the rules of evidence such as you have in any other courtroom, superior court, say, where the divorce will be heard. You're in a whole different ballgame in juvie under 169C. If you're Pennyworth, you don't ever have to be off base. You can carry the base with you."

Skip said, "Translate that, Stu."

"The Court views this as a child protection case. It will listen to anything it thinks pertinent."

"But this is a divorce," Gamble said. "It belongs in superior court—"

"District court—which is juvenile court—has original and exclu-sive jurisdiction under 169C. For you that means Rutherford B. Stickney."

"He's going to decide what happens to *Justin?*" Gamble said. "My child? Ford *Stickney* is?"

"He may," Bredwell said. "But first he's got to hear you at the preliminary. Then, if he thinks there is probable cause that Justin is neglected—"

"*That's absurd!*" Skip said.

"Then he will set a date for an adjudicatory hearing."

"That's where the real contest takes place," Bagley said. "If there is one. That's where you take off the gloves. The judge listens to the fray and then decides whether Justin is neglected or not."

"What," Gamble said slowly, "if he decides Justin *is* neglected?"

"Then," Bredwell said, "he sets a date for a dispositional hearing."

"That's when the returns come in," Bagley said.

"If he decides that Justin is neglected," Bredwell said, "he could take Justin away from you. He could place Justin in another home."

"*But Justin doesn't want that,*" Gamble said.

"I hope he's communicated that to his attorney," Bredwell said.

"His *attorney,*" Gamble said. "I can't believe it." She looked at Skip. "Our little Justin."

Skip said to Bredwell, "You're saying it's *possible?* Justin could be taken from us?"

"Unlikely," Bagley said. "He might write some orders, though."

"What sort of orders?" Skip said.

"I have no idea," Bagley said.

"I think the only person who knows what sort of orders all of this is aimed at is Weld Pennyworth. Though he might have given some indication to Justin. Suggest to Justin that he be open with you about it."

"What does that mean?" Gamble said.

"Pump him," Bagley said.

"I *will* not." Gamble looked across the table. "And don't you either, Skip."

"Fine," Bredwell said. "Let Pennyworth run the show."

"Is that what it means?" Skip said.

"We don't even know what he's *seeking.*"

"Can he stop the divorce?" Gamble asked.

"No way," Bagley said. "It's the wrong court, anyway."

"Speaking of which," Bredwell said, "Pennyworth—"

"Pennyworth is *despicable,*" Gamble said. "This is *my* son and this man is . . . he's *abusing* my son."

"*Our* son," Skip said. "But she's right."

"Speak softly when you speak of abuse," Bagley said. "No one's mentioned abuse yet. It's the other part of 169C."

"You should be warned," Bredwell said, "that if the Court does not dismiss the petition at the preliminary, it will probably order an investigation."

"An investigation of what? What sort of investigation?" Skip asked.

"An investigation of you, of Gamble, and of Justin as regards the alleged neglect. The investigation can take different forms. A mental health evaluation is one of them—"

"A *shrink?*" Gamble said.

"Why does the idea of a shrink frighten you, Gamble?" Skip said.

"Shut up, Skip. I am not frightened."

"No, just bonkers."

"Ease up," Bagley said. "It can take the form of an investigation by the guardian ad litem—"

"Nelle," Gamble said, smiling.

"Ah, no," Bredwell said. "Mr. Pennyworth has had himself appointed Justin's guardian ad litem—"

"He *what?*" Gamble said.

"Can't you object?" Skip said.

"We could, but it's done and Ford Stickney does not like his handiwork messed with. Just accept it. You've stipulated Nelle as guardian ad litem to superior court and she no doubt will be appointed such—unless Pennyworth objects."

"There could be a fight," Bagley said. "A real fray. That would be fun to watch. Pennyworth and Vance going at each other. Though of course," he added quickly, "we are not in court for purposes of amusement."

Bredwell continued. "As guardian ad litem in Judge Stickney's court, and relative to the alleged neglect of Justin, you can expect to hear from Pennyworth shortly. He will want to call upon you personally, or have you come to his office, to interview you."

"I cannot *stand* this," Gamble said. "The man is insufferable."

"He has set up an office in Manchester."

"Just for *Justin?*" Gamble said.

"He is apparently taking this case quite seriously. I don't know why."

"It would be an invasion of privacy, wouldn't it?" Skip said. "Poking into my personal life."

"No, Skip," Bredwell said, "it wouldn't. I suggest you both cooperate with him. Cautiously, of course."

"Show him you're each just such a loving parent and all you want is the best for Justin," Bagley said.

"Suppose what *he* wants isn't the best for Justin?" Skip said.

Gamble said, "Suppose it's not what *I* think is the best for Justin. Or Skip. His parents."

"Then it's up to the judge. It's up to the judge finally anyway."

Bredwell looked at his watch. "Let's get on with this. I've got a noon tennis date."

"It's pouring," Gamble observed. "There is thunder and lightning."

"The *indoor* court," Bredwell said.

"Goddamn it," Skip said, "I'm glad that came up." He turned on Gamble. "Just where the hell do you get off claiming the stock in the indoor club?"

"I wrote the check. A check for five thousand dollars from my account."

"And I deposited twenty-five hundred dollars in your account."

"No, you did not, Skip."

"I goddamn well did! I'll get the canceled check, I'll—" He realized something suddenly. Quietly he said, "All right, I didn't put it in your account. I put five thousand dollars from *my* account into the ski vacation we had in Klosters—"

"Yes, Skip. What else did you put into that trip to Klosters? There was that lonely Latin beauty. A young widow from Argentina. So lonely, so beautiful. Skip kept her company all the time—"

"That's a damn lie—"

"Please, folks," Bagley said.

"It is joint property," Bredwell said to Bagley.

"Well, Stu, there's some question about that."

"My name is on the stock certificate," Gamble said to Skip. "I'm afraid there's no name on the Klosters vacation. But you're welcome to the memories—"

"That was a *good* time, Gamble, goddamn it."

"Maybe for you, not for me."

"Ted," Bredwell said, "are you going to make an issue of the tennis club stock?"

"It seems to me my client has a legitimate claim to sole possession quite apart from any division of joint property."

Bredwell turned to Skip. "Let it go, Skip. We'll discuss it."

"*Let it go?* Are you going to let this money-grubbing—"

"Calm yourself, Skip," Gamble said pleasantly.

"—and her *chiseling* representative—"

"I didn't hear that, Skip," Bagley said. "Just don't repeat it."

"Listen to him," Gamble said.

"Ever," Bagley said.

Bredwell said, "I've a mind to walk out and leave the three of you to Mr. Pennyworth's mercies, whatever they may be."

Bagley said, "Good point, Stu." He looked at Gamble and Skip. "You folks still haven't heard what the old devil is pulling in superior court."

"Well?" Skip said.

"Letters from him yesterday. 'Dear Brother Bagley,' 'Dear Brother Bredwell' . . . *Brother*—that's a term of address lawyers sometimes use with each other."

"When they wish to indicate exactly the opposite," Bredwell said.

"Mr. Pennyworth has asked superior court for a continuance of the preliminary divorce hearing until the third week after the present date. Third week is significant. What he's attempting to do is, he's switching judges on us. Instead of Jack St. Marie, who's inclined to be mechanistic about divorce, old Pennyworth has done himself some research and come up with Judge Turner Haskins, a judge who is inclined to examine all the fibers and loose ends in a domestic fray."

"That's not so bad," Skip said.

"Yes and no. In this case, our mutual case, there is this very definite unraveling that Pennyworth is attempting. She—"

"She?" Skip said. "Who?"

"Judge Haskins."

"She's a woman?" Skip said.

"Why does the idea of a woman judge *upset you so,* Skip?" Gamble said sweetly.

"Shut up, Gamble. I'm not upset."

"Good. I'm glad to hear it."

"What I think Pennyworth is hoping—"

Gamble went on, "Women in this country, Skip, have achieved independence, professional status, a lot of things that are different from, say, the tenth century, a state of affairs that you refuse to acknowledge—"

"Now, Gamble," Bagley said, "this is not serving—"

Gamble looked at her attorney. "He still thinks I'm his chattel, Ted. I told you that. He thinks wives are chattels and every other woman is a sex object. I'm not your chattel anymore, Skip."

"You never were. You're so goddamn self-absorbed—"

Bredwell stood up angrily. "You two had better get yourselves together or Mr. Weld Pennyworth may just have his way with you."

"Whatever way that may be," Bagley said.

"Surely *you* two can stop him," Gamble said sarcastically.

"Not if *you two* are helping him," Bredwell said.

"He's just another attorney, for chrissake," Skip said.

"No, no. He's the Devil," Bagley said. "Really he is. In the courtroom he's the very devil."

"And out of it," Bredwell said. "This motion for continuance. So he can get the one judge he thinks might be sympathetic to whatever it is he's trying to make happen."

"Object," Skip demanded. "Object to the continuance. Keep the judge we've got."

"Ah, well, you see," Bredwell said, "there he's got us both ways. Normally attorneys accommodate each other when one of them seeks a continuance."

"Then don't be so damn accommodating," Gamble said. "Tell the bastard to shove it and let's get on with it. With Jack whatever-his-name. Can't you do that?"

"We can do that," Bredwell said. "File an objection. Say that we think Mr. Pennyworth is delaying and purposely leaving our clients dangling—"

"Well, do it," Skip said.

"Trouble is," Bagley said, "there's probably going to come a time when Brother Bredwell or I will desire a continuance. A conflict of appearances. Let's say I have a case in federal district court in Concord the same day there's a hearing on your business in superior court in Manchester. Let's say the client in the fed case takes precedence over you, Gamble. You want to appear in court alone? Or with a hastily prepared associate?"

"No . . ."

"Or Bro Bredwell has a conflict."

"I see."

"Bro Pennyworth says, 'Well, you boys didn't accommodate me in my motion for a continuance, I'm not going to accommodate you.' He'd like that. Only have to play against half the team—because make no mistake about it, we are all of us, Mr. and Mrs. Whitney, Bro Bredwell and Bro Bagley, we are all a team, we *have* to be a team, a team enterprise in opposition to Pennyworth. Or else there'll be the devil to pay."

"Then Pennyworth gets his judge," Skip said.

Bredwell said, "Pennyworth gets his judge."

26

PENNYWORTH FINDS A CLUB

PENNYWORTH HAD BEEN SEARCHING FOR A CLUB HE MIGHT use on the Whitneys and when he found it he was surprised by its serviceability. It was not the sort of thing one might expect to find lying about the forest floor at night when one is a young boy like Justin and there are animals aprowl in the darkness.

It was not a dark forest, however, and there were no animals present (at least not recognizable as such), just invited guests. Pennyworth was at a Saturday evening party given by Linda and Jim Giambelli in their house down the road from the Whitneys' house. Neither Whitney was resentful at not having been invited. Quite the contrary.

Gamble had called Linda a few days before, as soon as she had heard about the party at which Pennyworth was to be the featured guest. "I never knew you had such *hostility* toward me. Inviting *that man.* Don't you know he's trying to take my son away from me? Don't you know he's alleging horrible things about me? Don't you know he's trying to *ruin my divorce?"*

Linda Giambelli knew no such thing. She knew that Pennyworth was involved in some sort of extraordinary legal hassle that in turn involved a child, her dear young neighbor Justin; that Pennyworth had been *chosen* by Justin; and that Pennyworth was a professional acquaintance of her husband, had appeared on his show as a great favor a couple of years back, and was calling in that favor now by asking Jim to give a party and invite friends and neighbors of the Whitneys.

Skip had also not been thrilled by the prospect of a party for Pennyworth. He had called Giambelli and accused him of unneighborly activities.

There were forty-seven guests. Twenty couples and seven divorced singles, two of whom had been married to each other and still spoke. Linda had hired a bartender and a catering staff. She had never outgrown the excitement of contact with newsmakers and celebrities, glamour (even local Boston and New England glamour), or contest. She listened to most of Jim's programs, and not out of duty: She loved hearing the personalities, loved hearing the issues. Giambelli had never grown tired of it either, whether it was some dazed author on a tour, an actor or actress promoting a movie, a sports pheenom, or a pol with a POV to sell. The Giambellis had loved Pennyworth from the first, even before he had much of a name for himself. Pennyworth was a hell of an interview and Giambelli was looking forward to getting him on again as soon as Justin v. the Whitneys was concluded.

Pennyworth did not so much enjoy his celebrity status as use it.

At the Giambellis' he was generous in expressing his pleasure at meeting each of the other guests—and then he *listened*, after first having gently introduced the theme of Gamble and Skip Whitney, the neighbors of the Giambellis whom he had not yet met, though he knew young Justin Whitney (rather well), splendid lad, and, indeed, was embarked upon an enterprise—about which he could not speak just now—of some moment to young Justin.

"Oh, you mean the divorce," a pretty woman named Mrs. Hollander said. "We all know about that. My daughter Amanda's in Justin's class and she's been telling me all about it. How Justin got hold of you and he's going to stand up for kids. I think that's wonderful and kind of scary."

"Why scary, Mrs. Hollander?"

"Tracy, please."

"Why scary, Tracy?"

"Well, so many of us have been through it. As children. I know what I'd like to have done to my parents."

"What is that?" Pennyworth said.

"It's best left unsaid."

How curious, Pennyworth thought, that this woman doesn't understand that she is inflicting the same thing that happened to her on her own child.

"Tell me about the Canbys," Mrs. Hollander said.

"Tell *me* about the *Whitneys*."

Tracy Hollander furrowed her brow and looked at Pennyworth. "You mean it?"

"I will if you will," Pennyworth said in a measured tone.

And so it went with each of the individuals or groups Pennyworth interviewed, though no one but Pennyworth would have thought of so formal a word as *interview*. It was cocktail chatter. (During which

Pennyworth noted with curiosity the arrival of an interesting-looking woman who glanced at him and maintained the glance, before turning her attention to her host and hostess.)

At first the club appeared as a minor theme, but it was so recurrent that it became the major theme. The Whitneys' house.

"You haven't seen it? Wait till you see it."

"For this area, it's like modern architecture happening for the first time."

"I mean, they had *solar* panels."

"They got a Jacuzzi when we thought only people in Los Angeles had them."

"They love that house so much, sometimes I think they'd have to think twice which they loved more, Justin or the house."

"Really?" Pennyworth said.

"Oh, it's so beautiful inside. You don't have to like modern architecture to love it. So much light. It's so airy."

"Must be terrible to heat in the winter," Pennyworth said.

"They have to *open* the windows it gets so warm. The solar collectors."

"They built it themselves. I don't mean by hand. But, yes, they did some of that, too. Before Skip started making all his money. And then Gamble—after Justin was born. I mean, they designed it. They were both always working on it. They put so much of themselves into it."

"Then Justin was born and they got other people to do it for them."

"I'll have to see it sometime," Pennyworth said.

"Oh, you must. You'll never forget it. And if you'd grown up around here—"

"I did," Pennyworth said, immediately regretting the display of autobiography and ascribing it to the small amount of white wine he had drunk in over two hours of interview. "Though not in Carlton."

"Where?"

"Here and there," Pennyworth said.

"Well, if you grew up around here, used to even what passes for *modern* design here, you'd be *amazed* by Skip and Gamble's house."

"Is that right?"

"I'd fight over it too, if it was mine."

"There's the lake. They have the best site on the entire lake. They have their own tennis court. In the summer that lawn gets mowed *and* rolled where they have a croquet court—"

"The games room, the pool table, for the two adults—"

"It's really like a club."

"Is that so?" Pennyworth said. He decided it was perhaps time to have a martini and relax.

And when Pennyworth relaxed, he noticed again the woman across the room, the late arrival, who had curiously remained ever across the room from him, repositioning herself away from him whenever his course might take him to her vicinity.

Pennyworth decided it was time to close the distance.

Who was she and why had she been looking at him without approaching? Did she know something that he didn't know, something that he ought to know?

Besides all of which, she was not unattractive—a woman of apparent intelligence, of self-sufficiency, someone who observed, measured, and assessed, a woman who kept close counsel with herself, Pennyworth guessed, observing that she listened rather more than she spoke. An excellent poker player, Pennyworth would have guessed, knowing that his guesses were usually right on.

He asked Linda Giambelli to introduce him.

"Oh, don't you know each other? I thought you would. That's Nelle Vance."

Click: Justin's self-appointed guardian ad litem who had yet to be formally appointed as such by superior court. Pennyworth found her presence in the litigation an annoyance. He was going to remove that presence at the first opportunity—the preliminary hearing before the superior court, which court had already received his Objection to Appointment of Guardian Ad Litem, citing his own prior appointment to that office by another court and the fact that he was already fulfilling that function, there was no need for redundancy, a second appointment would divide the child's trust, confuse him, and bring additional stress to an already stressful situation from which the guardian in place was attempting to relieve him. Nelle Vance might have seen the motion by this time.

As he did in the case of any adversary, and had done as well with Bagley and Bredwell, Pennyworth had provided himself with basic intelligence about Vance. He knew what college she had attended (Hampshire), what law school (Boston College), her fields of expertise (personal injury, property law, labor mediation), her annual income ($68,210.72 on her last income tax), her place of residence (an old farmhouse she was restoring herself), her age (31), her sexual preference (hetero), her marital history (none), her lovers (no one presently), her religious affiliation (lapsed), her car (Subaru wagon), her interests (skiing, tennis, sailplaning), and so on. Had he wished, he could have provided himself with her bra size, her preferred means of contraception, and her credit rating, but at the moment none of that was pertinent.

What concerned Pennyworth about Vance was that if she were appointed guardian ad litem in the superior court proceedings, she could, in that capacity, make decisions and act on behalf of the minor child Justin. She could, in the capacity of guardian, file a motion to have Pennyworth removed as Justin's lawyer in the superior court proceedings.

She must be dealt with delicately, firmly, finally—and soon. Hence, his motion to deny her appointment.

No doubt Vance had provided herself with some of the same sort of intelligence about him. Or else she was a fool. There was nothing in her history to indicate that she was a fool. And all that sort of information about him was already public.

And so there was no need for Linda to make an introduction, although she went through the formality.

"Mr. Pennyworth," Nelle said.

"Ms. Vance."

Nelle offered her hand. Pennyworth took it. Nelle said, "I've never before met a man who objected to me before we even met."

"Is there a sexist content to that observation?"

"Its content is content to be what it is."

"It is the position that you would assume to which I object. Not the person."

"Oh, it's the position you find objectionable. By whose standards?"

"The standards of the office."

"We all have our standards, Mr. Pennyworth. I fly mine and I suggest you go fly yours."

Linda Giambelli had sensibly backed away, having no wish to be a party to a quarrel at her own party. There were problems enough with her married guests.

Pennyworth said, "I was not informed that you were abrasive at social occasions. We have taken off our wigs, so to speak."

"Have we? I rather thought you were here to do homework. I rather thought the occasion for this party was to provide you with an opportunity to do your homework."

"I always enjoy a good party. The Giambellis were kind enough to invite me. And you?"

"I invited myself. The one thing I've always admired about you, Pennyworth, is that you always do your homework."

"Only one thing?"

"So many of our colleagues don't."

"I speculate, Ms. Vance, that you are here to the same purpose I am."

"I already know everyone here."

"You don't know me."

"Until Whitney v. Whitney, I enjoyed that fortunate state."

"But now that you know me, I'm sure you'll come to love me."

"I don't fall in love so easily. And never with showboats."

"I don't think we're hotting it off, Ms. Vance."

"Let's start again."

"Where?"

"I find it interesting that you began practice as a juvenile defender."

"One must begin somewhere. I'm afraid, Ms. Vance, it is time to conclude our interview."

"But we've only just begun, Mr. Pennyworth."

"I know it's sad. But perhaps we'll meet again."

"We'll meet in court, Mr. Pennyworth."

"Perhaps not."

"Your absence would be in Justin's best interest. Exploiting Justin to enhance your own notoriety—"

"Justin came to me, Ms. Vance, I did not go to him. And let me point out, too, that he did not go to you. Your attempt to force your professional self on him is deplorable. In so doing you are aggravating his already considerable despair. For what? Self-aggrandizement? I beg you to withdraw, Ms. Vance, for the child's good. Justin does not want you."

"No, Mr. Pennyworth, it's you who doesn't want me. You're acting like a little boy who wants to make up all the rules. But the rules are in place."

"Thank heavens for that."

"Mr. Pennyworth, I'm a friend of Gamble's, and I'm a friend of Skip's, and most especially I'm a friend of Justin's. A very good friend. You are none of these things."

"I beg your pardon."

"Go to hell, Pennyworth."

"Madam, as of now, you are Nelle and void. Assure yourself of that."

27
MOTHER, FATHER, BOY, DEVIL

GAMBLE GOT BACK FROM HER REAL ESTATE CONVENTION and picked Justin up in midafternoon on Sunday. Justin was wary and noticed that she kissed him almost formally, the way he kissed his aunts when it was required of him. She asked him about Boston, the circus, what he had done last night, had he seen his father?

"You said I wasn't supposed to."

"I mean, did he come over or something? Did he go to the circus?" Justin was silent.

"Justin, I need to know. It's important."

"I wouldn't do something you told me not to do. You or Dad."

"It wasn't up to you."

"Nothing's up to me."

"I meant, it wasn't up to you to keep your father away. I mean, I just wanted to find out if he pushed his way in or not."

"Yesterday was the first decent day I've had in *years*."

"Not years, Justin. Did he or didn't he?"

"He didn't. But you want me to snitch on him if he did, don't you?"

"I asked you a simple question, Justin."

"Simple."

Justin felt that she tried to make it up to him when they got home. She'd brought pastry from Concord and they ate some together and Justin was just beginning to ease up when the big question came, the one he knew she'd get to.

"What's this about a charge of neglect against me?" She said it casually. But then she jumped at him. *"You know that isn't true. Not a word of it . . . This man, how did he get hold of you?"*

"I called him. I saw him on TV." Justin stood up. "I'm going to do guitar."

"Sit down."

Justin sat down. Whatever his mother asked, he answered her, one way or another. She was very angry at him. Then she was loving.

Then pleading. Then angry again. After a while Justin felt as if he weren't there anymore.

He began to think of the notes in his guitar book. What he was supposed to practice. He looked right at the notes and staff on the white page in the book open on the silver-colored music stand and he imagined himself seated on the stool, the guitar held in the classic style he had just begun learning, and he imagined his fingers playing the notes.

His mother was hugging him. "You just don't understand how difficult this is for me, Justin. It's really hard for me. I don't think you understand that. I know it's hard for you. But it'll be over, and then you'll be glad."

She didn't say about what.

His mother liked him to practice upstairs in the open library where she could hear him. But he took his guitar and music and stand and footrest and went into his room and closed the door.

He got Clyde's box out and examined it to make sure he had left enough food before he went away and then he carefully moved the damp soil around to make sure that Clyde was all right.

"It's all right, Clyde. I'm home now. You don't have to worry. I'll always come back and I'll always take care of you. I didn't take you with me because it's safer for you here. I'm going to play the guitar now. Do worms have ears? I'll have to look that up. Or call Dr. Blanchette. Anyway, I'll put you right here in front of me and maybe the notes will go into your home and you can feel the music even if you can't hear it."

His dad called while his mother was fixing dinner.

"How was the circus?"

"Okay."

"Just okay?"

"It was good."

"While you were off with Ryan, a policeman came to see me. Did you know about that?"

"I guess."

"Do you *really* think I neglect you?"

Justin was silent.

"This man Pennyworth—"

"I'm not going to talk about him. Mom tried to make me talk about him and I won't."

"Helping coach your soccer team, helping you build that box right away when you asked me, is that neglect?" His father then listed everything he could think of that he had ever done for Justin. "Does that sound like *neglect,* Justin?"

"I don't want to talk about it."

"If I were *there,* Justin—"

"Why aren't you here? Why aren't you and Mom together? Don't I count?"

"I hope you'll think about taking it back about my neglecting you. Because it's not true. And you're not a liar, Justin." Justin was silent. "Good night. I love you."

When he got off the phone his mother said, "Was that Dad?"

"Yes."

"What did he say?"

"That's private. What he says to me is private from you."

"*Justin.*"

"What you say to me is private from him."

"*What did he say?*"

"The same as you."

"Come sit down."

"I'm not hungry."

On Monday early, before either Whitney might leave bed, much less their houses, Pennyworth called each of them, identified himself by name and as guardian ad litem, explained what the guardian's task and duties were, and asked for the opportunity to meet with them in their own residences as soon as possible.

"It's *six-thirty in the morning,*" Gamble said.

"I did not mean immediately. But as soon as possible. Justin's well-being and mental health are in question—"

"What would *you* know about that?"

"I'm trying to find out, madam."

"Go to hell," Gamble said and slammed the receiver down—which was precisely the sort of response Pennyworth had hoped to provoke.

Gamble lay in bed with the warm company of her own anger. She remembered that she had been counseled to cooperate—or at least appear to cooperate—with Pennyworth, but the bastard had no right to come between her and her own child.

On the other end Pennyworth had set the receiver down gently. Gamble's admonition that he go to hell was becoming a familiar one—Vance had made the same suggestion. Pennyworth was pleased. He worked best in circumstances where other people were emotionally upset with him.

Skip Whitney was as easy as his wife had been. "What the hell kind of hour is this to call? Calling at this hour is harassment."

"As guardian I wish to pursue the facts of the matter as expeditiously as possible. I'm sure, as Justin's father, you'll want to assist me. You wouldn't want to neglect—"

"I've seen that shit neglect thing you foisted off on Justin. You leave my son alone or I'll come after you myself."

"Then you *are* willing to meet with me."

Skip Whitney hung up.

At seven Pennyworth called Mike Dunphy, Justin's teacher.

"Yes, I can talk to you for a few minutes . . . Yes, I'm concerned about Justin . . . All right, I'll tell you . . ." And finally, after Pennyworth had completed his questions and notes, "Okay then, I'll see you Friday. But you know, Mr. Pennyworth, I hate to get between parents and a child. For one thing, it's not going to sit too well with the other parents. And I don't think the school board is going to like it very much, either."

"Mr. Dunphy, you'll be doing your duty by Justin. Furthermore, you can only testify to what is so."

Pennyworth waited until midmorning to call Nelle Vance. It was, he thought, a move of great subtlety and it had occurred to him Sunday afternoon after he had had an unexpected and surprisingly erotic thought about her. What he planned to do with her, however, had nothing to do with the pleasures of the flesh and everything to do with the machinations of his own mind, machinations that Pennyworth thoroughly admired.

"Ms. Vance."

"Mr. Pennyworth."

"You suggested that we might have a date in court. I'm calling to suggest Friday afternoon at three in Carlton District Court."

"Justin's preliminary on your petition for neglect."

"Just so."

"I was planning to be there. I thought you might call. Now I have to reconsider. What is it you *actually* want me to do?"

"Ms. Vance, juvenile court is a closed proceeding. You have no standing in the instant case unless I provide it."

"Bagley or Bredwell can bring me in."

"Not if I object. Justin has the right of privacy. At the adjudicatory hearing, they can bring you in."

"If it gets that far."

"I have every confidence that it will. Judge Stickney will want to hear this out. Now, Ms. Vance, you have applied in superior court to discover and represent Justin's best interests as guardian ad litem."

"Ah, Pennyworth. You clever boy. It appears you *do* want me to show up at the preliminary. And for that reason I know I ought not to. On the other hand, if you advise the Court that you requested my presence and I don't show up, you'll no doubt suggest to the superior court that my interest in Justin isn't sufficient to warrant my appointment as guardian."

"No, Ms. Vance, I shall suggest to the superior court that your interest is of a frivolous nature."

Pennyworth glanced at a note on his Strategy & Tactics sheet. He had written: *Objective: Make Justin an equal among equals in the divorce proceedings. Then render his parents unequal.*

28
SOUNDING NEW WATERS

THROUGH ADROIT STAGE MANAGEMENT PENNYWORTH WAS able to cluster Justin, Michael Dunphy, and Nelle Vance to the rear of the small courtroom away from the Whitneys and their attorneys at the counsel table. Judge Stickney had not yet entered, and because of the rules guarding juvenile court, no one else was present.

Pennyworth went around to the front of the counsel table and, smiling cheerfully, offered his hand to Bagley and Bredwell. "Hello, I'm Weld Pennyworth. I'm glad to meet you. And these are your clients? Mrs. Whitney? Charmed. Mr. Whitney? I've heard so much about you both. I hear you two play a great game of tennis—"

"You are detestable," Gamble said. "Turning our child against us."

Us, thought Pennyworth. *Us?* Excellent. "A fine boy, Justin. You should both be very proud."

"Pennyworth," Skip said, "you should be skewered. You should be skewered, drawn, and quartered."

"I am a man of parts, that is true—"

"Turning Justin against his parents. You're trying to wreck this family," Gamble said. "You're vicious."

"Calm, calm, Mrs. Whitney. Our mutual endeavor here, all of us, is to assure Justin of as much calm as possible—in contrast to calamity. We have our different ways of going about it. The Court resolves our different approaches to Justin's benefit."

"All rise," the clerk of court said.

Judge Stickney, in his robes, entered, but before he sat behind the bench, he regarded each person in the courtroom individually. As he sat he said, "Mr. Pennyworth, witnesses are irregular at a temporary hearing."

"Your Honor, my brothers," and he indicated Bagley and Bredwell, "have informed me that they will contest Justin's petition hotly. I believe that Mr. Dunphy and Ms. Vance will provide the Court with convincing evidence that substantiates the petition. Therefore, I ask that they be heard."

"I'll decide about that later. First, I've yet to hear from Mr. or Mrs. Whitney. Justin, Ms. Vance, Mr. Dunphy, please be good enough to wait outside." When the door was closed, Judge Stickney said, "Mr. Bagley, Mr. Bredwell, your turn."

Bagley arose. "Your Honor, I'd like you to hear Mrs. Whitney."

"Go ahead."

Bagley nodded to Gamble and she got up from the counsel table and seated herself in the witness box. "Do you want me to swear her, Judge?"

"We can forgo that. Get on with it."

"Your name, please."

"I know who she is, Mr. Bagley. Just get on with it."

Suspecting what Bagley's line would be, Pennyworth was pleased that the judge was already showing irritation.

And, indeed, Bagley did what Pennyworth expected him to do. He caused Gamble to enumerate, at considerable length, every parental virtue she had ever visited upon her son Justin.

Pennyworth stared first at the American flag on one side of the judge's bench and then, after a while, he stared at the New Hampshire state flag on the other side of the bench. He allowed Gamble to orate on her own behalf for a full five minutes, by which time the accumulated tedium had become oppressive. Pennyworth estimated that Stickney would be appreciative of relief.

Pennyworth arose. "Your Honor—"

Bagley turned to Pennyworth. "Mr. Pennyworth, I am questioning the witness. You may inquire later."

"Your Honor—"

"Well, Mr. Pennyworth?"

"I foresee that this line of testimony will be extensive and that it will be followed by similar testimony from Mr. Whitney. Your Honor, in the interest of expediting this hearing, we will stipulate to

Mr. and Mrs. Whitney's being exemplary parents, that they have been the best possible parents in the world for Justin. We will in fact insist upon it. I might list their parental virtues myself. I have informed myself of them from Justin and from parents in this community who know both Justin and his parents. Their excellence as parents is well known. I could go on about it at length."

"That won't be necessary, Mr. Pennyworth." Stickney sounded tired. And chillingly patient.

"Perhaps, then, the honorable Court will accept our stipulation as to the Whitneys' sterling qualities as parents."

"Yes, Mr. Bagley, I think that's reasonable. Mr. Bredwell?"

Bredwell stood and looked at Pennyworth before looking at the judge. "Does the honorable Court accept as fact that Mr. Whitney is as Mr. Pennyworth has described him—an exemplary parent?"

"Yes, Mr. Bredwell. Consider it a finding of fact."

"Then, Your Honor, I move that this case be dismissed. The parents' care of the child is no longer in dispute. There is no foundation for the petition."

Stickney was sitting back in his chair. He adjusted his gaze slightly to Pennyworth. "I believe Mr. Pennyworth is about to inform us differently."

"Thank you, Your Honor. Mr. and Mrs. Whitney are in the process of recklessly depriving their child of the benefit of all those virtues we have agreed were *formerly* theirs. In the process of divorce, they are neglecting and impairing their child's mental health.

"Let's consider the conduct of these parents. They are removing the single safeguard the child knows—the protection and security afforded by their mutual presence. Parents are the natural guardians of their children. But where is the guardianship here? Abdicated. Abandoned in their own self-absorption. Certainly this is neglect.

"The parents are removing the safeguard of their collaborative protection of the child. They are removing it willfully and intentionally. Is that not neglect?"

"You are bending the Court's ear, Mr. Pennyworth. You are pulling its chain."

Pennyworth came out from behind his counsel table to stand directly before the judge. "Your Honor, if we were speaking of, say, *medication* that was being withheld from the child, there would be no question but that the case was one of neglect. I submit, Your Honor . . ." Pennyworth paused to look first at Gamble in the witness box and then Skip behind the counsel table and he thought that perhaps Gamble flinched when he looked at her and that the judge noticed. "I submit that these parents are not withholding medication from their child, they are willfully and intentionally withholding the very stuff of life from their child, the very stuff upon which the child is dependent for his mental health and emotional well-being. And that, Your Honor, I submit, constitutes neglect.

"For that reason, I hope that in due course the parents will be dealt with and chastised accordingly, the same as any other neglectful or abusive parents."

Bagley said, "I object. There is no question of abuse here."

Pennyworth looked and sounded distressed. "The child has been *emotionally battered,* Mr. Bagley. What would *you* call it?" Pennyworth shook his head. "The bruises of physical abuse may disappear. The bruises of emotional abuse linger a lifetime."

Stickney was still tipped back in his chair. "I see no petition regarding abuse here, Mr. Pennyworth."

"It is implicit, Your Honor, but I will not press the point."

"It is not a point you would take, Mr. Pennyworth."

"Your Honor," Bredwell said, "may I recall the Court's attention to my motion to dismiss?"

"Anything else, Mr. Pennyworth? Anything else I ought to consider before responding to Mr. Bredwell's motion?"

"Three items, Your Honor. The first is Mrs. Whitney's and Mr. Whitney's refusal to meet with me in my capacity as guardian ad litem. My attempts to interview the Whitneys on behalf of Justin prior to this hearing were rebuffed."

"Mrs. Whitney?"

"He called at six-thirty in the morning!"

"Monday morning," Pennyworth said. "To ensure the greatest opportunity for arranging a meeting prior to this hearing today."

"Mr. Whitney?"

Bredwell stood up. "My client is willing to meet with Mr. Pennyworth at any time of mutual convenience."

Bagley said, "Mrs. Whitney agrees to the same."

"All right, Mr. Pennyworth. Items two and three?"

"I pray the Court to allow testimony by Mr. Michael Dunphy, Justin's teacher, and by Ms. Nelle Vance, an attorney who is a friend of the family."

Stickney was silent for a few seconds. "It will not be necessary to hear from Justin?"

"I had hoped to avoid that."

"Good. If we can get through this without placing Justin in the position of having to testify, I'll allow the testimony of the other two parties."

Pennyworth went out, returned with Mr. Dunphy, closed the door, and directed Dunphy to the witness box.

Pennyworth said, "Please state your name."

"Michael Dunphy."

"Your profession?"

"I'm a teacher."

"And your relationship to Justin Whitney?"

"I'm his fifth-grade teacher."

"Is that a homeroom situation or a classroom situation?"

"Classroom."

"Would it be accurate to say then, Mr. Dunphy, that Justin is in your care throughout the school day?"

"Most of the day. Sometimes he's at music or art or gym or recess."

"But he is with you physically most of the day?"

"Yes. I wish I could say that he was with me mentally, too, but lately he's been spacey."

"In contrast to what? To when?"

"He used to be extraordinarily attentive. Until about two weeks ago when he suddenly found his parents were getting a divorce."

"Did he describe the situation to you?"

"Several times he said that both his parents were leaving him. That's the way he feels about it."

"What sort of student was Justin until recently?"

"Excellent. He was identified in first grade as gifted and he has been coded and tracked as such ever since."

"In the period since he learned of the divorce, has Justin's performance in school been substantially affected?"

"Yes. It's been a poor academic performance."

"Let me ask you about Justin's behavior in school, Mr. Dunphy. Has there been behavior that is atypical of him?"

"Yes. Outbursts of tears, outbursts of anger. At me and at his classmates and friends."

"As Justin's teacher, did you think this behavior warranted being in touch with Mr. or Mrs. Whitney?"

"Yes. I felt strongly that it was necessary."

"And were you in touch with them?"

"Yes, I talked with Mrs. Whitney by phone at her home and with Mr. Whitney by phone at his office."

"Mr. Dunphy, what was the substance of those conversations?"

"That Justin was suffering emotional upheaval."

"Did you make any request of Mrs. Whitney or Mr. Whitney?"

"Both of them. I said this was a very stressful time for Justin, obviously, and that I thought it would be helpful to Justin and to me if they each came in and we talked about how to handle things, at least in school, to make things easier for Justin."

"What was Mrs. Whitney's response to that?"

"She thanked me for calling."

"Did she come in to see you?"

"No."

"Has she called you since you called her?"

"No."

"How long ago was that?"

"A week."

"What was Mr. Whitney's response to your call to him?"

"The same as Mrs. Whitney's. He thanked me. But he didn't come in and he didn't call."

Pennyworth said, "My brothers may inquire."

Bagley started to stand and then paused partway up. "Stu?"

"Go ahead. You're already on your feet."

He came out from behind the counsel table and then leaned against it, his hands spread apart behind him. "Mr. Dunphy, how long have you been a grade-school teacher?"

"Seven years."

"You're an experienced teacher, then. Dedicated?"

"It's a fancy word, but, yes. You have to be."

"As an experienced teacher, Mr. Dunphy, do you find Justin's situation to be a new one or unique in some way?"

"That's kind of a broad question."

"Well, Mr. Dunphy, let me put it this way. Have you had other kids in your classes who were going through divorce?"

"Yes."

"Would you say that Justin's behavior is similar to that of other kids going through a divorce situation?"

"More or less. Yes."

"Thank you."

Bagley nodded to Pennyworth as he returned to his seat.

Pennyworth left Dunphy in the witness box and said, "Your Honor, the pain and stress for these children, the emotional and intellectual impairment, the mental harm, these elements remain the same no matter how many children are forced to go through divorce. The commonality of the experience makes it no less injurious."

"Yes, yes, Mr. Pennyworth. Do you have anything else for the witness, or are you going to let him sit there indefinitely?"

"One thing more, Your Honor. Mr. Dunphy, a week went by between the time Justin learned of the divorce and the time when you felt his suffering warranted attention from his parents to the school situation. During that week in which you observed Justin's anguish, did Mr. or Mrs. Whitney contact you about Justin?"

"No. Neither parent has contacted me about Justin."

Pennyworth looked up at the judge. The judge was bent over some paperwork. Pennyworth saw the top of his pen moving.

"Thank you, Mr. Dunphy. Would you ask Ms. Vance to join us?" As Dunphy left, Pennyworth turned back to the judge. "Your Honor, as a bridge between what the Court has just heard and what the Court is about to hear, I'd like to offer these ·thoughts."

"Would I be able to prevent you, Mr. Pennyworth?"

"That would be the Court's discretion, Your Honor."

"Go on." The judge went back to his paperwork.

"There has been a deprivation of familial relationships, Your Honor. A deprivation such that the healthy psychological development of the child is already being impaired. Nurture itself has been removed. And the normal protection that a child may expect from parents. I submit that this is willful neglect, Your Honor. Both parents are aware of the consequences of their selfishness. Neither parent could even be bothered to respond to Mr. Dunphy's request for a meeting at school. Once again, I say *neglect.*"

"Ah, Ms. Vance," Judge Stickney said as Nelle entered. "Please have a seat in the box."

"Your Honor." Nelle seated herself.

Pennyworth began immediately. "Ms. Vance, I believe you have been stipulated by Mr. and Mrs. Whitney as guardian ad litem in their divorce proceedings before superior court."

"That is so."

"I believe you have filed a motion for that appointment."

"Yes."

"I understand you proposed yourself to the Whitneys through their separate counsels, Mr. Bagley and Mr. Bredwell. Is that correct?"

"Yes."

"Please tell the Court what prompted you to seek this appointment."

"Concern for Justin."

"Concern in what way?"

"I want to protect him."

"From what?"

"At the time I did not know that I would be concerned with protecting him from you, Mr. Pennyworth."

"At the time, Ms. Vance, what did you think you wanted to protect him from?"

"Justin is a victim in all this."

"All what, Ms. Vance?"

"The divorce. I want to protect him from as much of it as I can."

"An admirable objective, Ms. Vance. But isn't that obligation, that responsibility, best left to the parents?"

"Usually. But not in the present situation."

"Aren't the parents protecting their child?"

"In a general sense, yes."

"But in the specific area of their divorce, they are not? Isn't that why you've sought appointment as guardian ad litem? To offer protection the parents have withdrawn from the child? To offer protection that the parents are neglecting to provide?"

"As an overall characterization—"

"You know the rules, Ms. Vance. Please answer yes or no."

"The rules of evidence and testimony do not obtain in juvenile court, Mr. Pennyworth, as you well know."

"Thank you for your confidence in my erudition, Ms. Vance. But as to the question, yes or no? Or do you want me to repeat the question?"

"No. The answer is yes."

"Thank you."

The judge said, "Mr. Bagley? Mr. Bredwell?"

Bredwell stood. "Your Honor, Ms. Vance is not the guardian. She is only representing herself and her personal interest, not Justin Whitney."

"Mr. Bredwell, you and Mr. Bagley stipulated her as guardian in superior court. Why?"

Bredwell looked uncomfortable. "She wanted it. She's a friend of Justin's. She knows everybody involved."

Stickney tipped back and looked out the window for a moment. Then he swiveled toward the courtroom again, still tipped back. "I think, Mr. Bredwell, you're telling me that Ms. Vance is intimate to the parties and the circumstances and that she is in an excellent position to observe and assess. Ms. Vance, I believe you answered yes to Mr. Pennyworth's question as to whether your ambition was to fill in and offer Justin the protection the parents are neglecting to provide?"

Nelle paused and then said, "Yes, Your Honor."

"If no one else has anything for you?" Pennyworth looked at Nelle speculatively. The judge looked at the attorneys. "Then you are excused, Ms. Vance. Thank you."

When the contestants were again alone with the judge, Pennyworth spoke. "Your Honor."

"Mr. Pennyworth."

"I ask this honorable Court to carefully consider Ms. Vance's testimony. In that Mrs. Whitney and Mr. Whitney are failing to provide the child with necessary emotional care, the parents are substantially neglecting Justin—"

"That is absurd, totally absurd," Gamble said.

The judge tipped forward and looked down. "Mr. Bagley, kindly advise your client to keep quiet."

Skip laughed and said to Bredwell, "That's a piece of advice Gamble has *never* taken."

"And you, sir," Stickney said to Skip, "you also will keep quiet. I suppose you have more, Mr. Pennyworth?"

"Neglect, Your Honor. Substantial and substantiated neglect. Neglect that has produced demonstrable emotional harm—"

"Your Honor," Bagley said, getting up, "I see no such thing demonstrated or substantiated. This entire excursion is frivolous and I join my brother in his motion to dismiss."

"I agree with you, Mr. Bagley," the judge said. "I agree that Mr. Pennyworth's purposes here are entirely obscure."

"Your Honor," Pennyworth said, "I wish to set in motion the initial steps to protect young Justin Whitney."

"What do you have in mind, Mr. Pennyworth?"

"Precisely, Your Honor: *minds.* I pray the honorable Court that Mr. and Mrs. Whitney be ordered to undergo mental health evaluation by a psychiatrist—"

"No way," Gamble said.

"She's right about that," Skip said.

"I'll hear from you later," Stickney said, "but you'd best keep very carefully quiet now, both of you."

"Thank you, Your Honor," Pennyworth said. "As guardian ad litem I have this week consulted with Joanna Rosen, M.D., Cyrus Roy, M.D., and Edward Senel, M.D. Dr. Rosen is Justin's pediatrician and has been so since his birth. Dr. Roy is Mrs. Whitney's personal physician and, in fact, delivered Justin. And Dr. Senel is Mr. Whitney's personal physician. On the recommendation of these three, together with that of the New Hampshire Family Services—here are the supporting documents, Your Honor—if the Court orders the evaluation, Lorraine Salmon, M.D., of Manchester is considered an appropriate selection. Dr. Salmon is a psychiatrist whose specialties are childhood and the family unit."

"Are you making a recommendation as to Justin then, as well, Mr. Pennyworth?"

"Yes, Your Honor. I believe it is central to obtain a psychiatric evaluation not only of the present trauma, but also of the future effects of the present trauma. It is to be hoped that the psychiatrist will, as well, provide the honorable Court with her own recommendations for Justin's well-being."

"Very well, Mr. Pennyworth, it's worth consideration." Stickney tilted slowly back and forth in his chair and rolled a pen between the fingers of his two hands. *"Now,* Mrs. Whitney, now it's your turn. You may address the Court from where you are."

Gamble started to speak, but Bagley said to her, "Stand up."

Gamble stood. She looked at Stickney. "Mental evaluation? *Mental* evaluation. I think I *will* go mental over this. I will not have my head examined by a perfect stranger. I will not. Nor is anyone going to examine *my* child's head without my permission."

"Is that all, Mrs. Whitney?"

"Yes."

"You may sit down, Mrs. Whitney. Mr. Whitney?"

Skip stood. "Your Honor, the way I see it, *this* man, Mr. Pennyworth, *he* is the lunatic. He needs his head examined. Walking in on someone's family. Grabbing a child off to sue his parents. Your Honor, the way I see it, he's trying to make a jackass of the Court. And if the Court goes along with it, the *Court* needs its head examined."

Stickney nodded and smiled. "Is that all, Mr. Whitney?"

"Yes, Your Honor."

"Please be seated then, Mr. Whitney. Are you comfortable now, Mr. Whitney?"

"Yes, Your Honor."

"Good. Mr. Pennyworth, you seem to be trying to get my attention."

"Yes, Your Honor. I pray the Court to take special cognizance of the therapeutic aims of juvenile court as mandated by statute."

"Thank you, Mr. Pennyworth, for reminding the Court of its duties. Thank you very kindly."

Stickney rubbed his nose with a knuckle and then studied the back of his hand. After a moment he bent over the paperwork before him and began writing.

After a while Stickney looked up. "This Court is reluctant to find the child neglected. But it is persuaded that further investigation is warranted. The child will remain with his parents according to the temporary orders issued by the superior court. The child and both parents are ordered to undergo mental health evaluation by Dr. Salmon—there being no objection to Dr. Salmon from counsel. Mr. Bagley? Mr. Bredwell? Very good. Mr. Pennyworth, I suspect you have already been in touch with Dr. Salmon."

"Yes."

"I want to set a date for the adjudicatory. One month hence? Will that give the psychiatrist time to conduct her interviews and make a report?"

"That's what she requested, Your Honor. A month. If the Whitneys cooperate by presenting themselves and Justin to Dr. Salmon at an early date. She requires a minimum of two hours with each, an hour at a time."

"Mr. Bagley, Mr. Bredwell. Please explain to your clients that they are under court order. Further, explain to them the consequences of failing to abide by the Court's order." Stickney sat back. "We are certainly in uncharted waters here and I mean to sound their depths."

29

PENNYWORTH CHATS WITH GAMBLE AND SKIP

JUST ABOUT THE WORST PART ABOUT SUING SOMEONE, Justin had decided—aside from how they felt about you for suing them—was all the waiting around. Waiting to get a lawyer, waiting for the lawyer to call, waiting to see how your parents would feel about it, waiting for court to happen, waiting for the judge, and then having to wait outside while all these people were deciding your life inside.

Nelle tried to kid with him, but Justin didn't go along with it. He remembered how she had held him and comforted him right after he found out about the divorce, but he still thought she could be a spy. Mr. Dunphy had gone home. And Justin's dumb books were out in his backpack with his weekend stuff in his father's car.

Occasionally someone would walk across the squeaky wood floor going to or coming from one town office or another. That was just about all the excitement there was. Though he had been frightened by doing it, Justin had also thought that suing would be more interesting than this. Instead, when you got to court, it was just boring. You just had to wait outside while all the good stuff was going on inside.

Outside the courtroom, Pennyworth said to Justin, "I'd like to spend a few minutes with you, my boy."

"He is not your boy," Skip said.

"Nevertheless, I'd like to spend a few minutes with him."

"No, definitely no," Gamble said.

"I'd like to explain to him what went on inside."

"*I* will explain to him what went on inside," Gamble said.

"Are you denying me access to my client?"

"I am denying you access to my son."

"You will force me to seek a court order."

"Seek all you want, Mr. Pennyworth, you're not going to see Justin today."

"That's not up to you," Skip said. "As of school release time, Justin is with me today and for the weekend. Remember? How long do you want, Mr. Pennyworth?"

"Skip, this man is *corrupting* Justin's mind—"

"Fifteen, perhaps twenty minutes, Mr. Whitney."

"*Skip.*"

"Shut up, Gamble—"

"I will not release him to you again—"

"That's stipulated—"

"Not in so many words—"

Pennyworth was looking at Justin. Justin was crouching away. "See what you two are doing to him," Pennyworth said.

Nelle said, "I see what *your* contribution is, Pennyworth."

Justin decided that he was right about Nelle.

"A *shrink?*" Justin said. "*Me?*" The boy seemed more amazed— even entranced, Pennyworth thought—than fearful. "Jeezum."

"She'll just talk to you for a while. I think there may be some games."

"Mom and Dad, too?"

"Just as I said."

"My mom and dad are good at playing games."

"I agree. I've seen them at it."

"When did you ever see them playing games?"

"Just now."

After Pennyworth left him, his mom and dad's two lawyers came over and sat on either side of him. "Hello, Justin."

"Hello, Mr. Bagley. Hello, Mr. Bredwell."

Bagley said, "We just thought we'd see what you think of all this."

Justin put his head down.

"What say, Justin?" Bredwell said.

"Do I have to answer?" Justin said, looking at his sneakers that didn't quite make it to the floor.

"We can't *force* you, Justin," Bredwell said, "but we could ask the judge to ask you."

"He knows already."

"Then why not tell us?"

"It's private between Mr. Pennyworth and me. You're on the other side."

"*Other* side?" Bredwell said. "Incredible. Suing his parents and—"

"Hey, Justin," Bagley said. "This isn't a soccer game, young feller. This is for real marbles. It's hardball. Do you understand that?"

"Yes."

"Did Mr. Pennyworth push you into this?"

"No."

"We just want to know how you feel about what's going on."

Justin continued to look at his sneakers. He aimed the toes at each other and touched them together. "It's fine with me," he said quietly.

"Now look," he heard his mother say from above him, "you've got to *stop* this, Justin."

"Then *you* stop it," he said, still not looking up.

Back inside the courtroom, Bagley and Bredwell had sat the Whitneys at a counsel table, but themselves remained standing.

"Apparently you two weren't paying attention when we advised you," Bredwell said. "Pennyworth is succeeding at just what we warned you against. He's dividing you. He's dividing your opposition to Justin."

"I'm not opposed to Justin," Skip said.

"Your opposition to Pennyworth then," Bredwell said. "Call it any blessed thing you wish, Pennyworth is dividing it."

"You're playing his game," Bagley said.

"Speak of the devil," Bredwell said.

Pennyworth had come in the door. "Justin is ready to go with you, Mr. Whitney. But before I leave this charming company . . ." Pennyworth pulled a chair around to the head of the counsel table and sat down. "As Justin's court-appointed guardian ad litem, Mrs. Whitney, Mr. Whitney, I am required to act as a finder of facts. We should make our interview appointments right now."

"I really am quite pressed for time right now, Ted," Gamble said to her lawyer.

"Mrs. Whitney," Pennyworth said, "I'm sure your dance card is filled to capacity. But it is your obligation as a parent to cooperate with the guardian ad litem."

"Not if he's prejudiced."

"You may decline, of course. But I'm sure you would prefer an interview with me to an investigation by an officer of the Division of Child and Youth Services."

Gamble looked at her lawyer. Bagley said, "He can get that order." Gamble sighed.

"Monday then?" Pennyworth said. "Your house? Love to see it. Justin's home. Heard so much. Two P.M.? Fine." Pennyworth entered it in his diary. "And Mr. Whitney, I'd like to see you in Justin's other home. Noon all right?"

"It's a nuisance. But I'll be there."

Pennyworth made the notation. "Ah, and speaking of the family homestead," he said to Bagley and Bredwell, "have you fellows agreed upon an appraiser yet—or will there be separate appraisals?"

"*Appraisal?*" Skip said. "Of my house?"

"*Whose* house?" Gamble said.

"We haven't gotten to that yet," Bredwell said.

"Surely that should be tended to as soon as possible. It's a major issue. The worth of the house and its disposition."

"There has been some tentative discussion," Bredwell said. "But Mrs. Whitney, being a realtor herself, has some reservations about the candidates who have been mentioned."

"Candace Carrere is well thought of," Pennyworth said. "She's used by a number of firms in Manchester. I took the liberty of contacting her this morning and she has agreed to do the appraisal Monday afternoon."

"Some other woman tramping around my house?" Gamble said. "Sizing it up? *No sir.*"

"Mrs. Whitney, it is Justin's right as a party in this—"

"I don't believe that is so," Bagley said. "He has no equity in the property."

"He has a right to a guarantee of his educational expenses. *Polk v. Polk, Grenier v. Grenier,* RSA 169E. The value of the house has a direct bearing on that guarantee. Therefore I will have it appraised on his behalf."

"Ted, *do something.*"

"Gamble, it may as well be Candace Carrere as anyone. And it may as well be done now as later. At least we'll know what we're talking about. If her figure isn't in our ballpark, we'll get our own designated hitter. Stu?"

"She's all right with me."

"Monday afternoon, one P.M.," Pennyworth said.

"You are insufferable," Gamble said.

Pennyworth was delighted with himself. Everyone was angry at him. He had just about killed the parents in juvenile court. Suddenly in the midst of his satisfaction, he found himself faltering at the wheel of his car, his foot easing off the accelerator to compensate for an attack of dread just when he had been feeling so good.

The Voice said, You really did. You just about killed them in there.

Pennyworth found he was sweating again.

"How do you feel about going to see this psychiatrist?" his father asked Justin as they drove to Skip's new place.

"It's okay."

"Did Pennyworth discuss it with you? Or did he just go ahead and do it?"

"That's private."

"Oh. Private from your father."

"Private to me."

"You know, I didn't start this stuff, Justin. Your mother did."

"I don't care."

Nelle said to Bagley and Bredwell, "Pennyworth is getting away with murder with this judge."

"Stickney holds that everything so far has met the requirements of the statute," Bredwell said.

"I think old Ford B. is just having a little fun," Bagley said.

"At everyone's expense," Nelle said, "especially Justin's."

"And, I think," Bagley said, "he's just waiting for something to come along that *doesn't* meet the requirements, and then he's going to dismiss the petition and Mr. Pennyworth all the way back to hell and gone."

"What if he doesn't? What if he finds that divorce is an act of parental neglect?"

"He's not going to find that," Bredwell said. "What would he do with it?"

30
DIVORCE CITY

IT WAS A STRANGE HOUSE HIS FATHER TOOK JUSTIN TO IN a strange neighborhood called Deer Meadow, a development of attached houses almost as far away from home as another town.

What Justin had to do was already familiar to him after only one experience. Find where to put his things. Look out the window to see what could be seen. Find where the bathroom was. Go downstairs and see what else there was in all this strangeness. And in a strange house Justin was strange to himself, as if he were watching himself and neither the person watching nor the person being watched were really himself.

"Of course, it's not like our home," his father said. The new house was rented and pretty empty of furniture "and going to stay that way until we're both back in our own home. But I did get this . . ."

It was a whole new stereo. "But we already have one," Justin said.

"Not as good as this—and that's at the other house. That CD is three years old. There've been lots of improvements since then. This is top of the line, a five-disc changer. Look at these speakers. They'll do a hundred watts. What do you think?"

"It looks great," Justin said quietly.

"Wait till you hear it. *And* I got interlocking remote control, too. We can get stereo from the new TV or you can turn a speaker on anywhere in the house or change from phono to FM or—*Hey!* What's this?" He indicated a box. "Open it."

It was taped closed. "Oh," his father said, "I guess you'll need a knife. Open this." He handed Justin a small box wrapped in white paper.

Justin opened it. It was a Swiss army knife just like his dad's. "Gee, thanks, Dad." Justin was pleased. He opened and closed each blade and instrument. *"Thanks."*

"You're old enough for this now. Of course, you can't take it to school."

"I know that."

"And be careful not to lose it."

"I won't." He opened the box. There were CDs and tape cassettes, some classical, some rock, some folk.

"It's to start your collection for here. Later I hope we'll be taking them home. The woman at the record store helped with the rock stuff. How is it?"

"It's fine. They're all good."

"You can exchange what you want."

"These are fine, Dad."

"Put something on." Justin kept changing recordings because his father wanted him to, so he could experience the whole range of sounds the system could deliver.

After a while, his father said, "Won't this be great when we get it back to our own house? You can hardly turn it up here. It'd blow the walls down. Won't it be great?"

"Sure."

"I almost forgot. I want a glass of wine. Come into the kitchen."

In the kitchen there was an eighteen-speed mountain bike. "What do you think of that?" his father said.

Justin almost cried when he saw it and realized it was for him, but the tears had nothing to do with pleasure at getting the bike.

His father came over and put his arm around Justin. "I'm glad you like it. Now you can keep up with me on hills. I got it a little big. Come spring you're going to need something bigger than that old horse you've got at the other house."

It wasn't old. His father and mother had given it to him two years ago. It still fit him. He'd just barely grown into it right. He looked at the new bike and heard the new stereo playing a new CD of his own and he felt the weight of the new knife in his pocket and he couldn't remember anyone, his mom or his dad, saying *I love you* to him almost since the divorce started.

"Anyway, we don't have to transport a bike back and forth now." His father poured himself a glass of white wine. "It's too late to try it out today. We'll go riding together tomorrow morning."

"I've got soccer."

"Oh, yeah. Tomorrow afternoon then. Have you had steak this week?"

"Unh-unh."

"I thought not. C'mon, look at this." His father opened the back door. There was a brand-new propane grill outside. "It can do lots more than the one at the other house. Won't it be great on our deck when we get it back home?"

* * *

That night, in the strange room that was his here and where even the air from outside had a strange smell, Justin told himself an awake dream where Mr. Pennyworth had done everything so well that his mom and dad got back together again and they really loved each other and Justin especially for getting them back together, and they lived at home again, all three of them, and home didn't anymore have that strange new feeling to it.

It was a happy awake dream and then Justin thought of Clyde all alone in the dark back in his room and he began to cry, but not so that his father could hear him.

At the soccer game the next morning, Justin was afraid his father and mother would have an argument in front of everyone again, like before. But they didn't even stand near each other, and Justin didn't know whether to be relieved or sad. He felt both.

Walking together over to the sidelines after the first quarter, Ryan was angry at him. "You had a good chance at a goal there. You didn't even shoot."

"I'm living in a new place," Justin said and knew that wouldn't make any sense to Ryan as an answer because it didn't make any sense to Justin.

Mr. Dunphy said, "You're not concentrating on the game again, Justin. It's not fair to your teammates. I want you to sit down the second quarter and pay attention to what's happening."

A few minutes later, when the team was back on the field, Justin heard his father say to Mr. Dunphy, "It's not fair to Justin. You know he needs to be in there. You know that."

"I don't know that. I don't know what he needs except what I see, since you and Mrs. Whitney won't come in and discuss what he needs."

"Listen here, Dunphy, I'm a taxpayer and that places you in my employ—" And so, Justin thought, it wasn't going to be a fight between his father and his mother, it was going to be a fight between his father and Mr. Dunphy.

Justin felt a hand squeeze his shoulder. He looked around. It was his mother. "Sorry for the way your father is."

Driving back to Deer Meadow, Justin said to his father, "I wish you wouldn't say that stuff to Mr. Dunphy. He was right."

"He was right? You think so? How does *he* know what my schedule is? How do *you* know what my schedule is? It pays his salary, that's all he needs to know."

"He was right to sit me down. I wasn't paying attention."

"How can you *not* pay attention to a game you're *in*, Justin?"

Justin didn't answer.

"Well?"

"I don't know."

Justin learned the eighteen speeds right off, and his father was right, he could take hills a lot better with the new bike, even though it was a little big.

When they got back, there were some kids playing a pickup game of soccer on an open stretch of grass on the other side of the parking area.

"Put your bike away," his father said, "and get something to drink or eat—I got you those Dove Bars."

"Gee, thanks."

"Then go on out and say hello to those kids."

"I don't know."

"They're your neighbors."

"I guess not."

"Why not?"

"I just don't want to."

"Look, Justin, the reality is, you're living here and you've just got to face it. Now, get something to eat and then go over and say hello."

When Justin came out, he didn't go over to the other kids. He just sat on the front step. He felt ashamed not to be living at home. He felt ashamed that he was living here because his mother and father were getting a divorce.

The kids were just kicking the ball around. They weren't very good.

After a while one of the players left the group and walked over toward Justin, his head down. It was Chick. He stopped a few feet away from Justin and barely looked up. "Hi."

"Hi," Justin said.

"You living here now?"

"Yeah. When I'm with my dad. You?"

"Yeah. With my mom. I was awarded to her mostly. I thought that was your dad. I saw him moving in. I figured you'd be here."

"Yeah. Well, I'm here. For this weekend."

"Heather's here, too. She lives here. And Derek. He was awarded to his father, mostly. No one knows why. Not even Derek. That's unusual, you know?"

Chick was looking down at the ground. Still, it was more words than Justin had ever heard him say at one time.

"You want to come over to my house and play?" Chick said.

"Sure. Let me tell my dad."

The car outside Chick's was a big one from a long time ago. It was white and rusted in places. Inside, the house smelled of disinfectant spray and Chick's mother smelled a little of something like wine, only stronger.

"My little chicken home to roost," Chick's mother said, grabbing him in her arms. "Hello, who's this?"

"That's Justin Whitney. He's in Mr. Dunphy's class."

"How do you do, Justin." She put out her hand. Justin shook it. "I'm Fawn Ross. Call me Fawn. Isn't that funny, a Fawn coming to live in Deer Meadow with her little Chick?"

A man came in from the kitchen with a drink in each hand.

"That's Glen," Chick said.

The man handed a drink to Fawn and said to Chick, "Who's this young gentleman?"

"Justin," Chick said. "He just moved in. For weekends, like."

"Well, Justin, can I offer you a drink?" Glen laughed. "Just joking, of course. Hey, you must be the Mercedes. Damn, I bet. Right?"

"Yes."

"I said to Fawn, we got Camaros, we got Firebirds, we got Subarus and Volkswagens, we got a Taurus wagon and a Saab 900, and now we even got a Mercedes. Place is looking up."

Chick was looking down again.

"You want something?" Fawn said to Chick.

"Naw, we were just going out."

"What'd you come back for?" Glen said.

"I forget," Chick said.

"Must have been something," Glen said.

"Naw, nothin'." Chick started to walk toward the front door.

"Don't walk away from me, son," Glen said in a level voice.

Chick stopped, but did not look up. "Sorry."

"What did you come back for, son?"

"I told you, I forget."

"I don't like lying, son. I've told you that."

"He just wanted to show me where he lives," Justin said.

"Oh, Mr. Mercedes. Thank you so much for remembering for him."

"I guess we'll be gone when you get back," Fawn said. "Get yourself some cereal. There's CupASoup and crackers. I forgot milk, so forget about the cereal. We'll be back, I don't know when. Okay?"

"Sure."

"If your father calls, tell him he owes me thirty-five dollars from when I had that road call taking you over to him and he's not going to see you till I get it."

"But I want to see him, Ma."

"Not till he gives me the money he owes me."

"Don't be a hangdog," Glen said. "Look up, son, have some pride. Look your mother and me in the eye."

"He's not really my dad," Chick said outside. "They're not even married."

"I got that," Justin said.

The sky had turned a dark blue above and was red in the distance. The air had turned from cool to cold. The soccer game was breaking up and kids were walking off to the different groupings of attached houses.

"You still got a home? Where you grew up?" Chick said.

"Yeah. My mom's there. Till the court decides. You?"

"My home got sold."

"That's sad."

"It sure is."

Justin looked back at Chick's house. Except for the car in front, it was the same as his house. "You gonna just have cereal for dinner?"

"I can't have cereal for dinner, 'less I eat it dry."

"Oh, yeah."

"CupASoup and crackers, I guess."

"That's *all?*"

Chick looked back at his own house. "Divorce wouldn't have to be so bad if you had a real home, you know?"

"Come over to my house for dinner," Justin said.

"Naw—all the way back to—?"

"I mean here. Dad won't mind."

In the gathering darkness a girl and boy had come over from the grass area. "Thought that was you," Heather said. "See, Derek? I told you." She looked at Justin. "Welcome to Divorce City."

"I think you need to know about this," his father said.

"Stop it, I want to go to sleep."

"But you've got to understand, I tried to save the marriage—"

"I don't care—"

"I tried to get your mother to go to a psychiatrist, I don't know how many times—"

"*I don't care.* I'm not interested."

"But you should care. You should be interested—"

"I'm not!"

His father was silent. Justin lay absolutely still, as if, if he moved, it would start his father again.

"I'm sorry, Justin . . . I see you here alone . . . and everything's smashed, and I just want to explain. I guess I'm trying to explain it to myself."

Justin turned away. "Don't explain it to me."

"Okay, you're right." He put his hand on Justin. "It's hard not to, sometimes. I mean, you *know* both of us—"

"Don't start. *Please.*"

"Okay . . . What a sad little boy your friend Chick is. He was glad to be here, I think. Do you think he was glad to be here?"

"He had fun. Yeah. He looked up a lot. He usually won't look at anybody. He had a good time."

"You know, when I was saying about being alone and talking to you because sometimes I don't have someone to talk to?"

"There's the shrink, Dad."

"That's not funny."

"Yeah, I understand. I feel that way, too, sometimes."

"I hope you have someone to talk to, Justin."

"Yeah."

"Ryan?"

"Ryan sometimes. And Clyde."

"Who's Clyde?"

"Oh, just someone."

"A friend of *Mom's?*"

"I don't think so."

"Justin?"

"Yeah?"

"I love you."

Justin rolled back and flung his arms up for his father. "I love you too, Dad."

Outside the new house cars kept going and coming as Justin tried to get to sleep in the new room.

Hearing the cars start and drive off, Justin thought that he would never be going home again nor would his father, no matter what his father said about going back there, because no matter who got the house, it wouldn't be the three of them there together and so it could never be his home again. Justin wondered if he would ever have a home again. How old would he have to be?

It was not until the cars in the parking area below his window had stopped interrupting the darkness that Justin finally got to sleep.

He dreamed that Mr. Pennyworth had gotten his mom and dad in a cage and shut the door on them and even that wasn't any good because though his mom and dad were together, Justin was outside and couldn't be with them.

31
REPEAT PERFORMANCE

GOING BACK HOME, JUSTIN REALIZED HE'D LEFT HIS LEGOS at his father's. Actually, it *wasn't* like going back home anymore. It was like two huge magnets getting together with the same poles aimed at each other. Justin could *feel* the resistance.

When his mother kissed him at the door, Justin knew something was up from the smell of her. She had on perfume the way she always did for something special at night. She was wearing fancy slacks and a fancy blouse and *jewelry*. She smelled like a party.

She tried to keep his father from coming in, but he went in anyway. He needed to get more towels, he said.

There was a man in the living room. He stood up.

"Justin, Skip, this is Dr. Campbell."

"Ralph," the man said. He extended his hand. "Glad to meet you, Skip, Justin, glad to meet you, son. Keep hearing about you."

"Yes," his father said. "I haven't heard word one about you. What are you doing in this house?"

"*Skip*. This man is a guest here. He's interested in some property of mine—"

"That sounds right, anyway."

"Ralph is a cardiovascular surgeon. He's going to operate in Baltimore tomorrow. I'm driving him to the airport in Manchester. They're sending a plane for him."

"That's unusual, isn't it, Ralph? Don't they have cardiovascular surgeons in Baltimore?"

"The procedure needed is a specialty of mine."

"Well, Skip, I'm sorry you can't stay, but I'm very rushed and I want some time with Justin . . ." His mother stopped. "Is this all you brought home?"

"Yes." Justin didn't understand.

"Where are your Legos? Your big box of Legos? Are they out in the car?"

"I forgot them," Justin said.

His mother studied him. "And the blue rugby you wanted? That I got you? Did you bring that back?"

"It's in the laundry, Gamble," Skip said.

"He should have brought it back."

"He's wearing a *new* shirt," Skip said.

"I want the one I bought him. What goes over to your place, Skip, I expect to come back here."

Skip laughed. "Gamble, don't be so rigid."

"*Rigid?* Don't make me laugh, Skip."

Dr. Ralph said, "Sounds like you two could use a little divorce counseling."

"Shut up," Skip said.

"Does wonders for some people," Dr. Ralph said.

"I don't want wonders," Gamble said. "Just Justin's things that belong here."

"The Legos," Skip said, "I bought the—"

"And, Skip, in case you've forgotten, you owe me ninety dollars for replacing the shocks on the station wagon after I lent it to you and you overloaded it and ruined a few other things."

"I didn't over—"

"Shaw's Service Station said you must have. You loaded the bed and the rear shocks had to be replaced."

"I told you they had to be replaced last summer—"

"Ninety dollars, Skip. And those clothes. Before Justin spends another weekend with you."

"I shouldn't be concerned," Skip said with a tight smile, "but I'm sure you're making a real great impression on Dr. Ralph here."

"Don't bother 'bout me, sounds just like home. Both homes. Hers and mine."

"Have you got children?" Skip said.

"Two girls."

"How do they like it?" Justin said. "Two homes."

"I guess they don't have much to say about it," Dr. Ralph said.

"You're going now, Skip," his mother said.

"Look, sweetie," his mother said to him, "I'm sorry I have to leave you, but I've got to drive Ralph to the airport and we're going to stop off for a bite to eat at the inn."

"That's okay."

"I got your favorite Stouffer's. Chicken fettuccine. He's a real gourmet," she said to Dr. Ralph. "How's that?"

"Fine."

"You just nuke it for three or four minutes. It says on the package. I left the right kind of bowl out, okay?"

"Sure."

"And I made you some salad and there's French bread and I got you a chocolate croissant with almonds for dessert, okay?"

"Fine."

"Be sure to have milk."

"Okay."

"Before that, you take a bath and shampoo, okay?"

"Sure."

"And don't forget guitar," she said with a special smile.

"Sure."

"Now, before I go out, there's something I want you to see. A surprise. I want you to try it out. It's behind the couch."

Justin went behind one of the couches and found a new guitar case, a hard, smooth one, the kind that cost a lot of money no matter what's inside. This was a narrow case. He knew it wasn't an acoustic guitar. He knew what it probably was.

"Bring it out and open it up."

He brought it into the middle of the living room.

"Careful when you open it, son, might be a rattlesnake inside," Dr. Ralph said.

Justin opened it. It was an electric guitar, a real good one—just about professional grade.

"What's wrong, Justin? Isn't that what you've always wanted?"

Justin felt tears coming to his eyes again. "Stop it," he said. "You and Dad just stop it."

His mother was kneeling down in front of him, a look of fear on her face. "What's *wrong*, Justin? You were so disappointed when you didn't get one on—"

"That was different."

"Aren't you even going to play it?"

"Later."

"There's the speaker, the *pickup*, it's a really fine one, Justin, all you have to do is plug the cable in and, look, I'll show you—"

"I know how to plug the cable in—"

"Then why don't you—"

"I'll do it later," Justin said quietly. "I'm going to take my bath now."

"Justin," his mother said, *"please."*

"Son," the doctor said, "don't turn your back on your mother, son. Turn around and come try out this fine instrument, son."

"All right."

Justin plugged one end of the cable into the guitar and the other into the pickup. He tried out the sound gently. The sound was okay, he didn't know, he didn't know anything about electric guitars, just some heavy metal sounds he heard on recordings. Then he turned the volume and the distortion on the pickup way up and started playing whatever his fingers found as fast as his fingers could find it.

Over the sound he heard his mother crying out, *"Please! Justin!"*

When his mother got home Justin was in bed looking at comics.

She came in and sat on his bedside. He smelled the perfume—though not as strongly as before—and felt or even smelled the cold night air on her skin.

"I'm sorry about the guitar," he said. "I really like it. Thanks."

"Why did you act that way?"

"I guess I was tired."

"Stay up late at Dad's?"

"No."

"How is it over there? Deer Meadow. *God.*"

"It's okay."

"Just okay?"

"I don't know yet. We just got there."

"We?"

"Dad and me."

"I guess maybe you were just tense from being there."

I was tense, okay, Justin thought, tense about you guys going head-to-head back here.

"You know, that's why I have to get this divorce. Your father made me tense, too. All the time. Every day for years. I guess you're old enough to understand that."

"I don't know."

"Well, your dad is that way. I know he's a good pal sometimes, but he can make you tense if he doesn't get his own way. Justin? I'm talking to you."

"I hear you," Justin said, his eyes closed.

"I think you need to know some of this about your dad."

Justin pulled the pillow over his head and pressed it against his ears. His voice muffled, he said, "I don't need to know anything."

His mother removed the pillow. "You're not the only one with a right to be angry around here, young man. Talk about tension. You know you're killing me with all this, Justin? You and Mr. Pennyworth. The two of you together. This was supposed to be a nice, *simple* divorce, *damn it,* Justin."

His mother started to cry and Justin sat up and put his arm around her and comforted her. And that felt *weird*. As if the strange room he had been in at his father's was a room inside his head and he was inside the room inside his own head.

"I'm sorry, Mom, I'm really sorry, I'm sorry."

"Your father *forced* me to get this divorce," his mother said.

Justin didn't say anything and his mother wept for a while and then got quiet. She used the folded-back part of the sheet to wipe her eyes and there was a smudge of black eye makeup on it afterward.

"Well, anyway," she said, patting her eyes with the balls of her hands, "it hasn't exactly been a joyful reunion, has it? But I love you. Believe me?"

"Sure."

32
PENNYWORTH GOES VISITING

DEER MEADOW, PENNYWORTH SAW, DRIVING UP TO number 58 and parking his Porsche next to Skip's Mercedes, would not have been the residence of choice for either auto by their manufacturers.

"Don't judge me or what I can provide for Justin by this," Skip said. "It's purely temporary. It's the only sort of place you can get around here where the maintenance is taken care of for you. You can just come and go, keep dry, keep warm, sack out, and have none of the household nuisances to take care of."

"Do you mind that? Household nuisances?"

"Not at all. Not at home. That's where Gamble is now. I love taking care of that place. No, this place here is just till I get my home back."

"What if you don't? What if it's awarded to Gamble? I understand you'd threatened to burn it down."

"Just my half," Skip said. "The court has to award me a half interest. It's joint property. So I'd just burn down my half."

"I trust you are jesting, Mr. Whitney."

"I'd try to buy it out, Weld, that's what I'd do. And if I couldn't do that, I'd try to force the sale of the place. I have a right to get my equity out."

"Perhaps, Skip."

"But I will not let Gamble live in it. Anyway, I have equal claim to it—the court may award it to me. There are some factors operating on my side. For instance—"

"I'm here to talk about Justin, Skip. Justin's best interests."

"Well, there you have it, Weld. That house is a hell of a place for a boy to grow up with his dad."

"Why are you seeking the divorce, Skip?"

"I'm not seeking it, Gamble is."

"You filed a cross-libel for divorce."

"Well, that's what you do, you know. You've got to protect yourself. You know that, Weld. Gamble's been nothing but trouble to me. She's impossible to live with. Another reason is, it's in Justin's best interests."

"The divorce?"

"Yes."

"Why is that?"

"We were arguing all the time. I tried to protect Justin from it, but it was impossible."

"You two seem to have a pretty flexible visitation arrangement, Skip."

"Yes."

"Is the arrangement stipulated or is it by mutual consent?"

"It's stipulated that we'll try to do it mutually."

"How is that working out?"

"Sometimes it does, sometimes it doesn't."

"Has Gamble refused you visitation?"

"She's threatened to."

"Has she?"

"Not yet."

"Justin told me one night his mother had to be in Concord for a late meeting and instead of getting a sitter she had him stay over with you."

"Yeah. That's the sort of way we managed things when we were married."

"You're still married."

"You mean in God's eyes? I don't believe in God."

"In the state's eyes."

"Next you're going to tell me we'll always be Justin's parents, the three of us will always be a family."

"I wouldn't be so rash, Skip. So that's the way you worked things when you were living together?"

"Yeah, it's about the only thing that worked when we were living together. And if I had to go away on a trip, Gamble took care of Justin and everything at home. If she had to be away, I did."

"What if Justin got sick?"

"One of us would leave the office and take him to the doctor or stay with him."

"Would you say that was predominantly Gamble or you?"

"Oh, no. We shared it."

"I understand you two aren't disputing custody. I haven't run across any motions to that effect."

"No, we're pretty much in agreement about Justin. At least we were. I'm not so sure now. The way Gamble says I can't see him till I bring the Legos back. Do you know about that? The Legos?"

"I'm afraid not. But before we get to the Legos, Skip, just follow up on the nature of the agreement you and Gamble were in about Justin."

"It's pretty simple, actually. We both love him. We both respect each other as parents. Justin loves both of us—I mean, look at the crazy lengths he's going to to try to keep us from getting a divorce." Skip paused and thought. "I guess it's mutual dependency. Gamble and I are dependent on each other to take care of Justin so we can keep up with our professional lives and still give Justin first-class parenting."

Parenting? the Voice said. *Parenting?* That word ought to be prohibited. I've said so before. You never knew what it was anyway, did you?

Yes, Pennyworth said back, I did.

Gamble knew Candace Carrere by reputation and from casual encounters at professional meetings and she knew that Candace was a power in the state realtors association, but when Gamble saw her driving across the meadow to *intrude* herself into Gamble's house and *appraise* it, Gamble felt considerable animosity.

With effort Gamble conducted Candace through the house and, with no effort at all, treated her with nasty politeness.

Candace said, "It's never pleasant having your house appraised, is it? Even when you want to sell."

"I don't want to sell."

"It's an intrusion," Candace said.

Gamble offered her a cup of tea. They exchanged small talk about professional matters.

When Candace left, Gamble's brief feeling of agreeability also departed. Gamble felt violated. Not by Candace but by Mr. Weld Pennyworth who had inserted his dirty self into her house. Gamble had been angry at Pennyworth. Now she hated his guts.

Gamble watched the smartass drive up in his smartass Porsche with the telephone aerial and some other aerials. She let him wait at the door a full two minutes before she went to it.

"I hope I'm not early, Mrs. Whitney," Pennyworth said.

"Wiseass." Gamble closed the door behind him.

Pennyworth remained just inside the door. "What a lovely home. So full of light. So airy. It reminds me of some of the better domestic architecture in California." Pennyworth dropped the names, like falling leaves, of a few superstar film and recording people.

Gamble found herself warming to the intruder. "Oh," she said. "Does architecture interest you?"

"Passionately. When I'm able to move outside the city, I hope to build something like this."

"Oh, then let me show you around. Have you the time?"

"I'll make the time, Mrs. Whitney."

"Please call me Gamble."

"So kind of you. You must call me Weld."

"All right, Weld. What does Justin call you?"

"Mr. Pennyworth."

"Well, just come along, Weld."

"As I was driving across your field, I was struck by the amazing proportions of the house. Who designed it?"

"I did." Gamble paused. "Well, actually, Skip and I designed it together. It just sort of grew as we lived together and added on and remodeled."

"No professional help?"

"Just builders, if that's what you mean."

Pennyworth and Gamble stood on the deck overlooking the lake. The foliage had passed its peak. Much of it had fallen. Stark black trunks and boughs stood along the shoreline, interrupted here and there by the white of birch, the deep green of pine rising on the hills beyond.

"This is an *ideal* place for a young boy to grow up in, don't you agree, Weld? Look around. There's swimming and sailing at his back door. And canoeing. In the winter we skate from here. You should see the skating parties. A big bonfire. Kids and adults. Hot chocolate. After school Justin brings some of his pals home and they play hockey.

And there's tennis and badminton and croquet—I mean a *real* croquet court. And horseshoes and a place for skeet shooting. Bocci. Inside there's a ping-pong table, and fooseball, a pinball machine, a pool table. And all sorts of electronic games and Justin has his chemistry set and train table—"

Very much like your old Kentucky home, is it not? the Voice said.

Pennyworth was silent.

Perhaps the boy is spoiled, the Voice said.

No, he isn't. His head is on straight.

Perhaps you were spoiled, the Voice said.

My head is on quite straight, thank you, Pennyworth replied.

"Fishing. I forgot fishing," Gamble said. "Justin can fish right from his very own dock. You wouldn't want to deprive him of all this, would you? He belongs with me right here."

"How is visitation working out?"

"Oh, I've had to be strict a couple of times, put my foot down. Skip tends to take advantage. That's a major fault of his. You have to stand up to him. That's a big reason for the divorce."

"I understand you threatened to withhold Justin. Something about Legos?"

"Oh, that. The Legos are just symbolic. I expect Skip to return whatever I send over to his place."

"I understand that the Legos belong to Justin."

"Well, of course, do you think *I* play with them? They're building blocks, for heaven's sake. I play with real houses."

"I understand you're good at it."

"Yes. Thank you."

"What if Justin got sick and, say, you were in the middle of a closing?"

"It would depend on how sick."

"Oh, the school called you. He isn't feeling well."

"If it were an important closing?"

"Yes."

"I'd call Skip and see if he could handle it."

"No hesitation about that?"

"No. Why? I'd expect him to do the same thing. Of course, he doesn't have Justin during the week, so that's not likely to happen."

"But you trust him to take care of Justin?"

"If you're trying to trap me into saying Skip ought to have primary custody, I'm not going to say anything like that."

"That isn't my intent, Gamble. But as long as you've brought it up, who do you think *Justin* wants to be with?"

"Well, that's *clear*, isn't it?"

"Is it?"

"Of course it's clear. He wants to be with *both* of us. You of all people should know that."

Of all people, the Voice said.

"How do you feel about that?"

"Quite honestly, Weld, I resent, I very much resent your intrusion."

"I asked how you felt about Justin's desire?"

"I think it's sweet. Totally impossible, but sweet." Gamble paused. "It's loyal and loving, too. I very much resent you leading him on in this fantasy of his, Weld. *That* is abuse. You are abusing his trust. You are offering him the hope of something that hasn't the slightest chance in hell."

"I appreciate you sharing your feelings with me, Gamble."

"Sending *me* to a shrink and it's *you* who's building up this fantasy world for my child. Talk about unreality."

"The shrink is there for therapeutic reasons as well as for purposes of evaluation. Dr. Salmon has an excellent reputation. Well, I don't want to keep you anymore. I appreciate the guided tour."

"It's always a pleasure."

"Speaking of reality, Gamble—and inquiring strictly in my capacity as guardian—have you given any thought to plans for Justin and yourself were the Court to deny you this house?"

"That's impossible."

"Skip has a joint and equal interest in the house and property."

"Then I don't think either of us should have it. If Justin and I can't live here, then Skip shouldn't either. My office should sell it. Or your friend Candace Carrere. Neither of us should live in it then."

Pennyworth had timed the interview with Gamble so that it would conclude just about the time Justin got home from school.

"Let's go for a walk, Justin," Pennyworth said.

"I have to get back to the office," Gamble said. "You can stay here. Justin will need to replenish himself. There's cider in the fridge and fresh donuts in the bag." She nodded. "You, too, Pennyworth."

"I am in your debt, madam."

Pennyworth had not had a donut in a very long time. Certainly not one like this. He studied it on the plate before him. It was raised and glazed. The smell of it brought back a bakery he had once known and Halloween. He had not had cider in he did not remember how long. The taste of it brought back fall and Halloween costume parties at town hall. He chewed the bites of donut delicately and reflectively, as if turning the pages of an art book. He sipped the cider with as much deliberation as he would have applied to a noble wine. What he received in return was a sweet and awful evocation of his own childhood. "How was your weekend?" he said to Justin.

"Shitty. It started outside the courtroom and got worse all the way till last night."

"Ah, last night was better."

"Last night was worse."

Pennyworth used the paper napkin Justin had set out and carefully wiped away all lingering traces of childhood from his lips. "Tell me."

"I don't want to talk about it."

"You have to. Eat up and drink up and then we'll take a walk."

"I really don't want to talk about it."

The country ground felt both strange and familiar to Pennyworth beneath the soles of his city shoes. "Then there is no reason for me to be here and we will dissolve this relationship."

"No."

They walked for another few minutes until Pennyworth discerned a likely looking boulder. "Let's hang out on that."

"Mr. Pennyworth, I know you want to sound like my generation, but that didn't make it."

"Let's sit down then. Now tell me about the weekend."

Once Justin got going it came in a torrent. The new place, the new bedroom, the gifts, the nighttime inquisitions and lectures by his mother and father, Nelle, Mr. Dunphy and soccer, the kids at school, the judge he didn't even see anymore, Dr. Ralph.

Pennyworth nodded and then listened to the woods. The afternoon was chilly now and he wasn't dressed for it. But he didn't need to be. He was hot with anger.

"You're a juggler, aren't you?"

"Huh?" Justin said.

"You're juggling all these people. Your mother, your father, Nelle, even me. Here you are ten and a half and you're trying to keep all these people happy."

"How do you know that?"

"It comes back to me."

"I'm not very good at it. I keep getting angry at them. Or sad. It's not fun."

"You'll get better at it. You'll become very good at it. You'll become very good at being a diplomat. Later on, you could even become a professional diplomat. Or a lawyer."

Justin stopped. "What comes back to you? What?"

"How it is when your parents get a divorce."

"Were you a divorced kid?"

"Once upon a time," Pennyworth said.

You still are, said the Voice.

"I guess you know then," Justin said.

"I guess I do."

Justin nodded solemnly.

It had been decades since Pennyworth had volunteered that information to anyone.

"I've got to change for soccer," Justin said as they walked back to the house.

"I loved that game when I was your age."

"I don't know who's picking me up today. I don't know if it's Dad or Mrs. MacKenzie or if Mom's mad at Dad and forgot about getting me to practice." Justin stopped in the driveway. "What's gonna happen now? I mean, with all this."

"You go to the shrink, Justin, and I go to Barbados, and then when I get back, *we* go to court."

"Which one?"

"Superior court this time."

33

IN WHICH HEADS ARE EXAMINED

THE MURGANWHEELER–NEW YORK CONNECTION PROVED so fortuitous that Gamble flew down to the city to make a slide presentation of her properties and the Carlton area on a Thursday evening. And that, in turn, meant that Justin would spend the night and the weekend with his father. "Only because your father was a good little boy and returned the Legos and your rugby."

But Justin was feeling uneasy about seeing his father and telling him what he had to tell him.

His father was going to pick him up after soccer practice. Justin felt so tired he could hardly move around, but Mr. Dunphy didn't say anything.

It was almost dark when practice was over and his father picked him up.

"Hey, sport, I thought we'd drive over to Manchester and have a Chinese dinner." Justin's weekend stuff was stowed in the trunk and they were pulling away from the soccer field. "We could go out for pizza, if you want. Or I can get something to cook at home, it's up to you."

Justin knew what he had to say but couldn't say it. There had been some moments at home when he'd felt panicked.

"Well," his father said, "what do you say?"

"Dad, I can't find my Swiss army knife."

"Really?"

"Yes."

"I'm disappointed."

"I'm sorry."

"It's expensive."

"I know."

"I told you to be careful with it."

"I was, I swear."

"Where did you have it last?"

"On my night table. It was out on my night table. That's where I keep it. And when I looked for it after school today, it wasn't there."

"Did you look under the table? On the floor? Under your bed?"

"I looked everywhere I could think of."

His father was silent. Justin watched the black trees by the side of the road come at them slowly in the headlights and then jump quickly into darkness.

"Your mother took it," his father said.

"No, it was me."

"I doubt it."

"Dad was so angry." Gamble was down on her hands and knees beside Justin's bed next to his night table. "I told him I didn't even know you *had* the stupid knife, much less *take* it. Well, what's this?" Her head was down almost under the bed and her voice came out from underneath it. She pushed Clyde's home out. "Aha." She reached underneath the bed and her hand came out with the knife.

"Oh, gee, great, thanks. But I *looked* under the bed, Mom."

"You couldn't have looked very hard. If it had been a snake, it would have bit you," she said, standing up. "What's that?" she said, tapping Clyde's home.

"Just sort of something."

"I can see that it's sort of something. What sort of something is it?"

"It's my pet."

"A box of dirt?"

"It's his home. My pet's home."

"What sort of pet, Justin?" Gamble said, moving a step backward.

"His name is Clyde."

"What is Clyde's full name and identification?"

"His name is Clyde Worm."

"A worm?"

"An earthworm."

"Outside. I don't want it in this house."

"Why?"

"Just because I don't. They make me feel creepy-crawly."

"But he lives in here, in my room."

"He could crawl out."

"Jeezum, Mom, where's he gonna go? He's not like a snake."

"Justin, I don't want to hear about it. He belongs outside."

"But this is his home! He's domes—he's *domesticated* now. He belongs with me. He's mine."

"He goes back outside."

"No. He's mine. I take care of him. He's going to stay with me. You're not going to do to Clyde what you're doing to me."

"What do you mean by that, young man?"

"Clyde has a home and he's going to keep it. I'm going to protect him. He knows what to expect out of life and I'm going to keep it that way."

Dash, dash, dash, dit, dit—the VOR at Seawell.

The sea turned greener and brighter as Pennyworth let down toward it and it became shallower. The white crests of waves furled the surface. Off his right wing was the green and yellow landscape of the island of Barbados, already warm to the eye after the gray chill he had left behind in Boston hours before.

Pennyworth dropped the right wing into a bank, aligned himself, and came further back on power. "Bridgetown Tower," he said formally, "Lear Jet One-one X-Ray is now on straight-in final for runway two-seven."

"One-one X-Ray, clear to land."

"One-one X-Ray."

Pennyworth swooped in like a bird from the sea, flared to a near standstill in the air, and settled bumplessly to the gleaming surface.

"One-one X-Ray, contact Ground one-two-one niner."

"One-two-one niner. Thank you, sir, and good day. One-one X-Ray."

What he was doing and what he needed to do on his return was subtle and required the greatest subtlety. He needed rest. Pennyworth was exhausted, and not from flying, flying was always refreshing. He was exhausted from the subtleties and subtle manipulations. Tuttle, back in his law offices in Manchester, had been right: Pennyworth was in over his head—in over his head in subtlety.

He needed rest and objectivity. Barbados promised sufficient geographic and psychological distance for renewed objectivity.

Pennyworth had had the nightmare that he might lose control of Justin's situation and that Justin would suffer more than if Pennyworth had never entered the situation.

The Voice had asked, What sort of ego brought you into this, Pennyworth?

Pennyworth had come to Barbados to stay with his former lover, and now good friend, the very celebrated actress Caroline Hunter who now presided over a beachside estate. Caroline was currently married and currently faithful to her current husband. Otherwise Pennyworth would not have come. What Pennyworth enjoyed was the protection of the married home.

Pennyworth shut down and stepped out into the sudden heat of Barbados.

The first snow of coming winter was falling—though it was only October—when Justin got home from school.

Gamble was dressed in a most peculiar way, Justin thought. Sort of as if she was real relaxed and casual and sort of as if she was going to go someplace sort of formal—a little bit as if she was going to a friend's for brunch and a little bit as if she was going to New York for a meeting.

"I want you to change right away," she said to Justin. "Go on up. I put the clothes I want you to wear out on your bed."

"What's wrong with these?"

"You've been wearing them all day."

"I *always* wear them all day."

"Now don't argue, Justin, go and do it."

"What's the big deal?"

"We have to be at the psychiatrist's by four."

"Today?"

"Today. Now get going."

"Jeezum, why didn't you tell me?"

"I put your good new rugby out and your best cords."

"Can't I have a snack first? I'm starving."

Gamble sighed. "I suppose you better. I don't want you to get crumbs all over your good clothes."

"I tried to get your father to go to a psychiatrist I don't know how often. To save the marriage."

Justin tried to shut his ears to it and watch the snowflakes zoom at the windshield.

". . . rigidity," his mother was saying. "Has to have everything his own way all the time . . . Surely didn't bring him any happiness, getting his own way all the time . . ."

They drove through downtown Manchester and then out to where there were streets and houses instead of buildings. Justin had expected to go up into one of the modern buildings downtown. He figured that's where a shrink would hang out. But his mother turned onto Oak Street and had him watch for number 418. It was a white frame house just like where real people lived.

Justin expected bright walls and paintings, all in cheerful colors, just like Dr. Rosen's, his pediatrician. But Dr. Salmon's waiting room was more like someone's living room, although not so big, and the furniture wasn't modern, it was sort of old, like it was part of a real living room, and the walls weren't bright and there weren't any pictures. Just some magazines on a table, kids' magazines, even comics, and grown-up magazines, and some boxes of toys and a play area over in the corner.

Justin couldn't concentrate on the magazines, not even the comics. They didn't seem real. He had that feeling again like being inside a room inside his own head. There were some playthings out on the floor, and he eyed them, but he was too old for that. Besides, he figured they'd watch him (someone would, from somewhere) and he didn't know the right way to play.

But after a while, bored and nervous, he went over and sat on the floor and began building a cabin with Lincoln Logs.

"Hello, I'm Dr. Salmon."

Justin got up. She was shaking hands with his mother. Dr. Salmon had a nice face, a real smile, and big glasses. She was cheerful and Justin didn't see anything to be cheerful about.

What was it like? Ryan asked later.

We just talked.

What about?

Everything. We even talked about you.

Me? What did you say?

We talked about Clyde, too.

Me and a stupid worm?

Dr. Salmon didn't sit behind a desk in her office. She sat in a regular chair by a table that was the right size for Justin but a little small for her. Justin sat at the table.

"What do you think a doctor like me does, Justin?"

"A shrink? Checks out people's heads. What's in their minds."

"Well, yes. But I'm not a mind reader. I want to hear what you have to say."

"About what?"

"What's going on, Justin?"

What did you tell her?

Everything I could think of.

Just like that?

She just got me going, I guess.

"Everything's bad."

"What's bad, Justin?"

"Everything. I don't want to talk about it."

"Well, let's talk about something happy. Do you have any pets?"

"I have two pets. One lives with me and one has to live away from home at Ryan's house. Well, that's his home, too. His name is Blackie. He's a rabbit."

"Why can't he live at your house?"

You talked about Blackie? To a shrink?

She wanted to.

Seems like a terrible waste of money. Is this shrink any good?

Justin stopped talking and looked at the floor. Dr. Salmon didn't say anything. After some silence, Justin said, "It's just hard."

"What's hard?"

"Everything."

"Give me an example."

"Like with Clyde last night. I built him a home in a box of dirt. He lives under my bed. Mom wanted me to stop taking care of him. She wanted me to put him outside. It's getting so cold, I don't know if Clyde could take it, he's used to being warm and cozy."

"How do you know that?"

"I just know."

"How did Clyde feel about this?"

"You mean me, don't you? How I feel?"

"Yes."

"I feel real mad sometimes and real sad sometimes."

"What do you do about that? What do you do when you feel mad or sad?"

"I don't know. I get tired."

"Anything else?"

"I almost hurt Clyde once. I got mad at him and I almost threw his house across the room and broke it. But Clyde trusts me, so I didn't do it."

"Why did you get mad at him?"

"I don't know. My mom and dad made me feel so bad, they had a fight in front of my friends. But I took care of Clyde, I didn't hurt him."

"Anything else you do when you feel mad or sad?"

"Well, I'm trying to stop the divorce."

"How are you doing that?"

"I've got this lawyer, Mr. Pennyworth? Maybe you've heard of him?"

"Tell me about him."

What about me? Ryan said. You said you talked about me, too.

She wanted to know who I talk to when I get mad or sad. I said I talked mostly to you. And sometimes I talk with the other divorced kids.

"That's when you're mad or sad. Who do you talk to when you're scared?"

"Clyde, I guess. And sometimes Mr. Pennyworth. I told him about not wanting to be alone."

"What did he say to that?"

"He said he knew exactly how I felt."

"Do you think he does?"

"I guess so. He remembers things from when he was my age sometimes."

That's all there was about me? Ryan said.

Well, Jeezum, Ryan, I was there to talk about me, not about you.

"Justin, do you know that it's probably impossible to stop your parents from getting divorced if they want to get divorced?"

"I know. Mr. Pennyworth told me."

"Then what do you expect to come out of what Mr. Pennyworth is doing for you?"

"First, he'll try to stop the divorce. I know it's making Mom and Dad real unhappy."

"What is?"

"Getting the divorce. But also me trying to stop it."

"But if Mr. Pennyworth can't stop the divorce?"

"He says he's going to make things better for me, that's all I know. Do you want me to draw pictures or something?"

"Would you like to draw some pictures?"

"I don't care. It's something to do. I'm sort of tired of talking."

You draw pictures, Justin? Ryan said. You're terrible. You're even worse than I am.

Dr. Salmon thought they were pretty good.

Did she have her glasses on or off?

Justin drew pictures of his mother and his father and himself, individually, together, on the *Yar*, at home, back when they were together, at home now and at his father's new place.

"They're not very good," Justin said.

"The people or the drawings?"

"Both."

"What's wrong with the people?"

Justin studied them. "They're not having any fun."

"I see Clyde over there in the corner in some of the pictures. How does Clyde feel about all this?"

"You mean me, don't you?"

"You speak up for Clyde this time."

"Clyde doesn't know what to do. He feels sorry for *everybody*. He'd help, if he could, but he's only a worm."

"Does Clyde have any fun at all?"

"He can't."

"Why not?"

"It's in the air. Not having fun."

You should have told her what I think, Ryan said.

What do you think?

I think I'm lucky my mother went away and left me and Dad together so he could meet Marcia and we could have fun together and there wouldn't be any of this divorce shit.

"Justin, it's time to stop now. But I'd like to tell you something before you go, something that's very important."

"Okay."

"In a divorce, a lot of times kids feel they can't have any fun till their parents are having fun again. But it's not a rule. You're allowed to have fun. People who are getting a divorce often don't have fun for a long time. But kids don't have to wait around all that time. There's no rule that says you—or Clyde—can't have fun. You don't have to wait until your parents are having fun again."

"Okay."

"I'm very glad to have met you, Justin."

"Am I going to come and see you again?"

"Do you want to?"

"I guess."

"I'll talk to your parents about it. But I can't promise."

"And the judge and Mr. Pennyworth?"

Then what? Ryan said.
Then I went out and my mom went in and I read comics.
What comics?

Dr. Salmon noted how, when Mrs. Whitney was invited into the office, she stood up very straight and tugged her top down, like a soldier preparing for inspection or battle.

Mrs. Whitney was wary throughout the interview, except when she was discussing possessions. She was at ease—became somewhat less tense—whenever she could list possessions or professional accomplishments.

"There seems to have been an incident involving a set of Legos, Mrs. Whitney. Would you tell me about that?" And after she had listened, "On the subject of Legos, Mrs. Whitney, the general subject, what comes to mind when you think of Legos?"

"Honestly?"

"Whatever comes to mind."

"Toys. They're toys. Making houses, forts, castles. Justin playing with them, building things. And that bastard Skip using them to get back at me because I'm in the house and he isn't."

When Skip came in a day later, Dr. Salmon categorized his dress as stockbroker casual: impeccably cut dark gray pinstriped suit, white shirt, aggressive and flamboyant red tie with white polka dots.

"There seems to have been some dissension over a collection of Legos, Mr. Whitney."

"Justin just forgot them."

"And about a Swiss army knife you gave him?"

"Gamble took it to get back at me about the Legos. Then she gave it back to Justin because he was so upset."

And later—"I understand the house you and your wife occupied together is quite important to both of you."

"Gamble just wants it to keep me from getting it. The house is an accomplishment. I regard life as an accomplishment. The house epitomizes what I have accomplished."

"Mrs. Whitney feels the same way."

"Mrs. Whitney needs a shrink. She's selfish. She's still a little girl who thinks she ought to have whatever she wants because she's so cute."

"I take it you disagree with that?"

"People should earn what they get." By example Skip listed a number of possessions that he felt had come the Whitneys' way solely as the result of his own labor.

"You and Mrs. Whitney each take Justin into your confidence."

"We do?"

"I brought it up to Mrs. Whitney and I bring it up to you now, Mr. Whitney, because it's causing him considerable distress."

"How so?"

"These briefings you each give him on the other's activities at his bedtime."

"I just tell him what I think he needs to know."

And that, of course, was what Gamble had said.

"Perhaps he doesn't need to know so much, Mr. Whitney."

"He's got to protect himself."

"From what?"

"From being used by his mother."

"Used in what way?"

"To help her keep the house."

34

SEEK, AND YE SHALL FIND, NOK, AND THE DOOR WILL OPEN

"WELD, HONEY, TELEPHONE. IT'S YOUR CALL COMING back."

Pennyworth opened one careful eye, well guarded behind sunglasses. Through the lens he saw long, tall Caroline Hunter approaching him in the nearest thing to nudity, a string bikini that was just about too small for her. He was vaguely concerned that Caroline had reawakened his old physical attraction to her. But in the golden sun of Barbados and the heat of Caroline's proximity, Pennyworth had gotten the idea of keeping himself faithful to something he could only identify as a premonition. Besides, there was Caroline's marriage, and Pennyworth devoutly respected marriage (while keeping a solemn personal distance from it) as long as the partners were not suing each other for divorce, coupling outside of their vows, or mistreating each other verbally, all of which had been part of his personal experience.

"Thank you," Pennyworth said, taking the phone, closing his eye, and resting his head once more against the back of the lounger. "Hello, this is Weld Pennyworth."

"Dr. Salmon, Mr. Pennyworth."

"Thank you for returning my call."

"Who could resist a call from Barbados? Winter is early here. Two days ago we had snow. Yesterday we had sleet and freezing rain. Today we have snow again."

"Television signs off at ten-thirty here," Pennyworth said. "They conclude with the weather forecast. I've been here for five days and the forecast has been the same each night. 'The weather tomorrow will be the same as today.' "

"Ah, if life were so simple."

"You and I would be out of business."

"Out of the pain business, Mr. Pennyworth. I'd be glad for that opportunity."

"You have interviewed Justin and the Whitneys?"

"Yes."

"You will be preparing your report?"

"Yes."

"I will be leaving here on Saturday. May I consult with you before you put your report in final form?"

"About what, Mr. Pennyworth, specifically?"

"I am concerned about Justin's care for Clyde Worm and Clyde's home. Blackie the rabbit may also have some relevance."

There was a pause and then Dr. Salmon said, "I think that's worth discussion."

Clyde Worm was warm and safe inside his climate-controlled box now atop Justin's desk where Gamble might check for outward-bound trails whenever she became wary.

Outside, the snow had turned to sleet again and was spitting against the window. Inside, the sounds came from Justin's guitar, the vibrations produced by the guitar, Justin hoped, soothing to Clyde, though what he was working on was not meant to be soothing.

"Hey, what is that?" Ryan said.

"Sort of a song."

Because of the rotten weather there was no soccer and Ryan had come home with Justin. He had brought along his saxophone from his weekly in-school lesson.

"I like it. But it doesn't sound like a song."

"Well, it's actually a talking blues. You play the blues on the guitar and you sort of talk the words."

"It's cool. Did you make it up?"

"It's sort of a copy of something called 'Talking Union Blues' and some other stuff, too."

"I could like play the melody on my sax. In between. Like when you finish each verse, before you start the next."

"Fearless," Justin said.

After a while Ryan said, "How come you did this?"

"I've been working on it ever since Chick said that stuff about kids ought to get together and have like a union."

"Aw, c'mon, Justin, we can't do that. How're we gonna do that?"

"I call it NOK. N-O-K. National Organization of Kids." Justin changed melodies and sang, "Seek and you shall find, NOK and the door will open, rock and the walls come tumblin' down."

"Let me hear the talking one again."

"Yeah, but it's all the same song. I want to work on the words. The words are hard. I know what I want to say, but it's got to rhyme and all that."

After listening for a while Ryan said, "You said a swear."

"I know."

"Can you say a swear in a song for kids? Can we *say* 'shit'?"

"That's what it is, isn't it?"

"Yeah, but I don't think they're going to let us sing it."

"Who?"

"You know. Like parents, teachers, like that."

"Tough on them. They gotta hear it the way it is."

Pennyworth filed for Miami International as his airport of entry. On the ground there—bright, but a little cool by Bajan standards—he attended customs inspection of his aircraft closely. Opposition had once tried to embarrass him with a drug find on One-one X-Ray at Customs, and though charges had been dropped before trial, it had been a serious inconvenience. Cleared, he continued north to Dulles and an overnight in Georgetown where he ate and drank well enough but where the central entertainment was a political conference at senate level.

Late the next afternoon he stopped briefly at Logan where a member of his staff met him with the Whitney file, and then he leapfrogged to Manchester where he settled himself into the suite he had had booked at the Center of New Hampshire across the street from Hillsborough County Superior Court, where, later in the week, he would argue on behalf of Justin in Whitney v. Whitney.

"You found the element that I was sure was there," Pennyworth said to Dr. Salmon in her office at eight the next morning.

"How could you have been so sure it was there?"

"I know my client."

"And who is your client, Mr. Pennyworth?" But Pennyworth ignored the question just as Dr. Salmon had thought he probably would. "In effect, you want the boy to have custody of his parents."

"In effect," Pennyworth said. Dr. Salmon showed no reaction. "It is a matter of the degree of emphasis in your report." Pennyworth sipped some tea. "I hope you don't perceive this as an attempt to sway your professional judgment."

"I'm quite used to attorneys visiting me in custody cases, Mr. Pennyworth, and attempting to sway me."

"How did you find Mr. and Mrs. Whitney?"

"Interesting. I don't mind going into that. They each blame the other's personality for the disintegration of their marriage. But the interesting factor is that their personalities are so much alike. Do they dislike the mirror image? Or are they so narcissistic they can't abide a mirror that doesn't present perfection? Or do they simply dislike themselves and their own images? I don't know yet. But I do know this. They are both material minded, success oriented, very much concerned with appearance—and the house is their most important and intimate piece of clothing. I imagine each gave excessive thought to what he or she was going to wear when they came to see me. I imagine that happens every morning, as well—and before every occasion, no matter how trivial, even shopping at the local market. One must appear both smart *and* casual. What a waste of energy."

Dr. Salmon sipped her tea reflectively. "Curious matter here. A financial profile of most foundered middle-class marriages will show that as economic security declined, so did the relationship between the partners—just as in the business world.

"But here you have a marriage in which each partner has become quite successful financially. And what has happened? Each has developed a keen desire to explore that success entirely independently. Each has, I'm sure, fantasies of affairs—or even marriage—with the most extraordinary people, *famous* people. Ah, the independence. But note: Each would have the security of the home they have created together. They each want to hold on to *home*. But without the other partner there."

"Do you see any possibility of reconciliation?"

"I don't think it would even be worth the attempt. They have each discovered they like being alone—or at least apart from the other person. Usually there is some remorse, some sadness, some wish that the marriage and the partner could be returned to. But I see none of that here. No. I see no possibility of reconciliation."

Pennyworth smiled.

Dr. Salmon looked at her watch. Her manner became less leisurely. "I am preparing a report for juvenile court, but you are asking that the report be prepared for use in superior court as well."

"An evaluation for juvenile court. And then an addendum for superior court. The addendum will be of no use or merit before juvenile court. The addendum has no applicability there."

"The concern you want addressed usually isn't an element in a custody case."

"Yes, that is true. But usually the child himself is not a litigant."

"I don't like that at all, Mr. Pennyworth. I have my reservations about your role in this. Those reservations will find their place somewhere in my report."

"In the meantime . . ."

"In the meantime, there is no way my report will be ready for presentation before superior court this week."

"I would not want to use it this week in any event. Next week before juvenile court—less the addendum. Sometime later before superior court *with* the addendum."

"The contents of the addendum, Mr. Pennyworth."

"I am not asking you to interject something that isn't there, Dr. Salmon. I am asking you to give consideration to this only if it *is* there. I am asking you to represent it on behalf of Justin only if, in your professional opinion, *the matter is there*."

"Certainly it is there."

"Bully," said Pennyworth.

"It's central to his adjustment inventory. As you've observed yourself, look at Clyde Worm. Clyde is Justin in Justin's happiest state. And why is that? Clyde has a loving, protective parent and a safe, protective home."

"Yes. Isn't that what we all want?" Pennyworth said.

"Of course. But look who's providing it here and to whom."

But, as Dr. Salmon had thought he would, Pennyworth avoided the double reference entirely. She knew Pennyworth preferred to think that her remark referred only to Clyde and Justin and she resisted saying to Pennyworth, Tell me about your childhood. She didn't think he would take it well.

Mr. Dunphy was in Mr. Boudrieau's office. Mr. Boudrieau was the principal of Carlton Regional Elementary School and he had called Mr. Dunphy in to find out why parents were calling him about some secret society of children reputedly centered in Mr. Dunphy's room.

"Mike, a couple of parents are concerned about Satanism, God help us," Mr. Boudrieau said. "Parents from another town. Do you know anything about it?"

"I don't know a thing about Satanism, Phil."

A harsh sort of undulating moan entered Mr. Boudrieau's office. Both men listened to it in silence. After the moan there was a brief silence from outside and then a rather more full-voiced sound.

"What is that?" Mr. Boudrieau said.

"Kids."

"*I know.* But what is it?"

"I think it's the lunch room."

They departed for the lunch room.

Justin with his guitar and Ryan with his saxophone were standing on a bench along with Amanda. "One more time," Amanda said. "From the top," and Justin began to play and talk the words.

> "Well, you're sittin' there alone and you're
> feelin' pretty sour,
> Can't do squat alone, you ain't got the power,
> Your parents don't care, they've gone and got
> split,
> And you're all alone and you're feelin' like
> shit."

"Oh God," Boudrieau said. "We can't allow language like that. Maybe it *is* Satanism."

"Let's hear the rest of it. Maybe there's even more reprehensible language. We ought to be fully informed, Phil."

"Really?"

"Oh, I think so," Mr. Dunphy said. "We owe it to the Forces of Light. In the crusade against Satanism."

"Maybe," Mr. Boudrieau said.

The children continued singing:

> "Seek, and ye shall find,
> NOK, and the door will open,
> Rock, with our own good sound,
> Till the walls come tumblin' down."

Then Ryan played his sax solo—a harsh, moaning sound. Justin followed again with the guitar and the words.

> "Well, you want to get some power, I'll tell
>   you what to do,
> Got to talk to the kids in school with you.
> Come and get them all together and sing
>   them this song,
> Gonna try to make it right when it's comin'
>   down wrong.
>
> "Parents split, ageists all around,
> Got to get together and make a big sound,
> All together now, take off our lids,
> Gonna make 'em hear us, all us kids . . ."

"Curious," Mr. Dunphy said, "part talking blues and part rap," as the chorus of "Seek, and ye shall find, NOK, and the door will open" began.

"Rap? Here in Carlton, New Hampshire? Isn't there supposed to be a teacher in here?"

"Me," Mr. Dunphy said, "but you called me to your office."

> "NOK, till the walls come tumblin' down."

The music stopped and Amanda raised her fist. What followed was like a cheer at some game with which Mr. Boudrieau was entirely unacquainted.

> "Hey, hey, N-O-K!
> Hey, hey, N-O-K!
> National! . . . Organization! . . . of Kids!
> Rayyyyyy!"

"My God, where does that come from?"

"Not from Satan, Phil."

35

PRELIMINARY HEARING, SUPERIOR COURT, TOGETHER WITH SURPRISE WITNESSES

COURTROOM 3 OF HILLSBOROUGH COUNTY SUPERIOR Court, Manchester, New Hampshire, was staidly contemporary, carpeted, wood paneled, and indirectly illuminated with fluorescent light. Pennyworth wondered what Daniel Webster would have made of it. Pennyworth stood in it alone. If he were going to argue before a jury, a knowledge of the physical terrain would be useful. Sometimes even the ambiance of a courtroom could prove useful.

Nevertheless, that was superficial stuff. To Pennyworth the environs of a courtroom were all the same: They were the environs of the chessboard and all the action took place in the mind. His pyrotechnics might be useful for purposes of demonstration or emphasis before a jury, but under any conditions they had the more satisfying and rewarding effect of distracting opposing counsel from what Pennyworth was really up to.

It was almost nine-thirty. Litigants and counsel were gathering in the large public lobby that served the four courtrooms. Pennyworth had eschewed the hospitality of the attorneys' rooms beyond the lobby—he did not want to offer Bagley or Bredwell or Vance any brotherly courtesy or chitchat prior to confronting them before Judge Haskins.

As in the early moves of a game of chess, the preliminary hearing was for developmental purposes and usually took place in chambers where the lawyers presented Offers of Proof—statements of what the evidence was going to be. There would also be temporary orders—the preliminary decisions as to who was to live where, drive which car, and pay which bill—all of which the Whitneys, together with their attorneys, and despite their disharmony, had managed to agree upon with admirable mutual cooperation. It was the final disposition over which they were prepared to fight without quarter, and the centerpiece in that matter was the house and property, not Justin at all.

In fact it all might have been done in chambers had Pennyworth not seen to it that it wasn't. His opening moves were dependent upon the context of the courtroom. He had secreted his two primary game pieces across the street in his suite. He could have them in court within ten minutes of the time when all persons having to do with *Whitney v. Whitney* were requested to draw near.

Pennyworth's opening moves were intended to gain control of the center board and the middle game—and to distract the opposition from the entirely unconventional and newborn configuration that would be Pennyworth's endgame. It was too bad he hadn't old man Webster as his adversary.

The Whitneys' lawyers went through their motions and recitals with all due perfunctoriness, the event being a pro forma occasion in which nothing of any moment was to occur. Judge Turner Haskins glanced up at counsel from time to time but largely attended to paperwork with a pen that was occasionally visible over the sidebar. Pennyworth nodded sleepily now and then as if his own attendance were only pro forma. He was aware, though, that Nelle Vance regarded him rather more closely than she did either Bagley or Bredwell.

Beneath the cloak of weary boredom he had drawn about himself, Pennyworth was keen with pleasurable expectancy at the prospect of his own performance, due to begin rather soon. He sat back and listened while Bagley and Bredwell set the table for him.

As to tables, the Whitneys and their respective attorneys sat at separate ones while Nelle and Pennyworth each sat at one end of those separate tables. Neither the Whitneys, nor their attorneys, all of whom were attentive to the judge, saw Sue and Bart Murgan-wheeler enter and take seats at the very back of the courtroom.

Judge Turner Haskins, Pennyworth had informed himself, was forty-three years old, the product of Washington University Law School in St. Louis, and the mother of a teenage boy and a teenage girl. For a period of several months, when the children were young, she had once been estranged from her husband, an MIT astrophysicist. She was paying no more apparent interest to the proceedings presently before her than was demanded, which was little. But, Pennyworth had also informed himself, Haskins possessed the ear of the reliable judge no matter where her attention seemed to be focused —rather like the pilot who carries on a flight deck conversation but is instantly responsive when his own number is called amidst waves of extraneous radio traffic. And, no matter what Bryce Tuttle's belief, Haskins's decrees were not so very predictable, though they were inclined to be swift and unassailable.

Judge Haskins looked up and said, "Is that all for now, Mr. Bredwell?"

"Yes, Your Honor. Both parties agree and pray the Court for a hearing on merits at the Court's earliest convenience."

"Thank you, Mr. Bredwell. The remaining issue is that of the appointment by this Court of a guardian ad litem for Justin Whitney. I have Motions for Appointment by both Mrs. Whitney and Mr. Whitney requesting Attorney Nelle Vance. I have a Motion for Denial from Mr. Pennyworth acting as Justin's attorney and," she paused, shifting papers behind the sidebar, "I have a Motion for Appointment nominating Mr. Pennyworth as guardian ad litem and signed by Mr. Pennyworth as attorney for Justin Whitney and by Justin. Is Justin in the building?"

"I appear," Pennyworth said, rising slowly and looking about as if he were unaccustomed to courtroom appearances and the matters at hand. "I thought it in Justin's best interests that he attend school as usual today. I am pleased to say that his parents concurred. He is absent and in school by agreement between Mr. and Mrs. Whitney as well as with me."

Pennyworth cast a sleepy glance at Bagley and Bredwell. He saw that they hadn't a hint of where he was going from that innocuous beginning, that still invisible foundation.

"I think that is wise."

"Thank you, Your Honor. If the matter of the appointment of guardian ad litem cannot be resolved here today, I'd move that the Court interview Justin as to his desires in camera and with no one else present. I'll make that a formal motion, if you wish, Your Honor."

"Unnecessary."

"As to the issue being the sole remaining one . . ." Pennyworth seemed lethargic and unfocused. But Bagley and Bredwell and both Whitneys were intent upon him and the judge regarded him speculatively. Pennyworth turned back to the table and dug into his attaché case and produced some papers. He looked up hesitantly at the judge. "May I approach, Your Honor?"

"Is that for me, Mr. Pennyworth?"

"Yes, Your Honor. And my brothers."

She looked at Bagley and Bredwell. "Gentlemen."

At the bench Pennyworth handed the original to Judge Haskins and a signed copy each to Bagley and Bredwell.

"All right, step back." Judge Haskins looked at the document briefly.

"This is outrageous!" Pennyworth judged that Gamble Whitney had just read the document.

"It damn well is!" Skip Whitney said from the other table.

Without humor the judge said, "You are being playful, Mr. Pennyworth. This Court will not be played with. You are not in California. Neither are you in Massachusetts."

"I assure Your Honor there is nothing playful about this. I am in dead earnest."

"Read your motion aloud, Mr. Pennyworth."

"A waste of time," Skip said. "A waste."

"You're a lunatic, Pennyworth," Gamble said.

"Counsel will please instruct your clients," the judge said.

When the caution had been delivered, Pennyworth resumed, the lethargy now entirely absent from both his posture and his voice. "Motion for Marriage Counseling. Now comes Justin Whitney, minor child of Gamble G. Whitney and Conrad J. Whitney, in the above-captioned matter and moves as follows—One: That pursuant to RSA 167B:1 and 458:7-b the parties be referred to an approved family service agency within the jurisdiction of this Court for marriage counseling for the reason that said counseling may assist the parties in reconciling the differences between them, which would be in the best interests of the parties and their minor child. And Two: For such other relief as may be just. Respectfully submitted and forwarded, etc."

"Objection," Bagley said. "Frivolous."

"Objection," Bredwell said. "Facetious. Capricious. It is not playful, Your Honor, it is an insult to this Court."

"It robs our clients of the dignity of their divorce."

"A last-minute, desperate device for a foundless venture," Bredwell said.

"I agree with my brother," Bagley said. "I object to this last-minute delivery. Surely Mr. Pennyworth had time not only to prepare this curiosity but to forward copies to Mr. Bredwell and myself prior to this hearing."

Good work! Pennyworth silently commended Bagley. Aloud he humbly said, "Not so, my brother. It was only on Monday, in my capacity as Justin's guardian ad litem—"

"Objection," Bredwell said. "Mr. Pennyworth is attempting to insert himself in the position at issue by extension from another court."

"Mr. Pennyworth, your tactic is a petty exercise at best. This Court is aware of your position vis-à-vis juvenile court. However, that position has no standing before this Court."

"Your Honor, I wish only to establish the capacity in which I have had the benefit of consultation with Dr. Lorraine Salmon, the psychiatrist making the evaluation of the Whitneys and Justin."

Bredwell rose laconically. "I object, Your Honor. We do not have the psychiatrist's report and the psychiatrist is not present to offer oral testimony. We have only Mr. Pennyworth."

"Your Honor," Pennyworth said, "my brother was all-fired eager to be advised as to why this Motion for Marriage Counseling was not brought to him yesterday or the day before. It was only on the day before that that I was accommodated by Dr. Salmon, in the interests of the child Justin, and had the benefit of her preliminary remarks. It is from that conversation, as well as other events, that I came to understand that marriage counseling is in the best interests of the minor child."

Bagley said, "All this is so *mysterious,* Your Honor."

"Do you have the psychiatrist's report, Mr. Pennyworth?"

"I shall see that a copy is delivered to the Court as soon as it is available, Your Honor. Probably late next week."

Bagley said, "In the meantime, Your Honor, are we expected to suffer Mr. Pennyworth's representation of this nonexistent document?"

"I say to the Court and to my brother, I have not sought to represent the document at all. How could I? It is not written yet. I simply responded to my brother's concern as to why the Motion for Marriage Counseling was delivered now, rather than yesterday or the day before."

Why, said the Voice, don't you need a shoehorn, Pennyworth?

Because I got all that in without one.

"Mr. Pennyworth," Judge Haskins said, "why do I have the feeling that you are attempting to fit the Court with a shoe that is too small for it?"

"Your Honor, do you wish me to reply to that?"

"Yes."

"My reply is that it is an unaccustomed pleasure to argue before so *sensitive* a court."

"Thank you, Mr. Pennyworth. Please take my observation as a caution. A serious caution, Mr. Pennyworth."

"Good for her," Gamble whispered to Bagley.

"We will return to the motion for counseling in due course."

"She's not going to take that seriously?" Gamble whispered.

Skip whispered to Bredwell, "Is he really going to get her to consider that? *Marriage counseling?* She's as crazy as he is."

"Pennyworth is not crazy," Bredwell whispered back. "What we have to be afraid of is, Her Honor is *interested.*"

"In this bullshit?" Skip said.

"We have strayed from the agenda," said Judge Haskins. "The

Court is considering the appointment of a guardian ad litem. Mr. Pennyworth, you have objected to Ms. Vance." The judge looked at the motion.

"That my sister has no prior experience as guardian ad litem nor has she completed the course of training and education as codified in Chapter 103 (HJR 3), Joint Resolution Relative to Selection of Guardians Ad Litem in Marital Cases."

"Ms. Vance?"

"Your Honor, I am unfamiliar with the resolution. I ask the Court's leave for the opportunity of reviewing it."

"Your Honor," Pennyworth said, "intending no derogation of Ms. Vance's other professional qualifications, it seems to me that someone who seeks appointment as guardian ad litem ought, in the best interests of the child, to familiarize herself, or himself, with the qualifications for that appointment. It would seem the least one ought to ask of oneself."

Pennyworth looked over at Nelle with sad compassion and then back at Judge Haskins with similar sadness.

"You have completed the course, Mr. Pennyworth."

"I have the certification, Your Honor."

"Ms. Vance, I won't rule until you've had the opportunity to look at the resolution. However, the Court notes Mr. Pennyworth's point regarding awareness and preparation."

"Thank you, Your Honor."

"We'll address the issue of marriage counseling. I hope that will give you sufficient time. In any event, that's all the time you have."

Pennyworth felt cautiously relieved. The threat was that if Nelle were appointed guardian ad litem, she would have a position superior to his in this court in regard to Justin. She could, in fact, burn Pennyworth: She could, as guardian ad litem and as she had pointedly mentioned, file a motion to have him removed as Justin's lawyer in superior court and Pennyworth would no longer have standing in Justin's behalf in superior court.

Nelle ran in panic to the law library in the courthouse. As usual, it had been vandalized by other lawyers and there was nothing current. The resolution that she needed to read was not there.

"There have been some minor disagreements relative to the disputed property between the Whitneys, such as the use of their sailboat, but where Justin has been concerned, they have shown exemplary cooperation with each other." Pennyworth turned to Bagley and Bredwell. "Is that in dispute? Because if it isn't, I would like the fact stipulated. It would save me inquiring of Mrs. Whitney and Mr. Whitney and therefore save the Court its valuable time."

Bagley and Bredwell consulted with each other and then with their clients and then with each other again. Bagley addressed the Court. "It may be so stipulated, Your Honor."

Pennyworth went on. "The Whitneys, then, are in harmony as to the care and well-being of their only child, Justin. Justin is not an issue, Your Honor. The disposition of the homestead property, together with some investments made in one name or another, is the major and *only* dispute between the Whitneys. It is, in fact, the sole dispute presented for the consideration of the wisdom of this Court. But the major consideration that ought to be before this Court is the well-being of the child Justin Whitney. And it is for that purpose I have brought the Motion for Marriage Counseling.

"Your Honor, I beg the Court's patience while I review our law so that I may get to the heart of this matter.

"First of all, in order to grant this divorce, there has to be some grounds for the divorce.

"As grounds, the Whitneys allege irreconcilable differences.

"But are they not cooperating in the ways in which they care for Justin? Are they not mutually dependent upon each other for the care that they provide for Justin? Do they not call upon each other for assistance?

"Furthermore, are they not concordant, through counsel, in opposition to my very presence and in contesting my efforts on behalf of their son?

"I submit that in the hearing on merits, when complete testimony will be heard, there will be no differences discovered between the parents.

"I submit that Mr. and Mrs. Whitney are having a squabble that has gotten somewhat out of hand, but not so far out of hand that they cannot cooperate with each other as a married couple, and not so far out of hand that the marriage could not benefit mightily from marriage counseling, and not so far out of hand that the family unit might not be preserved not only to the enormous benefit of Justin's growth and emotional and psychological well-being, but also to the great benefit of Gamble and Skip Whitney themselves."

Bredwell rose. "Your Honor, I grow weary of Mr. Pennyworth's verbosity. His argument for marriage counseling is, at its very best, loose and fugitive and I ask that the Court deny the motion so that we may get on with the business of guardian and get out of here."

Pennyworth said, "Your Honor, with the Court's permission—I know it is not customary at a temporary hearing—I would like to present two witnesses who will give testimony bearing upon the salvageability of this marriage and the usefulness of marriage counseling at this juncture."

"You will have to establish, Mr. Pennyworth, or I will cut it off."

Pennyworth turned around. "Mrs. Murganwheeler? Would you come forward, please?"

Nelle called five law offices, including her own, before she found an attorney—a child advocate—who not only knew of the resolution, but had it on hand.

"It's something the legislature passed in '86 and handed on to the administrative office of the courts. It's been in development. It's law, but it's been up to the individual court to honor it till the system gets going. There's some relief language."

The attorney read Nelle the resolution and she wrote down the most pertinent passage, though it gave her no personal relief:

> Resolved by the Senate and the House of Representatives ...
> That no individual be appointed as guardian ad litem until he has completed one course of training and education program for guardians ad litem in marital cases unless the Court finds that he is otherwise qualified by past training and experience ...

"Are they irreconcilable actually?" Pennyworth asked. "Let us see.

"Mrs. Murganwheeler, you and Mr. Murganwheeler visited with Mr. and Mrs. Whitney and Justin at the Grayson house on Carlton Lake on Saturday, September 22nd, this year, is that correct?"

"Yes."

"Your Honor, this was fifteen days after Mrs. Whitney had filed for divorce, ten days after Mr. Whitney had filed his cross-libel, and eight days after Mr. Whitney had been served, and only three days since Mrs. Whitney had been served. Now, Mrs. Murganwheeler, if you would tell the Court about that occasion."

Sue Murganwheeler described the sail across the lake in the *Yar*. The greeting at the Grayson house and young Justin, what a very special boy. How Gamble had brought along food and wine and how Skip had prepared the Grayson house for their inspection and made everything ready for a delightful time of drinks and lunch on the deck. "Really, the two of them made such a glorious occasion of it, one might almost become suspicious."

"And did you become suspicious, Mrs. Murganwheeler?"

"Oh, no. Bart and I were enchanted by their company. We were so complimented by their attention to us and, well, the four of us just got on so well, right from the start, it was like being with family or old friends. We thought they were the perfect couple. They were so bright with each other. And their son. They entertained us so well."

"They were cooperative with each other? They got along?"

"Oh, yes. We thought they were the perfect couple. We had no idea they were getting a divorce."

"How did you learn they were getting a divorce?"

"Oh, later on sometime, we learned from other people."

"What did you think of Mr. and Mrs. Whitney then?"

"Well, at first we were shocked. Really shocked. Then we talked it over and thought they must be getting the perfect divorce."

"The perfect divorce? Would you explain that to the Court, Mrs. Murganwheeler, and to me?"

"Well, I just mean, they are so splendid together, I just thought anything they do together, even a divorce, they would do that splendidly together, too."

"You observed that much harmony between them?"

"Objection," Bagley said. "The question calls for an expert conclusion."

"Calls for just an observation since neither you nor I nor the Court was there—"

"But I *was* there," Gamble said, "and there sure as hell was—"

Bagley had turned toward his client as Judge Haskins said rather quietly, "We're not ready to hear from you just yet, Mrs. Whitney. Please be very conscious of that. Mrs. Murganwheeler, I'll allow you to state your opinion."

"About what? I've forgotten now."

"How Mr. and Mrs. Whitney were getting on with each other that afternoon."

"They were just so good to each other. That's why we thought they'd probably be getting the perfect divorce."

"Thank you, Mrs. Murganwheeler."

"You're welcome."

"You may inquire."

Bredwell and Bagley were in whispered consultation with their clients. Then the two attorneys talked to each other. It was Bagley who approached the witness.

"Mrs. Murganwheeler, toward the end of your visit at the Grayson house, do you recall if there were any contretemps between Mr. and Mrs. Whitney? Dissension?"

"I don't recall that there was."

"Mrs. Whitney was attempting to sell you the Grayson house, was she not?"

"I wouldn't put it that way. I mean, it was friendlier than that. Gamble and Skip didn't have to extend themselves that way just for Gamble to make a sale."

"Didn't Mr. Whitney make some remarks about the lake going bad from acid rain and the values of lake property being inflated?"

"But you see, wasn't that so fair and honest of both of them? That really convinced Bart and me that we could trust Gamble. They didn't hide their opinion."

"*They?* Did Mrs. Whitney agree about the inflated values of the property? The acid rain in the lake?"

"She just sat there. She was smiling. I took it that she agreed and her husband was speaking for both of them. She certainly didn't say anything to contradict what Skip was saying."

"You felt no tension between them?"

"None."

"Thank you, Mrs. Murganwheeler."

"You're welcome."

Judge Haskins said, "Mr. Bredwell?"

"I have nothing, Your Honor."

"Mr. Pennyworth?"

"Thank you again, Mrs. Murganwheeler, you're excused. Mr. Murganwheeler?"

Bart Murganwheeler gave much the same account as his wife. "It was a splendid luncheon party," he said. "A splendid day in splendid company."

"Any tension? Any dissension?"

"Not a word."

When it was Bagley's turn, he said, "Maybe there was some by-play that you missed. Any chance of that, Mr. Murganwheeler?"

"Wasn't a cloud in the sky and not a one on the horizon that I could see."

"Let me put it this way. How about some off-speed pitches, maybe an inside curve?"

"Went right by me. I'd say Skip was pitching pretty good and Gamble was catching, and between them, they got this batter just where they wanted. What a team. Too bad they're putting each other on waivers."

36
A CHILL OF DEFEAT

AT SCHOOL THE NOK GROUP WAS NOT ALLOWED TO HOLD what had become a daily luncheon forum on the Rights of Kids. Mr. Boudrieau said they could sit at their tables and talk about whatever they wanted, but they couldn't hold a meeting about it—not in the lunch room, not on the playground, not in the gym.

"We could if we were the Rotary," Justin said.

"You are not the Rotary," Mr. Boudrieau said.

"Why can't we?" Ryan said.

"Some parents have objected. On religious grounds."

"We never mention God."

"That may concern them," Mr. Boudrieau said quietly, more to himself than anyone else.

"This isn't fair," Amanda said.

"It's worse than that," Justin said. "I'll get my lawyer on it."

That's all I need, Mr. Boudrieau thought.

Ryan said, "It's just one more time grown-ups are taking away kids' rights. This time it's freedom of speech."

"Probably freedom of assembly," Mr. Boudrieau said.

"I'm going to call Mr. Giambelli, too," Justin said to Ryan.

Judge Haskins heard Pennyworth and Vance on the guardian issue in chambers during lunch break.

The judge said, "There aren't a whole bunch of lawyers out there who want to do guardian ad litem work. The ones who do are involved in and committed to children's issues. Now you two, with no prior interest, no prior experience, suddenly you're squabbling about who's going to be the guardian ad litem here."

"Because of my concern for Justin," Nelle said.

She looked up at Pennyworth. Pennyworth had a sudden feeling of intimacy toward her. He immediately suppressed it. "Because of my *commitment* to Justin's well-being," Pennyworth said. "A commitment, Judge, that I've already demonstrated. Besides, I've done the course."

"We can be sure of that," Nelle said.

The judge addressed Nelle. "The child makes demands on the guardian, Ms. Vance. The child says, 'I want to do this,' and the guardian has to say, 'No, you can't.' The child will make great demands on the guardian's time."

Pennyworth did not like the judge addressing these explicit, cautionary remarks to Nelle.

"I know. I'm prepared for that."

"Does it make sense to have *two* guardians?" Pennyworth said.

"As far as *this* Court is concerned, Mr. Pennyworth, there *is* no guardian ad litem at present."

"Ms. Vance does not meet the standards of the resolution."

"Judge, there is some relief language in the resolution. No one shall be appointed guardian without the course, 'unless the Court finds that he is otherwise qualified by past training and experience.' I have extensive training and experience as a mediator, and one of the prime functions of the guardian is to act as mediator. I am already acting as mediator between the two parties. I have been stipulated by them as guardian ad litem. Someone else might not be able to fulfill the role as well as I. I have extensive experience with all three of these people—"

"That's a loose interpretation of the word *experience* in this context."

Nelle turned on Pennyworth. "I could write a guardian report this minute that would be deeper, more detailed, and more knowledgeable than anything provided by someone who is just recently on the scene."

"Justin's attorney," Pennyworth said, "objects to the appointment of Ms. Vance."

"*Why?*" Nelle said. "You know nothing of my professional capabilities."

"I'm sure your professional capabilities are splendid. You do not meet the requirements of the resolution."

"That is still up to the Court, Mr. Pennyworth," the judge said.

Nelle said, "Judge, I am already quite familiar with the people and the situation. I can clarify the situation for the Court. I can minimize the traumatic effect upon Justin because of my existing relationship with him."

"Justin doesn't trust you," Pennyworth said mildly. "He thinks you're a spy for his parents. He thinks you're on their side."

"How can I be on *their* side when they're in opposition to each other? I wonder how Justin came to that perception, counselor."

"Can you be neutral in this matter, Ms. Vance?"

"As far as the parents are concerned, yes. As far as Justin is concerned, no. I would see my work as identifying and protecting Justin's best interests and to continue mediation between his parents."

"Mediation?" Pennyworth said. "Are you proposing yourself as marriage counselor as well?"

"Mediation where Justin's concerns are at issue."

"Judge, I am already in place as guardian ad litem."

"Yes, Mr. Pennyworth, as you have mentioned. There seems to be a concentration of powers in your person that is not necessarily in the best interests of the child. And it is the best interests of the child with which we are each concerned. You as his advocate and the guardian as an arm of the Court."

Pennyworth felt a chill of defeat in the air. It was weather to which he was unaccustomed.

Judge Haskins said, "I see no reason why the two of you can't function together in separate but complementary roles—each on behalf of the child. Therefore, Mr. Pennyworth, the Court denies your motion and grants the joint motion of Mr. and Mrs. Whitney to appoint Attorney Vance guardian ad litem to Justin Whitney."

Outside chambers, Nelle said, "I think I understand your concern about me, Pennyworth. I think you're afraid I'll fire you."

Whatever feelings of intimacy—no matter how suppressed and stifled—Pennyworth may have retained were spooked away.

"Now I'm looking forward to hearing the noted attorney argue the merits of marriage counseling for a couple in the process of getting a divorce."

You shall, you shall, Pennyworth thought, a little uneasy that Nelle's voice should sound so much like that of *the* Voice.

When court was convened, Pennyworth called Nelle Vance.

The look she offered him as she was sworn was one of an entirely different sort of oath.

"You have been a friend of the Whitneys for some time?"

"Six years."

"During that period did you notice any serious disharmony?"

"Only if you count a libel and a cross-libel for divorce serious disharmony."

"But that is all? No raging arguments?"

"No."

"No physical abuse?"

"No. Just the usual tennis-court sort of tiff. Who should have been playing where, who was poaching on whom."

"Did you ever hear the Whitneys described as a golden couple?"

"They are known—were known—as *the* golden couple. People just referred to them that way."

"I suppose it must be quite a strain being the golden couple, living up to that description?"

"I wouldn't know, Mr. Pennyworth."

"No, you're not a marriage counselor, are you?"

"Do you want an answer to that, Mr. Pennyworth?"

"Forget it, Ms. Vance. You have, haven't you, mediated between these two friends of yours?"

"Yes."

"You have an extensive background in mediation, don't you?"

"Yes."

"And that includes domestic mediation as well as corporate and labor mediation?"

"Yes."

"How would you describe your efforts at mediation between Mr. and Mrs. Whitney? Difficult? Very difficult?"

"I'd describe the Whitneys as unusually willing to accommodate each other—however reluctantly—and especially where Justin is concerned."

"In fact, their biggest problem is not who is going to get custody of Justin, but who is going to get custody of that house of theirs, isn't that so?"

"Broadly speaking, yes. That's their biggest point of conflict."

Pennyworth nodded and turned away as if he were going back to his seat at the counsel table. But at the table he turned around and said, "That business about the tennis court, Ms. Vance, about who was supposed to be where and who was poaching on whom?"

"Yes."

"A matter of territory, wasn't it?"

Pennyworth sat back and listened as first Bagley and then Bredwell inquired. But they were uncertain as to what it was they needed to inquire about.

Pennyworth addressed Judge Haskins—who had already disappointed him once. Had, in fact, failed to hold Vance to the letter of the resolution. Was Haskins *listening* to him now or simply sitting through his argument?

"In order for there to be a divorce, there must be grounds for the divorce. The Whitneys have agreed that their marriage must be dissolved because of irreconcilable differences. But I challenge those grounds. In fact, the Whitneys are very much alike. They have the same interests, the same friends, the same goals and endeavors, the same deeply felt love and concern for their child. Neither of them would willingly do anything to hurt Justin. Neither of them would willingly see harm come to Justin. When necessary, they join together to care for him.

"Are Gamble and Skip Whitney irreconcilable actually? Listen to the testimony of Sue Murganwheeler and Bart Murganwheeler. Two weeks after Gamble Whitney had filed for divorce she joined together with her husband in an endeavor that was both business and social. Ten days after filing his own cross-libel, Skip Whitney assists his wife socially. Their guests had a splendid luncheon and afternoon with the Whitneys. Their guests thought the Whitneys the perfect couple—*after* they had initiated divorce against each other. Does this sound like a situation of irreconcilable differences? I do not think so.

"This previously excellent marriage, this golden couple, this epitome of the great American marital alliance . . . A golden couple who are together experiencing temporary spousal difficulty as all married couples do from time to time. Is a marriage of such repute and worth to be thrown away? Ought not the partners to have the opportunity to hear themselves and each other outside the intimacy of the bedroom and the cold confines of a court of law?

"And what of Justin? Are not the child's interests superior to those of the parents? Is it not the court's right and duty to extend every protection to the child and to extend every avenue of possible relief to him? In the instant case, marriage counseling for the parents—which may yet preserve that canopy of domestic protection to which the child is entitled from birth.

"Your Honor, I submit that this divorce would be a significant disservice to the Whitney family unit and that, furthermore, it would have a substantially adverse effect upon the child Justin.

"On behalf of Gamble Whitney—"

"On behalf of *who?*" Gamble said.

"On behalf of Skip Whitney—"

"Who *the hell* is he *on the behalfing of?*" Skip said.

"On behalf of Justin most of all, I remind the Court of the statutory provisions for marriage counseling—"

"I can't believe I'm hearing this," Gamble said. "This is a divorce!"

"And I pray the Court, by its honorable order, to extend that opportunity to the Whitneys and insist that they take it. For you see, Your Honor, all evidence indicates that there are no irreconcilable differences here. Thank you."

"Mr. Bagley?"

"Your Honor, I am almost tempted to admit that I am speechless."

"I take it you are not going to give in to that temptation."

"It's a sad day, Your Honor, when two perfectly decent people can't go about getting a divorce without the meddling of an outside attorney who represents neither of them." Bagley went on to describe "the utmost antipathy between the two parties of the divorce."

"A sad day, indeed," Bredwell said, following Bagley, "when the great institution of divorce is trivialized by the suggestion that it ought to be addressed with marriage counseling. That is absurd. And these two people, Your Honor, Mr. Pennyworth's golden couple, they don't like each other one iota."

Judge Haskins folded her hands and looked out toward the opposite wall of the courtroom—where there was no window. She remained that way for a moment or two and then refocused on the people seated at the counsel tables in her courtroom.

"I am not entirely convinced that there is hope for reconciliation. Nor am I convinced that the parties are as antipathetic as counsel would like to represent them. The Court *is* an authorized representative of the child, as Mr. Pennyworth was at pains to remind us. Motion for Marriage Counseling is approved."

"They will take me kicking and screaming," Gamble said.

"If necessary," Judge Haskins said. "Mr. Whitney?"

"I won't do it."

"Yes, you will. I am entirely willing to find you both in contempt if you don't. Consider this, if you wish, not marriage counseling, but divorce counseling—to help the parents accommodate and deal with each other and with Justin. Sometimes the bitterness of divorce can be mitigated in these sessions. Sometimes the acceptance of divorce that follows allows for the resolution of other issues . . . The Court will continue these proceedings awaiting the report of the psychiatrist, the report of the guardian ad litem, and the conclusions of the marriage counselor."

Judge Haskins stood.

"All rise," the bailiff directed.

The judge said, "Ms. Vance? Mr. Pennyworth? In chambers."

"I am going off for the weekend with my husband and my teenagers," Judge Haskins said. "I have been reflecting upon married life and parenthood today. You've drawn my attention to it.

"I take your argument, Mr. Pennyworth. What I hope to God is, in this or any custody case, I hope I do as little ill as I possibly can. I will partially rely upon you two to keep harm to Justin to the minimum. You are both his advocates. I hope you will resolve your differences and get on with Justin's best interests. If I don't see you doing so, I will have one or both of you dismissed and replaced."

You're all alone, Pennyworth, the Voice said. You lost one and you won one, but what you won is temporary, and you're all alone. You're alone here in this building and you're going to drive home alone and when you get home you'll be alone.

The Whitneys and their counsel—the four of them—were together in the waiting room.

Skip said, "God *damn* you, Pennyworth!"

Gamble walked up close to Pennyworth, even as Bagley attempted to stop her, and said, "Get the fuck off my back. Get off *our* backs."

"Now you're talking," said Pennyworth. "Take it up with the marriage counselor."

Pennyworth, of course, already had the appropriate counselor in mind, someone whom he felt secure would consider Justin's interests superior to those of Gamble and Skip.

Outside the courthouse the day was bright and still, pleasantly cool, a return to football fall in early November. Pennyworth paused and looked up at the calm blue sky. Around him people were quitting the courthouse to go home for the weekend.

"Nice sky," Nelle said. Pennyworth had not realized she was there. "Have you ever had engine failure?"

"No."

"Probably too careful, I imagine. That was a terrific performance in there, Pennyworth. I particularly liked it when you wrapped the Whitneys' marriage in the American flag. I was frankly surprised when Judge Haskins didn't gag."

"You were a wonderful witness, Ms. Vance. Very convincing."

"You took quite a chance. You didn't know what my answers were going to be."

"I know what the truth is. I assumed you would be guided by it."

"I thought you called me to try to get back at me for the appointment to guardian. I thought perhaps your intent was to discredit me before the judge."

"Ms. Vance, I had every intention of calling you no matter who was appointed guardian."

"We are going to have to live together in this arrangement, Pennyworth. I suggest we begin accommodating each other."

"I am in agreement."

"For Justin's sake."

"Of course. Your place or mine?"

"What do you mean?"

"To begin to live together."

"You have a poor reputation, Pennyworth, for living with anyone."

"I see the possibility of reforming myself, Ms. Vance."

Both of them paused and listened to what Pennyworth had just said. Of the two, Pennyworth was the one who most doubted that he had said it.

"You see the possibility," Nelle said.

"It is dimly upon the horizon."

"Let's ignore it, then. In the meantime, my place."

"*D'accord.* When?"

"Tomorrow morning. Nine o'clock. Dress casually."

37

SOCIAL EVENTS

ENGINE FAILURE. THAT WAS PENNYWORTH'S OCCASIONAL fear—those times when he was not in direct control of his life, whether waking, sleeping, or fantasy.

Now, dressed casually, he was twenty-five hundred feet in the air in a sailplane and being towed to three thousand feet. He was alone with Nelle Vance. She had the forward seat and he had the rear.

Ahead there was the vague clatter of the towplane. The control stick between Pennyworth's legs was being gently manipulated by Nelle. Controlling the sailplane's ascent, she moved her stick and Pennyworth's followed.

Pennyworth appreciated the smoothness with which, under Nelle's direction, the sailplane was climbed to altitude, but he was not entirely at ease. He preferred being in control himself and he preferred power.

There was an audible thump. Three thousand feet. Nelle had released the towline. She banked to the right, and ahead of them, the Cessna that had been towing them seemed to sprint forward as it banked away to the left.

Pennyworth was alone with Nelle at three thousand feet with no power.

"I'm in your hands," Pennyworth said.

"Don't you just wish," Nelle said.

She leveled the wings. There was a quiet and serenity that quite surprised Pennyworth, not because he hadn't anticipated it, but because he took to it.

"We'll go look for thermals," Nelle said, "and then I'll give you a lesson."

Pennyworth was well aware of the glide ratio of the sailplane, but still he said, "Don't go too far from home."

"Don't worry, Pennyworth, you're not going to get hurt."

You heard that one a long, long time ago, didn't you, Pennyworth? the Voice said.

Friday night at his mother's, then Saturday at his father's. That was just splitting him up too much.

"Where are you going, Justin?" his mother said.

"I'm just going bike riding."

He wished he could have the new mountain bike over here, but his father wouldn't let him, so he had to use his old dirt bike, which *was* getting too small for him after all. It was draggy having to have what belonged to him split up in two places.

Mr. Giambelli was still in pajamas, robe, and slippers when Justin went into the kitchen. He was sipping coffee and staring out the window.

"Justin, I am so glad you called. Hot chocolate, milk, sticky buns?"

"What's that you've got?"

"Burrito. Want one? It zaps in two minutes."

"Sure."

Mr. Giambelli went to the freezer and then went about the little business of readying the burrito for the microwave. "I was going to call you," he said. "Today."

"What about?"

"You called me. What's that about?"

"It's about NOK," and Justin explained what that was. "It's about NOK and how they're messing with us at school. Taking away our rights. Like free speech. On your program, you talk about things like that a lot. I thought maybe you could talk about Carlton Regional Elementary School not letting kids talk about what's on their mind."

Giambelli listened and then said, "How would *you* like to talk about it?"

"*Me?* You'd do it better."

"Before you get to NOK, I'd want to talk to you about your suing your parents not to get divorced. People would be interested in that. But you couldn't make any charges against your mother or father. Then we can talk about kids' rights. One leads into the other. What do you think about that?"

"*Fearless.*"

"You'd need your parents' permission."

"I'll talk to Mr. Pennyworth about it."

"Not bad, Pennyworth. Pretty good for a power pilot the first time."

"A pleasant start to reconciling our differences."

"I don't think they're irreconcilable. We have so much in common."

Indeed, Pennyworth thought. With that first flash of intimacy the day before, he had thought as much. Law. Flying. Skiing. Indeed it was unsettling. He saw in Nelle Vance a female counterpart to himself, someone with whom he already shared much, someone with whom there was already a shared intimacy. A companion *and* a colleague.

And he rather liked her face—that askew smile and a playfulness in her eyes. He discovered that he had a feeling of comfortable familiarity with her, and that startled him.

They were standing on a grass strip waiting for the tow Jeep and the line boys to retrieve the sailplane. Pennyworth's companion and colleague was dressed in Wellingtons, slim denim pants, a shirt over a turtleneck, and a denim jacket, all of which served to emphasize her femininity rather than disguise it.

Pennyworth found that Nelle was looking at him, the gangly boy who had disciplined himself into the upright man—tall, black haired, and bespectacled with the aviator glasses he wore when he was not in the courtroom.

The Voice said, She's looking at what *you* consider casual. Slacks, sweater—and a tweed jacket.

She's looking at the man, Pennyworth said.

She sees the boy, the Voice said.

A well-knit man, Nelle was thinking, athletic. She rather liked the dry humor in his fancy language, and she thought to her surprise, she was beginning to rather like the man himself. There was something in Pennyworth's face, something fleeting, that she was beginning to see and to respond to in a favorable way—a boyish vulnerability, as if a boy occasionally peered out from behind Pennyworth's careful control.

"How *was* the guardian ad litem course?" Nelle said.

"Entirely inadequate for the average attorney."

"Of course. I have lunch for us back at the house. We can discuss Justin."

Get out of this, Pennyworth, the Voice said.

But Pennyworth always strove to do the opposite of what the Voice insisted upon.

His father picked Justin up at his mother's after lunch. It was funny how home felt like home, but it felt less so when both his parents were in it together as now, though that was what Justin wanted.

And they talked together—*together*—privately from him. What was going on? Were they getting together again? Were Mr. Pennyworth and the judges getting them together again?

His mother kissed and hugged Justin good-bye. He was going to be with his father for four days—Monday was a teachers' workshop day (no school) and Tuesday was Veterans Day (no school).

In the car, his father said, "I've got a sort of surprise for you back at the new place."

"Not another present."

"What's wrong with presents?"

"I don't know. Too many of them lately."

"This isn't a present." His father drove along in silence.

"Can I put on my own music?"

"Sure."

Justin turned on the FM and pushed the preset button for his favorite rock station in Boston.

"You know I had to be in court all day yesterday?"

"You and Mom, yeah."

"I could've been out of there in ten minutes if it wasn't for that lawyer of yours."

"He's *good*, isn't he?"

"He stinks on ice."

"You get away with a lot of wild expeditions in court. You're a great actor, Pennyworth."

"I am only acting on behalf of my client. This wine is delightful. I think you ought to call me Weld. 'Pennyworth' seems rather formal. Or snide."

"Do you realize you haven't called me anything all day except when you said, 'Good morning, Ms. Vance'?"

"I apologize. That was rude."

"I don't think you were being rude. I think you were being very careful."

See? said the Voice. *See?*

The "surprise" at Justin's father's place was a woman named Gina. "A new friend," his father said.

Justin suddenly felt terribly lonely. He hung around his father's for as little time as possible and then he went out and looked for Chick.

Chick was over on the soccer area doing nothing. "It's getting cold," Chick said.

"Why don't you go inside?"

"Glen's there."

Justin looked around. "Where is everyone?"

"Most of them's gone to visit their fathers."

"Heather, too?"

"Yeah."

"My dad's got a new friend at our place. A woman."

"How is she?"

"I don't know. She says she's gonna cook dinner for us."

"Is she gonna stay over?"

"I don't know."

"You better tell your dad to be careful. Your mom might get angry. You're not supposed to do it in front of the children."

Pennyworth was imagining himself reaching out to place his arm around Nelle and embrace her. He was feeling considerable warmth and he knew that some of it came from the wine—Nelle had opened a second bottle—but that more of it was coming from some secret place inside himself of which he had been previously unaware. He wondered if it might be a burst blood vessel.

"I'd like to take you flying in the Lear, Nelle."

"I'd like that fine."

"Do you have an engine license?"

"No."

"Why not?"

"It never interested me. I like riding on the air."

"I like that, too. But today was the first pure experience. I don't think I trusted it."

"I noticed you were a little . . . *cautious* about straying too far from home."

"I was nervous about it. I didn't know a damn thing about you as a pilot."

"You didn't know a damn thing about me as a guardian ad litem either, Weld." (See, the Voice said, *see?* Now she gets you.) "But you trusted me with *your* life, so to speak."

"But not with Justin's. I can take responsibility for risks to myself."

"What about the risks you're having Justin take?"

"Like what?"

"Losing his parents' love. At least risking their antipathy."

"He's already lost their care. They only care about their damn divorce and who gets the house." Pennyworth poured some wine for Nelle and then for himself.

"You're risking his parents' affection, Weld. That's different from their love. Justin needs both love and affection. It's affection a child sees mostly. The little things. It's being withheld and he needs it."

Pennyworth set his glass down. "What do you know about what he needs and wants? I know what his desperations and sorrows are."

"You do?"

"I know them very well. You think you do, but you don't understand the boy."

"I understand the boy very well. It's the man who gets confusing."

"You don't understand him or his feelings. That's why I fought you on the guardian issue. I should have fought you harder."

"I didn't find much about you—historically." Nelle seemed to be changing the subject, but Pennyworth knew that she was not. His sudden alertness seemed to evaporate the alcohol in his system and the warmth he had been feeling. "Graduates *Harvard Law* and starts out as a juvenile defender? Odd, very odd. Idiosyncratic."

Pennyworth looked out the window. "I was after trial experience."

Nelle laughed. "You've hidden yourself very well. Except for the barest facts. Born right here in New Hampshire. Peterborough, 1950. Went to the George School in Pennsylvania. Then Yale. Then Harvard Law. Clerked in federal district court. All to become a juvenile defender. Some people consider that the dregs."

"Some people are right. I got out of it after two years."

"Two years of juvenile defendants is a long time, Weld. Some people would say that was a pretty long time."

"I was a slow learner."

"Then two years as a prosecutor."

"I was moving up in the world."

"Yes. Right into criminal defense and domestic law."

"Don't forget insurance companies."

"From the dregs to the pits. That's how you described divorce law, wasn't it? The pits?"

"I'm ready for some coffee, Nelle. I'm going to be driving back to Boston soon."

"Nonsense. You're staying right here. We're having such a cozy time."

Pennyworth, to his surprise, wanted to believe it—that they were having a cozy time and that he was going to stay.

Nelle topped off his wine. "Now, about your parents, Weld, were they divorced?"

Skip's friend Gina seemed a little disappointed when Justin brought Chick back for dinner, but Justin said to his father, privately, *"You* have a friend here and this is my home, too, isn't it?"

At dinner Justin told his father how "me and Chick and some other kids, Ryan included, we're getting together like a union. It's called the National Organization of Kids and Mr. Giambelli wants me to come on his show and talk about it."

"I don't know, Justin," his father said.

"Really?" Gina said to Justin. *"Jim* Giambelli? That's thrilling. How could you deny Justin that, Skip?"

"Gina, this is a domestic matter, a parental matter—"

"Oh. I'm only supposed to come in and do the cooking and . . . other things."

"That's not what I meant."

"It sounds like a wonderful opportunity. I wish *I'd* had a National Organization of Kids to belong to. Is it like the Boy Scouts? The Girl Scouts? Actually, the Girl Scouts sucked."

"It's about children's rights."

"Skip, you've got to let him do it," Gina said.

His father sighed. "Nothing in life is simple. I thought at least divorce would make life simpler."

"That was very good," Justin said to Gina, nodding at dinner.

"Chicken piccata."

"Strange, but good."

"I make a wonderful birthday cake. A traditional Italian birthday cake. Your dad tells me you have a birthday coming up, Justin."

"Not till after Christmas. Not till January."

"We deliver," Gina said, looking at Skip.

"She's trying to get on your good side," Chick said.

"I know." They were up in Justin's bare room.

"Glen was the same way when he first started up with my mom."

"Well, she got Dad to let me go on Mr. Giambelli's show."

"We've all got to listen. We got to call everyone and tell 'em when you're gonna be on."

"Yeah, and Ryan, too. Ryan's gotta come with me. And Amanda."

Justin had just *said* it was his home, too. It was sort of a lie and he didn't like himself for that. He recognized, though, that it was exactly the sort of thing Amanda and the others had said he should be doing—get things to work for yourself, take advantage of the situation.

And, too, he felt sort of scared about Gina being there, though he didn't think she was going to hit him or anything. The same with Dr. Ralph.

And it wasn't like being at home—either home—with Dr. Ralph or Gina there. It was like they took away what belonged to him.

Who knows, though? Justin thought. Maybe Gina was okay.

Anyway, she didn't stay over or anything. Justin heard her and his dad on the stairs around three in the morning and then he heard her back her car from in front and drive away.

Pennyworth's car was still parked, rather indiscreetly, in Nelle's driveway. The house was dark, her bedroom was dark, but the two occupants were awake.

"This is the most precipitous relationship I've ever been involved in," Nelle said.

"I agree," Pennyworth said. "I feel like I fell off a cliff."

"But you're all right."

"So are you."

Pennyworth thought that what had happened was that the tensions between them had been so insistent and overwhelming—and words had seemed to do nothing but increase them—that they had had no choice but to resolve the matter physically. Then, later, they had resolved the tensions again, when there weren't any.

And again in the morning when they awoke late.

When, toward the end of the afternoon, Pennyworth got ready to drive back to Boston, neither of them had yet referred to any companionable plans for the future.

At the door, before departing, Pennyworth kissed Nelle and said, "See you in court."

"In court," Nelle said.

38

JUVENILE COURT:
ADJUDICATORY HEARING

JUSTIN HEARD HIMSELF CRY OUT IN HIS SLEEP. OR THOUGHT
he heard it. At any rate he was awake. The sound of his crying out
was still with him in the dark and so was the dream that was, after
all, real life—that his parents were leaving him, walking away from
each other in opposite directions. And he was alone in the cold dark.
And no one to help him.

All of that was true enough.

Justin could not have defined the word *despair,* but it filled his
heart and mind and body.

All alone. No one to help.

Then he thought of Mr. Pennyworth. The dark was not so cold
—or so frightening.

And what was that? Pennyworth asked himself, awakening
sharply, as if from a frightening dream, but there had been no dream.
He thought he had heard a child—a boy—cry out.

Justin? No, it had been a very familiar voice crying out.

Go back to sleep, he told himself.

But a gloomy anxiety kept him awake. In fact, he had gone to
sleep with it. All the way back from New Hampshire, all the way
since he had backed out of Nelle's driveway, he had felt as if he were
being followed. There had been times in his life when he really had
been followed, and he had been appropriately concerned on those
occasions, but this was harrowing. This was not a reporter or a
private detective or someone hired by someone else or by some government agency to watch him or frighten him; this was a *presence,*
something that pulled closer to him the farther he drove from New
Hampshire.

Awake now in the dark, the gloomy anxiety welled within Pennyworth. And then, abruptly, the anxiety was overcome by a sadness
that brought him almost to tears. And after the sadness, an anger so
fierce Pennyworth could not remain in bed.

He got up and reviewed all the materials—including the psychiatrist's report—that he had at home. And then he dictated a very long memorandum for the file, a memorandum that would become the guardian ad litem report to juvenile court.

Typically, by the next day Pennyworth did not recall the *presence* or his anxiety or the attendant sadness and anger. It wasn't that these things hadn't happened; it was simply that he didn't choose to recall them, not unlike his running from Justin when Justin had first showed up at his office. Now, upon his return to New Hampshire for the adjudicatory hearing in juvenile court, his mind was on Dr. Salmon and the psychiatric evaluation.

Judge Stickney did not seem keen on the psychiatric evaluation. He had the four close-typed pages up there on the bench with him and he paused during argument and testimony from time to time to reread various passages. Then he glanced down at Dr. Salmon or at Pennyworth with grave suspicion.

"Dr. Salmon," Stickney said, "are you telling this Court that the Whitneys as parents are guilty of consistent mistreatment and neglect of their child?"

"In the matter of the divorce, yes, I am." Unknown to himself, Pennyworth smiled contentedly. Dr. Salmon went on. "The separation of parents from each other and the separation of the child from one or both parents feed into a child's greatest anxiety. The consequence is seen by the child as his own death."

"Shrink talk," Stickney said. "Fantasy, speculation. The parents are splitting up, the boy is upset. That's natural."

"Judge Stickney, the literature and clinical findings are quite clear. The parents' behavior adversely affects the child's emotional health. It results in an impairment of emotional health. There is clear danger of subsequent injury. The consequences are life-threatening. Justin exhibits the classic sequence of emotions. Anxiety, anger, fear, and despair that later, in adolescent years, may find expression in suicide. The suicide rate during adolescence among the children of divorce is significantly higher than that of adolescents whose parents are not divorced."

"Dr. Salmon, we are not discussing divorce here. We are discussing 169C and the criteria of 169C."

"Your Honor, the psychiatric evaluation finds a neglected child consistent with the definitions of 169C. The parents are not providing the care necessary for Justin's mental or emotional health. Not only is he likely to suffer serious impairment as a result, his very life is at future risk."

Pennyworth saw that Stickney did not like this at all; and that his dislike was not for Dr. Salmon's prognosis so much as it was for the legal cul-de-sac that Pennyworth had constructed and into which he had drawn the Court. Pennyworth almost expected Stickney to glance behind himself to see the door to the cul-de-sac closing.

Stickney fixed Pennyworth with a look of displeasure. "The report of the guardian ad litem concurs in the particulars."

Pennyworth arose. "The parents are preoccupied with the disposition of their material goods—such as their house. Justin is not an issue on their agenda and they have stipulated as much."

"Sit down, Mr. Pennyworth."

"Your Honor," Pennyworth said and sat.

"Mr. Bagley?"

"Mr. Bredwell will conduct our inquiry, Your Honor."

Bredwell stood and came around in front of the counsel table. He smiled at Dr. Salmon. "I have the utmost respect for your profession, Dr. Salmon." Then he smiled at Judge Stickney. "But sometimes it seems to me that a great, great deal of weight is placed on a somewhat flimsy foundation. I call Your Honor's attention to page 2, paragraph 4, of the psychiatric evaluation."

The judge flipped a page. He read. He looked up. "Clyde Worm," he said.

"Clyde Worm," Bredwell said. "Dr. Salmon, Clyde Worm takes on nearly mythic proportions in your account. We've all read it of course, but now I'd like the Court to hear the tale directly from you." Bredwell smiled at the doctor with the forbearance a parent shows a child—and then smiled at the judge, grown-up to grown-up.

"The proportions are not mine, Mr. Bredwell, they are Justin's. We are talking about repressed anger. Repressed anger is the fuel of teenage suicide—"

"Excuse me, Doctor, I thought we were talking about a worm named Clyde."

"We are talking about Justin's life, Mr. Bredwell. In a very literal sense Clyde Worm *is* Justin's life. During my interviews with Justin it was evident that there is a great deal of repressed anger. In the evaluation Clyde Worm represents one example. There are several others in the evaluation."

"I asked about Clyde Worm, Dr. Salmon."

"Justin sees Clyde Worm as an extension of himself, a self in need of care and protection. In this case a self for which Justin himself is able to provide care and protection, exactly the care and protection Justin misses from his own parents. Clyde Worm lives in a house that Justin designed and built. Justin provides Clyde with food and water and even music and conversation. He is *very* caring of Clyde and *very* protective of Clyde. Yet, in his anger at his parents one evening, Justin almost destroyed Clyde. That is, in a symbolic sense, Justin almost took his own life. The Whitneys had had an argument in front of Justin. Justin felt helpless. He also felt enraged. But where could he direct his rage? Not at his parents. So there in his room he picked up Clyde in *Clyde's* home and almost hurled him against the wall. He was ready to stamp on Clyde, he said. In other words, his anger had no place to go except against himself. Justin was ready to destroy himself."

"But he didn't."

"Not now. Not yet."

Pennyworth saw that Stickney was listening closely, his eyes now fixed on Dr. Salmon, the expression on his face either one of disbelief or of apprehension.

Bredwell smiled indulgently. "Do you really expect us to attach such life-and-death significance to a worm?"

"I expect you to attach such life-and-death significance to Justin's message."

Pennyworth thought that Bredwell looked as if he were having an attack of gas pains. When he had recovered from the seizure, Bredwell said, "Dr. Salmon, I thought the worm had a more phallic turn in your iconology."

"We are discussing Justin's iconology, Mr. Bredwell, not yours."

"However, yours is but one opinion."

"It is the opinion solicited by the Court."

"Thank you, Dr. Salmon."

"I do have one question," Nelle said, getting up.

"Proceed, Ms. Vance," Stickney said.

"Dr. Salmon, here on page 4, paragraph 2, you express reservations about Mr. Pennyworth's association with Justin."

"Yes."

Pennyworth stood up. "That is not an issue before the Court, Your Honor."

"It is now, Mr. Pennyworth. Go ahead, Ms. Vance."

"Thank you, Your Honor. We are, Mr. Pennyworth, concerned here with Justin's best interests, not exclusive of his life apart from his parents. Dr. Salmon, please tell us the gist of your reservations."

"Justin has a fantasy that he can sue his parents back together again. Mr. Pennyworth is abetting that fantasy. It is unrealistic on Justin's part to think that he can prevent his parents from obtaining a divorce. Simply put, this is not a time to hold out false hopes to the child."

"Do you think that Mr. Pennyworth ought to be removed as guardian ad litem before this Court?"

"I think that Mr. Pennyworth ought to confine himself to Justin's realistic prospects."

"Isn't it true that abetting the fantasy, holding out false hopes, is harmful to Justin?"

Pennyworth stood quickly. "I will stipulate to that, Your Honor."

"Really, Mr. Pennyworth."

"Such conduct would be harmful. But there has been no such conduct."

"Your Honor, it seems that I'm going to have to question Mr. Pennyworth."

"Well, do it now so that we may be advised by Dr. Salmon."

"I'll save you the trouble," Pennyworth said. "From the beginning I have told Justin that what he was asking was unrealistic."

"And what was he asking, Mr. Pennyworth?"

"He wanted to sue his parents not to get a divorce. I told him that was unrealistic."

"But isn't that what you're doing, Mr. Pennyworth? Suing the Whitneys not to get a divorce?"

"Where is there a motion to that effect, Ms. Vance? There *is* no motion to that effect."

"No," said Gamble, "you're just making it damned uncomfortable."

Stickney sighed. "Appearances to the contrary, Mrs. Whitney, this is not a roundtable discussion."

"What are you doing then, Mr. Pennyworth?" Nelle said.

"What I am doing is between my client and me. If Dr. Salmon thinks that I am abetting a fantasy, we'd better get Justin in here to tell everyone, including the doctor, that that is not so. I have tried to make the distinction, Your Honor, Dr. Salmon, between what Justin wants and what is realistic. I think that what Justin may have expressed was more in line with his desires than with his legal counsel."

"Dr. Salmon?" Stickney said.

"I don't suggest that Mr. Pennyworth has deliberately fostered the fantasy. I do say that simply placing Justin in the process fosters the fantasy."

"Granted," Pennyworth said. "We all have our hopes and fantasies. Is Justin to be denied a part in the legal process because he is a child? Are his hopes of less value than any of ours? I daresay that his hopes are of a purer nature than those of anyone in this room—with the possible exception of the Court, of course."

"Thank you, Mr. Pennyworth," Stickney said. "Ms. Vance?"

"I don't think I'm getting anywhere with this, Your Honor."

"No, I don't think you are. You've either got to argue that the child ought to be denied the opportunity of the process, or you've got to argue that the process itself fosters a detrimental fantasy."

Skip pointed at Pennyworth. "That man *placed* my son in this mess."

"I suppose we were bound to hear from you, too, Mr. Whitney," Stickney said.

"No, Mr. Whitney," Pennyworth said politely, "I did not place your son in this mess. You and Mrs. Whitney did. Justin came to me for help."

"All right, everybody," Stickney said, "creative playtime is now concluded, free expression is henceforth prohibited. Mr. Pennyworth, you are still on your feet."

"Your Honor, I would like to offer a closing statement *before* Dr. Salmon steps down."

"And then no more from you, Mr. Pennyworth?"

"So stipulated, Your Honor."

"Why then, proceed, Mr. Pennyworth, do."

"Your Honor, Dr. Salmon has testified to the present trauma being inflicted upon Justin by reason of parental neglect. Furthermore, she has testified to resultant suicidal tendencies in Justin's adolescent years. She has testified that Justin has already been placed emotionally at risk. I submit that the testimony of this expert witness is exactly in accordance with 169C, part 3c."

Pennyworth sat down.

Stickney swiveled to face Dr. Salmon. "Dr. Salmon, in your professional capacity you are familiar with RSA 169C."

"Yes."

"This is not your first encounter?"

"I have done numerous evaluations with reference to petitions brought under 169C."

"In your professional opinion, are your findings in accordance with the criteria set forth by 169C?"

"It is the parental duty to serve the best interests of the child, but the Whitneys are clearly not doing so. Justin has been placed emotionally at risk. There is demonstrable trauma. There is a suicidal factor engendered by neglect."

"But the neglect here is the parents' attempt to get a divorce."

"That is the nature of the origin."

"Dr. Salmon, I am persuaded that your findings meet the criteria of 169C. However, a ruling by this Court to that effect would present an untenable precedent: that divorce is an act of neglect on the part of parents. Divorce must always cause stress for the child. Nevertheless, it is a right of married people to get a divorce. Are we to penalize every parent who seeks a divorce? Do you wish to do away with divorce for married parents, undo that entire system of relief for tortured marriages?"

"I was not asked to address a hypothesis of legal consequences. That is not my field of expertise. I was asked to evaluate, from a psychiatrist's point of view, real people and a real situation."

"All right, Dr. Salmon, thank you, you may go." Stickney sat back and said to no one in particular, "You place the Court in a most uncomfortable position." Then he was silent for a moment before he spoke again. "All right. The guardian ad litem has found in accordance with 169C. I'm not going to put much stock in that. It was expected and self-serving. But the psychiatrist has found in accordance with 169C and her testimony was convincing. Therefore, the Court finds the child Justin Whitney to be neglected by his parents Gamble G. Whitney and Conrad J. Whitney. The present custodial orders remain in effect. The dispositional hearing will be held thirty days hence."

Bagley said to the Whitneys, "That's the longest he can put it off. By statute he can't put it off any longer than that."

"Why is he putting it off?" Skip said.

Bredwell said, "Maybe he wants a lot of time to think about it. In that event, I would be worried."

"What could he do?" Gamble said.

"Just about anything."

Bagley said, "He may be putting it off in the hope that he won't have to do anything at all. That the situation will become moot."

"How so?" Skip said.

"If your divorce were granted in the meantime."

"Well, that could happen," Gamble said.

"Not if Pennyworth blocks it," Bagley said.

"Can he do that?" Gamble said.

"I think we'll have to wait and see."

39
ON AIR

IN THE STUDIO THE SOUND OF THE COMMERCIAL WENT DEAD in midsentence; the On Air sign lit up red; the engineer behind the glass partition looked at Giambelli, nodded, and pointed at him; and Giambelli paused as he listened on an earphone and then said, "My first guest this hour is a young man who is suing his parents not to get a divorce."

Each of the parents was at a radio in their private offices, the doors shut, the secretaries instructed to put through no calls, *no matter what,* for the next hour.

Gamble had bitterly opposed Justin going on the radio. But there he was, sixty miles away in Boston, on a fifty-thousand-watt clear-channel radio station about to wash the family laundry in public on a signal that could be heard all over New England and as far south as New York City and God knew how far north into Canada, where, fortunately, neither Gamble nor Skip had any relatives or friends who might be listening. Thank God it wasn't nighttime. The station carried to the Midwest and Florida then.

Pennyworth had canceled his three o'clock and had himself also left instructions that he was not to be interrupted for the hour *by anyone.*

Pennyworth had threatened to get off Justin's case if Justin went on the radio. But Justin had asked for reasons and Pennyworth had suddenly felt himself as vulnerable as a child. *He had no reasons.* All he had was a gut feeling that Justin on air would jeopardize *him,* Pennyworth.

And, of course, that made no sense.

But the Voice made sense of it: *Little Weld* wants to be the center of attention, as always. So, for an hour, is it going to kill little Weld if *Justin* is the center of attention?

It would be useful, Pennyworth had come to realize, if public attention were drawn to Justin: Superior court and juvenile court would both have to examine Justin's complaints closely. Those complaints could not then be simply dismissed for the convenience of the parents and the convenience of the courts in their protection of divorce. It would be useful in getting Justin's position taken seriously.

In the way, there were the parents and Nelle, not one of whom wanted Justin anywhere near a microphone.

Nelle wanted to protect Justin's privacy. "You just want to make him into a *People* magazine person like yourself," Nelle said.

"I am not a *People* magazine person. The typical *People* magazine person is ephemeral."

He said to the parents and their attorneys, "I am sorry, Mrs. Whitney, Mr. Whitney, Justin is *not* going on the show to discuss you, he will not even mention you. I know that comes as a great disappointment to each of you. Justin is going on, with two other children, to discuss divorce from a child's point of view. That is part of the agenda. Part 2 is a new political movement called the National Organization of Kids, or NOK. Am I to go on the show myself as in opposition to freedom of expression under the First Amendment? To show that you two are attempting to suppress and destroy an incipient political movement whose sole purpose is to represent and enhance the rights of children? For your own immediate, selfish interests? Am I?"

Gamble and Skip each consulted the liberal and conservative constituencies within their own heads and were reluctantly forced to come out on the side of the First Amendment.

Nelle had no such difficulty. As Justin's superior court guardian ad litem, she had asked for an injunction against Justin's appearance. She had filed in both New Hampshire and Massachusetts. Her motions had been denied.

She thought she might have had *some* chance, but Pennyworth had orchestrated things so that she had virtually no chance. Justin was not to go on the show alone, he was to be accompanied by the other two executive officers of NOK, Amanda Hollander and Ryan MacKenzie.

If the *president* of NOK wasn't there, why?

Neither Nelle nor the Whitneys had been able to counter that.

All that Nelle salvaged was her fury at Pennyworth for making Justin a public animal.

"Mr. Giambelli, this is a longtime caller from Brockton."
"Yes, I recognize the voice."

"And I think what you're doing is atrocious. Letting children turn against their parents on radio! Encouraging it."

"I don't think they're turning against their parents, ma'am. You all love your parents, don't you?" Giambelli said to his three guests. "They're all nodding yes, ma'am. They're asking for more consideration in their own lives."

· "I have two children of my own, Mr. Giambelli. A boy and a girl. And I'm not listening to your show ever again."

"I pity those two kids," Ryan said. "Like our friend Chick says, it's tough work being a kid."

"Is it really tough work being a kid?" Giambelli asked. "We'll find out more about that after this."

The engineer ran three commercials. Then Mr. Giambelli repeated his question.

Justin said, "I just wish my parents would get back together," but it was bleeped with a repetitive sequence of musical notes recorded from a synthesizer.

Mr. Giambelli said, "Remember, no references to your parents. You have to talk about parents in general."

Back on air, Justin said, "Parents split the kid, like he was some sort of something they owned or something, like a bunch of Legos or something."

A caller said, "If they can stop divorce, they can commit murder. I mean, what are laws for, Jim?"

A woman's voice said, "Hello, Jim? What these kids are saying is terrifying. They want to take the law into their own hands—"

"Divorce law."

"That's right. They want to take divorce law into their own hands. What do they know at that age? *They've* never been married. What they want, it's terrifying. I know. I've been divorced twice."

"Thank you," Giambelli said. "Hello."

"I'd like to address my question to Justin."

"Go ahead."

"Justin, are you a Christian?"

"Good-bye to that caller. I don't see the relevance. We're talking about children's social rights, not religious affiliation. Go ahead, caller, turn your radio down."

During a commercial break, the engineer's voice came into the studio from a speaker. "Jim, the board's been lit up solid almost since the start."

Giambelli smiled.

"What's that mean?" Justin asked.

"More people are calling in this hour than anytime since Iran/Contra."

"I think you ought to get those kids off the air, Jim. Send them home where they belong. When I was their age, my father'd tan my hide for talking like that . . ."

"What kind of monsters *are* these kids, talking against grown-ups?"

"I thought this was an adult show, Mr. Giambelli. Adults talking to adults for adults to listen to. Here's one listener you've lost permanently."

"If you'd just hang on for one minute, caller, I'd like to ask you a question."

"Well, all right."

"Why do you feel so threatened?"

The caller hung up.

In separate places, but of one mind, Gamble and Skip each thought of a number of questions they would themselves like to ask, questions framed along the lines of, "Well, Justin, you seem to think you've been badly treated. Don't you remember any of the wonderful things I've done for you all your life? Let me list a few thousand. No, make that a few million."

Nelle, in spite of herself, rather liked what the kids were doing.

And Pennyworth, along with little Weld (whose presence Penny-worth did not acknowledge), just beamed.

"I'm against abortion," the caller said, "but I'm beginning to wonder."

"A national organization of kids? That's scary, Jim. I mean, we've already got to deal with the blacks and women like they were people—kids, too?"

"Keep it up," the caller said in a small, tentative voice. "Good-bye."

"Hey, all right!" Ryan said. "One of *us*."

"Jim, I'd like to direct my question to the president of NOK." Justin recognized the voice of his mother. "Justin, your parents have always—"

Giambelli ran over her with the synthesized music. "No references to specific people, caller."

"Well then, you're interfering with my freedom of speech under the First Amendment."

"We're not discussing the Constitution, ma'am. We're discussing parents and children."

Gamble hung up.

Skip liked that a lot. He, too, had recognized Gamble's voice. It was so deeply satisfying to hear her bleeped, however musically, and then hear her throttled. He decided to try his own luck. He was sure she'd still be listening.

"I think you guys are real great."

"Thanks," Amanda said.

"Like, could I join up with you? Could I do that?"

"Sure," Amanda said. She looked at Justin and Ryan. "I guess."

"Young lady," Giambelli said. "I take it you are a young lady?"

"Yes," the caller said.

"Write them care of the station here and we'll see that your letter gets to them. They can take it from there."

"Gee, thanks."

There were several more calls asking for the address. Giambelli began giving it every few minutes.

"I suppose the next thing you want to do is lower the age for president from thirty to ten or seven or something."

"This question is for the young man called Justin." Justin recognized the voice of his father. "You there, Justin?"

"Yes."

"First, I'd like to make a comment, and then I'll ask my question."

"Go ahead," Giambelli said.

"Selfishness is a personal quality usually associated with children, right? Well, I, for one, run across it much more often in adults than children."

"Good point, caller. Go on."

"Yes. Adults are a lot more selfish than children. I think your guests would agree. In fact, adults often exert their selfishness at the expense of children. Would you agree to that, Justin?"

"Yes."

(In her office, Gamble was at both boiling and fuming points. She could guess what was coming.)

"Kids help each other out a lot. I've noticed that. Right?"

"Yes."

"Whereas adults can be very selfish with each other and with their children, too. Right?"

"Yes."

"Like you three kids have been saying, that selfishness comes out a lot in divorce. Now, when let's say the mother initiates the divorce and wants the child and the house and everything, wouldn't you say *she's* the selfish one?"

Amanda saw Justin looking away. She said, "We can't talk about things according to sex, caller."

(Gamble physically applauded Amanda. Chalk one up for womanhood, she thought, completely missing the point. Fuck you, Skip.)

"Seems like a lot of antikid sentiment out there," the new caller said.

"I take it you're not a kid," Giambelli said.

"I once was. I remember."

(Pennyworth found himself nodding in agreement and stopped.)

"I like seeing these kids standing up for the kid I once was," the caller said. "More power to you, and God bless."

"I'm concerned about this group that calls itself NOK," the next caller said. "I'd like to look at it from an historic perspective. Do you mind?"

"Go ahead," Giambelli said.

"I'm reminded of the Children's Crusade. That was back in the thirteenth century. It was started by two twelve-year-old boys. Of course they weren't inspired by anything as mundane as divorce. They had *angels* come and tell them what had to be done. Children had to go and reclaim the Holy Land. Read *innocence* and *security of childhood* for Holy Land, Jim. Anyway, bands of children came from all over Europe and joined together to go to Jerusalem. Some of the children were given free passage to what was supposed to be the Holy Land. Some French nobility provided the ships. But the children were taken to Africa and sold as slaves. Some of the other children—not many—but some actually got to the Holy Land. Once they got there, they disappeared. Forever. I just thought you listeners, and particularly the children, the ones interested in NOK, might like to know that."

Off air, Giambelli said, "They're out there, you take care."

During the hour's five-minute break for news, after their part in the show was over, the station manager came in and shook hands with Justin, Ryan, and Amanda and said, "There're a bunch of kids downstairs in the lobby, walk-ins from the street. They said they heard you on the radio and they want to meet you. Couple of adults, too." He turned to Giambelli. "*Big* response, Jim. *Big*. The lines are full." He turned to Justin. "I was just talking to the manager of our

TV station and he wants you to come on 'The New England Show.' "

"I saw Mr. Pennyworth on that."

"It's syndicated. That means you'll be seen all over the country one time or another. It'll be a big thing for NOK. If you're really serious about it."

Serious about NOK? *Serious?* Neither Justin, Ryan, nor Amanda could believe the *manager* was serious.

40

ALARM

WHEN JUSTIN, RYAN, AND AMANDA CAME DOWN FROM THE studio, they were met with applause from the kids waiting for them in the lobby, every one of whom wanted to talk and to join NOK. It took almost an hour before Giambelli was able to get his guests free to go home. They stepped outside into cold and dark, and Justin cried joyfully, "Snow!"

It fell out of blackness and suddenly became white and visible in the illumination from the parking-lot light. Giambelli looked at the steady fall, and there was no joy in his voice as he said, "This is going to be a hell of a commute."

In the car, Justin thought Mr. Giambelli was sort of grim the way he made everybody check their seat belts.

The snow flew at them through the beams of the headlights. It flew against the windshield and stuck until the wipers pushed it aside. Justin was thinking of frozen winter and he felt warm. He was thinking of ice skating and his birthday, a month away in January. His parents would *have* to get together for his birthday.

Out on Route 128, going north toward the New Hampshire turn-off, it was pretty, the red taillights of the cars strung out ahead like Christmas lights in the darkness. But Mr. Giambelli looked tense. A couple of times Justin felt the car lose traction and begin to skid, but then Mr. Giambelli got control back and they continued on their way home.

An eighteen-wheeler came up fast on the entry ramp next to them and seemed to be racing them for position. It angled into traffic several cars ahead of them, but then it kept going right across *all* the lanes. The red lights ahead got brighter at the same instant and the trailer stretched across the road blocking everything coming at it and sliding and the cab jerked around *facing* them and Mr. Giambelli cursed and braked and turned and the car slid and all the other cars were skidding and Justin felt a deep stab of terror and, simultaneously, his mind raced ahead to his birthday again and, just like someone had videotaped it for him, he had a clear picture of his parents there together on his birthday, but he wasn't there. Then the windows were filled with a blurry red light and his body was snapped against the taut restraint of his seat belt.

". . . On 128, state police report a multicar accident on the north-bound side just south of the Concord exit where a tractor-trailer has jackknifed. Traffic is backed up all the way to the Mass Pike off ramp. Police are advising alternate routing."

Gamble, Skip, Nelle, and Pennyworth were each still tuned to Giambelli's station listening to calls and commentary about NOK that continued to come in to the next talk-show host. Gamble and Skip separately had the same frightening thought: Justin would be coming home on 128. And then, with relief: But he would have left a lot earlier, right after the program.

". . . We have a report now that our own Jim Giambelli and his young guests from this afternoon's show were in a car involved in the multicar collision northbound on 128. We're waiting for further word."

Gamble, Skip, Nelle, and Pennyworth each started calling the station and the Massachusetts State Police. But the lines were busy.

Skip called Gamble. "Have you heard anything?"

"No."

"I'm frightened, Gamble."

"Me, too."

"I mean, I'm really scared."

"That's two of us. Remember, I didn't want him to go to Boston. Not at all. He'd be safe at home now."

"If you hadn't started this whole fucking thing with divorce," Skip said, "he *would* be safe at home now."

"Is this all you can think of to do with the phone—attack me?

What if he's trying to get one of us? It was *Pennyworth* who got him into this," and Gamble hung up.

Pennyworth felt something he hadn't felt in many, many, many years. He felt helpless.

He had remained in his office in case Justin—or *someone*—called. He had been on the phone with Giambelli's station manager. Nothing. He had been on the phone with a captain in the state police. The accident victims had been triaged to three separate hospitals. The captain didn't have any names yet.

Pennyworth sat in gloom. For a few seconds he heard what he suspected was young Weld's voice, but he couldn't make out the words, and then the phone rang.

"I'm terrified," Nelle said. "Whatever's happened to Justin, I blame you for every bit of it. You and your craving for attention. That's what got Justin into this."

Pennyworth squared off. "Justin deserves every opportunity to make his case in court and in the media."

"The case in court, Pennyworth, is going to be your ass. You're fired as Justin's lawyer."

"Yes? Who's firing me?" But Pennyworth knew full well.

"His guardian ad litem is firing you."

Gamble started when the phone rang out in the silence of the house. But then she was furious when it was Skip again. "You're blocking both our lines!"

"I'm getting off right away. I just want you to know that was me being scared about Justin, that's why I jumped on you. I'm sorry. It wasn't fair."

"Well, I'm scared, too. I told you."

"I'd be there with you if I could, if I didn't have my own phone to mind."

Gamble heard herself being gentle with Skip and it felt comfortable. "I know. I'd want you here if it wasn't for that."

"Call me as soon as you know anything."

"Of course—and you, too."

"Of course."

"*That 128 situation continues to back up traffic all the way to the Mass Pike off ramp, but one lane has been opened northbound at the site of the accident. State police report thirty-six injuries requiring medical attention, but there are no reported fatalities.*"

*   *   *

Pennyworth debated calling Gamble or Skip to see if they knew whether or not Justin, the other children, and Giambelli were safe. But he did not want to alarm either parent if they did not yet know that their son might have been in an accident. Besides, Gamble and Skip hardly considered him a family friend. He debated calling Nelle. Perhaps she had been in touch with the parents. Finally he remained in his gloom, unconnected to anyone.

Nelle also had misgivings about calling either Whitney and for the same reason as Pennyworth—that they might not yet know that Justin had been in an accident. But after half an hour of uncertainty, she called Gamble.

Gamble knew nothing. She wanted to keep the line open for Justin, but she was terribly worried, she was distraught, she needed to talk to someone, she felt so alone, and then, abruptly, she said, "But I've got to get off, I've got to," and she hung up.

Nelle called Skip. Gamble answered. Nelle said, "I'm terribly sorry, Gamble, I was trying to get Skip. I must've dialed your number."

She hung up and carefully dialed Skip and got Gamble again. "I'm sorry. I don't know what it is. My phone must be fucked up." Nelle hung up again. But she was too rattled to try Skip another time.

She sat there in her office, her radio continuing to give her information about road conditions around Boston, but nothing helpful about Justin and Giambelli. How did they *know* that Giambelli had been in the 128 accident? The station manager didn't know. He'd said, "All I know is, someone called it in, but we got cut off, the woman who took the call got cut off. But we got a pretty good eyewitness account of the accident first. Though she said the call kept fading away, she could hardly hear the caller. Then, nothing. Zilch."

When Gamble heard the doorbell, she jumped. She hurried to the door, but she had to force her legs to move. She was afraid she'd open the door and a police officer would be standing there with horrible news. But when she opened the door, it was Skip.

"*Oh, God,*" she said, thinking he had gotten the horrible news himself and could not bear to have told her over the phone.

"What *is* it?" Skip said, clearly alarmed by Gamble.

"Nothing, nothing. Is it okay?"

"I don't know. Have you heard something?"

"No . . . Skip, why aren't you at your phone?"

"I told a pal at the telephone company I have an emergency situation. I told him about Justin. He got me hooked up to call for-warding. My calls will come here."

They looked at each other, sharing their mutual helplessness and dread for a few seconds, and then they took each other in their arms and pressed themselves together tightly.

Giambelli had done something extraordinary. Or fate had done something extraordinary for him. At the moment of multiple colli-sions all about him, he had managed to maneuver in such a way that, when he was both front- and back-ended, and hit again on the driver's side, none of the children were injured. Somehow his shoulder got pummeled and his head struck the window next to him, but there was no blood and the car ran without hesitation or any sounds of imminent malfunction.

When it was safe to do so, he got out. The drivers around him were eminently polite and also subdued and shaky, just as he was. They exchanged insurance information and commended each other for being alive and relatively uninjured.

When he got back into his car, he picked up the phone and called the station. Whomever he was talking to didn't seem to hear him so well. He couldn't hear *her* so well. It was either the weather conditions or something wrong with the phone because of the accident. Finally the phone quit entirely.

Eventually the police came along and sorted out what had hap-pened and then got the cab of the tractor-trailer pulled out of the way. The traffic slowly filtered into the single lane going north.

A few minutes up the road there was a turnoff to a Roy Rogers and a gas station and Giambelli followed the turnoff, but when he saw the lines of people waiting to use the outdoor telephone booths, he just kept going and got right back on 128. The plows had been out up here and the going wasn't bad at all if you took it at about thirty-five to forty. A couple of times he tried the phone again, but it had become useless.

There were no roadside facilities along the highway to New Hamp-shire and it was almost eight o'clock before Giambelli got to Nashua and pulled off at a service station and called the kids' parents.

"Oh," he said to Gamble, "Justin's fine. They're all fine. But I'm going to have to make another stop before I bring them home. They're a little hungry. They're ready to eat the upholstery."

41
BLACKIE'S HOUSE

AFTER GIAMBELLI'S CALL, SKIP GOT OUT A BOTTLE OF Scotch for himself and a particularly good bottle of white wine for Gamble. He started to ice the wine. Gamble watched him and then said, "No. I need something strong. Give me some Scotch."

When he brought it to her and she reached for it, he saw that her hand was trembling. He put the drink down and took her hand in his.

"I do miss your touch sometimes," Gamble said.

"I miss touching you sometimes."

"Well, we did one thing right. Justin."

"Yes."

They touched their glasses together and drank.

"Two things, actually," Skip said, and grinned.

Gamble smiled back. "The house," she said.

"Right on."

They had the same sense of humor.

When Giambelli drove up to the Whitneys', Gamble and Skip were outside before he'd even stopped the car.

Justin was unprepared for the way his parents greeted him. They each embraced him as if they would embrace him right into themselves. Then it was as if his parents had never argued. They were kind to each other, even touched each other, warm together in their mutual love for him, and Justin sensed it all.

He was very tired and they both came up to his room with him, and after he'd brushed his teeth and gotten into his pajamas, they sat with him and told him he didn't even have to go to school the next day, he could sleep as late as he wanted.

Mr. Pennyworth called while they were sitting with him, and so did Nelle, and Mr. Pennyworth got him on the phone to say good night, and so did Nelle. And then his mother began to read to him and Justin saw his mother begin to cry and his father placed his hand on his mother's and then placed his arm around her shoulder and took the book and continued to read. After a while Justin was vaguely aware of the guitar music off in some sleepy night distance and his mother's lips on his cheek and then his father's on his forehead and he went to sleep in the sweet kindness of his best dream having come true.

But sometime in the dark he awoke and heard his parents arguing downstairs and then he heard his father's car driving away.

"Look what Blackie did," Ryan said. "See this? I let him out of the house for his afternoon walk? And he got out in the snow and boy was he surprised. He just looked around, his ears twitching, you know? So all of a sudden he got busy and he got digging like crazy. I never saw anything like it. Look. He made this hole. It's a tunnel. It goes all the way back here, see? Underneath here, he made himself a snow home. And this is his escape passage coming out over here, see? Pretty neat, huh?"

Justin looked at it for a minute and then he ran and tramped down the tunnel and jumped on the snow home until he had crushed it down, Ryan yelling at him, *"Hey! Hey! Quit it!"* and trying to grab hold of Justin long enough to stop him, but Ryan couldn't, and Justin went on and destroyed the escape tunnel as well.

"What'd you do that for, Justin?"

"This isn't his real home," Justin said. "His *real* home is inside."

"You're crazy!" Ryan said. "Blackie worked so hard. Look at all the work you ruined."

"His real home's inside."

Justin listened to Nelle and Pennyworth arguing. The three of them were in Nelle's office and Nelle and Pennyworth were arguing about who was going to take care of him in court. It was grown-up arguing, sort of polite, but it was arguing and it was like they were each appealing to him in some way, like he was the judge. It sounded a long way away. It had to do with whether Mr. Pennyworth was fired as his lawyer or whether Justin wanted to tell Nelle that Mr. Pennyworth was still his lawyer before Mr. Pennyworth had to leave and go someplace. It just went on like that.

"You two sound like my parents. *Stop it!*"

"We should never have done that in front of Justin," Nelle said.

"I have never been out of control in front of a client before," Pennyworth said.

"Were you really out of control? I thought you were just putting on one of your jury acts."

"You dragged me down," Pennyworth said.

"I would characterize it differently. Two drowning people dragging each other down."

Pennyworth thought. He sighed. "Fair enough."

"Justin is very important to both of us."

"Thank you for acknowledging my concern."

"I thought you were using him, Weld."

"What changed your mind?"

"Justin's trust in you." She looked at Pennyworth from her seat behind the desk. "I bow to that. I trust Justin."

"That's a specious sort of reasoning."

"It's a reasoning of the heart rather than the mind, I grant you. But I suspect there's more heart involved on your part than you're willing to acknowledge. Sometime you must tell me exactly why you took Justin on." Nelle studied Pennyworth again. "Do you know?"

Pennyworth thought. "In all honesty, I can't answer that question."

The restaurant they decided upon turned out to be mediocre, but it was neutral territory—neither of them had been to it—and that seemed to be important. The more neutral the setting, the more likely something important might come of it.

Pennyworth said, "My friend Tuttle filled me in on your argument in Swain v. Conroy. I'm pleased to say I'm impressed. So was Tuttle."

"I wound Mr. Tuttle's clock in that one."

Pennyworth placed his knife and fork carefully near the edge of his plate. He looked at Nelle.

"Are you waiting for something?" she said.

"It's your turn to say something to me."

"All right." She put her knife and fork down and touched her lips with her napkin. "After I fired you, I realized a more objective view of what you've been up to on Justin's behalf. I can't say I really understand it. I see pieces of it here and there, but I don't know how they relate. The way you're doing this is not any way I ever gave much thought to. Like Capablanca, I am not much interested in positions that don't occur in real play."

"Ah, but Nelle, we are in real play. If you promise not to attempt to fire me again, I will explain the strategy and the tactics."

"I have a board back at my place."

"I remember. We could go there and play with real positions."

42

THE DISPOSITION OF A JUDGE

WHEN, THE NEXT MORNING, PENNYWORTH WENT TO SEE Linda Gray, the marriage counselor, he felt an uneasiness that he soon identified as yet another premonition. If he were fool enough to get married, he might end up seeing a marriage counselor professionally, though not as an attorney.

What placed that thought in my mind? Pennyworth wondered.

You did, the Voice said. The thought of marriage has crossed your mind.

Well, yes, there was Nelle, sweet Nelle, the intellectual sharpshooter, his thrilling bedmate, his partner now in the safe conduct of Justin through the trials of divorce. Justin and Nelle, between them, had put Pennyworth in serious mind of fatherhood for the first time in his life.

You already have a child, the Voice said.

Yes? Who?

Young Weld.

"I've spoken to Dr. Salmon and she's in agreement," Linda Gray said. "The Whitneys are hopeless. I don't see what you or the Court hope to accomplish by forcing them through further counseling."

"Dr. Gray, in your profession you are subject to a great deal of ventured manipulation."

"All the time."

"And you spot it all the time, as I do. Therefore, I will not attempt to manipulate you. I will tell you straightforward what I hope may be accomplished here. I hope that you will come to find the interests of the child to be superior to those of the parents."

"Then what?"

"Counsel them accordingly. Bring them together."

"Neither you nor I can save that marriage."

"It's not the marriage I'm trying to save. It's Justin."

Dr. Gray looked about herself as if she had lost something in the room.

*　*　*

That afternoon was Dr. Gray's first session with the Whitneys together. Her prior interviews had been with them individually. Now she would see if indeed there was some underlying structure of commonality between them.

"When you thought Justin might have been in an accident," she said, "you had warm, affectionate feelings about each other."

"I was scared shitless," Gamble said. "The feeling passed as soon as I knew Justin was safe."

"Skip?"

"Gamble was the only one who could understand how I felt. I mean, she's the only other parent of Justin."

"I see."

"Then we got into an argument. She threw me out of the house. My house."

"No more than half of it is your house," Gamble said. "And maybe not that much."

As she had feared, Dr. Gray had once again come across the Whitneys' underlying structure of antagonism.

"Sometimes," Dr. Gray said, "the house seems more important to you two than Justin."

"We are not arguing about Justin," Gamble said.

"No, indeed," Skip said. "I can tell you one more thing Gamble and I aren't arguing about."

"What's that?"

"If we weren't each under court order, we wouldn't be going through all this bullshit with you."

Dr. Gray began to consider Pennyworth's suggestion that perhaps the child's interests might be superior to those of the parents.

The child, that night, slept in a sleep so deep he could not rouse himself from it no matter how desperately he wished to escape it.

Someone was chasing Justin through the house with an ax. Justin ran into furniture, stumbled against walls, fell down the stairs, but the axer did not touch the house at all. The ax was for Justin. The axer was going to split Justin head to crotch and Justin would die.

He ran outside into the darkness. In the woods there was a figure ahead of him, just some motion Justin glimpsed, but he was sure it was Mr. Pennyworth and he cried out to him.

Pennyworth was back in his house, alone again, alone in bed, but not alone in sleep.

He was in a dark place, hurrying away from something dreadful, he did not know what. A voice was crying out to him, pleading for him to stop, wait. Pennyworth began to run, but no matter how fast he ran, he made little progress.

Now he knew his pursuer was Justin. Exhausted, he turned on Justin.

"Stop following me!" Pennyworth cried at Justin. But it was not Justin. It was young Weld.

Gamble and Skip, Bagley and Bredwell, Nelle and Pennyworth assembled before Rutherford B. Stickney for the dispositional hearing in his courtroom. The door was shut—juvenile court was in session. Justin was in school.

Stickney sat hunched forward behind the sidebar, his eyes making a slow review of the attendees at the counsel tables.

"In the matter of the petition brought under 169C, it is of considerable pertinence to note that this Court has jurisdiction over the parents as well as the child.

"The Court is charged with doing everything within its power toward the rectification of any situation that jeopardizes a minor. I hope you all understand that.

"I have heard testimony here that can be neither skirted nor denied.

"The psychiatrist spent several hours with all parties in interview and evaluation. She testified to the present harm and future peril to which Justin is subject. She testified that the behavior of the parents, as it is constituted in their divorce proceedings, seriously and adversely affects the child. She testified as to a real element of life risk. She testified as to the danger of subsequent injury to the child—specifically and in particular the danger of adolescent suicide.

"I cannot ignore the findings of the psychiatrist.

"Both parties have neglected the child by pursuing the divorce.

"The findings of the psychiatrist meet the criteria of 169C.

"Therefore, the Court orders the following.

"That marriage counseling, which I understand has already been initiated, be continued and that after an appropriate length of time, to be determined by the counselor, the counselor will report to the Court.

"That Mr. and Mrs. Whitney and Justin, together or individually, continue consultation and therapy with Dr. Salmon. It is the Court's intent in so ordering that Justin be afforded every opportunity through prophylactic therapy of undoing the harm and lingering peril caused him by the divorce. . . . We want to do whatever can be done now to get rid of the life risk in the adolescent years.

"The Court permits the child to remain with the parents under the arrangements stipulated and presently in effect.

"The Court makes the following orders of protection for the child.

"That the parents henceforth refrain from harmful conduct against the child.

"That the parents refrain from acts of commission or omission—as defined by the psychiatrist and set forth in the written order—that tend to afford the child present harm and future peril."

Both Bagley and Bredwell had risen.

"You'll get your turn, gentlemen. Let me finish mine." Stickney addressed himself to Gamble and Skip, looking first at one and then at the other, as if he were following a tennis match. "Mrs. Whitney, Mr. Whitney, I have stopped short of ordering cohabitation—which might be construed by los supers as cruel and unusual punishment. Now, counselors, who's first?"

Bagley got up and said, "The orders of protection, Your Honor. They strike me as pretty loose. What do they mean?"

"They mean, Thou shalt not get divorced."

"With all respect, Judge Stickney, I don't think you can order that."

"I can order anything I want. The divorce court can't override it."

"Thank you, Your Honor." Bagley sat down. Bredwell didn't get up.

"Is everybody crazy here?" Gamble said.

She did not expect an answer, but she got one—from the judge. "Mr. Pennyworth, at any rate, is not." He looked around. "Anyone else? Ms. Vance? Mr. Bredwell? . . . What have we here? Silence in the court. Without admonishment? I find it eerie.

"Well, before I leave you good people to burn my ears in my absence, I will add this. I hesitate to imagine the chilling effect other decisions of this sort would have."

Stickney got up. Pennyworth said, "All rise."

"The man is crazy," Gamble said. *"Crazy."*

"What we have here," Bagley said, "is a rogue judge."

"Where did he go to law school," Skip said, "planet X?"

"It would seem," Bredwell said, "that he went to the Pennyworth School of Law and he attended very recently."

"I don't like what that implies," Gamble said. "Are you implying that Pennyworth paid him off or something?"

"No. I'm saying straight out that Pennyworth schooled him. In fact, brother Bagley, he took us all to school."

"Does that mean I can't get my divorce?" Gamble said.

"Oh, no, no, it couldn't mean that," Bredwell said. But he looked at Bagley.

Bagley was biting his thumbnail. Bredwell, Gamble, and Skip waited on him.

"That sonofabitch Pennyworth," Bagley said softly. *"That sonofabitch.* He's made a fucking tar baby." He looked at Bredwell. "Every time we move we get more stuck."

"That's certainly been what he's managed to do," Gamble said.

Bagley went on. "I don't think superior court divorce orders can supersede juvenile court orders."

Bredwell nodded. "It's an interesting point of law. One that we are now impelled to explore."

Bagley said to Gamble and Skip, "Divorce court is *part* of superior court, but . . . Oh, we can move to override juvenile court in superior court. But the authority pursuant to the divorce statute cannot override the authority pursuant to the child protection statute. We get nowhere in divorce court . . ."

After some silence, Skip said, "Do I have to stay married to her?"

"Do something," Gamble said. "What can you do?"

"We go to another arm of the superior court. Another judge. We appeal Stickney's ruling. We get heard by another judge."

"A third judge?" Skip said.

"A third judge. We start over in an entirely new process in a new court. We have a de novo process on only the question of neglect."

"Oh, God," Gamble said, "a *third* court."

"Pennyworth's certainly having his way with us, isn't he?" Bagley said, with a little admiration in his voice.

"You've certainly had your way with this Court," Stickney said to Pennyworth in Stickney's chambers.

"I prefer to think that Justin is the beneficiary of justice."

"You know I'll get overridden. Nobody's going to stop divorce."

"I don't recall that you specifically ordered anyone not to get a divorce," Nelle said. "Not in writing. It was oral. I thought that was clever of you."

"Foresighted, Ms. Vance. Now, Mr. Pennyworth, as we sit here chatting about cleverness, your cleverness is a wonder by half, isn't it? By more than half, I suspect." Stickney looked at Nelle. "Do you know what he did? Why he came to juvenile court with this preposterous petition?"

"He explained it to me."

"Well then, let's see if I'm properly appreciative. It began to come to me when I saw how far you had brought me with Dr. Salmon and her evaluation."

"Your astuteness has been a pleasure, Judge," Pennyworth said.

"I think we will suspend and continue regarding my astuteness, Mr. Pennyworth. You couldn't go to divorce court and get an order for the litigants to go to a shrink, could you? No, indeed you couldn't. So you came to juvie where you could, and I did, and furthermore you procured this fantastic ruling out of it, entirely fantastic, but ineluctable given the evidence you presented. I shall be a laughingstock. I feel as if I had been transported by the little people during the night, fairies or goblins or something that picked me up there and transported me here. I wish I had never met you, Mr. Pennyworth."

"It was the Devil made you do it," Nelle said.

"Yes, I've heard that about Mr. Pennyworth. Do you know where we are? Of course you do, you orchestrated it. You have two courts at odds with each other and I foresee a third court entering."

"I suspect so," Pennyworth said, "if Bagley and Bredwell are on their mettle."

"Do you have visions of it going to the Supreme Court, Mr. Pennyworth? Los Supremes?"

"The state supreme court possibly. But before that, Judge Stickney, I foresee that you will be recognized as possessing the wisdom of Solomon. I foresee you doing much to resolve the discord among the three courts."

"Ah, Mr. Pennyworth. So kind. Are you going to inform me as to how this is to happen?"

"I believe, Judge, in your wisdom, you'll find your way to it yourself."

43

"WHAT THE HELL ARE WE DOING HERE?"

THE PSYCHIATRIST'S REPORT FOR JUDGE HASKINS IN superior court was of a markedly different substance from that for Judge Stickney in that it addressed issues over which the juvenile court had no jurisdiction.

Copies of the second evaluation were duly forwarded to Ted Bagley, Esq., Stuart Bredwell, Esq., and Nelle Vance, Esq., but Pennyworth elected to hand-deliver Judge Haskins's copy himself. He wanted to sound out Judge Haskins's reaction and intentions as a result of Judge Stickney's orders.

"Of course I've seen it," Judge Haskins said. "It tells the Whitneys to cease and desist from the process of getting a divorce. At least, that's what I believe its intent is. Is that your understanding?"

"Yes," said Pennyworth.

"And so you've come to see me to try to find out what I'm going to do about it." She picked up the psychiatrist's report. "I'm sure this is very interesting reading, but not so urgent you had to bring it yourself."

"I think you'll find it interesting, Judge. It leads to some rather novel judicial conclusions regarding the Whitneys."

"But what you've really come for is to try to find out what I'm going to do about Judge Stickney's orders."

"You see right through me, Judge."

"From the beginning, Mr. Pennyworth. Though sometimes you are so transparent as to be invisible. Then I have a wee bit of trouble following you. What I'm going to do about Judge Stickney's orders is nothing."

"I had a professor in law school who advised the very same— whenever possible."

"I don't believe you, Mr. Pennyworth." She picked up Dr. Salmon's report. "Is this really interesting reading?"

"For a psychiatrist's report, it's a page-turner. For our purposes, anyway."

"Yours and your client's."

"And the Honorable Court's."

"Well, Mr. Pennyworth, I am aware of the impending proceeding before Judge St. Marie here in superior court. But I intend to proceed here with *Whitney* regardless. The juvenile court order is directed to the parents and has no authority over this court. This court will be in session as long as the Whitneys care to proceed. How they respond to Judge Stickney is up to them. How Judge St. Marie responds to Judge Stickney et al. is, for now, a separate matter and the business of the other court. How does that sit with you, Mr. Pennyworth?"

"Quite comfortably, Judge."

Pennyworth had a meeting across the waiting room in Jack St. Marie's chambers with St. Marie, Nelle, Bagley, and Bredwell. Bagley and Bredwell would get Dr. Salmon's report in the next day's mail. Pennyworth wondered if they'd see where the report aimed the court.

He rather thought not. The concept was a unique one—the concept that Pennyworth would extract from the report and propose to the Court.

Judge Haskins reread portions of Dr. Salmon's report not so much for the psychiatrist's observations but to attempt to foresee what Pennyworth would make of them:

No distinction can be made between these two parents as nurturers. . . . Apart from the divorce and the mutually antagonistic behavior of the parents toward each other, Justin enjoys beneficial and mutually reinforcing relationships with each parent. . . .

This is a dual-career household. Both parents work and there is no distinction to be made between them as to parental time they have in the past or will in the future afford Justin. Indeed, that situation continues to be in effect even though the parents are separated and Justin's time is divided between two households. Parenting continues to be shared and because of the demands of their business careers (which may necessitate travel out of town or work late into the evening), the parents are dependent upon one another for Justin's care when one or the other is not available. This is an arrangement they have accorded each other throughout Justin's life and that they continue even now. Nor do they have any argument with each other about the child's need for each of them.

However, in their mutual antagonism during this period, the parents have each provided unstable environments for Justin. I will return to this after some further explanation.

I have spent four hours with Justin, one hour at a time. I have spent two hours with each parent, one hour at a time. Of the three, Justin presented as the most mature, the parents as the most childish.

The parents exhibit their oddly childish behavior in their mutual obsession with who is going to gain custody of the biggest toy in their lives, that being the house that they caused to be constructed together and that they both worked on as well, contributing their own labors.

Both parents exhibit a keen interest in things they own or would like to own or would like to retain in order to prevent the other from gaining. The parents are very material and status minded. Possessions are very important to them as status symbols, as indicators of attainment. The house is to each a symbol of his or her accomplishments. No symbol, no accomplishment. The toy then is perceived as much more than a toy in this context. It becomes a life and death issue.

The house is also the spoils of the marriage. Whoever gains possession of the house has won the war between the two antagonists and, for bonus, deprives the other of the personal work the other has invested in it. It is thus that because the house is so important to each of them that each wishes to gain sole possession of it.

Thus each parent sees the house as both the prize and the battleground. In our interviews neither parent lent very much emphasis to the house being a place of shelter or nurture. They each, however, betrayed an interest in Justin as a key to who will gain residential possession of the house. (And here I do not wish to suggest that either parent is deficient in love for Justin.)

By example, Mrs. Whitney treated herself as a property she was representing and attempted to sell herself (her cause) as if she were herself a house and I was a potential buyer. Mrs. Whitney made an error of speech. She said, "I will take much better care of the house, I mean Justin, than Skip will." And Mr. Whitney assured me that Mrs. Whitney was undisciplined and irresponsible in her housekeeping responsibilities but that he himself saw to these "duties" daily (rather as if the house were being toilet-trained) and that he would see to it that the house was properly maintained for Justin not only now, but for Justin to inherit. I feel this demonstrates again the life and death nature of the dispute over the house.

Justin, on the other hand, who is the most vulnerable of the three, finds that the house itself provides a stable and stabilizing and reassuring environment (see my earlier references to Clyde Worm and Blackie the rabbit) when the parents, in their antagonism with each other, are providing exactly the opposite.

Before proceeding to my recommendations I would like to say again, and emphasize it, that both parents love Justin and not to the exclusion of the other. In dramatic contrast to the rest of their behavior toward each other, wherever Justin is concerned, the partners can reach agreement. To this I must add that the primary objective of the recommendations that follow is to disrupt the child's life as little as possible.

Ah, Pennyworth, Judge Haskins thought, putting the psychiatrist's report down, you brought it all together. For surely Pennyworth had discussed the report with Dr. Salmon prior to its being written. Where are we, Judge Haskins thought, but back in that house, that wretched house?

Pennyworth still had his case to make, he still had to demonstrate clearly and convincingly that where he was headed was where the Court ought to follow. Without danger of appeal and override. Which made her think of Jack St. Marie and what might be proceeding in his court that could affect hers.

She was interested by Pennyworth, but he was exhausting. And one can overdo the wearing away.

In chambers, Jack St. Marie, still in his robe and also deprived of the opportunity for a private sandwich during lunch break, looked across his desk at Pennyworth, Vance, Bagley, and Bredwell and said, "All right, lady and gentlemen, what the hell are we doing here?"

Bredwell began to speak, but St. Marie went on. He said to Bagley and Bredwell, "How could you two be so incompetent? You let a district judge in effect bar your clients from getting a divorce."

"He's a rogue judge," Bagley said.

"I suppose," said St. Marie, "we have Mr. Pennyworth to thank for this order. But it was Judge Stickney who signed it. Well?"

Bredwell said, "I ask Your Honor to consolidate the two cases. The divorce and the petition for neglect."

"Stuart, you said that as a joke. I *know* you said that as a joke. We have two statutes in conflict here. The statute governing divorce and the statute governing child protection. Do you know where that leaves us?" He looked around as if someone might actually answer him. "It leaves us in never-never land. We are in the twilight zone of law and make no mistake about it."

He looked at Pennyworth without affection. "We run a nice, stable judicial system in this state, Mr. Pennyworth."

"It is truly admirable, Your Honor."

"I thought you'd probably ask me to suspend and continue, Mr. Pennyworth."

"No thanks, Your Honor."

"The motion would have been denied. Ms. Vance, anything to offer?"

"I'm not sure Ms. Vance has any standing in this matter," Pennyworth said. "I'm not sure she should be here."

"She's here because I invited her. Well?"

"The psychiatrist's testimony was convincing."

"Ah dear, ah dear." St. Marie sat way back in his chair. "Then there is nothing to do but go through the entire de novo proceeding. I hope you're all being well compensated."

"A penny on the dollar, Your Honor," Pennyworth said.

"Pro bono," Nelle said.

"My client is going to be very unhappy about this additional expense," Bagley said.

"This was just going to be a nice, simple divorce," Bredwell said. He looked at Pennyworth. "Do you realize you're going to cost these people *thousands* before this is through?"

"It's not going in my pocket," Pennyworth said.

St. Marie sat forward. "Never-never land. Twilight zone. I'm going to need a long time to search and think about this. Then we'll hear the petition from the beginning. I'm setting a date six weeks from now."

"What about the other court?" Bredwell said.

"I know nothing about the other court. I'm hearing an appeal of an order from a district court."

Outside, Bagley, somewhat dazed, said to Bredwell, "He's right. What the *hell* are we doing here?"

"It was going to be just a nice, simple divorce," Bredwell said again. "We agreed we'd do our best for that, didn't we, Ted?"

44

A DEVIL OF A BIRTHDAY

CHRISTMAS.

Justin spent Christmas Eve to Christmas Day noon with his mother. Then his father picked him up and he spent the rest of Christmas Day on until noon the following day with his father. He received much the same presents from both parents (new cross-country skis from his mother, new downhill skis from his father, video game cartridges from both, etc.) and though he had thought he had wanted the presents he got, he didn't much care once he got them.

He was thinking about his birthday coming up in January. There he was on Christmas Day thinking about his birthday. Dumb. It didn't make sense—he didn't want presents on his birthday either.

But his birthday was different from Christmas. It had to do with his parents.

Dr. Gray, the marriage counselor, reported to Judges Haskins and Stickney that her efforts were futile, that the situation between the Whitneys was deteriorating, and that she had therefore scheduled only one more session, set for just after the first of the year, and that short of a dramatic change of attitude on the part of both Whitneys, efforts at marriage and divorce counseling would be terminated at that time and that she would offer a report and be available for consultation in chambers. "But, please, let's not protract this farce."

"Weld, Jim Giambelli."
"Yes, sir."
"This is about Justin Whitney."
"Go ahead, Jim."
"That NOK show we did—we got more letters on that than any radio show I ever did. People who listen to talk shows aren't letter writers—not usually. They get on the phone. Oh, we may get a stray letter or two here and there, but the NOK show drew forty-three letters."
"Mostly from kids?"
"Mostly from kids. They didn't hear it. They want a rebroadcast. The people here want Justin on 'The New England Show.' "
"Television."
"Yes."
"I don't think his parents are going to be comfortable with that. It was a mean experience they went through."
"I appreciate that. But Justin's been in the newspapers now. Word is getting around. Outside Boston. Outside Manchester. There's interest in what he and his friends are doing."
"You'd have to talk to the parents."
"You have no objection that he do the show?"
"None. You'll have to talk to Nelle Vance about it, too. I think she's the key to any progress you might make with the Whitneys."
"All right."

"I presume you've spoken to Justin."

"Oh, yes. I brought him copies of the mail. Except for some of the lunatic adult stuff. The Whitneys got some letters, too. Direct, not through the station. Telling them to keep their little brat off the airways and home where he belongs."

Two weeks before Justin's birthday he handed out his party invitations at school and brought one to his father. His father opened it carefully, knowing what it was, and then seeing the careful, cursive, still boyish handwriting in the blanks of the card.

"I gave one to Mom, too."

"Well, she's giving the party."

"I invited her anyway."

"Look, Justin, your mom and I spoke about this already and she doesn't want me at the party—"

"It's *my* party!"

"So, we'll just have our own party here on another day and—"

"No!"

Late Sunday afternoon Justin was back with his mother. She saw him twitching with anger at her. "Why *can't* Dad be here? It's *my* birthday."

"You can have anyone you want, *anyone at all,* but your father is not entering this house. Not that day or any other while I'm here."

"But, Mom—"

"He can give you a birthday party himself. He told me he'd do that."

"I don't want two parties. I want one party here. It's the only present I want."

"A lot of kids would feel lucky getting two parties—"

"Then I won't go to it. I'll stay in my room. I won't come down."

"You'll change your mind. When your friends are here."

"No, I won't. Besides, I'm going to tell everyone *not to come.*"

"Justin, I will not have your father at that party. It's our party. Yours and mine."

Linda Gray was weary before she even started the final session with Gamble and Skip Whitney. Usually she was engaged by her work, stimulated by the work itself, and by hope; but the Whitneys simply wearied her. At least she had an associate in this last travail —Nelle Vance had asked to take part.

"No one's trying to force you to do anything, Gamble," Dr. Gray said.

"You've been trying to force me to get back together with Skip. That's the point of this, isn't it?"

"The point has been to try to get you two talking, one way or another. The idea is to address your problems, not divorce them."

"I bet you say that to all your clients," Skip said. "Wiseass professional cliché."

"Rooty toot toot for you, Skip. Right on," Gamble said. "I'd like to point out there's only one area where Skip and I need to talk and we do that very well. Justin. We are not divorcing him. We maintain excellent communication about Justin."

"Such as," Nelle said, "communicating straight out with Justin and Skip that no way is Skip going to come to Justin's birthday party."

"It's my party and I'll decide who's going to be there."

"Justin is very upset about this," Nelle said.

"I suppose you're threatening me with the guardian's report."

"I am concerned that Justin is being so needlessly upset. It's the *one* present he wants. *One* party with both of you there. It's *his* birthday—"

"I did it for him, Nelle, old girl. I gave him birth. Something you know nothing about."

"I know Justin's pain. I'm concerned by your refusal to alleviate it."

Gamble crossed her arms and sat back in her chair. She looked at Skip. "You sure seduced these ladies, didn't you? All right! You want to come to the birthday party, come ahead!"

"Thank you. Can I bring anything?"

Gamble ignored him. She spoke to Nelle in a patently sweet voice. "But you'll be there too, dear Nelle. To help keep the peace. As guardian ad litem. I was going to call you anyway. I told Justin he could have *anyone* he wants at the party and guess what? He wants you and he wants Weld Pennyworth." She spoke to Linda Gray just as sweetly. "Now isn't that just *the most beautiful* sort of cooperation? Why don't you come too, Dr. Gray? There's bound to be something for you to poke your nose into."

Nelle brought up the second issue she had to represent for Justin. But both Gamble and Skip were determined that Justin would not go on TV.

Gamble said to Skip, "You can't bring anything. But there are things you can do. You've done them before, so I don't think you'll have a problem. You can do the bonfire and you can clear the ice if it needs it. Also, you can supervise the kids out on the ice. You're good at that. Supervision."

"I'll be glad to."

"What a jolly party we're going to have."

In the evening, Nelle called Pennyworth. "Are you planning to spend the night here Friday?"

"That is my expectation."

"Then bring your skates."

"How very kinky."

"You do have skates, Weld, don't you?"

"I do have skates."

"Then bring them. We're going to a skating party on Saturday." She didn't say *birthday party*, because she was more thinking about the skates and because she wanted to surprise Pennyworth with whose party it was and for what reason.

Later, when Pennyworth accused her of outrageous duplicity, she thought that maybe something had been at work in her, some secret knowledge, that had censored any reference to a *birthday* party. She had even kept Justin's present out of sight in her shoulder bag.

Saturday was bleak with winter, gray with lowering snow clouds, the air chill with gusts of wind that intermittently carried sleet and snow showers.

Nelle turned off the town road and into the Whitneys' driveway between the pines.

"Here?" Pennyworth said.

"Justin wanted us both."

Pennyworth grunted.

"I don't think he knows we're an item."

"An item?"

"As his guardians ad litem, not his guardians ad item. I think that's why he wanted us here."

Pennyworth had dressed in knickers and boldly patterned knee socks—cross-country ski attire. His hockey skates from college were on the back-seat floor next to Nelle's figure skates.

They drove out from between the pines and into the snow-covered meadow, the golden-hued outdoor sculpture that was the Whitney house warmly lit from within and directly in front of them. Pennyworth looked at it grimly. As they drew closer Pennyworth saw activity out on the lake and the cheery flames of a large wood fire at lakeside. He turned his head away.

Sometimes one can forget what one needs to forget. Sometimes one can ignore it. But Pennyworth found himself filling with anxiety.

Pennyworth wanted to struggle. Something in him wanted not only to struggle but to run away. Something else within him, equally desperate, refused *now* to struggle or to run away. He felt within himself the desperate passivity of the patient awaiting surgery.

It is perhaps time, the Voice said.

But still Pennyworth did not know time for what—or what it was that was making him so fearful. He felt his heart driving like a poorly lubricated engine.

Nelle and Pennyworth walked around the outside of the house to the bonfire. It was stacked nearly waist-high with wood. The flames bustled orange and flared outward like pennants in the gusts that charged across the lake. Little figures—boys and girls—skated about in some design that was cosmic in its complexity out where the *Yar* would have been moored. Skip, in a bright yellow ski jacket, patrolled the periphery. Gamble, in a bright green ski jacket, skated with two other women.

Wooden benches had been set near the bonfire. Children's boots of many colors were scattered around them. Music played from speakers and there were beverage urns and stacked cups. Pennyworth glanced at Nelle and saw that she was ignited with inner pleasure. He himself felt numbed with anxiety. His mind would not tell him why he was so anxious. His heart maintained its excessive rate. They sat on a bench and put on their skates.

Justin detached himself from the moving design and skated over to them. "It's *great* you got here. *Fearless.*"

"Happy birthday!" Nelle said.

Birthday. Pennyworth would have left if he had had his own transportation—just as he would have backed away from any avoidable danger that threatened his life.

"Yes, Justin, happy birthday to you. I didn't know." He looked at Nelle. "Nelle didn't tell me."

Justin did something that Pennyworth found painful, something that intruded sorrow into his anxiety. Justin put his hand on Pennyworth's arm. "It's just like all my other birthdays. Nelle can tell you. My friends here. My mom and dad together. A skating party. There's hot chocolate and cider. And my dad stuck some wine in the snow."

"I think I'll have some wine," Pennyworth said and went to it unsteadily on his skates, poured a paper cupful and drank it and followed it with a second.

* * *

The wine and the motion and feel of the ice beneath the blades, once it came back to him, steadied Pennyworth. But he was still preoccupied with his anxiety.

"Pennyworth," Skip said, suddenly skating at his side, "Weld, if that's okay—"

"That's acceptable."

"Thank you for coming. Justin was really eager that you be here."

"I didn't know it was his birthday."

"That's acceptable. I'm sure you've done quite enough for him already."

Pennyworth kept moving and Skip kept right at his side. "Gamble and I always did this for Justin's birthday. This is a sort of re-creation of times gone by."

"So I understand."

"I guess we've got Nelle to thank for bringing it off."

"I guess we do."

"Uh-oh," Skip said, regarding a fallen and crying child. "At least there's no blood."

"There may be internal bleeding," Pennyworth said as Skip skated away to the child.

Then Justin was upon him with some of his friends. "Ah," said Pennyworth, extending a warmly gloved hand, "the famous Ryan . . . Ah, the famous Amanda and the famous Heather . . . Are these the representatives of NOK?"

"We're all NOK here," a small boy said in perhaps a defiant voice, but it was difficult for Pennyworth to tell because the voice was so small.

"And you are?"

The boy didn't answer. Justin said, "His name is Chick."

"No, it isn't," the boy said looking down. "It's Charles," he said tentatively.

There was a moment of splintering sleet. Pennyworth kept moving, skating away from what he was feeling. The sleet hissed against the ice. Pennyworth felt chilled to trembling, as if he had no protective clothing on at all. He felt his gloved hand taken in a gloved hand. He looked over. Nelle smiled up at him. Then she flashed ahead, still smiling, skating backward, and then was at his side again. "Did they ever teach you to do this in hockey? I bet not." She placed his arm around her waist, her hand in his. Pennyworth felt not only frightened but befuddled. The world had turned strange, confusing. "I shouldn't say this, Weld, but you can score with me anytime." Pennyworth could not think of what to say. He was at the mercy of whatever was going on inside him.

Gamble skated to their side. The three of them stopped. "So good of you to come, Weld, Nelle. I could have had a better birthday present than Skip, of course."

"Justin couldn't have," Nelle said. "The two of you here together."

"And what of it? What of it, Nelle? It's all over at five o'clock."

It was getting dark quickly. The children were over at the benches exchanging skates for boots. Skip was allowing the fire to die. The flames were little now, licking into the darkness. The sleet had become a steady, prancing snow. The house up above, lit golden from within, looked the warmest and gentlest of refuges. Pennyworth knew it was not. He would have gone anywhere but in.

The children were all about the table, looking toward the doorway to the kitchen, intent upon the celebration for Justin.

Gamble's voice started in slow song from the kitchen. "Happy birthday . . . to . . . you, . . . Happy . . ."

The children around the table joined in. Pennyworth looked out the window as if there were a driveway out there beyond the window. Instead of gray October there was black January. He felt infinitely more frightened than he had ever felt before. Indeed, he felt dread.

The children's voices had joined together as the cake with its crown of candles was brought in. ". . . birthday . . . dear Justin, . . . happy birthday . . . to you." The cake was set before Justin for him to blow out the candles.

"Remember to make a wish," Gamble said.

Pennyworth had forgotten to make a wish.

A gray and wet October day.

Pennyworth's ninth birthday. They were in the house on the country road outside Peterborough where Weld had spent his whole young life.

They were young Weld's mother, father, and a bunch of pals from Mrs. Ames's third-grade class. The kids had all come home from school together, and there were streamers and balloons in the living room, and the dining room table had been set with birthday-theme plates and napkins and cups and snappers and prizes and little paper cups of candies.

The games had been played and everyone was at the table singing "Happy birthday to you, happy birthday to you, happy birthday, dear We-eld," when Weld saw the sedan pull into the driveway. On the door there was an emblem: Sheriff's Office, Hillsborough County. A man got out and went around to the kitchen entrance.

There was the cake in front of Weld with the candle flames hopping about and he was still small enough that he had to get so close to them to blow them out that he could feel their heat on his face. And he *did* blow them out. He looked up to see what his mother thought of *that,* but she wasn't even paying attention, not paying attention to his birthday cake!

She was looking out into the kitchen where his father and the sheriff were and then young Weld heard his father cry out, "No!" and then, "Mary-Ann! Goddamn it!" and Weld and his friends had been left to deal with the rest of the birthday as best they could.

From time to time Weld could hear the voices of his parents— from upstairs now, a safe distance from the party—and it was the same as all the arguing he had heard from the living room or from their bedroom at night, only not so loud now, and his friends didn't hear it, or pretended they didn't, but *Weld* heard it and it was something sudden, a surprise of sorts, because it had been so long since he had heard it—days or weeks—that he had almost forgotten it.

"She served papers on me," his father later told him, "right there at your birthday party. The divorce papers."

"*I* didn't know they were going to deliver them that day," his mother said. "I had no control over when they were going to be delivered."

Weld's father moved to an apartment in a house in town and Weld went back and forth between his mother and his father and he had things that belonged in one house and things that belonged in the other and things that he wasn't allowed to take back and forth no matter when he had gotten them or from whom. Sometimes he thought he wasn't allowed to take himself back and forth.

A while after the divorce, his mother married again and she and her new husband moved into a house in Nashua—forty-five minutes from Peterborough—and that meant going back and forth over a longer distance. It might have meant going back and forth fewer times (his mother had custody) except that his mother's new husband didn't want Weld around on weekends.

But weekdays Weld was in a new place with none of his old pals, none of the boys and girls he had been with every day since he had been a toddler. Even the trees were unfamiliar.

When Weld's tenth birthday came, he remembered that he hadn't made a wish after blowing out all the candles on his ninth-birthday cake. He hadn't known back then what to wish for, and now that he did, it was too late.

When the tenth birthday came, Weld, who was having headaches at the new school, refused to have a birthday party, and when his mother gave one anyway, he went to his room and wouldn't come out and cried so hard his body shook. His mother's husband told him he was selfish and ungrateful and they were going to return all the gifts they had gotten him and Weld had said that was fine.

His father wanted to give him a birthday party back in Peterborough with all his friends, but Weld had refused it—he didn't want something else bad to happen and most of all he didn't want his friends to remember what had happened at his last birthday party.

A little while after that his father moved to Boston and the back-and-forth was longer and then his father got married again and his new wife already had two kids younger than Weld. His mother had a new baby, too. There were these two families and he didn't belong to either of them, though he thought the other kids did.

Soon enough he was sent to prep school in Pennsylvania and after that he returned to either parental home as infrequently as he could. He preferred to accept the invitations of classmates and friends to come home with them (to *real* homes, Weld felt) over holidays and vacations.

And when he was old enough, he found summer employment away from both homes.

As far as Weld was concerned, his parents were dead. He felt nothing. He had already mourned the loss of the parents he had had before his ninth birthday, mourned their loss so deeply and often when he was ten and eleven and twelve, that he had no mourning left within him.

Sometimes, though, there was a scream within him for the lost child, young Weld.

There is such a thing as to know something so well as to forget it because of its very familiarity. As he watched Justin blowing out the candles on the cake, Pennyworth recalled that the anniversary of a trauma may re-create the trauma.

Justin blew out the candles in one try. I hope you made a wish, Pennyworth thought. Justin looked over at Pennyworth.

The children were gone. Pennyworth would have left before anyone, but Justin had asked that he and Nelle talk to him before they left.

"It's about NOK," Justin said quietly, the three of them sitting on the lower steps of the cantilevered stairway. "Mr. Giambelli says that if I can come on 'The New England Show' and talk about it, people'll see it all around the country."

"I think that's up to your parents, Justin," Nelle said.

"But they won't let me."

"They're still your parents," she said.

Pennyworth might have been monitoring the conversation from outer space—he was a long way from it. Another voice was crying out to him from a long way away.

"Do you want some help cleaning up?" Nelle said to Gamble.

"I can help, too," Skip said.

"It's time for you to go, Skip."

"And *happy birthday* to you, too, Gamble."

"It's *my* birthday," Justin said. "Don't start. *Just don't start.*"

Pennyworth was hearing the Voice crying out, getting nearer.

"I hope you had a happy birthday with your friends," his mother said. "But it's not over. I have some presents for you."

"Me, too," his father said. "You'll get them next weekend."

Justin said, "I made a wish and I blew out all the candles. If you could, would you give me the wish?"

"I don't know," his mother said.

"What is it?" his father said.

"Let me go on 'The New England Show' so I can tell about NOK."

"No," his mother said.

"No," said his father.

"I *need* to tell about it. I'm the head of it."

"*No, Justin.*"

"No."

From right inside himself, finally caught up with himself, so loudly that he thought the others must surely hear, Pennyworth heard his young self, young Weld, cry out.

Pennyworth said loudly, "He has a right to be heard! Do you want me to go to court about it?"

"My God, Weld, you *scared* me. Did you have to be so loud, so *vehement?*"

"Yes."

Nelle could hardly hear his voice above the sound of the car.

Back at her house, Nelle did not know what to do with Pennyworth. He was as remote as if he were in another country. She asked him if he wanted some wine. He asked her if she had the makings for martinis. She said yes. She didn't recall that she'd ever seen him take a hard drink before. He asked for a pitcher. When he made the martinis, she felt as if she were watching a ritual.

In spite of Pennyworth's odd behavior, Nelle felt cozy. The forecast was for snow throughout the night and well into the next day. A major nor'easter. There was oil in the furnace, wood for the wood-stove, and the makings of some good meals in the refrigerator. She felt cozy, but Pennyworth sat across the room by the woodstove with his martini—and the pitcher on the table beside him—and he held his arms about himself as if he were chilled through.

Nelle gave up trying to talk to him. When she found herself getting angry at him, she took her glass of wine and went into the kitchen to make dinner.

Why *didn't* I let my father give me that party back in Peterborough? That's where I wanted to be. Those were the friends I wanted to be with.

Pennyworth thought about it a long time.

He noted that the Voice held back in respectful attention, without commentary, as Pennyworth deliberated with himself. Young Weld was there, too, but he was sleeping a sleep of exhaustion.

When Pennyworth got up he found that he had nearly finished the pitcher of martinis and that his feet were not entirely reliable. He found Nelle in the kitchen checking something in a Dutch oven.

Pennyworth began talking to her. He sounded to himself as if he were summing up for a jury. But the jury was himself. He needed to hear himself out.

"All this time I've been trying to get back at my own parents. All this time that I've been beating up on other parents. I thought it was for young Weld. It *was* for young Weld.

"But that's not what today was all about. Today young Weld came *back*. He *insisted* on coming back. I remembered him. He's been following me around and getting closer and closer . . . but I tried not to pay any attention to him."

Pennyworth began to cry. "I did something terrible, terrible." Nelle came over to him. She wanted to touch him, but she didn't want to interrupt him.

"I *remembered* young Weld today. I rediscovered *myself*. I redis-covered the little boy *I* abandoned back there during the divorce. *I* abandoned him. *I* abandoned me."

Nelle held Pennyworth and he held her and he put his face against her hair and smelled her perfume and the freshness from the time outside and felt his own tears on his cheeks and then wet in her hair.

Pennyworth released her and took a handkerchief from his pocket and addressed his face and eyes and nose with it.

"I'm going upstairs for a while. I'm very tired," he said.

45
THE DEVIL AWAITS

PENNYWORTH WAS PREPARING HIS FINAL ARGUMENT FOR Whitney v. Whitney and extrapolating from that the questions and responses he would need to emphasize most when he examined Dr. Salmon.

He was in his office and the pre-set timer turned on the television set. "The New England Show." Six-thirty on a Sunday evening. Just the time when no one else in the universe would be watching. But Pennyworth watched approvingly.

". . . So Amanda and Heather and me, and I guess it was Chick's idea first, and Ryan, we thought kids ought to have an organization. So we started one at school, but some parents got down on us, so we can't have it there anymore. . . . We call it the National Organization of Kids because we want it to be for all kids and it's not just for divorce, though that's how it started. Like Chick said, it's hard work being a kid and that's why we want to get together and see if we can help each other sometimes. You know, *kids* . . ."

Justin is unsuitably dressed, Pennyworth thought. A blazer, tie, and shirt. Something he would otherwise only wear to weddings and funerals. Gamble's doing, Pennyworth thought.

He got up from the dispersed pages of Justin's file and went over to a bookshelf. He picked up the paperweight and inverted it, righted it, set it on the shelf again, and watched the tumbled snowflakes storm around the trees and cabin, the ever-secure cabin.

Early the next morning, with Gamble's thoroughly reluctant permission, Pennyworth picked up Justin and drove him to school. He told Justin what he hoped to accomplish in the courtroom during the next two days.

"Jeezum," Justin said.

"If I am successful and that is the judge's decree, how would you feel about that?"

"Fearless." Justin paused. "Do you think you can do it?"

"I am going to give it one hell of a try, Justin."

"Fearless."

"I'm going to try to get the judge to see you alone in chambers. Just you and the judge. She'll ask you some questions, you say how you really feel. How would that be?"

"Fearless."

"Is that the new word? *Fearless?*"

"It's your word. I learned it from you."

"Not in the same employment, I don't think. Everything I've just told you, we must keep it a secret. Can you?"

"Yes."

"Fearless," Pennyworth said, following a yellow school bus into the turnoff to the school and then pulling over to a stop in the parking area. Pennyworth reached behind his seat and handed Justin a heavy fist-size object wrapped in taped-together office stationery.

"What's this?" Justin said.

"Your birthday present."

Justin unwrapped the glass paperweight with the swirling snow and trees and cabin inside.

Pennyworth said, "It's old-fashioned, but I liked it very much when I was a boy."

"Gee, thanks, Mr. Pennyworth," Justin said, already entranced by the scene.

Pennyworth explained a little about himself when he had been young Weld. "He wasn't a bad boy, Justin, young Weld wasn't. *I* wasn't. We both have to remember that about ourselves. The divorce *wasn't* our fault."

"It's hard to believe that a lot of times."

"Don't give up on yourself."

"Okay."

"That's something I like about you, Justin. You don't give up on yourself."

"Sometimes it's hard."

Pennyworth looked carefully at the boy. "Do you ever feel like killing yourself?"

Justin looked away. "Yeah," he said, his voice hardly reaching Pennyworth.

"I did too back then. A lot. In a way, I did. . . . Justin?"

"Yes?"

"Forget it."

Justin sat still for a moment and then nodded.

"I can't prevent the divorce. I knew that all along. I told you."

"Yes."

"But here we are. You'd be surprised where we are. Your mom and dad are going to be surprised. And Mr. Bagley and Mr. Bredwell also, I think."

With one brief exception, Pennyworth sat silent as *Whitney v. Whitney* passed from morning to afternoon and eventually from Gamble's libel and pleadings to Skip's answer and cross-libel.

At first both Whitneys were relieved by Pennyworth's silence and abstention. But as Pennyworth *remained* seated and silent, as they began to *hear* his silence, and as their own attorneys began taking quick, anticipatory glances at Pennyworth, both Gamble and Skip became uneasy.

Custody was not an issue. Much of the testimony was a catalogue of material possessions (especially the house, furnishings, appurtenances, and land) and earnings, bank accounts, investments, and real estate holdings.

Custody was not an issue. Joint custody was a judicial presumption and neither litigant opposed it. Gamble asked for primary physical custody and Skip answered with his own plea for primary physical custody.

Bagley questioned Gamble at some length about her merits as a mother and homemaker before offering her to Bredwell for inquiry. Bredwell spent most of his time establishing joint ownership or contesting Gamble's allegations of proprietory rights to the house and other assets. His questions to her about custody merely emphasized that Gamble and Skip had shared parental care of Justin—protecting Skip, Pennyworth saw. "And on that occasion you asked Mr. Whitney to take Justin and care for him . . . ? And again on . . . ? Thank you, Mrs. Whitney."

Judge Haskins said, "Mr. Pennyworth."

Pennyworth got up. "Thank you, Your Honor, no. I reserve the right to recall the witness."

Gamble felt thorough relief. She stepped down. She was followed by witnesses who testified as to the circumstances of acquisition and ownership of various possessions and properties of the Whitneys. Cross-examined, they in turn were followed by character witnesses who testified to Gamble's exemplary care of and love for Justin. Pennyworth questioned none of them.

Skip's case was presented in the same manner. It challenged Gamble's assertions as to ownership (particularly the house, etc.) and participation. Then Bredwell questioned Skip in such a manner as to show him to be an exemplary loving and caring father. Bagley offered no cross.

Both attorneys were presenting positive parental cases, promoting their own clients without attacking or belittling the other parent, a strategy that was entirely agreeable to Pennyworth.

After Skip was presented, Haskins again invited Pennyworth.

This time Pennyworth arose and came out before the judge and Skip. Oh, shit, Skip thought, he's going to try to take me down about Justin some way.

Oh goody, thought Gamble, the bastard's going to challenge Skip as a father.

"Mr. Whitney," Pennyworth said, "did you listen to the testimony Mrs. Whitney gave relative to her role as Justin's mother?"

"Yes."

"Did you listen to it closely?"

"Yes, I did."

"Mrs. Whitney asserted that she takes the role of being Justin's mother seriously and discharges her role with great care and deep love." Oh Christ, Gamble thought, feeling herself imperiled. "Does that accurately describe Mrs. Whitney's testimony as you heard it?"

Skip hesitated. Then he said, "Yes, it does."

"I notice that you hesitated, Mr. Whitney. If you have any doubts or qualifications as to Mrs. Whitney's self-confessed ableness as Justin's mother, I ask you to present those doubts or qualifications to the Court now."

"I have none."

"All right. You listened to the witnesses who followed Mrs. Whitney and testified as to her worthiness as Justin's mother?"

"Yes."

"You attended their testimony closely?"

"I did."

"Do you have any disagreements or qualifications as to their testimony?"

"No, sir."

"Thank you, Mr. Whitney."

Gamble whispered to Bagley, "And this is the man who stuck Skip and me with neglect?"

"It is, it is," Bagley said, watching Pennyworth reseat himself—as if Pennyworth's posture might suggest where the devil the fellow was headed.

Bredwell followed Skip with a file of witnesses to matters of property, etc., and after their cross-examination, with witnesses to Skip's outstanding character and performance as father of Justin. There was no cross.

Pennyworth rose and said, "I'd like to recall Mrs. Whitney at this time, Your Honor."

Skip thought, The sonofabitch set me up. He sandbagged me! He got me to say all those nice things about Gamble and now he's going to let her tear me down.

"Mrs. Whitney, you listened closely to Mr. Whitney's testimony about himself as Justin's father?"

"Yes, I did."

"In his self-characterization he's a very good father, is he not? Did you hear it that way?"

"Yes, I did."

"Now, Mrs. Whitney, do you agree or disagree with that self-characterization?"

"I have to agree with it."

"I see. You and Mr. Whitney hold each other in high regard as Justin's parents. Is that a fair statement?"

"Yes. It is."

"You listened to the witnesses testifying about Mr. Whitney's performance as a father."

"Yes. I did."

"Pretty flattering testimony, wouldn't you say?"

"Yes."

"Do you wish to dispute any of that testimony?"

"No. I guess not."

"I don't want a guess, Mrs. Whitney. I want your seal of approval on those witnesses or your reason for not giving it."

"I'm not going to argue with them. I know all those people. Their testimony was accurate."

"Thank you, Mrs. Whitney."

Skip said to Bagley, "He's turning everything around. First he says we *neglect* Justin, now he seems to be helping to tell the Court we're *great* parents."

"That, at any rate, is what he *seems* to be doing," Bredwell said.

Judge Haskins looked at her watch. "We'll hear from the guardian ad litem next. But considering the time, we'll leave that for the morning. Who is Justin with tonight?"

The attorneys consulted their clients and Bagley rose. "He's with Mrs. Whitney, Your Honor."

"Mrs. Whitney, what time does Justin get out of school?"

"Two o'clock."

"Mrs. Whitney, please make arrangements for Justin to be here after school tomorrow."

Justin was wonderstruck when he heard the automatic garage door opening and looked outside and saw not only his mother's wagon pulling in, but his father's Mercedes pulling up outside on the drive. He ran down to the kitchen where they would be coming in from the breezeway.

His mother bent and kissed him, her cheek cold with the winter night. Justin smelled the Chinese food his father brought in even before he looked up and saw the brown paper bag all full and flat sided with the cartons inside. His father put the bag down on the counter and hugged him.

"Would you like a drink, Skip? Want to fix something for us?"

Justin put the back of his fist, the knuckles, to his lips and looked at his parents with astonishment and anticipation. What had happened in court? Did something happen? Were they back together?

His father took his mother's coat and went off to hang it up. His mother began unpacking the Chinese food and transferring it to pots for reheating. "How was your day, Justin?" His father came back. "Anything interesting in school today?"

Justin felt like fleeing to his room before the tears started. "Same as usual," he said. "What about court?"

"Same as usual."

"Wine?" his father said.

"I feel like something strong. A jolt. How about Scotch rocks?"

"Just the thing," his father said. "As the lawyers say, I concur."

He went to the cabinet where the drinks were kept in that end of the house and got out a black bottle and went to the refrigerator just as if he still lived there, Justin thought.

"The judge wants to see you in court after school tomorrow," his mother said. "Your dad's going to get someone from his office to drive you over. I want you to wear your blazer and a tie."

"Why?"

"To show respect for the Court," his mother said.

"Do I have to?"

"I don't want you leaving this house looking like a bum."

I don't look like a bum, Justin almost said, but if his parents were getting together again, he didn't want to do anything bad or say anything bad to make them split up again. "Okay."

The telephone rang and Justin went to it because his parents were both doing things.

"Justin," the voice on the other end said, "this is Pennyworth."

"Oh, hi," his parents heard.

"The judge wants to see you in court tomorrow."

"Yeah, I know," his parents heard.

"I want you to wear a rugby, cords, and sneakers."

"I'm not supposed to."

"You do it anyway. Can you?"

Justin thought. He looked at his parents together in the kitchen. "I don't think so. No. But why?"

"I want you to look like a kid."

"I guess not."

"Got you doing the blazer-and-tie routine, huh?"

"Yes."

"You're more appealing in sneakers and a rugby."

"I can't do it."

"Okay, Justin, see you in court."

"Who was that?" his mother said.

"Mr. Pennyworth."

"What did he want?"

"He's just telling me about coming to court tomorrow. Same as you."

They sat at the kitchen table and his mother and father were having wine with the Chinese dinner and they joked with each other and with Justin.

"That Mr. Pennyworth," his mother said. "He sure is shrewd."

"No wonder they call him the Devil," his father said. "He sure does some devilish things."

"Do you know what he did today?" his mother said.

"No."

"Guess."

"I can't. What did he do?"

"You tell us," his father said. "Mom and I can't tell at all."

"I don't know."

"He must have told you some of the things he wants to do, some of the tricks he's going to pull. Didn't he?"

"Some, maybe."

"Like what?" his father said.

His mother put down her chopsticks. "It's important for your father and me to know."

Oh, Justin thought.

"For our well-being," his father said.

Oh. "Are you guys getting together again?"

There was silence.

"Like now?" his mother said after a while.

"No. *Together.*"

"We can get together like this," his father said. "That's something, isn't it?"

Justin was silent.

Before he went back to Deer Meadow, his father asked Justin to walk out to his car with him. "Can't you tell me anything about what Mr. Pennyworth is up to, Justin?" his father said.

"No."

"All right. You've got a right to your privacy even if you know. But tomorrow, Justin, I want you to be very careful what you say when the judge asks you questions. It may decide whether we get to live here together again."

Then his father bent down and kissed him and hugged him and the terrible thing was that Justin knew his father loved him very, very much.

After his mother had tucked him in, she said, "Justin, if you know, it's very important that you tell me what Mr. Pennyworth is trying to do."

"I know. I mean, I know it's important to you."

"Won't you tell me something, anything at all, about what Mr. Pennyworth is up to?"

Justin stared at the line where the ceiling met the wall and shook his head.

"All right. Tomorrow, when the judge asks you questions, I want you to be very careful how you answer her. The answers you give her could have to do with the whole rest of your life and how much time you and I will be together and where. Do you understand?"

Justin nodded to the line.

His mother bent down and hugged him to her and kissed him and said, "I love you very, very much."

"I know," he said.

When his mother had left the room, Justin thought about his father and mother and the next day. He turned on his bedside lamp and got up. He peered at Clyde's home to see if Clyde was visible, but Clyde was safely snuggled in somewhere beneath his own covers down there in his own house.

Justin took his books out of his backpack and then some papers and junk from down below that had probably been accumulating from the first week of school. He threw all that out, except for a few pieces of good junk, and then he packed in his sneakers, a pair of cords, and a rugby shirt. Then he put his books back in on top.

46
THE BOY, THE DEVIL AND DIVORCE

"WE WILL NOW ADDRESS THE QUESTIONS OF CUSTODY AND visitation," Judge Haskins said. "Ms. Vance?"

Nelle's guardian ad litem report had been in everyone's hands for almost a week. She recommended as nearly equal a division of time between Mrs. Whitney and Mr. Whitney as possible. She had, in fact, prepared her report in concert with Pennyworth's preparation of his own case and argument for Justin.

They were both Justin's advocates and once they had agreed upon his best interests—strongly governed by Justin's own desires—they cooperated with each other.

"We don't want to give it away in the guardian report," Pennyworth said. "Let the consequence, the fruit, emerge in court. We don't want Bagley and Bredwell all prepared and stoked up to argue against the guardian's recommendation, the foundation. The structure, so to speak, will appear in court."

"We have to rely, then, entirely upon what you do in court."

"Do you have misgivings?"

"If you bring it off, I have no misgivings. If you don't bring it off, I will be very angry with myself that I didn't have it in the guardian's report."

Pennyworth seemed barely to pay attention as Bagley and then Bredwell examined Nelle. Even Nelle was annoyed. He might at least look up from time to time, she thought. But he didn't even make notes. Once again it was as if Pennyworth were in some other place with some other company.

At the conclusion of Bredwell's inquiry, Judge Haskins said, "Mr. Pennyworth?" Pennyworth stood, declined, and returned to wherever he had been. "Is there anything the guardian would like to add?"

And Nelle found the opportunity to offer the single observation both she and Pennyworth wanted stated as conclusively as possible. Nelle said, "Justin *intensely* desires to live with *both* parents."

"Ms. Vance, are you suggesting to this Court that a divorce not be granted in this case and that the parents be compelled to live with one another?"

"I wasn't aware that that argument had been offered here, Your Honor. No."

Nelle returned to the counsel table.

"Mr. Pennyworth," the judge said, "I believe it's your turn."

Rising to address the Court, Pennyworth, with no forethought that he was going to do so, first addressed himself.

This, Pennyworth said to young Weld, is it.

And thereafter Pennyworth was conscious of young Weld's presence as he spoke.

When Pennyworth had been reintroduced to young Weld during the trauma of Justin's birthday party, the reacquaintance had been startling and painful. But set free of Pennyworth's imprisoning custody, young Weld had become an admiring and admired presence Pennyworth was no longer at pains to hide from himself.

At some point Pennyworth had realized he had no reason—*never* had had any reason—to blame young Weld for his parents' divorce and that, in fact, he loved the boy. At that point Pennyworth moved from the chill and bitterness of fall and winter into springtime, an almost-paradise regained. He was still somewhat numbed and bewildered by it and he did not know whether to trust himself entirely in court.

"Your Honor, counsel for the minor child will call one witness and one witness only. Dr. Lorraine Salmon." Pennyworth peered at Dr. Salmon as if to be certain that she was really there. Then he glanced at Judge Haskins as if to make certain that Judge Haskins saw her there, too.

Dr. Salmon was sworn and stipulated as an expert witness.

Pennyworth took the psychiatrist through her report and the judge stopped paying complete attention to the repetition until Pennyworth employed it to demonstrate the happy home Justin had known and to emphasize the danger of adolescent suicide.

"Is it your testimony that the present arrangement is harmful to Justin's growth as an individual?"

"Yes."

"I hope to demonstrate to the Court," he said to Judge Haskins, "a resolution that will return Justin's life to as complete a degree of harmony as is possible under the present circumstances."

Pennyworth walked a few paces, his head down, seemingly consulting with himself. He looked up at the judge. "Here we are in divorce court. *And, ah . . .* the *impossibility* of the Court's goal.

"Your Honor, allow me the presumption of quoting your learned colleague, the Honorable Charles G. Douglas, former associate justice of the Supreme Court of this state, who, in his book *Family Law,* has written of that goal, 'The marriage may have failed, but the divorce should be a success!'

"Justice Douglas goes on to admonish us that 'Divorce should reorganize a family, not dissolve it.' "

The judge interrupted. "Mr. Pennyworth, as you are well aware, the proper time for argument and summation is *after* you have finished questioning."

"Your Honor, I only wished to state for this Honorable Court the intended destination of my inquiry."

"Get on with it, Mr. Pennyworth."

"Dr. Salmon, would you define, in chronological terms, what is usually meant by 'the tender years'?"

"It's a loose concept, Mr. Pennyworth, but it's meant to characterize those years when a child is most dependent upon parents and before the child is able to make mature judgments about his own well-being. It varies from child to child. Loosely, in years, from birth to eleven, twelve, thirteen, or fourteen."

"How old is Justin?"

"He just recently had his eleventh birthday."

"Dr. Salmon, do you consider Justin still to be a member of the tender years' set?"

"No. In fact, as I noted in my report, Justin exhibits more maturity in the divorce situation than do his parents."

"Do you think Justin has sufficient maturity to make a sound judgment about his own custody arrangements?"

"I do. I think a great deal of weight ought to be given to Justin's view of his situation."

"While we're on the subject of the parents' maturity, you found that they have a very strong feeling for material possessions, did you not?"

"I did."

"That's outrageous," Gamble said to Bagley. "What am I supposed to do, give up the house I built?"

Skip said to Bredwell, "This is horseshit. Is it immature for me to want to hold on to the house I built?"

"Are the parents treating the child as a possession?"

"In reference to the house, they are treating Justin as the key to the house."

"The house is very important to both Mr. and Mrs. Whitney, is it not?"

"Extremely important."

"More so than the child?"

"It is of paramount importance to each of them. Justin has been set aside in importance in that conflict. Save as a key to the house in the event that one or the other of them is awarded physical custody. Then custody becomes the key to the house."

"Dr. Salmon, would you advise the Court that one or the other parent ought to receive primary or physical custody?"

"As you know, in my report, I advised against any such distinction. But the reality is that such a distinction must be made. It can't be avoided."

"With all due respect, you may leave the law to the Court, Dr. Salmon. Interesting and creative results can come of law, even divorce law. That's why we have learned judges."

"Point against Pennyworth," Bagley said to Gamble. "Haskins does not suffer butter gladly."

"Dr. Salmon, would you repeat for the Court here, orally, what you stated in the report about the child's parental preference?"

"Justin wants to live with both parents."

"What do you think of that?"

"Apart from the divorce, Justin enjoys a positive, nurturing relationship with both parents."

"Within the context and time frame of the report, Dr. Salmon, what sort of environment have the parents provided Justin during these recent months? Since the time of their announced intention to divorce each other."

"It's been an *unstable* environment for Justin. Mr. and Mrs. Whitney have each provided an unstable environment."

"Dr. Salmon, I've read over your report a number of times. It would be accurate to say that it has become bedside reading for me."

"I'm sorry to hear that," said Dr. Salmon. "I can think of more recreational bedtime activities."

"Oh, I haven't limited myself to the report. But to return to it, you have just testified that the parents have provided an unstable environment for Justin. But at the same time you say in the report that the house itself provides a stable and stabilizing and reassuring environment when the parents don't. Is that a fair summary?"

"It is. The house nurtures a sense of security that the parents have not provided in recent months—due, as I said, to their legal actions against each other and, as a matter of fact, due to their preoccupation with the house itself."

Pennyworth introduced the subject of Clyde Worm.

Skip saw Bredwell making notes. "What's he doing, that stuff about environment?"

"I'm not sure."

"Well, what are all those notes?"

"I'm just trying to keep track of him. He's a moving target."

"*Clyde Worm?*" Gamble said to Bagley. "Haskins must be busting a gut."

"Don't be too sure."

"Why not?"

"I'm not sure."

Dr. Salmon was saying, "When Justin, in that instance, almost destroyed Clyde Worm's home, he was actually turning his anger on himself."

"But he didn't destroy Clyde Worm's home," Pennyworth said.

"No, he didn't. And that is significant. Just as Justin preserved Clyde's home, he would preserve his own home. It is Justin's perception that his home affords him the only protection he now has."

Pennyworth was quick and emphatic now. "His parents don't?"

"No."

"But the house does."

"Yes."

Gamble and Skip came to the same realization at the same instant.

"My God!" Gamble said to Bagley. *"He's going after the house!"*

"Thank you," Pennyworth said to Dr. Salmon. He turned to Bagley and Bredwell. "You may inquire."

"Dr. Salmon," Bagley said, "a house is just a house, isn't it? It's the love in it that counts, isn't it?"

"Yes. But in the absence of love—or preoccupation with other matters—it's the house that counts. The familiar environment."

Dr. Salmon was not to be dissuaded or persuaded into qualification. Bredwell tried.

"The home is a place of security, a predictable place," Dr. Salmon said.

Bredwell persisted.

"Mr. Bredwell," Dr. Salmon said, "there are studies that indicate that the biological parents need not even be present when the breakdown of a marriage is severe enough. The home itself provides the modicum of continuity that the child is desperate for. A surrogate parent, such as a relative or good friend, may then provide the emotional environment the child needs."

Bredwell withdrew.

Bagley was already in consultation with Gamble. He went over to Bredwell and Skip.

"Dr. Salmon," Judge Haskins said, "to whom does Justin turn when he's hurt or has a problem?"

"He has friends in school, of course, Your Honor. The NOK group. But my impression is that usually he goes to his room and consults with himself. Sometimes through Clyde Worm, but usually in loneliness."

"What about his parents? Can he talk to them?"

"Since his parents are the wellspring of his problems, he has learned to keep his own counsel. But I must insist that he loves his parents *deeply* and when they are not involved in a divorce issue, they provide him with equally deep love. Their love is Justin's sunshine. But the divorce has eclipsed it."

"Thank you, Dr. Salmon. You are excused."

"Your Honor," Bagley said, standing. "Mr. Bredwell and I both request a thirty-minute recess so that he and I may consult with Mr. Pennyworth and Ms. Vance."

"To what purpose, Mr. Bagley?"

"To see if we can arrive at a mutually agreeable order that this Honorable Court would see fit to approve."

"Very well."

The consultation, however, took considerably less than thirty minutes. Pennyworth listened to Bagley and then to Bredwell. He said, "Nelle?"

She spoke to Bagley and Bredwell. "I believe that Weld is pursuing Justin's best interests. The guardian passes."

"Weld, come along, be a good fellow," Bredwell said. "Let's work this out here and now and save all of us a lot of scratching and fighting."

"In the best interests of Justin," Bagley said. "Let's pass the ball around and see if we can all salute it."

"Gentlemen," Pennyworth said, "I see no reason to negotiate. My client is in a no-lose situation."

Pennyworth felt young Weld pat him on the back—and then embrace him.

We still have to convince Her Honor, Pennyworth cautioned.
Nelle said, "Counsel for the minor child has the ball."

47
THE DEVIL DRIVES

PENNYWORTH AROSE AND PLACED THREE SHEETS OF TYPE-
written paper face down on the counsel table. Then he moved to the
front of the table.

"In preparing this summation, I found myself reflecting again and
again upon that marvel of domestic architecture, the bird's nest,"
Pennyworth said, more as if he were addressing himself than the
Court.

"What does that mean?" Gamble whispered to Bagley.

Bagley had already shot a look at Bredwell. "The worst."

"He can't be serious," Skip said to Bredwell.

"I'm afraid he's most serious."

"An extraordinary piece of work when you consider it," Pennyworth said. "And how kindly the arrangements between parents and
fledgling, and between parent and parent . . .

"Well, the mind takes strange flights and we are here before this
honorable Court to consider the situation of young Justin Whitney
and what should be done about it.

"Up until the 1920s, children in this country were considered to
be the rightful chattels of the male parent. They were considered the
papa's property and if he wanted them, that's where they went in a
divorce.

"In the twenties, the courts across our land received the revelation
of psychological insight, the doctrine of the tender years was estab-
lished, and most custodial awards went to Mom.

"In all this, precious little attention has been shown to children's
rights. The parents' rights are always considered superior to those
of the child. That includes the child's right to his own life."

"Is he saying Justin ought to run his own life?" Gamble said to
Bagley. "That's outrageous."

"Kids ought to have rights," Pennyworth said. "The papas had
their shot. The moms had theirs. It's the kids' turn."

"The man is mad," Skip said to Bredwell. "Does he think kids ought to bring themselves up?"

"We don't know what he's proposing yet."

"In Justin's case, we do have some precedent right here in his native state. In *Del Pozzo v. Del Pozzo,* the Court, in considering the best interests of the child, took careful account of the environment of a proposed home and its likely influence on the children who were at issue."

Pennyworth adjusted himself to face Judge Haskins directly. "Justin is no longer a member of the tender years' set. I shall ask this honorable Court to take into account Justin's specific desire as to where he wishes to live.

"Not only where he wants to live, but in what arrangement. It is recognized that the desire of a minor child as to the geographical location of his residence ought to receive the closest attention from the Court and given great weight, not only in awarding custody, *but also in terminating parental rights.*" Pennyworth turned to see the effect of this last shot of verbiage upon the Whitneys. They were suitably shocked and Pennyworth was gratified.

"In *Butterick v. Butterick,*" Pennyworth began.

"The Devil quoting Scripture," Bredwell said.

". . . the Court held that, in considering a change of custody, if there were to be a change of custody, it would be necessary to show that where the child is currently residing subjected the child to peril or harm. Dr. Salmon has testified to that harm. But I would like to broaden the scope here. It is not only where the child is living, but *how* the child is currently living. How *is* Justin currently living? He is being shuffled back and forth between Mr. and Mrs. Whitney. Shuffled. Subjecting him to pain and inconsistency. Subjecting him to enforced instability. Subjecting him to harm now and in the future.

"In *Perreault v. Cook,*" Pennyworth went on, without notes, "the Court found that, and I quote, 'the shuffling of a child back and forth between father and mother can destroy his sense of security, confuse his emotions, and greatly disrupt his growth as an individual.' "

"Christ," Gamble said, "is he going to try to take Justin away from one of us?"

Equally alarmed, Skip said to Bredwell, "Is he trying to rig a sole custody order?"

"I submit to this honorable Court that, as Dr. Salmon has testified, there is a strong possibility that Justin will suffer grievous damage, in addition to the damage he has already suffered, if the Court permits or orders him to continue to live under the present arrangement."

"But everyone said that's the one thing Skip and I are good at," Gamble said to Bagley.

"Hell," Skip said. "We're fair about Justin. We make that work."

"What is wanted here," Pennyworth said, "and what can and must be provided here for Justin, is a stable home environment and stable family relations within it, a place of familiarity, predictability, and stability.

"No doubt the Court, over the years, in case after case, has given great thought to the impossibility of that objective in the context of a divorce. Without, I hope, being presumptuous, a method by which that goal might be reached would be of interest to the Court."

Judge Haskins cocked her head. "If you are not being presumptuous, Mr. Pennyworth, it would indeed be of interest to the Court."

"I find it interesting, and perhaps even tragic," Pennyworth went on, "that in building their magnificent new house, the Whitneys destroyed their old one, that older humble home where they spent the early years of their marriage. And at the same time, as they each began to realize their financial ambitions, they drew away from each other and destroyed their marriage. That would be of little interest were they not Justin's parents." Pennyworth found himself looking at the Whitneys sternly. He chastised himself. It was not an attitude he wished to project. Nevertheless, Gamble looked away in one direction and Skip looked away in the other.

"I quote Justice Douglas again. 'The marriage may have failed, but the divorce should be a success.' And we do here have the opportunity of making the divorce a success.

"Again, Douglas. 'Divorce should reorganize a family, not dissolve it.' Shortly I shall propose an order for reorganization, a reorganization, Your Honor, that provides as little disruption as can be conceived in Justin's present and future life.

"I ask this honorable Court to consider, as I have, the bird's nest. While one parent is away in search of food for the young, the other parent is at home nurturing and protecting."

Pennyworth returned to his counsel table and picked up the three sheets of paper. He turned to the Court.

"On Justin's behalf I took it upon myself to draft a custody order that is as close to a continuation of the original family as is possible. I submit it, Your Honor, for the Court's esteemed consideration."

Pennyworth handed a copy to the bailiff who delivered it to the bench while Pennyworth handed a copy each to Bagley and Bredwell.

"The intent of the proposed order," Pennyworth said, "is to minimize the breakup of Justin's family structure and to allow him to benefit from the mutually reinforcing relationships he has previously enjoyed with both parents. I am advocating that Justin spend equal time with each parent, but in a continuous environment."

Pennyworth heard Gamble gasp behind him and he knew she had read the specific terms of the proposed order.

"I am proposing that we do away with the shuffling back and forth of Justin between the father and the mother. I propose to do away with the shuffling of the child altogether and to shuffle the parents instead.

"In fact, let us, at the same time, do away with the principal contest between the two parents. If it please this honorable Court, I propose that the heatedly contested homestead property be awarded in trust to the minor child Justin until he reaches the age of eighteen, or finishes high school, whichever occurs later; that the parents alternate monthly residence with the child, and that the parent in residence pay the bills accrued during residence, and that the parents jointly pay for the general upkeep, maintenance, insurance, and real estate taxes on the homestead property."

Gamble was stunned. "She won't do that, will she?" Gamble said. "Make me visit my own son? Take my house and give it to him?"

Skip said, "I can't believe any judge in his right mind would do such a thing."

"Her right mind," Bredwell said.

Judge Haskins said, "Is Justin in the building now?"

Bredwell rose. "Yes, Your Honor."

"I will see Justin in camera without parties, legal counsel, or the guardian ad litem."

Gamble was scandalized when Mrs. Minerva from Skip's office brought Justin into the courtroom. Instead of Gamble's neat little gentleman, Justin looked more like . . . *an urchin,* Gamble thought. A neat urchin, but still an urchin. Dirty sneakers, worn cords, and an old rugby shirt. A *scamp.* The way Justin was dressed would reflect *terribly* on her, Gamble thought. And she had *seen* Justin off in the morning in his tie and blazer. . . . On the other hand, Gamble thought, the way Justin was dressed, maybe Judge Haskins wouldn't pay any attention to him.

Judge Haskins shook hands with Justin and then smiled down at him. "This isn't your first visit to a court, is it, Justin?"

"I was in Judge Stickney's court, but mostly they kept me outside."

"Well, here you're inside."

Judge Haskins removed her black robe and Justin was surprised that she was dressed in a skirt and blouse just like a regular woman. He was just as surprised by some of the things she got him to talk about—soccer, reading, even Clyde Worm.

And even Blackie the rabbit and how he didn't want Blackie going back and forth between two houses, not even the house Blackie had dug in the snow. She was interested in his Legos and how he had one bike in one place and one bike in another and how a lot of his things were split up and couldn't be taken back and forth even though they belonged to him.

Both of his parents were waiting for him when he came out to the lobby.

"How'd it go?" his father said.

"Okay."

"What did you talk about?" his mother said.

"Things," Justin said.

"Like what?" his father said.

"Soccer, reading, Clyde Worm."

"You're joking," his mother said.

"My Legos, too."

"I guess I'm not surprised. Look at how you're dressed." Gamble decided not to make an issue of it. It was probably because of the way Justin was dressed that Haskins hadn't discussed anything serious with him.

Skip watched Justin walk away with Gamble to go home. He still thought of it as home even if he lived in Deer Meadow. "What happens now?" he said to Bredwell.

"Hard to say. I doubt if Haskins and St. Marie know exactly what to do. In the normal course of things, Haskins would write a decree and that would be that. But there's Stickney's order and your appeal. I suppose it could keep going to the state supreme court."

"How long would that take?"

"Six months to a year."

"Who would take it there?"

"We might. Pennyworth might. I have a terrible feeling that Stickney himself could."

48

THE DEVIL TO PAY

"FORD," JACK ST. MARIE SAID TO STICKNEY, "YOU HAVE placed me in an exceedingly uncomfortable position."

"I'm familiar with the position and its discomfort. It was all mine, Jack, till the Whitneys kindly appealed it out of my court and into yours."

"Vexatious, Ford. I must either overturn you or uphold your order that the Whitneys not get a divorce."

"You won't overturn me on the basis that I ever ordered the Whitneys not to get a divorce. I'm too smart for that, Jack. My order is loosely phrased in the language of 169C itself. I ordered them to abstain from harmful or offensive conduct against the child or against each other. I ordered them to refrain from acts of commission or omission that tend not to make the home a proper place for the child. Nowhere did I mention the word *divorce*."

"Too true, but that is the intent. Presumably. I understand that you elucidated upon the order orally to that effect."

"Nowhere is it in writing."

Turner Haskins said, "If they obtain a decree of divorce, would they be in violation of your orders?"

"That is not for me to say. It is out of my hands now. It's all a nice little bundle for Jack."

"A de novo proceeding on a 169C petition for neglect. I can tell you right now, I'm not going to enjoin those people from getting a divorce."

"You haven't heard the evidence. Or Mr. Pennyworth. They are both persuasive. You will find Mr. Pennyworth entertaining, Jack."

"Have *you* found Mr. Pennyworth entertaining, Turner?"

"He has interesting views."

St. Marie said to Stickney, "I'd like to put everything in Turner's hands. I'd like to put everything in the hands of the divorce judge. She and I have discussed it."

"Yes, Jack, what have you discussed?"

"One, I grant the divorce," Haskins said, picking up some sheets of legal yellow notepaper handwritten in black ink, "and, two, here are the orders that go with it. The question is, Would that comply with the intent of your orders?"

Stickney accepted the papers but did not look at them. "Even if it did, would the Whitneys drop their appeal?"

"I have to think they would," Haskins said, "if no one's going to get in the way of their divorce."

"Do you think Pennyworth . . . ?" St. Marie said.

"Pennyworth is a realist," Haskins said.

"Really?"

"It goes unnoticed," Stickney said.

Accordingly, three weeks later, a decree of divorce was entered in *Whitney v. Whitney.*

Justin said to Pennyworth, "I'm sad, but I'm glad, too."

"For once it comes out all right for the kid. Or as nearly so as we can get it, right?"

"*Fearless.*"

"The child has custody of the parents."

In the orders that accompanied the decree, Judge Turner Haskins offered an introductory summation: "We are not going to split up Justin's possessions. His possessions will all stay in one place and so will he." Pennyworth's proposed order had been adopted.

"This is *incredible,*" Gamble said. "*Outrageous.* Giving Justin the house."

"Only until he's eighteen," Bagley said.

"*I'll be forty-two years old,*" Gamble said.

"You'll still need a roof over your head."

"He got his way!"

"Who?"

Gamble wanted to blame Justin but couldn't. "Pennyworth."

Skip said to Bredwell, "Is Gamble going to appeal?"

"First, let me say that if there's going to be an appeal, I'm not going to handle it. And neither is brother Bagley."

"You're *satisfied?*"

"No one is satisfied in this sort of thing."

I bet Pennyworth is, Skip thought. "No appeal, huh?"

"That was Ted's advice to Gamble and she took it. That's my advice to you as well."

Skip nodded. "All right. I can live with it. It's not all that bad, is it? I mean, good going for Justin, right?"

"Right."

"There's just this one thing."

"What's that?"

"In seven years I have to be back in court with Gamble again about the house."

"You know what a kid said to me in New York?" Heather said.

She and Chick and Justin were sitting on the steps of Chick's house at Deer Meadow. Justin was back for Saturday and Sunday with his father in order to get all his possessions for removal to what was now—at least for the next seven years—his own house.

"She said, 'I'm NOKing,' N-O-K. I didn't get it. I thought she was saying k-n-o-c-k-i-n-g because it sounds the same. She said she saw your show and she was NOKing. Isn't that great. We're a *verb*."

"Fearless," Justin said.

Chick sat with his head down just as he had at lunch when Amanda and the other kids were talking about divorce the day after Justin had come home and learned about his own divorce.

"She said a kid taped it and there're copies all over the place now. Another kid from down there told me he's a NOKer. Or he's going to be. He wrote us, too. So they turned it into a noun, too. Isn't that great?"

"Fearless," Justin said.

Chick still sat with his head down. Without looking up, he said, "Mom 'n Glen're inside."

"So what's new?" Heather said.

Chick didn't reply. He looked down at his shoes. After a minute he said, "This is. C'mon."

"What is?"

"I'm gonna NOK. I'm gonna NOK ass."

Justin and Heather followed Chick inside.

Fawn and Glen looked up from where they sat on the couch, bottles of beer at hand on the coffee table, TV and music both on.

"Hey there, son," Glen said.

"My little Chick," Fawn said.

Chick looked at them directly, his head up. "I am *not* your son, Glen. And I am *not* a little chicken. My name is Charles."

Gamble was at home deciding what personal possessions had to go with her, what should stay, what she should ask to take along to her new place, and what she would have to buy. Being a realtor, she had already found an apartment that would have to suit her every other month. It was strange both leaving and staying in this house.

* * *

"Well," said Jim Giambelli to Justin, "you've become a celebrity on behalf of children's rights."

"And earned the enduring animosity of every parent who ever or will ever want to get a divorce," Pennyworth said.

They were in Giambelli's office at the station. "The number of letters is extraordinary. From all over the country. Over two hundred. And that doesn't count the ones from adults."

"Who consider you a danger to civilization as they know it," Pennyworth said.

"The kids want to know how they can become members of NOK. They sent money. Dimes, quarters, dollars. There're a couple of tens and twenties in there, too. Some of the stories are really sad. There's a check for a hundred dollars from a man in Toledo who says he knows exactly what you're talking about."

Pennyworth tipped his mental hat to the man. Inside that man was undoubtedly a young fellow who would recognize young Weld.

"You're going to have to acknowledge the money they sent," Pennyworth said to Justin.

Giambelli said, "We've heard from other stations that they've got bundles of mail to forward to us, but it keeps coming in."

"Damn," Pennyworth said. He looked at Justin. "Damn and *blast*. You are going to need an accountant. You are going to need a secretary." Pennyworth sighed. "You are going to need a lawyer."